Lapp

The Beach House

Sally John

HARVEST HOUSE PUBLISHERS

EUGENE, OREGON

Cover by Garborg Design Works, Minneapolis, Minnesota

Published in association with the literary agency of Alive Communications, Inc., 7680 Goddard Street, Ste #200, Colorado Springs, CO 80920

This is a work of fiction. Names, characters, places, and incidents are products of the author's imagination or are used fictitiously. Any resemblance to actual persons, living or dead, or to events or locales, is entirely coincidental.

For
Aliah Claire John
Welcome, sweetheart

Acknowledgments

As is true with all my stories, this one is the result of a joint venture. My heart overflows with gratitude to the following—

My readers: You are incredibly beautiful. Your gracious encouragement undergirds me day after day.

Contest respondents: Reading your real-life stories about fortieth birthdays was sheer delight. I laughed and cried and found a common thread. It was a turning point, either remembered by those over forty or anticipated by those not yet there. Thank you for the peek into your hearts. They are gold mines of feminine wisdom.

The suggestions for character names were much appreciated as well and carried me way beyond "name your baby" books. I used names provided by *Carol L. Hoefs, Peggy McShane, Sherrie Kuster Burton,* and *Peggy Hadacek.*

Bill and *Jane Hull:* for sharing your lives with us in so many ways, not the least of which has been through words, especially those "Hull-isms."

Trisha Owens and *Joyce Lax:* for introducing me to reflexology, patiently answering questions, and keeping my nerves in order.

Kim Moore and *Gene Skinner:* for *sashimi.*

Harvest House: for the whole range of your tireless efforts toward excellence in editing, marketing, page and cover design, and sales. What a privilege to be part of the family!

Kim "the Exceptional Editor" Moore: for knowing my characters better than I do myself and for taking such extraordinary editorial care of them.

My family~

Sandy Carlson: for real-life research.

Tracy John: for boogie boarding and brainstorming.

Elizabeth John: for volleyball, a myriad of other researched information, and a last-minute, first-class editing job.

Christopher and Tracy: for introducing me to the Northwest.

Tim, Christopher, Tracy, and *Patti John:* for first read-through, critiques, and support.

And *Tim,* my anchor, for giving me San Diego.

The Beach House Ladies

Jo Zambruski ~
Lives in California; single; OB/GYN doctor

Char Wilcox ~
Lives in the Chicago area; married 17 years to Cam, dentist; mother of Savannah, 15, and Cole, 13; active as volunteer

Andie Sinclair ~
Lives in Wisconsin; married 20 years to Paul, real estate agent; mother of Jadon, 17, and Zach, 16; reflexologist

Molly Preston ~
Lives in Oregon; married 12 years to Scott, forester and pastor; mother of Eli, 11; Betsy, 9; Abigail, 7; and Hannah, 5; substitute teacher

"Let be then: learn that I am God."
Psalm 46:10

Prologue

May
Del Mar, California

Dr. Josephine Zambruski studied the five-by-seven framed photograph in her hands and tried to remember when she had stopped displaying it on her desk.

Perhaps it was during that idiotic redecorating phase that had taken hold of her like a bad perm. There was no escape. She had to play along, even if it meant boxing up her entire past. Chrome sculptures and watercolors were in, funky photos were out.

"At least I saved it."

She rose from the floor and stepped around the cartons that cluttered her home office. Settling into her leather desk chair, she propped her bare feet against the desk's edge.

"Hi." She spoke softly to the picture still cradled in her hands, to the four young women caught for eternity in the midst of a belly laugh.

Jo smiled as that raucous guffaw echoed in her mind down through the years. How many had it been? She and her friends stood on the sunny steps of Saint Matt's, their childhood suburban Chicago church. Obviously it was the day of Molly's wedding which was…when? She glanced at the back of the frame and saw she had written July sixteenth twelve years ago.

The photo drew her attention again. Oh, they had known how to laugh. There was Molly in her billowy white wedding gown of a thousand and one rhinestones, the others in chartreuse taffeta. The bride was inelegantly bent over nearly double and leaning sideways into Jo. Petite Char clung to Molly's other arm, mouth wide as all outdoors. Gangly Jo, with toothy grin and eyes squinted, hung on to Andie's shoulder. Redheaded Andie clasped her hands at her chest, eyes large as saucers and lips forming a giant *O*.

A feeling of homesickness swept over her.

What a bunch of sentimental hooey!

Jo chuckled in surprise. The phrase was trademark Molly. Char would have responded with "Sugar, you've got your heartstrings all crisscrossed with your brain." Andie would have gripped Jo's arm, tears pooling in her eyes, and said she knew exactly what she meant.

Where had the dozen years gone?

She swiveled around and gazed through the large window behind the desk. The scene included the early evening sky, the Pacific Ocean, and little else. Miles separated her from the beach, but the home's hillside perch eliminated other houses and much of the lush vegetation from view.

She watched the sun touch the water. The notion struck her that that was where the years had gone. Simple arithmetic. Twelve times 365 equaled one day at a time, melding into a blur of cross-country moves, work, and—for the other three—marriage and motherhood. Only the sending and receiving of annual, all-purpose Christmas notes broke the continuum.

The homesick feeling returned. She suspected it was more than sentimental hooey. Somewhere in the last twelve years she had lost touch with a basic part of herself. Was that why she had stopped displaying the photo? Because to look at her friends was to know something was missing from her life?

The thought struck a hopeful chord. If that were so, then the time had come to remedy the situation.

They would love her ocean view. Better yet, they would love the beach down in San Diego. They could rent a place near the sand and go barefoot and remember when dreams tickled their imaginations.

As the sun set on Jo's fortieth birthday, she reached for her address book.

One

September 24
A Chicago suburb, Illinois

When her teenage daughter created a scene in the master bedroom at 7:10 on Tuesday morning, Charlaine Wilcox stopped folding the turquoise silk blouse. It lay half in and half out of the suitcase while she glided her tongue along the backs of her teeth. *Slowly,* she commanded herself. Feel each individual tooth bump...the flatness of the front ones. Top row. Bottom row.

Any old body can count to ten, her mama—God rest her soul—had said on more than one occasion. Georgia-born-and-bred Ellen Cummins Stowe née Wentworth learned the gliding trick from her own mama, Edith Huntington Wentworth née Cummins. Women in the family controlled their tongues. They did not spout off in anger like common riffraff. They did not even raise their voices much above a soft whisper.

"Mom!"

Char sighed inwardly. The legacy hadn't quite taken hold of fifteen-year-old Savannah Stowe Wilcox yet.

Char glanced at her daughter. "I said no."

"You are such a flaming fossil!" Her voice screeched her pet phrase of the week. "Dad said this outfit looks great!"

9

"Savannah, sugar, your daddy can't see for beans at six-thirty in the morning." She resumed folding the blouse as she spoke. "I am a bit concerned about his early-bird patient today. That man might walk right out of the office with a perfectly good tooth whittled away to make room for a crown." She patted the blouse neatly into the suitcase, curved her lips upward into a tiny smile, and sat on the edge of the four-poster king-size bed to face her daughter.

"Ha-ha." Savannah crossed her arms and scrunched her pretty face into a tight mass of wrinkles.

"Your hair's lovely, all curled like that. It'll look extra nice in a ponytail for tonight's game." Her daughter's ash-blond hair and eyes the color of sliced almonds mirrored her own features. "But your makeup's going to make funny lines if you keep up that frowning."

"Mom! I need an answer!" Her voice rose again above the *Today* show on the television. "You're the one who let me go shopping! Everyone wears these skirts from Abercrombie! And that's what we decided to wear today! The whole entire volleyball team!"

"Skirt" was hardly an accurate term for the precious few inches of fabric hanging from her daughter's hips. "Sugar, let me put it this way: You look like a strumpet."

Savannah gave her a blank stare.

Char sighed inwardly. What were those schools teaching? Obviously not vocabulary. "A slut."

"A slut? Mom! Thanks a lot!"

"Well, you know, the boys are going to get all hot and bothered. They won't be able to focus on their geometry. And your teacher will ask why—in the name of all that is sane and holy—would a mother allow her daughter to step out of the house with the sole intention of disturbing every male who crosses her path?"

Char had already lost one battle over clothing the previous month. Hers had been the lone voice of reason against the girls' so-called uniform, which consisted of T-shirt and spankies. *Spankies!* The name was as loathsome as the purple bun-hugging shorts themselves. On a diapered toddler they would have looked cute. Not so on a gaggle of young ladies with the muscular thighs of serious athletes.

No, she was not about to lose a battle in her own house over what constituted decent school clothes. She finished the lecture. "Go put on that nice new sage green outfit I bought for you last week."

"I hate you." Savannah turned on her heel and stomped out the door.

Heart pounding, Char remained seated on the bed, breathed deeply, and finger-combed her short hair. She was not in a popularity contest. She absolutely was not.

A scuffling noise came from the hallway.

"Get out of my way, brat!" The barked command was a typical Savannah address to her thirteen-year-old brother.

Cole laughed heartily. "Yo, mama! Lookin' good!"

Char smiled to herself. His insolent compliment would send Savannah racing to her closet to pull out the first outfit her hand touched.

A shriek was followed by the stomping of feet. Cole entered the bedroom then, his distinctive lopsided grin in place, and leaned against the doorjamb. The child was far too rakish for his age.

"Cole, honey, I owe you one."

He held out his arms, palms up. "Consider it a freebie. Reverse psychology zings her every time. So where's C.P.?"

Not up for another battle, Char let the disrespectful reference to his father, Camden Pierce, pass without reprimand. Like Savannah's angst, it was simply another adolescent phase, here today, gone tomorrow. "He had an early appointment."

"So how are you getting to the airport? Your car's in the shop." He paid close attention to anything with wheels attached.

She opened her mouth to say "Kendra," but she caught herself before making a peep. Kendra, dearest of dear friends, who—unlike a husband—did not get her knickers all tied in a knot at the mere thought of making a round trip out to O'Hare. *Oh, puh-lease.* Kendra's eyelashes had fluttered. What was one more stop for a master car pool driver? Unload the kids at their respective schools, breeze through Starbucks, enjoy an extra gab fest on the 294, and arrive with time to spare. Duck soup.

Char was tired of duck soup. She wanted chateaubriand. Complexity and effort, aromas that defined luscious, food that danced on the palate. She wanted out of Chicago without further ado, even if it meant sitting at the airport an extra two hours.

She flipped shut the suitcase lid. "Taxi, Cole. I'm taking a taxi."

And hang the extra cost.

Two

September 24
Madison, Wisconsin

"You're absolutely sure about this?" Paul Sinclair snapped his starched white collar upright and draped an electric blue tie beneath it, watching his reflection in the dresser mirror. "You could cancel this trip for a hundred bucks. Small price to pay for peace of mind."

Andie stood in the doorway and watched her husband knot the tie with meticulous care. He twisted one half just so around the other, now up and over, creating a noose into which he tucked an end.

He gave the tie a smart tug and folded the collar back down into place. "I'm just thinking out loud. Giving you options you might not have considered." Splaying his fingers across the silk, he patted his completed project. His well-groomed nails glistened, as did the diamond on his right pinkie.

The tie belonged to his "power collection." It signified a lunch or dinner meeting would take place that day with high-level clients, the kind who paid for the ring through record-setting purchases of multi-million-dollar buildings.

He stepped into the walk-in closet momentarily and emerged with a black suit coat. Slipping his arms into it, he said, "We could use your ticket next spring. All of us could fly down to Florida over the boys' school break."

Andie followed him down the hallway as he elaborated on other possibilities. She heard his words through layers of nuances that disguised his meaning. What was he really saying? It couldn't be a complaint about the money for her trip. She had gotten a great airline deal and paid for it from her own earnings. It couldn't be because Jadon and Zach needed her at home. They were seventeen and eighteen, two of the most independent boys she knew. It couldn't be that Paul would miss her all that much. With his crazy work schedule, most weeks they barely found time to talk beyond first thing in the mornings and on Sunday nights.

Was it concern for her peace of mind? True, she was a little nervous. She had never flown across the country by herself or even spent a night away from home without him, not counting hospital stays for the kids' births. What would she do for an entire week with old friends who by now were practically strangers? In a huge place like San Diego? And there were her clients, who would miss their regular reflexology treatment with her; the elderly ones especially might suffer setbacks. Then there were school and church committee meetings she would miss, information she would have to catch up on. Maybe she should stay home. Life would be a lot simpler. It wasn't as though she *needed* to go, to get away—

"Andrea, where's my coffee?"

Paul's voice bowled through her thoughts, knocking aside her questions. In a flash she knew what he was really saying. He was concerned about his own peace of mind.

They stood in the kitchen not far from the coffeemaker with its steaming contents, not far from the cabinet in which sat his travel mug. Who would grind the beans tomorrow and turn on the pot and retrieve the cup? Who would launder his underwear and pick up his starched shirts from the dry cleaner? Who would feed the dog when the boys were at football practice?

In another instant she remembered why she was going. Soon after Jo's phone call in May, Andie sat in church and listened to her priest explore Jesus' admonition to "fear not." Up until that point she had believed herself to be a fearless woman. Nothing daunted her. She faced spiders, snakes, and teenagers. Without so much as batting an eye, she cooked meat and potatoes for the football team one day and gourmet for a team of real estate agents the next. She ran her own business. She was a Proverbs 31 woman. Well, as near as possible, anyway. She didn't sew.

That day of the sermon she realized that two things scared her witless: disappointing Paul and being by herself. Now, in one fell swoop, she was going to conquer them both. With the Lord's help, she was going to obey Him.

Smiling at Paul, she brushed off his padded shoulders. "I'll get your coffee, dear."

Three

September 24
Southern Oregon Coast

"I don't want to go." Molly Preston cocked a hip and planted her fists at her sides, elbows akimbo. "Pure and simple. End of story." For emphasis she raised a shoulder and whipped her head around to look over it. Her ponytail flicked an eye. Through watery vision, she saw her husband half buried in the car trunk. He'd missed her prima donna rendition.

"What?" Scott called, his voice muffled.

She shifted her weight to the other foot and turned back again to the street. From her vantage point at the end of their gravel drive, the Pacific Ocean was visible. It lay at the bottom of the hill, across Highway 101, the other side of a low craggy cliff. Just a pie slice of pearl gray through a tunnel of conifers beneath an overcast sky.

The car trunk thumped shut. "Sweetheart, what did you say?"

Molly flounced again to look at him, posing hip, shoulder, and face to underscore her declaration. "I said I don't want to go."

He walked down the drive, a slow smile creasing his cheeks, and shrugged nonchalantly. "So don't go."

"You think you're calling my bluff, but I mean it. Take my bag out of the car this instant."

Beside her now, Scott took one of her hands from its perch on a hip and laced his fingers through hers. "Hey, you've been waffling since Jo called four months ago."

"This isn't a waffle." Was it?

"I thought we covered all the bases." Scant more than a vibration of vocal cords, the low pitch of his voice soothed. "There is no reason for you not to go. The kids and I will be fine for a week. You had money stashed away in your little nest egg, which you're allowed to spend on yourself once every forty years or so. And last but not least, a change of pace will do you good."

She turned, pulling his arm across her waist, and leaned back against his chest, snug as a bug in a worn flannel shirt of a rug. At 5' 11" he did not tower over her. When she wore heels, they stood eye to eye. Goldilocks would have declared him just right.

Scott hooked his other arm around her and kissed her neck. "Careful, Mrs. Preston. The neighbors will start wagging their tongues about what a fresh upstart you are."

His teasing brought a halfhearted smile to her face. That bit of gossip had circulated years ago. It was based on old Mrs. Bassett's observations, which she gathered while peering out from behind her front yard cedar across the street.

Scott tightened his hold. His breath warmed her ear grown cold in the early morning. She knew he was waiting for her to explain why she did not want to go. He was a patient man.

She reached back and ruffled his short hair. Premature gray strands had woven themselves through the coffee brown, the only discernible physical change after twelve years of marriage. Outdoor work kept him as fit and trim as the day she first spotted him in a pickup softball game.

Molly savored the moment. The distant surf whished faintly. A bird twittered. She drank in thick coastal air laden with an exquisite blend of every single tree rooted in the Northwest. Fir, cedar, pine, myrtlewood, spruce, hemlock—

"Moll, you're going to hyperventilate."

She elbowed his ribs and normalized her breathing. "Look down there. At the rock." She referred to a monolith-like boulder sitting offshore. Though distance minimized its size, in reality it was enormous.

"Mm-hmm. Your sentinel."

Just one of an army of sentinels scattered along the Oregon coast. Five years before, when she and Scott and the children first traveled down the 101, thick fog had encased the entire route. It hovered over the town of Port Dunmore as they moved into their home. Three days later Molly walked out to the mailbox at the end of the drive. Lightning quick, a shaft of sunlight pierced through the mist and bounced off the ocean like Fourth of July sparklers. She spotted the boulder out there in the water, solid and silent. It was fixed in place and dependable, a soldier on guard. An instant sense of safety overwhelmed her.

"Scotty, this is home. Why would I want to leave?"

"To visit with your friends and not cook or clean."

"You know what San Diego's like. Crowded, noisy, no clouds, no sentinels."

"You're a Northwest snob with a temporary case of cold feet."

"I suppose they'll warm up in San Diego?"

"Definitely." He turned her around to face him and took hold of her arms. "Look, I know life has taken a nosedive, but we're pulling up and out of it. We are not going to crash and burn. You're still just reeling from the swoop. Things will balance out. *Maybe* in San Diego. Okay?"

She saw the faint freckles on his narrow nose, the concern in his hazel eyes that the smile couldn't hide. "Okay. Who knows? Maybe Superwoman will die there."

"I love my Superwoman, but I also love my vulnerable wife who asks for help." Pulling her close, he murmured, "Come here. I want to give you a goodbye kiss that'll knock Mrs. Bassett's socks off."

Molly found her voice. "Is she watching?"

"With binoculars."

One thing about Scotty was that he knew how to kiss. His adroitness cost her some minutes and poured confidence into the doubting spaces. It very nearly consumed her reluctance to leave home.

Nearly. But not quite.

Four

September 24
San Diego, California

Inside the bustling San Diego International Airport terminal number one, Jo spotted Molly moving at a snail's pace. She was boxed in on all sides by hordes of passengers, some coming with her from the gates, others lined up and going the opposite direction toward security checkpoints.

Molly hadn't changed a bit. Still tall as Jo. Still slender. Her nut-brown hair still straight and pulled back into a ponytail to reveal a face full of character with its high forehead, ski-slope nose, and full lips. That tiny upward curve of her mouth was still there, a perpetual suggestion of an imminent smile.

"Jo!" The suggestion burst into a full-on grin as Molly noticed her.

"Molly!"

With a laugh, they hurried to one another and embraced. Ignoring others who had to dodge them, they hugged long and hard. A dozen years melted away.

"Moll, let me look at you. You have not changed one iota."

Molly glanced down at her long denim skirt, roomy matching jacket and loose-knit ecru sweater. "The baggy outfit covers hips that quite obviously accommodated four kids. But at forty, who cares?"

Jo smiled. Molly had always felt at home in her own skin. "You never cared at any age."

"Nope. You look as spiffy as ever, perfectly put together. How is it casual still looks elegant on you?"

Jo shrugged away the compliment and felt a stab of guilt. She'd always had the money to buy the best. Her tan chinos and long-sleeved white blouse were simple, but classically styled and made of fabric blends not found in chain department stores.

"Hey," Molly said, "I'm about to toss my cookies, to quote my son. Too much stale air. Do you mind if we go outside?"

"Of course not. The baggage won't be here for a few minutes." She took Molly's elbow and steered her toward a door. "I can't guarantee how fresh the air is, though."

"As long as it's outdoors and away from all these people!" She shuddered in an exaggerated way. "I just need eighteen inches between me and the next guy."

"No one would guess you grew up in Chicago."

Automatic doors swished open and they walked out onto a sidewalk ablaze in sunshine.

"Ah." Molly inhaled deeply. "This is great. It's so warm!" She set down her backpack and slid off the jacket. "Scotty says I'm a Northwest snob."

Jo laughed. "Well, the Northwest must suit you. You look great."

"Thanks. The area does suit me. I love it."

"How is Scott?"

"He's…" Her pause was almost imperceptible. "…fine." She nodded. "He's good. Preaching up a storm in his own laid-back way on Sundays, planting trees and finding corners the rest of the week."

"Finding corners?"

"It's a type of surveying." She tied the jacket around her waist. "And how are you, Dr. Zambruski?"

"I'm…" Jo rummaged in her purse for sunglasses. "…fine." Slipping on the glasses, she caught Molly's gray-green eyes studying her.

Okay, so she had paused too. Okay, so Molly had heard it.

The dozen years had indeed melted away, throwing the two of them right back to where they connected like sisters. It was a vulnerable situation because they had not shared on a deeply personal level for ages. The masks would have to come off now.

Jo felt a sudden weight on her shoulders. Was she capable of all that would entail? Too much time had passed. How could they ever catch up? Maybe she shouldn't have orchestrated this gathering. What was she thinking? The trouble was, she hadn't been thinking. She'd been riding a tidal wave of emotions.

"Jo."

She realized she was gazing at her feet and lifted her chin. "What?"

"I am so glad you came up with this reunion idea."

"Yeah?"

Molly nodded. "Yeah. I didn't know how much I missed you until just now."

The weight lessened considerably and shook loose her uncertainty. Jo smiled. "Ditto."

Molly grinned. "Thank you, Josephine."

"You're welcome, Mary Catherine."

"Don't call me that."

"You started it."

"You could end it."

Jo's giggle rumbled from somewhere far away. Probably from the third grade.

Five

San Diego surprised Molly. They had lunched outdoors on the bay, a spot so peaceful she could hardly believe more than a million people lived nearby. Her cold feet began to warm up. Jo helped the process, of course. Being with her was like shrugging into an old comfy sweater.

Actually, Jo sort of resembled an old comfy sweater, somewhat haggard in appearance and swimming in her chinos and long-sleeved blouse. When Molly commented on her thinness, she murmured about work and stress. Her hair, pulled back into a banana clip, was still light brown, long, and straight, but when she tucked a strand behind her ear, the familiar gesture seemed a nervous motion. The slate blue eyes, though, danced as sassily as always.

Back at the airport after lunch, they stood in a crowded hallway, off to a side away from the streaming beeline of passengers buzzing toward the baggage claim area.

Jo laughed. "There they are."

Char and Andie appeared on the escalator, bringing up the tail end, gabbing like a couple of magpies oblivious to their surroundings.

Without warning, Molly burst into tears.

Oh, Lord! Ninety minutes ago she had greeted Jo with laughter. Now tears?

22

Jo swung an arm around her shoulders and gave a quick squeeze. "Aww, honey. I thought you always liked Char and Andie. I'm afraid it's too late to ditch them. They're waving at us now."

A sob won out over a giggle, and Molly dug into her skirt pocket for a tissue. Due to a recent onslaught of such unexpected crying jags, she always carried a bunch of them. One of the elderly ladies at church promised to get her some lace hankies. That was just what she wanted.

Jo went on. "In all fairness to the girls, I don't suppose you're crying because you don't want them here. Let's blame the old standby."

She sniffed. "What's that?"

"You know. The female's multipurpose solution for every baffling malady under the sun." She raised her brows.

Molly knew. It was what she suspected. "Hormones."

"Yours have malfunctioned."

She nodded and wiped her eyes. "They're totally out of whack."

"Menopause is just around the corner, dear."

Her protest fizzled. Jo was an OB/GYN. She knew whereof she spoke. She probably knew plenty of fortyish women already experiencing menopause.

If there was such a thing as a natural-born doctor, Jo was it. She had diagnosed and offered treatment her entire life. One early memory was of her caring for Molly's skinned knee after a bicycle accident. It had been no simple slapping on of a Band-Aid. A thorough cleaning, ointment application, a lecture, and a follow-up visit were involved. They were nine years old at the time.

Jo patted her arm now. "We'll talk later about it. Check out those two. They haven't changed much, have they? Char's still cute and petite. You can tell by the look on her face that she's never met a stranger. Andie's still pretty. What is it about her that makes you feel all warm inside? She emanates freshness or something. Oh, Moll. How did we grow apart?"

It was a rhetorical question. Molly blinked away the last of her tears and waved. What Jo said about Char and Andie was true. Their features expressed their personalities.

Char was a sparkplug. Her hair, still short and blond, stuck out in every direction, evidently moussed that way on purpose. On most women the style would look downright frowzy. On her it looked good, as did the faddish outfit of floral capris and blouse. She was still in tune with fashion and displayed it well.

Andie's hair was less bright than in the past. Its old vivid red color had faded to a subdued copper, its wild style replaced with neatly curled layers falling just above her shoulders. Her brown pantsuit revealed slightly rounded angles, as if she had found the thirty pounds or so that Jo inadvertently lost. The bit of plumpness gave her a matronly appearance, which only augmented the sweetness of her smile.

Carry-on bags and handbags thumped to the floor as they all squealed and took turns embracing one another.

"How y'all doing?" Char drawled in her whispery voice.

Andie giggled. "Oh, my! Isn't this wonderful?" Her soft voice was pitched high like a little girl's. "Where do we start?

Jo pointed down the walkway. "Baggage claim. Then to the beach house!"

They gathered their things and strolled through the airport, all chattering at once. Molly thought how easily they slipped into old roles. Jo led. Andie encouraged. Char sprinkled glitter. And she, Molly, followed half a step behind, the teammate ever alert to back up the others.

The past rushed at her, and tears filled her throat again. The stale air closed in, a suffocating blanket. A passerby cannonballed into her and raced off without apology or even backward glance.

It was time to regroup.

She noticed a row of pay phones. "Hey, guys, I told Scott I'd call when we all got here. I'll meet you at the escalators?"

"Yes."

"Sugar," Char said, "don't you have a cell phone?"

"Last woman on the planet without one."

"Then take mine."

"I can use these—"

"Don't be silly. Those take forever and a day." She produced a slender silver contraption and placed it in her hands. "Just push the send button. Give him our love."

"Thanks."

As they walked on, Molly stumbled toward the sunshine.

⌐

Seated on a sun-drenched concrete bench outside the airport, Molly held the phone to her ear. All around her people moved about. Cars stopped briefly at the curb. Police urged drivers not to linger. She closed her eyes.

The answering machine in her kitchen picked up the call. All six Prestons said their names, then Scott finished with the requisite "Please leave a message." She pictured the kids coming in after school, excited to see the blinking red light on the device she referred to as Gloomy Gus. Most times it delivered only cheerless news that demanded immediate attention from Pastor Scott.

Lord, thank You for Gloomy Gus, this wonderful invention that allows me to be there when they walk in the door. I promise never to curse him again.

She chatted nonchalantly, describing her flight and what she had seen of San Diego so far. She spoke to each child individually, reminding them of school projects.

"Okay, that's that. Love you, kiddos. Be good. Now let me talk to Dad. Scotty." The lump returned to her throat and her chest tightened. She swallowed. "This is such an emotional thing. All at once I'm—I don't know. I'm a forty-year-old body in a twentysomething head. It's like my past just crashed into my present and they're not gelling."

She opened her eyes and glanced around. Was she making any sense to him? "It's kind of…" She almost said scary, but realized curious Betsy would very likely still be listening to the machine. "Scary" would disturb her. "It's kind of weird. But in a good way. So thank you for encouraging me to come. Bye. I love you."

Through a process of elimination, Molly figured out which button to push and broke the connection. Lifting her face to the sun's warmth, she shut her eyes again.

Lord, I'm waffling. Still. A doubter like a heaving sea ruffled by the wind. Is he really okay without me at home?

The ludicrous question echoed in her head. A smile pulled at the corners of her mouth.

Amazing how His peace could wind its way even around malfunctioning hormones running amok in a strange city.

Six

Jo groaned. "It's hidcous!"

"Nooo," Char purred in disagreement. "On the contrary, it's got character painted all over it."

"It's fire-orange," Andie piped in, patting her reddish hair. "Everyone knows fire-orange indicates character."

Molly laughed. "I vote with Char and Andie. It's perfect."

They stood at the edge of a flagstone patio. A short distance behind them the ocean whooshed peacefully, but their attention was glued to the monstrosity sitting before them: a so-called beach house.

Jo stared at her friends in disbelief. "Are we all looking at the same ramshackle house?"

They nodded, and Molly read the stenciled sign nailed above the door, "Thirty-four hundred Oceanfront Walk."

"Ladies," Jo said, "you will not hurt my feelings if you agree with me. It's absolutely appalling."

She had arranged to rent the place *by telephone*. Why, oh why, hadn't she made the thirty-minute drive and visited it in person? Why had she entrusted the decision to a property manager she'd never met?

Maybe because she had been in the midst of an impossible work situation. Maybe because she had only asked the stranger for four things: She wanted the house located on the beach itself, midway between the pier and the roller coaster, within a certain price range, and with four bedrooms. Those were verifiable facts. The woman had thrown in the adjective "lovely" for free, an opinion Jo did not stop to question or truly even consider. Until now.

The place was a dreadful one-story weathered cottage with reddish-orange shingles and dirt brown trim, the likes of which she would not have guessed still existed in that particular neighborhood. With beachfront property at a premium, buildings were packed together like sardines as far as the eye could see in either direction. But this house was literally scrunched between two homes, each of which soared to three-story walls of glass and gleaming white stucco.

"I am so sorry," she said. "It's dreadful. It looks like a huge foot wearing a rumpled sock, and it's so big it had to be shoehorned into place."

Andie looped an arm through the one Jo had propped on her hip and grinned. "Hey, we're together in San Diego for an entire week. Right out there is the Pacific Ocean, which I have never, ever seen in my life. The sun is shining. It's almost October, yet I'm wearing short sleeves, and flowers are blooming in all these pots like it's springtime. And last but not least, we are not cooking tonight. Good heavens, what more could we possibly want?"

Jo looked into her friend's peacock blue eyes. They were laughing. But then, that was Andie. Compassionate, empathetic, not one to make waves. If she had a negative thought, no one would know it. Her vote didn't count.

Neither did Molly's. Though she spoke her mind, her lifelong opinion toward material items was that they were not important. She would have been pleased with a tent on the beach.

Char, on the other hand, could be finicky. After she cooed positive encouragement in a voice that carried images of white wicker, a large Georgia wraparound porch, and a tall glass of mint julep, then she would get to her point.

Jo said, "Char, what are you really thinking? We can try to get another place. There are resorts nearby."

"Jo, hon." She smiled. "You've gone to all this effort to get us together and find us a place. We don't mind in the least that it wasn't built in this century, do we, girls? Or even in our lifetime. Let's take a peek inside. It's got to be just as cozy as the exterior." Her focus strayed over Jo's shoulder. "Hello there."

Jo turned. A man stood a few feet behind them, on the other side of a low white picket fence that separated the patio from the public sidewalk.

The corners of his mouth lifted slightly, crinkling his eyes behind rimless, rectangular-shaped glasses. "Hello. You must be this week's tenants." He spoke in a low, cultured tone. His accent sounded of British Isles origin. "Welcome to—" He paused and stretched his arm toward the reddish-orange monstrosity as if a drumroll should precede whatever it was he was going to say. "The Beach House."

Jo heard capital letters in his emphasis of the three simple words and nearly laughed. *Beach House, my eye.*

Char immediately stepped over to him, hand extended. "Why, thank you. I'm Char, and these are my friends. This is Molly, Andie, and Jo."

They moved within handshaking distance and he shook each hand in turn. "My name is Julian. Hello. Hello. Quite pleased to meet you." His voice was Sean Connery-esque, deeply resonant yet hushed with a Scottish lilt. He tipped his head to his right, toward the boxy tiered structure easily worth a couple million. "I live next door."

Jo had been drooling over the neighboring home, especially its glassed-in balcony perched atop the first floor. Behind it an immense wall of windows rose two stories high. Hawaii was probably visible from up there.

Char turned to look at his home and said, "Oh, my! You live here full-time in all this splendor?"

"Yes, I do have that privilege." His full lips settled into a tiny smile.

Jo squinted against the sun shining behind him. He looked like a healthy specimen of an aging lifeguard, probably in his mid-fifties. His hair was dark brown, ultra thick and curly but neatly trimmed and brushed back off his high forehead. Tanned, barefoot, and dressed in cutoffs and a T-shirt, he carried the peculiar laid-back air of a Southern Californian who did not spend much time working.

Lifeguards didn't buy million-dollar homes. Drug dealers did. Nor did lifeguards speak in cultured accents. Drug dealers probably did. Not that she knew any, at least of the illegal sort.

She said, "Your house is beautiful."

"Thank you. I live in the lower portion."

She turned her head and studied the house again. Windows covered much of the front side of the first floor, which extended out from the rest of the building, creating the balcony space above. French doors opened onto a narrow patio enclosed with a low stucco wall topped with plexiglass, protection against ocean breezes. Given the choice, she would have opted for the upper floors.

He went on. "I lease out the upstairs. It's a separate apartment."

Her neck nearly snapped. "Anyone there now?" And she thought Char forward! "We're not too sure about this *Beach House*."

He chuckled. "You're going to hurt Faith's feelings. Have you been inside yet?"

"No. Who's Faith?"

"Faith Fontaine. The original owner. She was quite the lady, devoted to charity and the community. She passed away a few years ago. Her place defines character."

"That's like hearing your blind date has a good personality."

"Jo, appearances aren't that important to you, are they?"

Hearing her first name spoken in an almost intimate tone by a complete stranger bothered her. Somehow it made her feel chastised. She turned away.

She imagined her appearance told him she was a professional San Diegan. Well, what was wrong with that? Ninety-nine percent of her time was spent indoors, but her skin was lightly tanned, compliments of year-round unremitting sunshine. It gave her a healthy glow. The highlights in her hair, however, came from a hairdresser's formula. She wore casual slacks and loafers, the labels of which were found only in boutiques because who had time to drive to a mall and shop? The delicate gold chain around her neck cost probably more than Molly spent on groceries in a month, but it was the only jewelry she wore. Her late-model cream-colored SUV, parked in the carport behind the beach house, easily accommodated luggage for four—four *women*—and two grocery bags of nonperishables. One couldn't get more practical than that.

She probably struck all of them as a prig.

She looked again at the house. It truly was an unattractive place. Like a pair of large inquisitive eyes on either side of the front door, two picture windows reflected the scene behind her. The panorama included the little picket fence, people on the boardwalk passing by, and lots of sky and ocean. Definitely no view of Hawaii.

But the patio was neat and tidy, full of outdoor furniture and well-maintained potted plants.

Molly nudged her toward the door. Andie whispered something about needing a bathroom. Char, still chatting with the neighbor, sounded on the verge of inviting him to dinner.

And no, appearances were not all that important to her. Not really.

Jo went to the door, punched in the lockbox combination—conveniently programmed to correspond with the day's date—and yanked it open. The key fell into her hand and she inserted it into the door.

Char cheered. "Yay! We're in! Well, toodle-oo, Julian. Catch you later."

"Enjoy your stay."

Jo threw a polite smile over her shoulder and turned the handle.

"He's dreamy." Char was at Jo's elbow. "And from Scotland. Did you hear that? I wonder how he got here. Is he too old for you?"

Ignoring the temptation to deliver her "I'm single and happy" speech, Jo pushed on the door. It opened directly into a combination kitchen-living room, a wide-open area that ran across the front width of the house. The four of them stepped inside.

Molly laughed. "It's wonderful, Jo. It really is!"

Andie hurried across the room. "It feels familiar somehow. I'm guessing the bathroom is somewhere back this way…" She disappeared down a hall.

Char twirled around. "It is absolutely lovely."

Jo didn't respond. The last vestiges of her high hopes now crashed to the floor. A worn hardwood floor at that, sparsely covered with braided throw rugs. No gleaming ceramic tile bounced her hopes back up. No wall-to-wall carpet cushioned their fall. No vaulted ceiling held them aloft. They rammed into walls painted yellow. *Sunflower* yellow.

Char continued her analysis. "And it's utterly charming."

Molly said, "It's eclectic."

Well, that word summed it up. No rhyme or reason whatsoever tied the decor together. *Things* were everywhere. Doilies and knick-knacks obliterated the tops of end tables, coffee table, fireplace mantel, and kitchen counters. They vied for space on several bookcases overflowing with volumes.

Chairs and couches of every color, pattern, and fabric filled the area to the left of the front door. Immediately on the right was a rustic dining table in front of a picture window. On the side wall were pine cabinets, white appliances, and a window over the sink affording a direct line of sight into the neighbor's window not six feet away. Probably Julian's kitchen sink window.

A hallway opened at the center of the far wall. Andie emerged from it now, grinning. "The bathroom smells like lavender, and the tub has claw feet."

Molly hooted. "Yes! That's it!"

Char laughed. "Exactly! *That's* why it feels so familiar!"

Jo felt as though she missed an inside joke.

Andie must have sensed her puzzlement. "Jo, it's Grandmère Babette's place all over again."

Grandmère Babette. Andie's French grandmother. The little woman about whom they could write a book: *Everything I Ever Needed to Know I Learned from Grandmère Babette.*

She sank onto a nearby floral print ottoman. Perhaps the rumpled sock of a beach house was the ideal spot after all.

Seven

Jo stood in the doorway of Andie's bedroom and watched her unpack. With her moving between the suitcase on the bed and a tall wardrobe that covered half the left wall, there wasn't space enough for both of them to be inside the room at the same time.

"Andie, let me take this one."

"If you like it that much, I'll share it with you." She hung up a blouse and smiled. "I checked underneath the daybed. There is a trundle. We could pull it out at nighttime for you to sleep on."

"That would leave about two square feet to turn around in." The only other piece of furniture was a ladderback chair painted red. "I just want you to be comfortable."

"I am. This room is perfect for me." She slid open a drawer at the bottom of the wardrobe. "It's all the space I need. And I love the country theme."

"There's not even a closet in here!"

"But there's this nice armoire. Did you smell the cedar?" She pointed at the drawer and shut it. "I have that little window with cute lace curtains. And a reading lamp over the bed. What more could I want? I bet the room was originally a pantry."

"Mmm. A storage room of some sort, anyway." It was located off the kitchen, just past a bathroom and exterior side door. "I can't imagine two people using it."

"Two kids would do fine, Jo." She sat on the bed. "I like it."

"Really?"

"Really. It makes me feel...safe." She shrugged. "Listen, I know it's your nature, but you've got to stop feeling responsible for our comfort, Doctor."

"You came all this way—"

"Because you asked us to, but also because we wanted to. We didn't have to say yes. We could have insisted you come to Chicago or Madison or Port Dunmore. I for one wanted to get away. I've never been away by myself. Can you imagine that?"

Jo smiled and leaned against the doorjamb. "No, I can't."

"I suppose not. You've been independent your whole life. Not that I regret my life. I love being home with the boys even now while they're in high school. I'm able to volunteer for the school district and practice reflexology part-time as well."

"Do you still work in a chiropractor's office?"

She nodded. "What I really want to do is have clients come to my house." Her face grew animated. "We have this breezeway, just a little screened-in room between the garage and kitchen, that is not useful for anything except to sit in during the summertime when it's not too hot. It would be ideal. We could make it an all-season room with big windows. I wouldn't be in the anybody's way." She turned to her suitcase and lifted out a pair of slacks. "Paul's considering it."

Jo caught a subtle shift in Andie's tone, a nuance she couldn't pinpoint. "How's the real estate business?"

"It's great. He's awfully good at it, even when the economy is down." She carried the slacks to the wardrobe. "I don't have to work for the money. He can't understand why I would want the headache of people traipsing in and out of the house. And he cannot begin to comprehend why I want to rub their bare feet."

Jo chuckled. "That's an easy one. Because relieving people's pain is your nature too."

She smiled. "It's not always a pretty job, is it? And kneading bare feet doesn't even begin to compare to what you do delivering babies and performing surgery."

"But the results are the same. We help people. That's what counts. Getting back to your idea about a home office. The headache would be yours, right? And Paul doesn't have to touch a single bare foot."

"Well." Andie slid a drawer shut, closed the wardrobe doors, and turned. "That's the conclusion I reached on my birthday." She smiled. "Don't you think there's something special about turning forty? I feel like I swung around a corner."

Jo thought about the image for a moment. It didn't work. Instead of turning a corner, she felt as though she'd backed into one.

In the kitchen Char helped Jo unpack grocery bags while Andie found cupboard space for coffee, tea, bread, peanut butter, jam, crackers, and cookies.

Molly, pen and pad in hand, compiled a grocery list. "Jo, you've brought enough food to last us for days. I move the marketing can wait until tomorrow. Let's go outside."

Char said, "I second that motion!"

Andie said, "I don't know. Wouldn't it be best to get all organized first?"

Jo heard the hesitation in Andie's voice. Though she had always been prone to being cautious, the sound of fear was a recent development. Well, recent as in some time during the past twelve years.

Molly shook her head. "Boo, hiss. Andie, the sun will be setting soon. Into the ocean you've never seen before! Or dipped your toes into! Come on. Let's do it!"

"Just my toes?"

"Just your big toe, if you want." Molly was halfway through the front door. "Okay with you, Miss Hostess?"

Jo nodded. As far as she was concerned, they could eat every meal in restaurants and skip the grocery store altogether.

"Great." Molly shut the screen door. "I found some beach chairs in a shed out back. I'll go get them."

Within five minutes they each had a lightweight chair under an arm and were trooping through the gate onto the boardwalk, all barefoot save for Andie.

As usual, the scent of thick salt air energized Jo. The day's myriad of worrisome details fell like grains of sand shaken from a blanket. She set her sights on the ocean and pointed her feet directly at it. The straightest route from front door to water's edge appeared to be about a sixty-yard stretch. Not bad for one ugly beach house.

"Ahh!" Andie squealed as a roller skater swished past her.

"Heads up." Molly caught her arm and prevented her from losing her balance. "It's like a highway out here. Look at that! Yellow dividing lines? What is this?"

The walkway was broad enough to accommodate five or six people abreast. Jo pointed to the painted lanes and explained. "Northbound, southbound. Walkers here, runners and bicyclers there."

"It needs a stinking traffic light," Molly mumbled.

"Your Northwest snobbery is showing," Jo teased.

"Yeah, yeah."

They crossed to the seawall that ran as far as the eye could see in either direction. Jo could easily step over it, but her legs were much longer than Char's and Andie's. She sat atop it. "Just swing your legs up and over."

Andie winced. "I don't know."

"There are steps down that way. Not far."

"Okay." She headed south, sidling close to the seawall as far as she could get from other pedestrians.

Jo exchanged a glance with Molly. As if by silent agreement, they did not call attention to Andie's timidity by taking her route. Instead they followed Char, who had already flung her short legs over the wall and was walking through the sand.

The beach was a flat cushy expanse of dull beige. They trudged to where it was a dark gray and hard packed.

Jo planted her chair between clumps of gold-brown seaweed some feet from the water's edge and sat in the low-slung seat. "Have fun, girls."

Molly rolled up her pant legs. "You're not coming in?"

"Nope. I love just sitting here like this."

"Chicken."

Andie caught up. Jo almost felt sorry for her. She had no chance of escape, what with Molly on one side and Char on the other, tugging at her arms. They relieved her of her beach chair, insisted she slip off her sandals, and pulled her toward the water.

Molly said, "Just a big toe, Andie. You can do it."

"But, Jo—"

"Forget Jo. She lives here. She doesn't know any better. This is a major deal for someone who has never seen the ocean."

Char added, "It's exhilarating, Andie. And look. The waves aren't high at all. Roll up your cuffs."

Jo smiled as the three of them inched toward the gently lapping wave's end. They dipped their toes into undoubtedly ice-cold water and giggled like youngsters. As another wave rolled in, they scurried backward.

Molly called out, "Zambruski, you are a chicken. The water is bathtub warm!"

"What would you know from warm? You live in Oregon!"

The sun waned now, its warmth fading as the orange ball slid toward the horizon. In the distance surfers sat on their boards, catching no rides on the calm steely gray.

Jo heard Andie's giggle again. It was more a nervous sound than one of delight. Earlier she had worn a little girl's expression of wonderment. Since leaving the confines of her room, though, the look had disintegrated into one of controlled panic.

While Char and Molly ventured out into midcalf depth, Andie moved sideways like a crab, back toward Jo. She plopped down into one of the chairs. The ocean breeze hadn't mussed one red hair out of place, an incongruous cap to her facial expression.

Jo said, "Are you all right?"

"It's just so...*overwhelming*."

"I remember feeling that when I first came to California. It doesn't quite compare to Lake Michigan, does it?"

"Hardly. But I'm not just talking about the ocean. The ocean is downright *frightening*. I'm talking about the whole thing. I mean, did you see—well, I'm sure you see this stuff all the time. First of all there was that unbelievable traffic from the airport, bumper to bumper at eighty miles an hour. Then people over there are whizzing along the boardwalk. You could get killed by someone on *roller skates*. Did you notice the poor homeless guy muttering to himself? And the boys loitering and drinking beer right out in public in front of everybody? In broad daylight! The half-dressed girls. All the tattoos and the pierced…pierced *everything*. Then there's that odd bird neighbor, Julian. He's back there now at the wall, watching us."

Whoa. Hadn't Jo just been thinking Andie never expressed a negative thought? She didn't turn to look at the neighbor. "He's probably waiting for the sunset."

"Whatever. Jo, I don't mean to whine. I'm truly not complaining."

"Andie, your voice is so sweet I don't think I could recognize a complaint from you, no matter what words you use."

"Paul would disagree. Anyway, I can't tell you how glad I am to be here. It's just so—how do I put it?"

"Overwhelming?"

"Yes. It is definitely not Wisconsin."

"Molly's overwhelmed too."

"Molly is?"

"Yeah. I guess you two have left the big city far behind."

"I used to love Chicago. Remember how we'd take the train downtown? We were only teenagers. Mere children! I don't think I would let my boys—" She stopped in midsentence and clamped her jaw shut.

"What is it?"

She didn't reply for a long moment. "Oh, Jo. You were always the strong one. Will you do something for me?"

The strong one? Now that was debatable…

Not waiting for a reply, Andie continued. "I keep slipping back around that corner I thought I turned on my fortieth. I feel like a scared mouse who turned it and saw the cat in a pet carrier being carted out the door by the owner. Hooray! The mouse can come out!

Except once in a while she stumbles across a hunk of cat fur and panics. Is he really gone? Was it only her imagination that saw him leave?"

"Andie, what are you saying? Who's the cat?"

She gazed out at the ocean. "That's not the point. Will you just tell me to put a muzzle on it?"

"On the cat?"

She sighed. "On my mouth every time I sound fearful. I'm so tired of being fearful."

"What are you afraid of?"

Andie turned to her. "Life."

"Hmm. That covers quite a number of topics that may come up. Maybe we should literally tie a gag around your mouth."

"Maybe." She smiled in a self-deprecating way. "Right now I want to go hide in my little room. It's the only place I've felt safe since…" She looked at her watch. "Since five o'clock central time, which would be three AM Pacific time, which means over fifteen hours of discomfort." She lowered her arm and twisted her hands together. "Make that sheer terror."

"But you've hung in there."

She nodded once, as if unsure. "I guess."

"Andie, you have. So congratulations on fifteen hours of courage."

"Okay. But I'm about ready to bolt for my room. The only thing keeping me here is that I'd have to pass Julian to get there."

Jo chuckled. "If necessary I will sit on your lap to keep you put. You have to watch the sunset. It's a requirement. It…feeds the soul." She reached over and squeezed Andie's hands. "Let's tell Molly. She's the one who prays in this group."

"But she—" Again she fixed her jaw shut.

"You're doing a pretty good job of muzzling yourself, dear. Let me guess. Either prayer or Molly scares you?"

"Molly. You know how she is. She'll just tell me to get out from under the pile and trust God more."

Jo recognized truth in her statement. Molly never accepted excuses or shenanigans or whining. She'd always pulled them along, up to a higher level. It was why Jo knew Molly was the strong one, not herself. It was why she would have traveled to Port Dunmore if Molly hadn't come down to San Diego. But she had sensed a change, a bending.

"Andie, I think our oak has become a willow. You'll probably want to confide in her."

Her brows went up.

Jo was pleased. Uncertainty was better than panic. "Watch the sunset, dear."

On the horizon, the sun shimmered above the ocean's flat periphery. Slowly the great ball elongated until a funnel emerged from its underside and touched the water. Orange liquid poured lazily into steel gray.

Andie's breath caught. Molly and Char paused in their water play.

Jo smiled. It was working for her friends as well as for herself. For a few fleeting moments even she sensed God unveil Himself.

Andie whispered, "It's the same color as the beach house. Fire-orange."

Jo squinted at the melding horizon of colorless sea and sky, their meeting point defined by only a bright slice of…fire-orange. Exact same tint as those shingles behind her.

Swell. If that wasn't enough to ruin a good sunset, she didn't know what was.

The final glow vanished, and a sharp whistle pierced the quiet. Then came the noise of hands clapping.

Jo swiveled. In the twilight she saw Julian sitting on the seawall.

"Woo!" he called to no one in particular as he continued applauding. "Yes!"

On second thought, she did know what was enough to ruin a sunset.

Eight

Water lapping at her ankles, Molly laughed outright at the neighbor cheering the sunset. She added her own boisterous applause and turned back toward the ocean. "Bravo! Bravo!"

After the final shout, Char said, "Is all this clamor over a sunset a West Coast thing?"

"Not that I know of." She stuck two fingers at the corners of her mouth and whistled.

A subtle shift in Char's expression suggested her genteel manners were offended.

Molly smiled. "I can't contain myself. I mean, wow. What a display!"

"Julian's clapping?"

"No, the sunset."

"Yes, that was incredibly lovely."

"It was God showing off."

"Molly." A hint of skepticism laced Char's tone. "You're clapping for God?"

"Sure. I bet Julian is too. I wonder if he's a believer?"

"Something's going on with you. I haven't quite figured it out yet. You don't really look different, even after four children and living in the rain for years on end."

Molly pressed her lips together to hold in a laugh and gazed at her old friend, waiting for a response. Char had always considered her peculiar and never hesitated offering that opinion.

Char studied her right back. "The Mary Catherine McDonnell I remember could outshout a gaggle of cheerleaders or any coach, including the head varsity football coach during a playoff game. She wouldn't bat an eyelash yodeling at the top of her lungs outside the boys dorm on a dare. But as I live and breathe, she would never ever say God was showing off." Her pale eyes grew wide and her mouth formed an O. "Don't tell me! Our sweet Scotty has gone into preaching hellfire and brimstone."

Molly could contain the snicker no longer. "Not quite."

"Well, sugar, I must say your liturgical roots are definitely *not* showing today."

"No, they are not. I've discovered I like kicking up my heels now and then." She looked pointedly at Char. "Literally." She watched the infinitesimal lift of Char's eyebrows. "Out in the forest, anyway, where I can shout hallelujah at the top of my lungs and not disturb anyone. Of course, we practically live in the forest, so sometimes I just step into the backyard and let loose. To date only one neighbor has complained."

"My, my. You are not joking. Well, as the saying goes, it would never play in Peoria. Nor Saint Matt's, either." She named the church the four friends had attended as children. "Nor Saint Mark's, where we now belong. But, you know, different strokes for different folks. Whatever works for you is all right by me, hon."

Molly sensed the elusive jump from open exchange to defensiveness. People usually got to that point the moment they learned she was a pastor's wife. They felt a need to explain their approach to religion. But Char wasn't "people." Molly didn't want that barrier to go up between them. Their time together was too short.

She said, "Yeah, well, the Charlaine Wentworth Stowe I remember had a certain unique way of letting loose herself. Of course, she only did it when she wasn't concerned about being the prim and proper Miss Georgia Peach, Southern belle par excellence."

The tease hit its mark. Char straightened her shoulders and gave her head a slight toss. "I am not *being* prim and proper. I *am* prim and proper, and there is nothing wrong in maintaining decorum."

"But you're dying to let loose."

"Molly, you will not goad me into ridiculous behavior."

The banter echoed from their teen years. No matter the height of the defensive wall Char constructed, Molly more often than not scaled it. She suspected Char of giving in for the same reason she wouldn't give up the attack: The laughter they shared afterward was pure elixir. Life's woes disintegrated on the spot.

"Char, we're in San Diego, far from anyone who would recognize you." She winked. "And we are forty years old."

"I beg to differ on that second point. *Three* of you are forty years old." Her birthday fell later that week.

"Whatever. Come on. Give it a go. The Charlaine Wentworth Stowe I remember never passed up an opportunity to fully express herself. I hope that hasn't changed?"

"All I have to say is you are such a dip."

"And you long to be one too."

A grin finally split Char's elfinlike features. "You think my rebel yell will suffice?"

Molly smiled. "It will more than suffice."

Char took a deep breath, tilted back her head, lifted her chin skyward, and emitted the most horrendous, most unladylike whoop imaginable. She had created it one afternoon during an adolescent snit fit aimed at the other three for snubbing her. It rose and fell several octaves and combined the sounds of wolf, bobcat, elephant, and various other unidentifiable animals.

Overcome with laughter, Molly sank to her knees in the damp sand. Behind her Jo and Andie joined in.

Pure elixir. Molly imagined God was showing off again, dousing them with such a sense of happiness. She hoped she could tell Char about it before the week was over.

Their wild laughter continued throughout the evening. They strolled along the boardwalk, dark except for circles of pale light cast from evenly spaced pole lamps. At a nearby restaurant they teased their waiter until Char declared "poor thing doesn't know if he's afoot or on horseback." Returning to the house, they still drew smiles from passersby.

With scarcely a break in the conversational trip down what Molly called the sunny side of memory lane, they changed into comfy sweats and pajamas. Molly built a fire in the fireplace, all that was needed to eliminate the damp night air. Jo rearranged furniture, muttering to herself about the crowded room. Her changes placed the couch and loveseat opposite each other on either side of the coffee table and perpendicular to the fireplace. Andie plumped cushions and pillows and shook the afghans that neatly draped every piece of furniture. Her murmuring referred to a tiny lizard she'd spotted sunning itself earlier on the patio. Char prepared tea, exclaiming over each find of bone china cups and saucers, silver tray, teaspoons from more than a dozen countries, and teapot complete with quilted cozy.

As they settled onto the couches, Char served them. "Jo, I have to say it again. This is such a lovely place."

"Mm-hmm."

Molly said, "Oh, come on, you old spoilsport. Enjoy it. Look around. We have real wood burning, not just some gas flame like what's probably in those fancy-schmantzy condos. We have cups from England. Lace doilies from Belgium. Knickknack replicas of the Eiffel Tower, Big Ben, and a Dutch windmill." She glanced around. Every European country was represented in some whatnot on horizontal surfaces. On the walls hung Delft Blue plates, a Black Forest cuckoo clock, and photographs of the Alps. "Obviously Faith Fontaine was quite a traveler."

Andie said, "A Grandmère Babette clone."

Char added, "Lavender sachets everywhere."

Molly said, "And the bedrooms! A different theme for each. Ocean, desert, Oriental, and country. How many contemporary homes are this much fun?"

Jo chuckled with them. "Okay, okay. It's…quaint. It's just so *not* Southern California."

Molly said, "Like the beach and the ocean don't make up for that. And the hordes of people. I bet this community never sleeps."

"Probably not. I hope you can all shut out the late-night noise and get some rest."

"What kind of noise?" Andie's brow furrowed. She wrapped her arms around a decorative pillow as though it were teddy bear.

"There's the nonstop noise of the ocean, which can be soothing. But there's also partying college kid noise." Jo grimaced. "And sirens."

Molly laughed. "Now that is so Southern California. What exactly is the crime rate here, anyway?"

"I'm sorry."

"Josephine! Stop it!"

Andie's look of concern remained, and she clutched the pillow more tightly to her stomach. "Is it safe here?"

At that moment Molly put her finger on something that, up to that point, had only been a disconnected observance. She had noticed Andie backing away from the ocean and shrinking before the neighbor as well as pedestrians on the boardwalk. Already she had twice swept the unavoidable sand trail from the patio and inside the front door. The Andrea Michelle Kendrick she remembered…

"Andie, your spunk is missing."

Andie glanced at Jo on the couch beside her and turned to Molly. Her lips parted slightly as if she were about to say something, but she quickly closed them, her face unreadable.

Molly felt that she had overstepped a line. *Oh, Lord.* "Of course, we've all changed. I like to think I'm not quite as mouthy. Obviously I was mistaken. I didn't mean to put you down. At forty we can't be quite as spunky, what with all the responsibilities of career and motherhood and wife-dom."

"Wife-dom?" Jo asked.

"New word. For three of us, anyway. Obviously not for you. You're not married. Not yet. But being single has its own bag of responsibilities—Oh, nuts! I apologize to both of you. And to you, Char, in case

I said anything to offend…" She let her voice trail away, concerned that the old judgmental self had reared its ugly head and hurt Andie's feelings.

"Sugar." Char patted her arm. "Like you said, we have all changed. And I'm sure it's for the better. We all look better, I know that."

Jo smiled. "You want to hear my 'I'm Single, Happy, and Fulfilled' lecture now or later?"

Molly replied, "Uh, whenever."

"The title sums it up. I won't bore you with details. And you don't need to apologize. Candid observations always were our stock in trade. They kept us honest and close to each other. We've been away from them for a while, so maybe we're out of practice."

"Well!" The word exploded from Andie. She stood, her face as red as her hair, and thrust the pillow behind her onto the couch. "I have a candid observation or two! I don't look better, Char! I'm fat!" Her voice rose octaves higher than normal, which put it into the range of shrill. "Paul hates me! My sons won't even notice I'm gone! And I don't think I want to go home again!" She burst into tears, hurried around the couch, and fled from the room.

Molly exchanged surprised looks with Char and Jo. "Maybe her spunk isn't quite gone."

As one they rose and went after Andie.

Nine

Face mashed against the pillow, engulfed with uncontrollable sobs, Andie heard a familiar inner voice calmly assess a laundry dilemma her tears were creating. *The mascara should come out of the crocheted lace edging if you soak it immediately in a mild solution of bleach and detergent.*

But what if there was no bleach in the house? Not everyone stocked bleach these days. Spot remover might not be—

A new wave of tears gushed. A sob wracked her chest and bubbled in her throat. It drowned the voice of reason that never failed to keep her on task.

Gentle hands caressed her back. They were Char's, so much like those of Andie's own petite grandmother. She didn't know whether to give in to the comfort or to flinch. The essence of Grandmère Babette had been playing hide-and-seek since she arrived in San Diego. It was there in the cottage and in the conversations with her friends.

The sobs lessened. She rolled onto her side and saw three blurred faces hovering. "I am so sorry," she hiccupped.

"Now, sugar, why is that?" Char, sitting beside her on the bed, shifted her weight. "This is what friends are for, to let our hair down together and fall apart if need be."

Molly handed her a tissue. "I think we've cried as a group for most of our lives."

Jo said, "Definitely. As a matter of fact, I think I stopped crying about twelve years ago."

For a long moment, Andie stared at her, as did Char and Molly. Char broke the silence. "Oh, Jo, honey, that can't be true."

"Well, yes, Char, it can. Which might explain why I wanted us all together again. I felt a need to reconnect with…" She shrugged. "Something in myself? I'm not sure. All I know is I was down to two choices: call you or buy a bottle of vodka."

A tear slid sideways down Andie's temple. She remembered the times they had all cried together at college because of Jo's drinking.

Jo cocked her head. "Andie, it's okay. I called you and you came. Now what can we do for you?"

She basked in the loving concern emanating from all of them. At least Jo had not repeated Andie's earlier confession of fear. She could save some face in front of Char and Molly.

But…wasn't saving face a fear of exposing her true self? Wasn't that what she wanted to avoid? Besides, Molly knew. Her observation that she'd lost her spunk was on target.

Andie pushed herself to a sitting position. "I want my spunk back."

Molly smiled. "I'd say you just took the first step. What would your spunk say is the next one?"

The answer came without a conscious thought. "To admit my fears. What I said out there, it's true. I am overweight. Fat. And you can agree, Char. It won't hurt my feelings. I eat for comfort. It helps me not think how afraid I am of everything. Like of losing Paul, or of the boys growing up. Jadon's off to college next year already. And I'm afraid of being here." She took a deep breath. "I don't know where to start. Would you pray, Molly?"

"Of course. Dear Father—"

Char cleared her throat, a faintly disapproving sound. "Hon, I don't think she meant right this very moment."

Andie said, "I didn't." She caught Molly's gentle expression and smiled. "But why not?"

Molly said, "I don't mind praying here and now. If you're not comfortable, Char, you could just excuse us."

"Why would I be uncomfortable? Go ahead." She folded her hands and bowed her head.

Molly closed her eyes and started again. "Dear Father, thank You for this reunion…"

Andie felt the words fall about her like a soft mist, unobtrusive, cleansing. Molly's tone addressed an intimate, all-powerful friend.

"Jesus said to bring all our requests to You. I ask that You would remove Andie's fears, unearth their roots, and expose them for what they are. Plant faith in their place and give her the courage to say more often, 'Why not?'"

Andie looked up to see Molly smiling at her.

She gave Andie a thumbs-up. "Amen."

"Amen."

And to think Molly had scared her in the past.

Grateful that the others did not tuck her into bed with the admonition she'd feel better in the morning, Andie washed her face and rejoined them in front of the fire. She had been awake for nearly twenty-one hours, but the emotional outburst seemed to have energized her.

Char poured her another cup of tea. "We were just discussing a schedule."

Thank goodness they weren't discussing how soon they should put her on a plane back to Madison.

"You know," Char went on, "this place is an absolute gold mine for shopping. We're within easy driving distance of Tijuana and Rodeo Drive. Can you believe that? The trick will be in choosing just one. A week isn't long enough!"

Jo said, "We thought we'd all add a suggestion to the list. What do you want to do while you're here, Andie?"

"Oh, whatever." She noticed Molly's tender expression and took courage. "Let me rephrase that. I mean 'whatever' in a positive sense. As in I'd like to do everything."

Molly smiled. "As in 'why not?'"

"Exactly." She turned to Char. "We have to celebrate your birthday on Friday. That should be your day to be pampered."

Jo said, "I agree. I'll even drive us to Mexico or L.A. just so you don't have the kind of fortieth I had."

Molly and Char mirrored Andie's questioning glance.

Jo blew out a short breath. "I attended a sixteen-year-old girl's funeral, went through boxes of memorabilia, and thought long and hard about the vodka." She looked at Andie. "What did you do?"

"We went out for dinner with friends." She bit her lip. "That's not exactly true. We went out three days before my birthday with Paul's associates and their wives for something or other and he mentioned my fortieth was coming up, so they toasted me. On my birthday my mother called. And that was it. Paul remembered the day after. We had pizza with the boys."

Char clicked her tongue. "Molly, hon, please tell us a happier tale about your day."

"Well, Scott remembered. He and the kids served me breakfast in bed. Halfway through, one of the church members called needing to see him and the kids left for school. I cleaned a major mess in the kitchen. Then I found Scott at the church and told him I was done pretending life was A-OK. Needless to say, I ruined his day as well as my own. So." She held her palms up. "Friday is your day, Char. All I can say is beware. Turning forty can be hazardous to your health."

Ten

"As I live and breathe," Char purred into the cell phone, "it's true! We were all scrunched together in this teensy-weensy bedroom and Molly prayed like God Himself would bother to squeeze in there between us in order to hear about how Andie feels out of sorts."

A chuckle filled the earpiece. It was an Andy Williams sort of chuckle. Easy listening. As if the old singer had just crooned his rendition of "Moon River" and, after the last note faded away, enjoyed a little laugh in utter disbelief that millions of people adored the sappy tune.

The chuckle did not belong to anyone famous, only to Todd Brooks, friend, neighbor, and most nonsappy person on the face of the earth. He was a better confidant than her girlfriend Kendra because, unlike her, he was a night owl and therefore available at two AM central time.

"Charlaine," he said, "I had no idea your week in Southern California would be spent in a humble cottage with a group of Jesus freaks."

"Nor did I!" She laughed and leaned against the seawall just beyond a circle of yellow light cast by one of the lamps dotting the boardwalk. The beach rental sat within shouting distance. Despite the hour, occasional walkers strolled past, night owls like herself, enticed outside by mild weather and the soothing cadence of the waves. She felt perfectly safe, part of a community.

"Actually," she went on, "only Molly would fall under the Holy Roller category. Which makes sense, considering she's a pastor's wife, nonliturgical and even nondenominational, I believe. Jo may be drinking. She's asleep already. And Andie—poor Andie! No wonder she feels out of sorts. Married to that hunk Paul Sinclair and looking exactly the way her mother always did: chunky and ten years older than her age."

"Maybe Paul the hunk is now Paul the chunk."

"No way. He would never let himself go."

Todd chuckled again. "Charlaine Wilcox."

The sound of his soft voice pronouncing her name like that always tickled her ears and sent a flutter into her throat and down into her stomach. She imagined the flicker in his chocolate brown eyes as they reflected the computer monitor light. His glasses would dangle from his fingers. His jawline would be shadowy, in need of a shave.

He said, "How can you be so sure?"

"Intuition."

"Ahh. That is your forte."

"Well, also there was the recent family photo she brought along." Char smiled at his laughter. "Which only proved what I had already intuited! I'm sure by Andie not taking care of herself she has pushed him away. She used to be so pretty and certain of herself. I just do not understand what happens to some women after they marry."

"Maybe Paul's the culprit. You know what cads we men are. Not there for you in the way you expect us to be."

"Now, Todd, sugar, don't you go beating yourself up all over again. She left you because she was foolish." Char referred to his ex-wife, who had divorced him nine months ago, declaring that after fifteen years she no longer loved him. "What woman wouldn't give her eyeteeth to be the wife of a successful software designer who bakes a mean chocolate chip cookie and attends PTA meetings? Whose kids adore him? Who is kind and considerate, not to mention good-looking? As a matter of fact, some would even say the best-looking guy on the block."

"Now you're getting carried away."

"It's true!" She emphasized her words, teasing him out of the gloom that settled about him at times. He had probably talked with his ex that day. "We voted last week, Laura, Maci, Sondra, and I. You won, hands down."

"I'm sure you did not, but thank you for the encouragement."

"My pleasure, Todd. Well, I should get back inside. My roommates will be worried."

"Good talking with you, Char. "

"Back at you. Toodle-oo."

"See you."

Char folded up the phone and crossed her arms. Conversing with Todd never failed to make her feel somehow more womanly. Even if she and the other neighbors hadn't actually voted, everyone agreed he was the best-looking guy on the block, probably within several square blocks. But more than that, he was just downright fun. Outspoken and impertinent, yet outlandishly good-hearted. He connected with her in ways she wasn't sure her husband ever had. When Todd announced that his wife wanted a divorce, Char wailed on the spot. Her tears were misinterpreted as empathetic when in reality she was sickened at the thought of him moving. What would she do without him right next door?

In the end he got the house and remained her neighbor. Most of the time he had his two children as well. When he was in town, he worked from home, a situation that made him more available to their daily needs than did his ex's career schedule.

And so life went on. The fact that Todd Brooks was—technically speaking—free and clear did not really change things. After all, Char—technically speaking—was not free and clear. Their friendship remained more platonic than flirty and, aside from midnight calls, in the open.

But there were moments when she wanted to gobble him right up in a most unladylike manner.

"Evening, Char."

She jerked to attention and saw the neighbor approaching. "Julian! Hi there!"

"I startled you. I'm sorry." He stopped in front of her. "I thought you were looking right at me."

"I probably was." She laughed. "But my mind was a million miles away."

"Cell phones have that effect." He glanced at the phone in her hand. "I hope everything is all right?"

"What?"

"It's so late. When I noticed you talking, I thought something might be wrong."

"Oh. No. Everything is fine. Just fine." Fine with Todd. Fine with Savannah, whom she'd phoned first. "My daughter forgot to call me after her volleyball game." Forgot or deliberately chose not to? "And I forgot to call earlier this evening. I tell you, I feel like I'm in three different worlds, and it's wreaking havoc on my cognitive skills. I'm there in Chicago with my family. I'm here in a time zone two hours behind myself. Then there's all the reminiscing with my old friends, which puts me right back in high school! Whew! I'm not sure if I should comb my watch or wind my hair."

He chuckled. "Did her team win the volleyball game?"

"Yes. And guess who scored the winning point with a perfect spike?"

"Your daughter."

"Of course. Ha! Aren't I the nauseatingly proud mama!"

"As you should be."

"Do you have children?"

"They're grown and live in the East."

"Just you and your wife live here then?"

"I'm single."

"So is Jo! The tall, slender, lighter brown-haired one. She's a doctor in Del Mar."

"Ahh. And you are the shorter, married one from Chicago."

"Yes. Cam is a dentist. We've been married seventeen years."

"That's a long time nowadays, isn't it? And to think you still have middle-of-the-night, long-distant tête-à-têtes. I am encouraged. Romance lives."

"Tête-à-têtes!" As if by spontaneous combustion, she felt her hair roots burst aflame. "In the first place, I was not talking to Cam. He's never awake at this hour. He didn't even leave a message on my voice mail. He doesn't talk on the phone unless there's an emergency with a patient." Why the overwhelming urge to explain details to this man? "I was talking with my neighbor, and it was by no means a tête-à-tête! Goodness, we're just friends. He's just gone through a horrible divorce. Our sons are friends. They were all at the game. Sorry to disappoint you, but as far as my experience goes, romance after seventeen years is pie in the sky."

"I'm sure there's hope. Cam isn't dead, is he?"

"Close enough. Professionally he goes by his initials, C.P. They stand for Camden Pierce Wilcox the Third or Couch Potato. Take your pick." Oh, her tongue was in waggle mode!

"Have courage, Char. Even couch potatoes breathe. Do you know what I see when I look at you? An attractive, delightful blonde with an irresistible zest for life. Somewhere in old Cam's heart lingers a yearning to have a tête-à-tête with you."

No response came to her tongue, she was in that much of a tizzy.

He tilted his head in a gentlemanly nod. "Just a little neighborly encouragement. Goodnight. Sleep well." With that he sauntered away.

Of all the…! Cam had a yearning? Julian thought her irresistible? Was that supposed to be a compliment? More likely he meant it was her fault Cam didn't reveal his heart. If only she tried hard enough, she could coax that yearning right out of him.

Yeah, right.

Julian didn't know the first thing about Cam. Any yearning her husband might have possessed died some time ago. He had earned his moniker all by himself: Couch Potato. Oval-shaped and lifeless.

Forget Julian. She'd better warn Jo to stay clear of the meddling fool.

Eleven

Andie sat in the living room with Molly, watching the embers glow, reluctant to end the evening. She was feeling like that bold mouse again, the one who'd seen the cat make its exit. Not only had the corner been rounded, several steps had been taken away from the wall. It was time to explore, not sleep.

Besides that, Char was outside, alone in the dark. Molly had revealed bumpy times with Scott. And Jo slept in one of the bedrooms, hopefully the result of exhaustion and not alcohol.

"Andie," Molly said, breaking the quiet. "I hate to ask you to work on your vacation, but I would love a reflexology treatment from you. Do you think we could fit one in?"

"Oh, Molly, of course! I meant to offer that to all of you. It just slipped my mind."

"I still miss Grandmère Babette working on my feet. It balanced me somehow. If old lady hormones are like adolescent ones, maybe you can get me off this teeter-totter. At least for the week." She smiled. "I can't find a reflexologist in Port Dunmore."

"It's not exactly a well-known practice."

The door opened and Char breezed inside, her cheeks flushed.

"Thank goodness." Andie exhaled in relief. "I was worried."

Char shook a finger. "Now, now, Andrea, honey. We are grown women. Promise you will not worry about me every time I step outside this door."

"I guess it's just a mother's habit." Not to mention other things, like it being after midnight in a strange city with every manner of weirdo scarcely three steps the other side of their patio. Who knew? Maybe those people were *on* their patio right now.

Char smiled. "We are such hovering hens, aren't we? I finally got hold of my daughter. Now I can sleep. I woke her up, but since no one bothered to return my messages or call me after the game, I don't think that matters a whole lot, do you? There are consequences to ignoring Mom."

Andie said, "My boys would never hear the phone in their sleep or bother to pick it up if they did."

"It's a girl thing. Savannah sleeps with her cell. Actually, it's the best time to talk with her, she's so mellow. She even forgot to call me a flaming fossil!"

Molly chuckled. "I'm taking notes for when my girls become teenagers."

"You'll have three at the same time!" Char laughed. "Good luck! Well, I'm off to bed. See you in the morning."

They bid her goodnight.

Andie felt an old worry wriggle into the area reserved for Char. The concern wasn't specific, like when Char went outdoors. It was more a vague unease. Her friend's bouncy, carefree attitude had landed her in trouble on several occasions when they were young. How was it she hadn't matured out of that? How did her husband cope with the disordered wake she left? Come to think of it, she hadn't talked much about him. Hardly a mention. Then there was Molly's news, or half news, rather.

"Molly, what you said earlier about you and Scott?"

"Mm-hmm."

"Are you two all right?"

Her lips lifted in a quick smile. "We're redefining 'us.' It's quite an adjustment for me to be working outside the home. Even though that's only a few days a week subbing, it has been a major change for everyone not to have me in control of family details. It was a rude awakening for Scott. But, yeah, we're all right. " She paused. "Whenever you want to talk about Paul, I'm here for you."

Andie's throat tightened, and she blinked rapidly to clear her vision. "Oh, Molly. I was so afraid you'd just tell me to get out from under the pile."

She winced. "I really used to say that, didn't I?"

"All the time." She giggled at Molly's expression. "It's okay. We were young."

"I am sorry."

"But it truly helped sometimes. I mean, it was what we needed to hear."

"I still apologize for my youthful insensitivity. Let me say as gently as possible that our only hope is in Christ."

"I know," she whispered. "I just can't figure out what that means in practical terms."

"Pray. And I'll pray for you. Do you want to tell me where to start?"

She shrugged. "I worry—no, it's more than that. I'm afraid. I'm afraid of life. Kind of a huge topic, isn't it? It's like this: Not a moment goes by that I'm not fearful of something."

Molly's eyes grew wide.

"Go ahead." Andie fluttered her hand, making light of her words. "Tell me to get out from under the pile."

"Andie, I'm not thinking that at all. It's just difficult for me to fathom not having a moment free from worry. What's disturbing you right now? Right now this very moment?"

"That's an easy one. I'm afraid Char's devil-may-care attitude will get her into trouble like it always used to. I'm afraid Jo will start drinking. That maybe she never really truly stopped. I'm afraid I will use up every ounce of your patience. And mostly I'm afraid that while I'm away Paul will neglect the boys and spend more time with…" She swallowed twice. "His girlfriend." There, she'd said it out loud, in a matter-of-fact tone. *His girlfriend.* Her heart thudded…but she still breathed.

"Oh, honey. I am so sorry. How awful for you."

Andie accepted her sympathy with a nod, and they looked at one another in silence.

Molly said, "All those things you listed that frighten you, they're things you cannot possibly control. Those are the things we learn to let go of, to let God handle. I wonder, what are you afraid of for yourself?"

"For myself?" She thought about it. She was still breathing… "That I'd die on the spot if I admitted that about Paul. If I said 'girlfriend' out loud."

"And you didn't die on the spot."

"No, I didn't." She let out a breath of satisfaction. "One down, a zillion to go."

Molly smiled softly. "Narrow the worries to this time and space for yourself. Are you afraid to go to your room and turn out the light?"

"No. I like this house and my room. Now, the thought of stepping outdoors gives me the willies, but I don't have to step—"

"Let's go."

"Where?"

"Outdoors."

"It's after midnight."

"You haven't seen the ocean at midnight. It's an amazing sight. The question you need to ask is why not see it?"

"Because this city is not safe. You mentioned the crime rate yourself."

Molly chuckled. "Sitting in this room is not safe in Southern California. Do you know what the chances are a major earthquake could strike?"

"Oh, great. Give me something else to worry about."

Molly slid an arm under her elbow and pulled her to her feet.

～

"Andie, stop holding your breath. Exhale. Exhale! Thatta girl. Now inhale."

They stood at the seawall just across the boardwalk from the picket fence. Only the fence's small gate and a few feet separated Andie from the safe confines of the house. Still, if Molly didn't keep her arm entwined with hers, Andie knew she'd spin around and run straight for her little bedroom.

The breathing on demand exercise made her voice squeak. "This is crazy!"

"More deeply. Try again. Inhale. Smell that sea air. Ahh!"

"I'm wearing sweats, for goodness' sake!"

"And I'm wearing pj's. So what?"

"There are people out here!"

"Exhale. This air is different from my coast. Saltier or something."

"Molly, this can't be safe!"

She squeezed her arm. "Look out there. See where that spotlight catches the white water? Magnificent."

"There are two police officers talking to a gang of kids not fifty yards from here."

"Police? We're safe then." She took hold of Andie's chin and turned her head. "Out there. Look. Pretty spectacular, huh? And listen. Wow. Hear that soothing rhythm."

Andie realized Molly was not letting go of her. She tried to focus on the scene before her, but it wasn't happening.

How ridiculous they must look to people on the boardwalk! Her bright blue pants and sweatshirt were not for public viewing. She was quite certain Char would not be caught dead in them even indoors in private.

And then there was Molly. Well, what could she say about her outfit? Her friend's quirky sense of humor had not dwindled over the years. She wore a thin white sweatshirt and hot pink flannel pants dotted with white baby chickens sporting yellow halos and tiny wings. Molly called them her "angel chicks" and evidently did not care who saw them.

And people did see them. Andie could not believe how many passed by. It wasn't a steady stream, but given the time of night the number was phenomenal. There were those kids not too far down talking with police clad in shorts. Shorts! She had seen a skateboarder, a bicycler, and an ambler with a sleeping bag over his shoulder. One couple strolled by arm in arm and—perhaps it was only the dim light playing tricks on her eyes—but she thought they were both men.

All that since they stepped out the door three minutes ago.

"Andie, please try."

Oh, no! What if people thought they were like that last couple? Two women locked in an embrace— "Molly! Okay, okay! You can let go of me."

She did so. "Inhale all the way down to your toes."

"What am I supposed to see? It's total blackness out there." Most of the beach lay in shadows. The walkway lamps scarcely reached beyond the seawall.

"Look that way."

She turned her head slightly. A nearby spotlight mounted on a gift shop's rooftop and aimed at the water lit a tunneled area, making it bright as day.

"Now, inhale through the nose all the way to the toes." Molly threw back her shoulders and demonstrated.

Andie followed suit. Anything to get them back inside as quickly as possible.

And then something happened. Like deep calling to deep, her heart was touched by the abstract. The mystery caught hold. The Ancient of Days spoke.

"Oh!" The word was an awed whisper. "God is real. He is so real. He created all of this, didn't He?"

"Yes, He did."

Her senses awoke to the details. Thick, damp, salt-laden air. Rhythmic sounds…a gentle whisper of a wave rolling in; a momentary suspension of noise, as if it held its breath; then a hushed tone while it receded. Small birds flitted alongside the water, playing a game of tag with it. White water glittered in the spotlight. Pinpoints of light sparkled in the blackness where the horizon should have been. Fishing boats? Or stars dropping in for a midnight swim? A seagull cried.

She sighed again. "What in the world could I ever be frightened of? The God who made all of this actually knows me."

"By name." The deep male voice with its little accent came from the other side of Molly.

Andie nearly leaped out of her skin before she realized it was Julian, the neighbor. How long had he been standing there eavesdropping? Instantly aware again of her unbecoming sweatshirt and pants, she moved closer to her friend, mashing her arm against Molly's.

"And," Molly said, "He knows the number of hairs on my head. Kind of puts life in perspective."

"That it does," he said. "There was a seventeenth-century theologian named Angelus Silesius. He said if God stopped thinking about us, He would cease to exist."

"Cool. I don't know what in the world it means, but my husband will like it."

He chuckled. "Andie, I apologize for startling you."

He addressed her alone, no doubt because Molly hadn't jumped at his voice, nor did she cower behind someone, a deer-in-headlights expression on her face.

He propped a bare foot on the seawall and crossed his arms. "You were so enraptured with the scene. It is rather incomparable, isn't it?"

His voice floated on the breeze, soft yet crisp. It reminded her of her father's. Not overly deep nor tinny. Neither condescending nor accusing.

Not waiting for a reply, he went on. "I find the ocean is less fearsome than it is a thing to be admired and respected. For example, you wouldn't want to surf during a winter storm. Do you surf?"

"I live in Wisconsin." She smiled and straightened her posture, moving a quarter inch away from Molly.

Julian chuckled again. "I guess not then. How about you, Molly?"

"No. We're on the Oregon coast, though, and my son wants to teach me when he learns. I'm thinking of postponing his lessons until he's thirty. You probably surf here?"

"Most days. I can't seem to live a half-minute walk from the ocean and not literally immerse myself in it on a regular basis. Faith Fontaine, the woman who owned your house, used to say it was like holy water for me. Like a vast basin of cleansing power."

"I wish I could have met her." The words gushed from Andie without a conscious thought. "That's something my grandmother would have said."

"Was your grandmother a little offbeat, a little mysterious, and totally enthralled with every aspect of God's creation?"

"Oh, yes! Exactly. And the house is so like my Grandmère Babette's apartment."

Molly added, "It reminds all of us of it. Even Jo is coming round."

"I'm glad to hear that." He lowered his foot from the wall. "Let me know if you need anything. Goodnight."

They wished him goodnight and he left, strolling the opposite direction from his house.

Andie yawned, suddenly exhausted. "Whew. I feel like I just climbed a mountain. Are you ready to go in?"

Looking over Andie's shoulder, Molly murmured, "Wait a sec. I'm guessing he's going to talk to those homeless guys. Yep, he's stopping. Isn't he interesting? He talks like he's personally responsible for our comfort. If Faith Fontaine really was like Babette, I bet she taught him everything he knows about being neighborly."

"Well, an hour ago I would have said he was downright weird and we should avoid him."

Molly smiled at her. "Really?"

"Yes."

"Guess we killed two birds with one stone then. We went outside in the dark and bonded with the neighbor as well."

"Make it three birds. The dark, the neighbor, and being seen in public with you and your angel chicks!"

Twelve

Molly and Jo sat at a small round table on a dining patio high above the beach. The morning sky was overcast, the air cool. A handful of other diners spoke in hushed tones or read newspapers, respectfully sharing with each other the singular quiet of early morning. In the distance, visible over the misted plexiglass barrier around the deck, a few scattered surfers floated about in the placid water.

Relaxed in the Oregon-like environment, Molly inhaled a deep contented breath. "That black-bean-and-egg burrito was perfect. And a latte with soymilk? Well worth a twenty-minute, predawn walk. Can we come again tomorrow?"

Jo smiled. "And the next day and the next, if you like."

"Andie would enjoy it. Char, too, if she managed to get up before lunchtime."

"Apparently she hasn't changed into a morning person."

"Apparently not. I wonder if she packed that 'Do Not Disturb' sign or found it in the bedroom here?"

Jo smiled again. Molly thought she looked better today, refreshed. Her thick gray sweatshirt added bulk, hiding her thinness.

Molly turned and watched the surfers. How good it felt, the four of them together again! "Why do you think…" She fingered the paper ring encircling the coffee cup and reconsidered the question. Maybe she didn't want to go there. Given her haywire hormones and the emotional stress of recent months, she could give it a rest. The past was over and the morning so pleasant.

"Moll?"

She faced Jo. "Hmm?"

"Why do I think what?"

"Oh, nothing." Again she paused. "Looking backward can lead to such a can of worms."

Jo smiled. "Better open it now. That's what vacation is all about, to set those worms free. You only have a week."

Molly nodded. "It's this business about turning forty."

"Turn on the can opener!"

She flashed a smile at Jo's lighthearted tone. "I'm still processing things." A stab of homesickness struck her. For a change, it was not for her family but rather for "girl talks," the kind she'd only experienced with Jo. "Things like us losing touch. Why do you think that happened?"

"Distance and marital status."

"That was quick. I'd say you've thought about this."

"Of course. I bet you have too."

"Yep, and I reached the same conclusion. Distance and marital status. And kids. I sometimes feel guilty for being married and having children. It seemed to ruin a perfectly good friendship. We didn't have anything in common after my wedding."

"Moll, you still have a silly streak. We had our wacko mothers in common."

She groaned. "Let's not open that can!"

"I noticed you haven't asked about mine."

"And you haven't asked about mine." A long silent moment passed before Molly posed the question. "So how is yours?"

"Unavailable. Yours?"

"Ditto."

"Unavailable" was the adjective they'd finally chosen as the most apt to describe their mothers. "PTA" and "sleepovers" and "movies" were words that never crossed the women's lips. The thought of sitting on a bleacher, watching their girls' volleyball game, was as foreign to them as strolling through the slums of Cabrini-Green.

Jo smiled. "Back to us girls…Distance divided us first. I moved away, remember? Followed a guy I thought I wanted to marry halfway across the country."

"And I thought you came out here for med school." Molly winked.

"Yeah, right. No, first and foremost was Ernesto Delgado. I never regretted not marrying him."

"Then you truly are contented? Fulfilled?"

Jo leaned back in the chair. "I thought so, until this year. On my birthday I even asked myself if I did regret leaving Ernie. Maybe I've only been fooling myself all these years. But I don't think that's it. More likely 'it' is turning forty and realizing my career has not fulfilled me." She shrugged. "How about you? You don't really feel guilty for having a family, do you?"

"No. Marriage and motherhood have been my greatest joy, and on most days still are. But like you with your career, I have not been fulfilled by them. Which is what struck me on my birthday. And it scared me."

"It scared you?"

"Mm-hmm. When we got married, I was so in love, so happy to leave Chicago for a higher calling, and a year later so happy to care for my own child instead of a classroom of other people's kids. It never entered my mind I'd want something different someday." She paused. "And then I turned forty."

"What exactly happened on your birthday?"

"Breakfast in bed was a sweet gesture. It was great. Then Scotty had to leave and I had carpool duty since he reneged on his promise to do it. Later, as I was eating cold pancakes and scrubbing frying pans—the eggs and bacon that *they'd* burned—I realized I wasn't happy. Not really. The more I thought about it the more disturbed I got. I was fed up with being known as Pastor Scott's wife, mother of Eli, Betsy, Abigail, and Hannah. Where was *Molly?* Obliterated by marriage and motherhood!"

"But at the airport you said life was great."

"It was. Then all of a sudden, wham! I'm forty and guess what? I have succeeded: I *don't* look like my mother! But I don't look like Molly, either. I didn't lose myself in a career like your mom or in the social scene like my mom. I wasn't ever unavailable to my husband or kids. But I lost myself somewhere along the way. In being so *available*, I created five monsters. Well, four. Hannah's too young; she doesn't count. But the others depend on me for every single thing. I'm not just talking about picking up socks. I mean the whole kit and caboodle, every detail involving house and schedules and kids, not to mention running the Sunday school department."

"So what happened after you scrubbed the frying pans?"

"I marched right into Scott's office, interrupting his session with the guy who'd called and interrupted my birthday breakfast. And I let loose." She wrinkled her nose. "Screaming mimi."

"Eww.'"

"Eww is right. I said this stay-at-home business was supposed to be a joint effort. But while I'm doing laundry, he's out there in the world getting fulfilled."

"What'd he say?"

"He didn't get it. Totally clueless. He didn't understand how I could be perfectly content one day and ready for the funny farm the next. Truth is, I can't either." She shrugged.

"Maybe it's like Andie said about herself turning a corner. Her perspective simply changed."

"That's it. Life no longer looked the same to me, but it did to Scotty, and he refused to budge. Pastoring consumes him."

"He's probably on call twenty-four hours a day?"

"And then some. Neither one of us was very well balanced."

"Past tense?"

"Some days." Molly smiled.

"How'd you get to 'some days?'"

"I went on strike. Except for Hannah and myself, I didn't cook, clean, or do laundry. The rest of them lived on hot dogs and cereal and wore dirty clothes. I didn't remind anyone of schedules; I didn't keep track of homework or personal items. Eli was late for school twice. Betsy missed a clarinet lesson and failed a spelling test. Abigail forgot about soccer practice and had to sit out most of a game. Scott lost his Bible and sermon notes. That was one interesting sermon, by the way, completely off the cuff. Lots of rustling in the pews that day."

Jo doubled over in laughter. "They must have been begging you to come back. How long did this last?"

"A week."

"And did it work?"

Molly tilted her head from one shoulder to the other. "It helped, but now I feel so guilty. I keep wanting to call home and check in on them. It's like needing a fix."

"Oh, Moll."

"The good news is I started substitute teaching. I gave up running the Sunday school. I gave up my little job of after-school care for three other kids. I've given my four more responsibility. Scotty pitches in at home and tells me it's okay to whine like some angst-ridden adolescent trying to find herself." She paused. "The bad news is he feels he's not giving a hundred percent as a pastor. And on the days I sub, home life is absolute chaos. I can't imagine teaching full-time, which is what I want to do."

"The chaos probably adds to your guilt."

"Yeah. I didn't even want to make this trip. I keep slipping into the old role, thinking the real 'Molly' should wear Superwoman's cape. I forget it's Christ who fulfills me, not what I do."

Although the sun remained hidden, a brightness had begun to dispel the mist. Jo slipped on her sunglasses, not quite fast enough to hide a flicker of her eye.

Molly sensed she was losing a connection with her. She took a deep breath. That was the other thing that separated them: While her faith had deepened through the years, Jo had grown indifferent to spiritual things. It had begun in their college days.

Lord, give me the right words. Give her ears to hear.

Molly said, "I don't mean to preach."

"It just sounds so flippant. 'Christ fulfills me. He will take care of everything.' But how?"

How to explain such an intangible? Molly reached into their common past.

"Jo, what do you remember from church? From when we were little?"

She pondered the question for a moment. "Candles, incense, and incomprehensible jargon. Endless words. Words, words, words. Words so familiar we rattled them off without thought."

"They were Scripture, hon. And based on Scripture. They were alive, straight from a world we can't see but the one where God moves, where He answers prayer."

"I keep looking for something a little more concrete."

"They're kind of like…" She paused and lowered her voice to radio announcer depth. "The List."

Jo's quick smile was wistful. "Grandmère Babette. What would we have ever done without Andie's grandma and her list?"

"Hopelessly floundered. Remember why she gave it to us? It's not a list of dos and don'ts. She said if we took those words to heart and followed them the best we could, they would make a difference. They would help us grow into confident women."

"I remember."

"God says the same thing. It's not about dos and don'ts but about His words infused with power and changing us from the inside out."

Jo turned toward the ocean.

Molly knew the can of worms had indeed been opened. Now she could almost hear the contents being dumped into a Tupperware container, preserved for another time. She changed the subject. "So what was your favorite item on the List?"

Jo smiled and looked again at Molly. "'A real woman has eight matching plates, goblets, and a recipe for a meal that will make her guests feel honored.'"

"I was there once, right after the wedding. Then Eli was born. I now have five of each. Only two of the plates aren't chipped. My lasagna works every time, though, even on paper plates."

"I own twelve and have used them twice. Maybe three times. I served a great salmon dish."

"I like 'a real woman has a set of screwdrivers, a cordless drill, a hammer, and a black lace bra.' I trust you have those?'"

"Definitely. You?"

"Yes. Scotty has his own."

"All four?"

She grinned. "No. By the way, my nest egg paid for this trip."

"Ah, nest egg. Another thing a real woman has." Jo raised her coffee cup. "Three cheers for Babette. You could say her list got me here too."

"Which item?"

"The bit about how a real woman knows 'where to go—whether her best friend's kitchen or a charming inn—when her soul needs soothing.' I'd already done the inn thing." Her smile softened the bitter undertone. "Speaking of kitchens, we ought to go roust our roomies and hit the grocery store." Jo's demeanor snapped down the last corner of the Tupperware lid.

Molly accepted the hint and drained the last of her cooled latte.

Thirteen

Andie cradled a mug of tea in her hand and stood at one of the front picture windows. The ocean was silent this morning.

But that voice in her heart was not.

Mystery shrouded the silver-gray expanse. Perhaps the previous night's thought that it called to her was fanciful, but she could not deny a new ache. A craving to spend time alone with God was awakened. She longed to meet His challenge to come, to let go, to receive His love.

Unsure what exactly that meant, she declined Jo and Molly's invitation to breakfast in order to be with Him. Since they'd left, she had simply been waiting.

Recalling the precious sense of God's nearness while standing at the seawall last night, she stepped over to the door and placed her hand on the knob.

That's not a flattering style on you. Paul's voice stopped her cold. *Sweats? It's broad daylight and there are people out there. Have you considered coloring your hair? Where's my coffee? I need a blue shirt for tomorrow. This red tie has a spot on it. Marinara, I believe.*

"Dear Lord."

Andie shook her head free of words that would continue to kill her if she listened to them. Better to think of Molly's words of encouragement and God's presence.

In a burst of energy, she pulled open the interior door and then smacked the screen door. It banged against the outer wall.

"Oops," she whispered. "Sorry, Char."

Barefoot, hair matted, tea mug in hand, face unwashed, not one stroke of blush on her pale cheeks, and clothed in baggy sweats, Andie Sinclair stepped onto cold flagstones. She marched across the patio and through the gate. With a smile and a hearty "Good morning" for a bicycler, she waited for him to pass, and then she walked across gritty concrete straight to the seawall. She sat on it, swung her legs over, dangled them above the sand, grinned at the ocean, and felt downright spunky.

"Good morning, Lord."

She inhaled deeply several times and giggled to herself at the thought that some pedestrian might stop and ask if she needed oxygen.

"What a glorious, glorious morning," she murmured. "Thank You."

"Good morning, Andie!" Julian's voice rang out from a distance. Panic tightened her chest.

I'm such a sight!

Fighting down all-too-familiar unease, she turned to see him walk through the opening in the low wall that surrounded his patio. She called merrily, "Hi!"

He sauntered in her direction. Like yesterday, he wore cutoff blue jeans, a T-shirt—this one was white with faded lettering—and no shoes. He carried a large white mug.

And she felt safe.

What was it about him? The pitch of his voice was deep yet soft and crisp. So like her dear father's, it drew her in. Even the accent added a sense of familiarity. Not that Julian's Scottish lilt resembled her dad's odd mixture of French and English with a New England twist. It was just that neither sounded like the average American.

Julian smiled as he approached. She wondered why she hadn't noticed his gentle manner when they first met. Probably because she hadn't noticed much at all except for the fact she still shook in terror, visions of crashing on the freeway at eighty miles an hour dancing in her head.

"How are you?" she asked when he neared.

"Great." He slid onto the seawall and faced her, his back to the ocean. "Ready to dive in?"

Dive in to what? "Huh?"

"The ocean."

She opened her mouth, but no words came to mind. What an absurd question!

"You know what they say about fears. Meet them head on and poof! They're gone."

"I stuck my toes in it yesterday."

His eyebrows rose up and his glasses moved with them.

"That counts."

"Oh, yes, definitely." He crossed his arms and raised the cup to his mouth.

"It does."

He swallowed. "No disagreement from me. But." He leaned slightly toward her. "Does it take care of the situation?"

"Sure." She sipped her tea and stared out at the ocean. The thought of entering it made her legs feel like jelly.

"I started with boogie boarding. It's like a kickboard, only wider and longer. One just holds on to it and more or less floats. It's quite simple. No muscle or skill required. No need to venture out as far as those surfers are."

"Hmm."

"Faith's house has everything you need. The equipment is locked in that storage shed out back."

After a moment's hesitation, she asked in a low voice, "Equipment?"

"Boogie boards. Wet suits. Most novices find the water rather cold."

Another pause. "Anybody can use this…this equipment?"

"Comes with the house. You'll find a key in a kitchen drawer, far left end of the counter."

She turned in time to see the passing twinkle in his brown eyes and the corner of his mouth lift momentarily.

At once he was the sibling, the older brother she'd never had, the confidant, the alter ego. He was the bridge that spanned the gap between Mousey Andie and Spunky Andie.

He murmured, "It's all about letting go."

Fourteen

Jo led the way from Kono's dining patio out onto the wide board-walk. She and Molly passed the entrance to the restaurant. It was a funky little place she had known her vegetarian friend would enjoy. They turned right and strolled by the Crystal Pier, its gate just opened now at eight o'clock to the public. Two fishermen carrying poles and pails walked through it. Only the eastern half of the sky shone brilliant blue, but sunlight crept toward the ocean, burning off the gray cloud cover in its path.

A sense of contentment washed over her. *God, thank You for Molly.*

Like the wispy sea breeze now stroking her face, the words floated in her mind—and nearly bowled her over. When was the last time she had spoken to God? There was that screaming fit directed skyward four months ago. Not exactly a heartfelt prayer of gratitude. It didn't count.

She stole a glance at her friend. In that split moment she saw the two of them walking to an Alcoholics Anonymous meeting not far from their college campus. It was to be her first. Molly held her arm and never once told her to get out from under the pile.

That was the night Jo dubbed the phenomenon that had affected her for years. She called it the "Molly Effect." The Molly Effect both attracted and repulsed her. In it she saw the face of God, radiant love and fiery eyes. She always imagined the fire aimed at her for not being as good as Molly.

The notion was probably why she had drifted away from Molly…and why she had called her after all these years. She needed to reconcile the fire with the love.

A bicycler approached now; she and Molly skirted him. People of all ages and cultures, on foot and on an assortment of wheels, traversed the broad walkway, elevated at this point above the beach. An elderly woman in a broad-brimmed hat was setting up an easel and canvas, no doubt to capture the priceless view of pier and ocean.

Palm trees and assorted flowers lined the route. Four-story motels rose on their left, painted in soft Southwestern pastels, desert pinks and peaches. They were neatly landscaped. Steam rose from a pool and Jacuzzi in the middle of a courtyard surrounded by plexiglass dividers and lush green vegetation. Wrought iron encased balconies that faced the ocean.

Maybe they had rooms available?

"Molly." She glanced over her shoulder. "We could—"

Where was she?

Jo stopped and scanned the area. Six feet back, Molly sat on a concrete bench along the motel side of the boardwalk. Beside her was a black man, his arms wrapped tightly around a backpack, dressed in a coat too heavy for the day. Though…it would have served him well through the night.

Jo hadn't noticed him. But then homeless people were as prevalent as skaters, dog walkers, and bikini-clad girls. What was to notice?

She retraced her steps and approached the bench. Molly was stuffing bills into the man's fist.

Another feeling of déjà vu enveloped Jo. She had often backtracked for Molly, finding her engaged elsewhere, usually trying to help someone.

Molly stood and met Jo a few feet from the bench. She shrugged. Wordlessly they turned and resumed their walk.

Molly said, "His name is Jimmy Mack."

"Why am I not surprised you know his name?"

"He looked so forlorn, totally despondent. Other than his name, though, he didn't respond."

"He'll just buy booze."

"You don't know that for sure."

Jo leaned around until Molly met her eyes. "You don't know that he won't, either."

"So tomorrow I'll buy two breakfast burritos."

~

"Andie's what?" Jo stared at Char in utter disbelief. First the ugly beach house, then the unnerving neighbor, then Molly's unsettling questions about childhood memories of church and linking them with the List. Molly *knew* she would relate to the List! And now this.

Char, seated on the wall opposite the ugly beach house, stared at her over the rim of an ugly, multicolored, garish coffee mug. Her eyes, mere slits, proclaimed Jo's earlier assumption correct, that Char never had become a morning person. She was not about to waste breath repeating what she had already said moments before: *Andie's surfing with Julian.*

Molly laughed and pointed toward the ocean. "Look! There she is!"

Jo spotted the redhead as she emerged from a flattening wave. White water swirled around her legs. For all the world, she resembled a surfer! Clad in a black wet suit, hair plastered to her face, she grinned and turned to the man beside her. *Man beside her?* It was Julian, sans eyeglasses, his thick curly hair dripping.

Char murmured, "What is that orange thing?"

She noted the spongy raftlike object bobbing at Andie's knees as the wave receded. A cord led from it, ending in a strap around her wrist. "It's a boogie board. Something like a mini-surfboard. You lay your upper body on it, point it toward shore, and catch a wave."

Molly propped a thumb and forefinger at the corners of her mouth and let out one of her wild whistles. Andie looked their direction and waved like a mad woman. Before Jo finished raising her own hand in response, Andie had turned away and began heading back out into deeper waters. Julian followed her.

"As I live and breathe." Char's voice was barely audible. "Whatever possessed that woman?"

Molly only chuckled.

Jo thought of Andie's timidity at the ocean's edge, her avoidance of Julian, her tears the previous night. She thought of Molly's prayer, of Molly's rendition earlier about herself and Andie studying the midnight sea.

The Molly Effect.

Jo shrugged. "Well, Char, all I can say is Molly prayed."

Fifteen

Andie giggled like a ten-year-old and kicked wildly, clinging to the rough edges of the boogie board with both hands. Her black-sleeved arms spread out over the fire-orange slice of stiff foamlike material. Fire-orange again. It was everywhere. The beach house, the sunset, her hair. It was such a happy color. She felt slender, cellulite and rolls tucked snugly into the thick, sleek, neck-to-ankle wet suit.

A wave undulated toward her. From what Julian had taught her, she knew by its appearance it would break after rolling past her. She was not in position to ride with its curl. Instead, she waited, letting her legs dangle in the water. The wave flowed beneath her and lifted her gently. She glided down the back side of it, her face still pointed to China.

China. Absolutely nothing stood between her and that mysterious faraway country except seawater. The thought exhilarated her. Or maybe it was the realization that little Andie Mouse had stepped so incredibly far away from the wall. She had even rounded *another* corner and now stood in the midst of all that was unknown. The only thing she could control at that moment—well! She couldn't think of a thing she could control at that moment. She was in the *ocean*, and her feet could not touch bottom! She wore a swimsuit in late *September* when Midwestern leaves were turning gold. Her hair probably looked as if it were glued to her scalp. She hadn't even applied cheek blush. And, tucked in with all that cellulite, were a pair of decidedly nubbly legs.

Wouldn't Paul be— Oh, there were too many adjectives to describe what he would be!

"Andie!" Julian called from a short distance away to her left. He too wore a wet suit and floated upon a boogie board. "Get ready!"

An approaching wave heaved, much larger than the previous one. She quickly rehearsed what Julian had taught her over the past hour or so. Her position and the size of the wave eliminated the option to ride over it. She could wait for it to crash atop her and get tumbled about. The clothes dryer routine cleared out her sinuses but wasn't particularly enjoyable. She would have to dive through it, a maneuver she hadn't quite mastered.

Without further hesitation, she kicked and pushed herself downward, down into the bowels of the rushing tower. Instant quiet enshrouded her. A moment later she emerged on the backside of the wave and expelled her breath in a hearty laugh.

"I did it!"

"Woo!"

They propelled themselves out farther. The water rippled gently, and they drifted, giving their legs a rest.

Andie crossed her arms on the board and rested her chin on them. The exhilaration calmed too, and she sighed in satisfaction. The sun warmed the back of her wet head.

Who would believe it? Not Paul. Nor the boys. Even Char wasn't so sure, and she'd been right there watching her struggle into the wet suit.

How had she gotten there? Only Julian seemed to think it possible as he gently suggested a way to combat her fears. He had offered his assistance and patiently waited for her decision, never once pressuring. Twenty nervous, determined minutes later she met him on the sand.

"Andie!" he called now and pointed.

The sight of the incoming wave took her breath away. It raced toward them, blocking half the sky. There was no going over or through it. The thought of tumbling under it nearly strangled her.

"Julian!" she squealed.

"You can do it! Let's go!"

Like him, she grasped the front edge of the board and kicked around in a half circle until she faced the shore.

"Go, Andie! Go!"

The roar of water swallowed his voice. Not far to her left the wave began its curl, crashing over into white water, racing in her direction like a bolt of lightening. With all her might she kicked. If she didn't meet the white water at the exact moment it reached her, the wave would win and she would lose.

Lose. She understood losing. She'd lost her Grandmère Babette. She'd lost her dad too soon. She'd lost Paul. She was losing her sons, both off to college over the next two years. She'd lost her spunk.

She was tired of losing.

"Lord."

The wave lifted her. Higher and higher still. She froze, her teeth gritted and her heart pounding in her throat.

And then she realized she had done it. She had caught the wave! She was one with it.

Her locked jaw released itself as did something deep inside of her. Grinning, she flew on liquid glass, the power of a jet engine propelling her forward. The wind whistled in her ears.

A long breathtaking moment later the wave diminished, its power spent. Andie stayed with it, letting it carry her until her knees dragged on the sandy floor. Nearly overcome with laughter she stood and raised her hands Rocky style.

She turned around. Where was Julian? She must share the moment with him. There he was, far out still, floating on the board. He had missed the ride! She waved to him.

He raised an arm, his hand fisted, a thumb skyward. Then he headed back toward the horizon. He wasn't coming in to coax her out again as he'd done numerous times.

Andie felt as if she had graduated. Who would believe it?

With a giggle, she picked up the board and walked onto the beach.

Sixteen

"Molly. Sugar." Char heard a tinge of exasperation in her voice and paused to glide her tongue along the backs of her teeth. "You are truly welcome to pick up this cell phone and use it whenever and for however long you would like. It makes no never mind to me or Cam or the phone company. I never use up my allotted minutes." *Well, not every month, anyway.*

Molly sat at the kitchen table, her hands tightly clasped beside the phone, a forlorn expression on her face. "You're sure?"

Standing at the counter, Char traced the fronts of her teeth and swiveled around to pick up the coffee carafe. How could the woman be so out of touch with the twenty-first century?

"Molly, I am sure." She poured the last of the coffee into her mug.

"I would have used Jo's earlier, but she didn't take it to the restaurant. It must be hormones."

"What must be hormones?" Char turned to face her.

"This…" Molly waved her hands above her head and twirled her fingers. "This…I don't know! This out-of-body experience."

"You're having an out-of-body experience?"

"It feels that way. Like my brain detached itself. I don't feel in control. Not that I am truly ever in control, but this is like I don't know what's going to come out of my mouth until it's already been said."

"Sounds like caffeine overload. How much coffee have you had?"

"Only a cup, and most of that was soymilk. Ten minutes ago I was fine. And now look at me." She pulled the elastic from her ponytail and combed her fingers through her hair. "I'm totally unnerved because there is no telephone in this place!"

"There are three, hon. Three cell phones and you are welcome to use any of them. Jo would even turn hers on more than once a day for you."

Char sipped from what was her fourth cup of coffee. Evidently her caffeine tolerance surpassed Molly's. Only now did she begin to feel awake and ready to face the day, which appeared to be developing into a complicated one. Jo's moodiness remained intact after twelve years. She had disappeared into her room again. Char wondered if she should check on her. Or search the room for a bottle? No way was she climbing into a car with a drunk behind the wheel.

Then there was Andie. Spunky aside, she'd always possessed an eggshell exterior and, like last night, it was shattered on a regular basis. Nothing new there—until Char found her first thing that morning wiggling into a wet suit, asking for help with the back zipper. It was as if a hard-boiled interior had emerged, a totally uncharacteristic version of the soft woman she knew. Andie was simply the last woman on earth who would surf, especially with a stranger.

And Molly was the last woman on earth who would fall apart over a telephone. Maybe it had something to do with her fortieth and that business she mentioned about Scott, something about pretending their marriage was okay.

Molly fiddled with the phone. "It's just that I've never been away from the kids for such a long period of time."

Long period— What? "Twenty-four hours?"

"Well-l-l, it will be a long time before I get home."

"Honey, how are you and Scotty? You said something about your birthday…"

"We're fine. We're working on some issues. You probably know what I mean. You've made it to what? Fifteen, sixteen years?"

"Seventeen."

"Seventeen. That's great. We were just growing apart. I was feeling—" Abruptly she stood. "Will you excuse me, please? I have to call him." Without a backward glance, she palmed the cell, her long legs already in motion. She crossed the room and went down the hallway.

Char remained standing and drank her coffee. Molly probably wouldn't care to hear how she and Cam had made it to seventeen years. How a couple could just ignore the inevitable growing apartness. How she could find fulfillment in school and community affairs and innumerable friends. How he could be content fixing teeth and watching television and not be concerned that one of her closest confidants was the neighbor *guy*. Why go to all the effort of working on *issues?*

Oh, well. Different strokes for different folks.

Seventeen

Molly lay on her stomach on one of the twin beds in her room. With Char's tiny phone pressed against her ear, she counted the rings of the church phone at the other end, her nausea increasing with each. Hadn't he said he'd be in the office that morning? Though she had left a message yesterday, they hadn't talked since she'd left home. Maybe something happened. He had Jo's cell phone number, but she didn't know if Jo had checked for messages yet. Apparently not using the thing was part of her friend's vacation.

On the tenth ring Scott picked up. "Hope Church."

"I can't do this."

"Molly," he breathed her name as if in relief. "What can't you do, sweetheart?"

"Be this far away from you and the kids."

He chuckled. "That's the most pathetic thing you've ever said."

"I know. What's even more pathetic is it's the truth. And it makes me feel like throwing up."

"Okay, okay. You win. You miss me more than I miss you. I have no indication my breakfast is moving upward. What did you eat, by the way?"

She followed his lead down a rabbit trail of detailed chitchat about their mornings and the children. After a time her stomach relaxed, and her mind stopped swirling.

"Scotty, seriously, this is harder than I imagined."

"That's the best time to practice leaning on Him."

"I just feel so vulnerable."

"Like an adolescent trying to figure out who she is?"

"Have I said that?"

"Once or twice. Maybe six times. Moll, I do miss you, and not because I'm doing the housework."

She smiled. "Really?"

"Really."

"But you're fine?"

"I'm fine."

"And the kids are fine?"

"The kids are great. So go be strong. Be Molly Preston, not Mrs. Scott Preston, mother of the pastor's four wild rugrats who played hide-and-seek in the church during choir practice last night."

"They didn't."

"Ready or not!" he shouted. "Here I come!"

"Scott!"

"I was on the phone. After I got off, I tied them together in a pew."

She laughed. What a distance they'd come! Three months ago he never would have allowed them within shouting distance of the choir or his office while he worked.

"Sweetheart, why don't you give me Char's phone number?"

"I don't know what it is. How do I figure it out?"

"There's a menu. Check that."

"Hold on." She lowered the phone, studied the micro screen a moment, and put it back to her ear. "Gobbledygook. I'll have to ask Char."

"All right. Get Andie's too. Maybe you'll feel better knowing I have all three. I love you."

"I love you too."

"I'd better go." He rattled off his schedule, which included Bible study that night. The next two days he would do surveying work up the Elk River. Way up. Where pay phones were unheard of and the cellular kind did not function.

They had taken giant steps in their marriage. They were growing back together, balancing kids and work in a healthier way. She was off on her own, for the first time in twelve years, getting reacquainted with old friends, including someone named Molly Preston.

Life was full of God's blessings. Why in the world did she want to cry?

The flood of tears broke loose after they said goodbye. She bawled herself to sleep right there in the cozy beach house in the middle of a sunny morning, her hand tight around Char's phone.

Eighteen

Jo stood beside her car, gulped down half a bottle of water along with four ibuprofen, and kneaded her forehead.

Not a blade of grass in sight, the single-vehicle carport more or less was the backyard. It afforded a spot of shade amid the relentless glare of sunlight. She faced the one-way, alley-sized thoroughfare and squinted. Heat waves quivered off lofty stucco walls, parked vehicles, and concrete. A tribute to the tenacity of life, plants sprouted everywhere, in pots and through cracks in the hard surfaces: jade, azalea, bougainvillea, bird of paradise, and even a palm tree. The sweet scent of alyssum wafted from somewhere.

Jo's head throbbed, in sync with her pounding heart. What had she gotten herself into, inviting three strangers to spend a week in such close proximity? She felt like a bug under a microscope, limbs splayed and pinned down. No matter their common history, the women did not know each other. And to think she had been sober when she called them!

In an attempt to wriggle out from that feeling of being scrutinized, she scheduled activities. They could focus on things and Jo could ignore the feeling she just might pop. The ugly beach house, weird neighbor, and unaccustomed tenderness unnerved her.

The event-driven approach wasn't working. Already the original timetable was shot to pieces. Molly was napping. Char had wandered down the boardwalk in search of a newspaper and who knew what else once she reached all those souvenir kiosks. Andie was at the front of the house, hosing down a boogie board and wet suit, the bridge of her nose scraped raw from an impact with the ocean floor. If yesterday's hairstyle, makeup, and clothes were any indication, she was still at least an hour and a half away from being ready. When Jo walked past her on the way to the carport, Andie squirted Jo's sandaled feet and teased, "Tag, you're it, Zambruski!"

Jo rubbed her forehead again and closed her eyes. The sensation of pressure mounting refused to go away.

"Good morning!"

Jo looked up and saw a man walking in the narrow street. He stopped when he reached the carport, a few yards from her.

"Morning," she said.

He smiled, a dazzling flash of white against flawless ebony skin. Black braided locks sprouted from his head every direction like a fireworks display held in suspension. A trimmed beard covered the lower half of his narrow face.

"How ya doin?" he asked.

"Just—" The word "fine" tangled with her vocal cords and didn't make its way out. She wasn't fine, and something in his black eyes told her he knew it.

"Oh, sister, life can be hard at times, can't it?" The singsong cadence of his voice mesmerized.

She felt glued to the concrete. Something unearthly emanated from the stranger.

He said, "I find when I express my troubles out loud to another human being, they just sort of…" He spread his arms out like a band leader and wiggled his fingers. "Dissipate." He laid a hand to his chest. "The heart doesn't take on the full impact of unbearable pain."

What was this? A Rastafarian-looking shrink in faded blue jeans and white button-down shirt with rolled up sleeves?

"My name is Zeke." Now he held the hand out to her.

She crossed the distance between them and shook it. "I'm Jo."

"Nice to meet you." His eyes remained focused on hers. They were like magnets. "Your heart looks like it's breaking with unbearable pain, Sister Jo."

She folded her arms, locking them across her midsection. Her deep heart cried out that yes, the pain was unbearable. Unbearable and unspeakable.

Zeke shifted his stance. Expectancy was written in his posture and on his unlined face.

And then she knew he was right, to speak the anguish was somehow to bear it. She should tell her friends. They would give her sympathy and practical advice. Wasn't that, in all honesty, the reason she had called them?

Her throat ached from its tight grip on words of confession. They would be swallowed, though. She knew that by the time she met up with Char, Molly, and Andie, she would have talked herself out of saying them. She would dredge up old things between them and shove the words back down.

Zeke, on the other hand, carried no baggage. He called her "sister." In the twinkling of an eye he had connected with her on a deep level. Intuitively she understood he would offer something beyond sympathy and practical advice.

And he was available now even as her words clamored for release. She said, "How much do you charge an hour?"

"Time means nothing to the good Lord." He smiled. "I try to follow His example."

Jo hesitated for the briefest of moments. She saw no fire in the man's eyes, only acceptance.

"Four months ago I killed a sixteen-year-old girl and her baby."

~

Midafternoon Jo strolled with her friends along a walkway in Old Town between historical white stucco buildings with red tile roofs. Eucalyptus trees cast long afternoon shadows.

Char purred a sound of delight and pointed to an open-air gift shop on their left. "Look at those wind chimes!"

Almost simultaneously Andie pointed to the right. "A hacienda! History!"

The two of them laughed.

Molly pointed straight ahead and moaned. "I'm going there to that grassy spot and sitting down. No way can I shop or sightsee. I ate one too many tortilla chips!"

"Molly, honey," Char said, "perhaps it was the *grande* platter of tacos, enchiladas, refried beans, and rice you ate with the chips."

She smiled. "Perhaps. Come plop with me, and then we'll do something more tangible than digest lunch."

Jo thought lunch a misnomer. It was after three o'clock.

They reached a vacant wooden picnic table where Char and Andie sat on the bench seat. Jo chose the ground. She slipped off her sandals and folded her legs lotus style. Molly stretched out full length on her back in the grass, crossed her feet at the ankles, hooked her hands behind her head, and eyed Jo.

"Josephine, you've been quiet. The restaurant was perfect."

Andie nodded. "Yes. Great food. Reasonable prices."

"Sugar," Char sighed, "I swear I feel like a cow the way you insist on herding us about. It was not your fault we all got sidetracked this morning and then didn't eat lunch until four o'clock central time."

Molly chuckled. "Your stomach's still on central time?"

"I'm not sure what time it's on. I grazed my way through the grocery store, eating all those free samples. The cheese lady and I got to be on a first-name basis, I went back so many times. Speaking of grazing, that reminds me of the cow mentality. Shall we make some sort of schedule so Jo doesn't have to behave like a livestock farmer?"

Andie raised a hand. "I vote for boogie boarding every morning."

They all stared in obvious disbelief at Andie. Her face glowed. The scraped nose gave her the appearance of a little girl as did the straight hair and casual cotton top over blue jeans.

Andie said, "I mean for myself. You all don't have to do it. But you can if you want. I think I counted six boards in that storage shed. And wet suits. What are you all staring at?"

Molly thrust a fist skyward. "Yes. Andrea Michelle Kendrick lives!"

Andie smiled crookedly. "Well, at least when it comes to the ocean she does."

"I'm confident she will spill out into other areas."

Jo thought she already had. Andie's fears were fading before their very eyes. She had talked with the weird neighbor, did not wear yesterday's makeup mask, and ate a salad for lunch, leaving most of the tortilla bowl behind.

Molly said, "I vote for breakfast at Kono's every morning with whoever wants to come."

Char said, "I vote for sleeping in. How about you, Jo?"

"The one healthy habit I have is walking, so I guess a walk to Kono's is my choice. Then I can feed my caffeine habit without making a ruckus in the kitchen too early for some people."

Char crossed one leg over the other and swung it. "Maybe we should address habits. Like I'm a night owl. I may go outdoors after dark. I hope no one worries about me."

Andie smiled. "Guilty. I'll try not to again."

Molly said, "My habit is talking to Scott regularly and often."

Now the other three stared at her.

"What?" she quizzed them.

Andie said, "That is so sweet."

Char stopped swinging her leg. "I can't relate to it. Truthfully, I'm enjoying a little break in the daily routine of marital miscommunication."

Molly sat up and hugged her knees. "My birthday was a turning point. We'd been seriously growing apart. I was a diehard Superwoman. Now we're in prevention mode. That means an awful lot of touching base. Anyway, I can use my calling card at a pay phone I noticed today. It's just a few blocks from—"

They drowned her out with protests, offering the use of cell phones.

"All right, all right," she conceded. "I will ask for yours when I need to. Not asking for help is a bad habit of mine."

"Good," Andie said, "My bad habit is being afraid of my shadow. Obviously I'm working on losing it. I could use any help you three can offer."

Char patted her arm. "It's okay, sugar." She turned. "Jo? How about your habits? Good or bad?"

"Like I said, walking and caffeine."

"So nothing we can help with?"

Jo caught an undertone and suddenly recognized the real question. "Char, I haven't had a drink in eight years."

The collective sigh of relief was nearly audible.

Char's genuine smile spread across her face. "Good for you, sugar. Well, okay. We have the mornings figured out. Now I have a suggestion for afternoons and evenings. Because you all had less than stellar birthday celebrations, I think you should do them over again this week. Everyone can have their own day to celebrate in their own way, and the others agree to go along with whatever they choose."

"Great idea!" Andie said. "Do you still have that tourist pamphlet in your bag?"

As the others began to swap potential ideas, Jo followed a different train of thought. She could easily blame that stranger named Zeke— or thank him. With a few kind words and the softest eyes imaginable he had opened a corner of her heart that she both yearned and dreaded to reveal before her friends.

"Char." She blurted her name, abruptly interrupting the conversation. "Molly. Andie. Maybe I do need your help. No, not maybe. I do need it."

They stared, riveted. Molly gave a half nod of encouragement.

Ever the poised doctor, she presented her dilemma matter-of-factly. "I don't know which way to turn. That's why I wanted all of us together, to take me back to when I always knew which way to turn. No, let me rephrase that. Back to when if I didn't know which way to turn, you guys pointed me in the right direction."

Andie said, "Like you're turning a corner and you can't figure out right or left?"

"More like I'm still in a corner. The thing is, I'm losing my confidence in practicing medicine." She paused, savoring again the new taste of freedom in finally admitting that first to Zeke and now to her old friends.

Molly said, "What happened, Jo?"

"Remember the sixteen-year-old I mentioned? The funeral on my birthday? She and her mom were my patients. Mom brought in daughter for birth control pills. Problem was, it was too late. The girl was pregnant. Mom requested an abortion. I don't perform them. No doctor in our group does. I mentioned adoption. Mom went berserk. This is a wealthy, high-profile family. They don't do teen pregnancy. Mom then insisted on RU-486, the abortion pill. I don't do that, either, but we all know a clinic where it is available. Mom took her there."

Jo rubbed her forehead. "Using the drug is not exactly a no-brainer. There's the timing issue: It's effective only during the first seven weeks. The patient must make at least three doctor visits. Sometimes it doesn't work and surgical abortion is necessary. Severe side effects need to be addressed." She paused. "In this case, Mom left town. Dad wasn't clued in. The miscarriage-like symptoms were severe due to complications. She didn't get help in time. She died. The baby died."

Molly sighed as if in despair. Andie wiped away a tear. Char murmured consoling words.

Jo went on. "I feel responsible for her death. I can't stop playing the 'if only' game. If only I had insisted more, convinced them otherwise. If only I'd given them names and phone numbers for help. I even think that if only I had no convictions, I could have given it to her. At least that way I would have been in charge and taken better care of her."

Molly's arm was around her shoulders. "It's over."

"I know. And I know I can't grieve forever." Jo looked at Andie. "But I feel stuck in a corner, not turning one." She saw understanding and acceptance on all their faces. "I guess I need you three to pull me out and give me a push."

Andie slid from the bench and knelt in the grass before her. "We're here for you." She lifted Jo's right hand. "Remember?"

"What?"

"Oh!" Char sprang to join them and placed a hand on top of their two. "How could we forget?"

Molly leaned over and added her hand to the pile. "Good golly, yes, how could we forget? On the count of three. One, two, three."

In a flash, Jo recalled a slumber party. Eighth grade, at Andie's. That night they adopted the Three Musketeers motto for themselves, a rallying cry for four outcasts.

Now, in unison, they pronounced it: "All for one, and one for all!"

As one, the others hugged her.

Nineteen

Long after dark, Char sat on the seawall in the same spot she'd occupied the previous night. She swung her legs, gazing out at white-caps caught in a spotlight and listening to her husband's recorded voice.

"Guess we've missed each other again," Cam said. "Anyway…"

Char tuned out her husband's litany of household woes. His voice was not an Andy Williams croon. Cam's distinct basso approached foghorn levels.

As he droned on with "where's this, where's that, can Savannah do this?" ad infinitum, ad nauseam, her twinge of guilt dwindled. No wonder she had left the phone in the bedroom earlier right about the time she knew he might call. Who needed this on vacation? He was boringly predictable as well as emotionally not at home. Honestly, the break from him was such a breath of fresh air.

"Your mom—"

She tuned back into his voice.

"—wants to have us over for dinner. Didn't you tell her you'd be gone? I told her you'd get back to her—"

In the first place, the woman was not her mom. She met the min-imum requirement of stepmother: She was married to Char's father.

Beyond that no true relationship existed, certainly not the kind that included schedule sharing.

Char pressed the digit to erase the message and another one to call Savannah. She had chatted with Cole earlier in the day and dealt with most of Cam's questions through their son long before Cam thought to ask them.

"H'lo?"

"Savannah! Did I wake you? Why, it's only eleven o'clock there!"

"Mom? Hi."

"How was your day, sugar? Anything exciting happen at school?" Char gently prompted and listened as her daughter shared tidbits between yawns.

She cherished such moments with her daughter, even the volatile ones when Savannah flew off the handle. Peaceful or not, the moments were proof of a relationship, the kind snatched from her at the age of thirteen by a drunk driver.

Still, after ending the conversation, she felt an ache, an old longing. None of her family members had asked about her or about her day.

Andy Williams, aka Todd Brooks, answered on the first ring. "Hey, sugar." Obviously he'd checked his caller ID.

Char laughed. "Stop making fun of me!"

"Ah, but I'm not. Imitation is the highest form of compliment. I miss your honey-toned prattle."

"You just heard it last night."

"Oh, right. I guess what I miss then is the very attractive lips from which that prattle falls."

Goose bumps covered her arms. What a silly reaction to his glibness! He could be an absolute flirt.

"How was your day, Charlaine?"

The goose bumps multiplied, no flirtation needed. "F-fine." She scooted halfway around the seawall and drew up legs, hugging them to her chest. Ocean, beach, starlight, and occasional passersby faded from view as she recounted the day's activities. Knowing the compassionate nature of her listener, she felt deeply gratified to be able to talk freely about herself.

He repeated her words, "All for one and one for all? The three, or rather four, musketeers?"

"Something like that. We were there for each other from the time I was thirteen. You know, they were all nerds. Superintelligent. Numbers one, two, and three in the class. I don't know why they dragged me along."

"Because you're so adorable and so Southern belle. You added the *je ne sais quois*. Nerds lack *je ne sais quois*. The oomph. The zip. The sparkle."

"Molly used to call me something. What was it?" Sparkle. Bright. Shiny. "Glitter."

"That's it." He paused. "The glitter is missing from the neighborhood, Charlaine." The pitch of his voice had changed, giving it a somber note. "It misses you. I miss you."

His words, spoken without hint of banter, stunned her. "Todd, sugar, what on earth has gotten into you?"

"Reality. Thought I'd try straightforward for a change and admit without apology my loneliness without you next door."

Silence hung between them.

At last he said, "I hope I didn't scare you off."

She bit her lip. Without a doubt he had drifted into inappropriate. Underscoring his words was his voice. It cruised on by Andy Williams' melodic tone and hit sensual.

But goose bumps prickled now from the top of her head to the tips of her toes.

And he was two thousand miles away.

"Why, Todd, you don't scare me in the least."

Twenty

"Zachary!" Andie laughed into the cell phone squished between her shoulder and chin.

Her youngest had just offered a humorous rendition of his brother's performance at football practice. She had already heard Jadon's version. The boys could always make her laugh. They'd even teased her about the boogie boarding, once they got over their disbelief that she'd actually stepped foot into the ocean.

"Zach! Enough. I have to go. Molly's foot needs all my attention." Andie sat on a kitchen chair facing her friend seated in an overstuffed armchair. With Molly's leg extended and her bare foot resting on Andie's thigh, Andie could work while she talked. Kneading feet was second nature to her, not requiring all of her attention or even her eyesight. She caught Molly's wink.

"Mom," Zach said, "you're supposed to be on vacation, not doing reflexology." His deep voice was indistinguishable from his dad's. Jadon's was the same. She pictured them both: tall, handsome, and athletically built like Paul.

"Honey, this *is* vacation for me. I get to give my old friend a treatment just like your great-grandma used to do for her."

"I knew you were going to say that. You are weird." The loving tone of a teenager who sometimes appreciated his mom erased any derogatory implication. "Bye."

"Bye." *Give my love to your dad...* The words spun in her head. Instead of voicing them, she closed up the phone and set it aside.

Paul had not returned any of her calls. His assistant called once. That didn't count. Sherri had chatted for a few moments, put her on hold, and then came back to report Paul was on another line. Could they phone later? *They.*

At the moment Andie wasn't sure how she felt about him. Of course she loved him. Wives loved their husbands. He provided well, had an honest reputation in the business community, was nice to her. Polite, at any rate. She respected and honored and appreciated him. The word *love*, though, implied *like*. She didn't think she *liked* him—

"Yow!" Molly yelped.

Andie lifted her finger from behind the ankle where she'd been pressing. "That's a little tender there."

"Yeah!" Molly winced. "So how are your kids?"

Easily conversing while she worked, Andie moved her thumb in a caterpillar-like walk along the sole, searching for other areas that would feel tender to Molly and like cracking egg shells to Andie's fingertips.

"Oh, man!" Molly flinched again. "Good grief! I forgot how bad this hurt."

"*Oui.* But, zee pain means zee bad stuff goes kaput." She mimicked her grandmother's French accent.

"Speaking of Grandmère Babette," Molly spoke through gritted teeth, "Jo and I remembered the List."

"Mmm. Hon, try to relax. Ah, yes, the infamous List." It was a catalogue of classic, womanly traits. Or at least what a colorful, independent Frenchwoman believed womanly traits to be. Babette had always slipped life lessons into casual conversation with the four girls. They would then rehearse her wisdom on train rides home from her downtown apartment. While the others dictated, Andie wrote them in a notebook. For high school graduation gifts, she collected the sayings into what she called "The List," copied them in calligraphy onto thick linen paper and framed them. She still had hers on a laundry room wall out of everyone else's sight. Paul thought it silly.

Molly said, "Do you have eight matching plates?"

"Sixteen. And goblets and a dozen perfect recipes." She smiled. "With a real estate agent and community pillar for a husband, entertaining has become a way of life."

"What's your favorite list item?"

"I don't know. But I can tell you the impossible one. 'A real woman knows she can't change the length of her calves, the width of her hips, or the nature of her parents.' The hips have gotten wider, the calves never were right, and my mom…sheesh. I still feel thirteen years old when I'm around her."

"Inadequate?"

"That's it. Molly, you have a lot of hormonal activity going on."

"Tell me about it. Some days I feel thirteen and I don't even have to call my mom." She laughed. "Can you fix it? Make me normal?"

"Why would I want to make you normal? Anyway, I can't fix or diagnose what's going on. Jo does that. I can only tell you that things are unbalanced, but you already know that."

"How is your business?"

"It's good, slow but sure." She smiled. "I meet all these people through Paul, and when I tell them what I do, their eyes glaze over. 'I see. You unclog nerve endings. How interesting! And that releases energy to do what?'"

"Make me feel better," Molly supplied an answer. "And help the body heal itself. Ouch! The process, however, is not fun. Do you tell them that part?"

"Most of them are asleep by the time I get to details, but once in a while I pick up a new client. Molly, we really should do more of this tomorrow. You need to flush out the toxins with a lot of water. I doubt that at ten o'clock at night you want to drink a gallon."

"No, I don't. I always remembered Babette's admonition about drinking water. Your grandma taught us well, didn't she? About a lot of things."

"She did. I wouldn't have survived without her as buffer between me and my mom."

"Andie, you know she was saying to accept yourself for who you are and accept your mom for who she is and forgive her."

She gently set Molly's foot on the floor and straightened her back. "What do you think she would have said about fortieth birthdays?"

Her friend thought a moment. "That there's a strong possibility we'll feel lousy, but to take heart. It's a corner and corners are for turning. I think her wise granddaughter said something along those lines as well."

Andie smiled. "Let's go outside and count the stars."

Twenty-One

Molly and Jo sat again at the outdoor dining patio on Thursday morning. The scene was a repeat of the previous day complete with egg burrito, distant surfers, and overcast skies. Missing, however, was Molly's anxiety to call home. Another twenty-four hours of relating as Molly Preston had stifled Superwoman and infused her with courage.

She raised her latte and touched it against Jo's across the small table. "Here's to your second fortieth birthday, Josephine. How do you want to spend it?"

"I told you all, I live here. I don't need a day—"

"Hush. You gave us permission to pry you from that corner. This is our first attempt. You have to go along with it."

Jo pressed her lips together.

"Come on, Jo."

She narrowed her eyes. "I want to show you my condo and office."

"Great. We'd love to see them. Now that wasn't too tough, was it? See, we'll bring you out one baby step at a time."

"No yanking?"

"Only when absolutely necessary." Molly smiled. "The next step is you have to decide what we'll do for dinner."

Jo groaned. "And please one vegetarian, one meat and potatoes lover, one very finicky high-maintenance eater, and one fresh seafood devotee."

"Need I repeat? It's your day. Go for the fresh seafood. We can handle it."

"Easy for you to say. At least you eat seafood too." She gazed toward the ocean.

Molly watched her and felt a fresh sense of admiration for her old friend sweep over her.

Though it might be prying off the plastic lid from that container of worms, she decided to ask anyway. "Jo, was that the hardest thing you've ever done?"

Sunglasses were not in place yet. Her slate blue eyes resembled the ocean when the sun shone on it. Comprehension filled them. "You mean not drink on my birthday?"

She nodded.

"Yes, it was the hardest thing."

"I am so proud of you."

"Don't be. I am my mother's child. You know how Char does that thing with her tongue on her teeth because her mom taught her to do that instead of spout off in anger?"

"Mm-hmm."

"I remember a kitty dying, the runt of a litter. I was probably about four. I cried and cried. Dr. Christine Zambruski nailed me with one of her looks reserved for bungling nurses. She hissed, 'Death is part of life. You are not allowed to cry over it.'"

"Oh, Jo. How awful. I don't remember hearing that."

"I didn't think of it until recently. It was buried deep. I would cry now and then, but only with you and Char and Andie. Never in front of my mother. And never at a funeral. 'Death is part of life!'"

Molly recalled Jo's words from their first night together. She said she hadn't cried in twelve years. "You didn't cry on your birthday?"

"No. Didn't cry, didn't drink. I'm a big girl."

"But you asked for help. You called us."

Jo nodded.

"And you asked us for help to get you out of the corner."

"Progress?"

"Definitely."

"Someone else helped. I met him yesterday behind the house, a strange, wild-looking guy. Dreadlocks."

"Zeke."

Jo stared at her.

She laughed. "I met him too, out on the boardwalk. He's a street pastor."

"What in the world is a street pastor?"

"His church is the street. Or the boardwalk, in this case."

"Does he preach on a soapbox?"

"I don't think so. He walks around ministering to people he meets. He does a Bible study with a couple of the homeless regulars."

"Ministering. Hmm. I guess that's what he did with me. I told him the whole story about the girl before I told you and Char and Andie."

"Really?" Molly wondered why it was a stranger could connect with Jo where she herself hadn't. Another of God's mysterious ways. "He saw your pain, hon. Better than I did."

"I hid it from you as best I could. Don't give me that look. We're on vacation! I wasn't about to dump all my woes on you. Zeke just happened to catch me at a vulnerable moment. I had a splitting headache, and my three buddies were not following my prescribed agenda."

"How did he get the story out of you?"

"I have no idea." Jo shook her head. "His eyes."

"Yeah, I noticed those. They could do it. Rather otherworldly."

"Molly, you look pale. Do you feel all right?"

She unzipped her sweatshirt part way and pulled at the neck of her T-shirt. "Just a momentary yucky twinge. They're coming more often. I feel like a teenager. Out of control. My body surprises me with all sorts of things. I'm hot, cold, nauseous. I gain an extra five pounds unaccounted for. I wail one minute and laugh the next."

"Let's do a blood test today, find out just where you are hormonally."

"Jo, it's the natural order of things. My cycle is sporadic. Things are shutting down. It takes some adjustment."

"But you don't have to grin and bear it. There's hormone replacement therapy." She reached over and tapped the coffee cup. "And things like eliminating caffeine from your diet."

"Now you're getting a little pushy, Doctor."

"Well, it's my birthday. I can say what I want." She grinned. "And you have to go along with whatever I decide to do. Right?"

At that moment, seeing her hurting friend's rare wide smile, Molly would have agreed to do almost anything she proposed.

Molly carried a cup of coffee and paper-wrapped breakfast at her side in a napkin. She'd chosen the burrito with egg, ham, and cheese for Jimmy Mack, the homeless man she'd talked to the previous day.

A long line of people snaked out from Kono's open door and onto the boardwalk. She and Jo sidestepped it. As if on cue, the cloud cover dissipated above them, giving way to blue skies. She felt a momentary sense of exposure, of being unprotected. She missed her ocean rock sentinels, low-hanging fog, and uninhabited beaches.

And then she saw Jimmy Mack. The sight of him reshuffled her emotions. A sense of community enveloped her, as if she stood in God's living room with sky for ceiling and walkway for carpet. Tastefully decorated with ocean and plants, the huge area easily accommodated a crowd. She imagined not everyone there knew the host.

Jimmy Mack sat in the same spot on the same bench as before, his arms wrapped around a knapsack on his lap, his eyes at half-mast. He appeared to stare at nothing in particular. Drugs or alcohol…or utter despair?

She nudged Jo's arm with her elbow. "I'll be right back."

Not wanting to startle him, Molly approached slowly and sat on the bench a few feet from him. The salty air did not mask the odor of an unwashed body. Up close she saw yellow in the whites of his eyes, the roughness of his dark skin, the coarse black hair beneath the black stocking cap.

"Hi, Jimmy Mack."

He ignored her.

"I'm Molly. We met yesterday? I thought you might like some breakfast." She set the cup of coffee and wrapped food on the seat between them. "It's a burrito and coffee. Oh." She reached into her sweatshirt pocket and pulled out small packets. "Here's cream, sugar, and hot sauce, if you like."

Still no response from him.

"I talked to my kids this morning. Man, are they going to appreciate me when I get home! Scotty, my husband, gave them chores because yesterday's breakfast was such a disaster. Eli—he's eleven—was to get the cereal boxes out of the cupboard. Betsy was to set the table. Hannah was to help her daddy butter the toast. Then Abner—that's what I call Abigail—was to stack and rinse the bowls. They all complained like it was a major ordeal. Scotty told them if they didn't help, they would be tardy for school. *Again.*" She paused. "I should have let them help a long time ago. Taking on a little responsibility won't kill them."

"Kids need responsibility." The guttural voice was nearly indecipherable.

"I think so too. Do you have kids?"

No response.

Like before, when she asked a direct question, he clammed up. She changed the subject. "My friend over there is getting antsy. We're going to visit her office today. I think it's in some fancy neighborhood. She's a doctor. You know, if you were pregnant, she could take care of you."

The corner of his mouth moved, so slightly she wondered if she imagined it.

Molly slid the food nearer him and stood. "I'll see you later."

Across the boardwalk, Jo shook her head, an amused expression on her face, and mouthed the word, "Why?"

Molly weaved her way between runners and walkers and closed in on her. "Hey, maybe he's an angel."

A small man on a small bicycle with tall handlebars pulled alongside Molly. "Jimmy Mack ain't no angel." He grinned.

She saw gaps where teeth should have been, his ragged clothing, and dirt smudges on his face. "How do you know he's not?" she challenged him.

"He's done gone too far the other way. 'Jimmy, Jimmy, oh, Jimmy Mack, when are you coming back?'" Singing loudly off-key, the man veered the bike between her and Jo and pedaled away.

Jo looked at her. "Old song."

"Martha and the Vandellas."

"Miss Trivia Queen."

They resumed their trek back toward the beach house.

Jo brushed her shoulder against Molly's in a playful gesture. "I know why you do it. It's why you carried me off to AA when I couldn't stand on my own two feet. It's why you're going do your best to drag me out of this corner I'm trapped in. You're really Saint Jude reincarnated."

"I am not the saint of hopeless causes, Jo."

"Then you're Saint Molly, saint of the Molly Effect."

She eyed her friend. The phrase from their college days had always been uttered with disdain and a grimace.

Jo smiled. "It's okay. I think I'm ready for it. After all, you got Andie the scaredy cat talking to the weird neighbor and swimming in the ocean."

"All I did was pray for her."

"Prayer. Molly Effect. Same thing. I rest my case."

"You are not a hopeless cause. Neither is Jimmy Mack."

"Well, I ain't no angel and neither is he."

Molly glanced over her shoulder at Jimmy Mack. The knapsack was still cradled in his arms, but he held the coffee cup in one hand and the burrito in the other. She imagined then not angel wings but nail holes.

No, her friend and the stranger were not angels. Just wounded souls like herself in need of a touch from the One who hung on a cross.

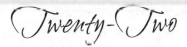

Twenty-Two

Jo stood in the center of her spacious private office while Molly, Andie, and Char oohed and aahed. It was a repeat of what they had done a short while ago at her house.

"Sugar, I am green with envy." Char trailed her fingers along the edge of the cherry desk and sat in one of the two matching sea green armchairs.

Andie moved slowly around the room, examining abstract art and framed degrees. "Char, *I* am green with envy. I'm the one who needs an office. You can be green with envy over her house."

Char laughed. "All right. It's a deal. Ocean view. Granite countertops. Stainless steel appliances. Mmm. Where do I sign up?"

"Where do I sign up?" Andie grinned. "Ocean view. Soft classical music, not a speaker in sight. Lovely green plants cascading everywhere. Gentle pastel colors. I don't need the desk. The leather loveseat will be nice, though."

Molly plopped onto the referenced couch. "It's very pretty in here, Jo. Professional and warm at the same time. Even the examining rooms. The reception area is downright gorgeous, and the magazines are current, not six months old. I imagine all that makes your patients feel secure."

Jo joined her on the couch. "Well, they used to, anyway. I'm officially on a self-appointed sabbatical of undetermined length. I've spent months casting patients off to the other doctors in the group. Letting my little mommies go. Convincing two women in imminent need of hysterectomies that the male down the hall is quite capable."

"That sounds like an agonizing process."

"Not as much as delivering babies. My first one after the funeral— I, um, I nearly lost the mother. Misread all the clues." She had called Alcoholics Anonymous that night. A counselor talked to her for nearly four hours while she bit her nails to nubbins. "Every delivery after that one was sheer terror. That's what I meant when I said I'm losing my confidence in practicing medicine. I don't trust myself anymore. That girl's death undid me."

Molly touched her arm. "A sabbatical is a perfect solution. You'll get grounded again."

"Oh, Jo!" Andie exclaimed and swung around from where she stood before a bulletin board. "I'm sorry. This is a different subject. Yes, of course you will get grounded again! But look at this!" She pointed to the board, a collection of baby photographs, some yellowed with age. "Did you deliver all these babies?"

Jo nodded. "The first dates back thirteen years."

"Oh, Jo!" she exclaimed again and turned back to the board.

"It's become a tradition." She shrugged. "A couple of my first mothers gave me pictures. Remember how we plastered our dorm rooms with photos of the four of us? I always liked that. Even—" She bit her lip.

They waited, three pairs of brows raised in expectation.

A sensation of letting go washed over Jo. It was fast becoming familiar. Why hold back now?

She swallowed. "Even wasted, I would gaze at those goofy pictures. I have no clue why that one of us at age fifteen standing around a pot of foul, boiling whitefish in Door County, Wisconsin, gave me hope. But it did. Anyway, I continued the practice and began displaying those first baby pictures. Every expectant mother notices the board, of course, and most of them add to it."

"Jo, honey," Char said, "what a tribute to your life's work. It is absolutely precious."

"I don't know if it's a trib—"

Molly squeezed her forearm. "Yes, it is. Just accept the compliment and say thank you."

She didn't deserve the compliment, but the Molly Effect had its way. "Thank you. The pictures give me hope. They ground me. I didn't understand that until recently. I just knew I liked them. You probably noticed how impersonal my home is?"

Molly did her head thing, an ambivalent shoulder to shoulder bob. "The photo from my wedding was on your bookcase."

"Some interior decorator convinced me to stash it years ago along with others. I unearthed that one on my birthday." She gave them an abject smile. "I almost got rid of these too."

Andie hurried to her side, knelt, and grasped the forearm Molly wasn't touching. "Oh, Jo!" she gushed again, sounding more and more like her empathetic grandmother minus the accent. "Promise me you won't ever get rid of them. They are a testimonial to you, to your wonderful work. Just imagine! All the new lives you've brought into this world. You must get grounded again. What do you need, Jo? What exactly do you want?"

It came in a flash, as if a curtain had been thrown aside. No. She smiled. It was as if she'd darted around a corner. She didn't know what caused it. The Molly Effect? The Grandmère Babette clone holding her arm? The nearness of long-lost, caring friends? It didn't matter. She knew right then and there exactly what she wanted.

Her smile broadened into a grin. Her cheeks ached at the unaccustomed stretch. "I'll show you right after I draw some blood from Molly's arm."

⌒

So much more than thirty minutes separated Jo's exquisitely appointed Del Mar office from the Hector Navarro Clinic.

Jo sat with Andie, Char, and Molly in her car parked at the curb across the street from the facility. The low, flat-roofed, stucco building with peeling aqua paint and its surrounding neighborhood would not have appeared out of place in Tijuana. Spanish was spoken as frequently as English, evident in the signage on businesses not boarded shut. There was no ocean view from any of them, not that the Pacific lay within visibility. Last week a drive-by shooting occurred two blocks over. At the moment a gang of kids clothed in baggy black and draped in copious silver chains loitered at the corner. They were probably exactly as they appeared: a gang. Children carrying guns, protecting turf, dealing drugs.

Tapping her fingers on the steering wheel, Jo eyed the trash-strewn sidewalk and waited for her friends' reactions. In the rearview mirror she caught Char's from the backseat.

Clapping a hand to her breast, Char exclaimed, "Oh, my! *That's* where you volunteer?"

"Jo," Andie breathed her name as if in awe. "You are a ministering angel."

She winced at praise she did not deserve.

From the front passenger seat Molly locked eyes with her. "Saint Josephine."

"I haven't done it for long, and I don't come often. Once a month, Saturdays. I missed a couple times ago."

Andie said, "But this is where you'd rather be, right? This is exactly what you want to do, serve in a poor neighborhood?"

Jo's imagination carried her back to when she was a third-year premed student visiting Chicago one weekend. Except for Christmas and occasional special events—her sister's baby shower, her brother's high school graduation—she did not go there. Three hours away, Champaign-Urbana became home with a capital *H* the moment she set foot inside that first dorm room, a suite she shared with Molly, Andie, and Char. A brand-new sense of freedom fell about her like a silky mantle. She vowed never to remove it.

Her mother and father were both physicians, Christine a gynecologist and John a surgeon. Distant and unemotional, they raised their three children at arm's length except when scrutinizing their performance. Years after the fact, Jo realized she went into medicine as a means of seeking their acceptance. By then she had fallen in love with her profession and had no regrets about her choice.

During college days when she visited them, they expected her to accompany them on hospital rounds. After all, she owed them the opportunity to review the wisdom of their investment in her education.

That particular Saturday in Chicago she met Ernesto Delgado, a resident serving his internship. Jo knew her parents' prejudices and recognized their disdain of the Hispanic. That fact only enhanced Jo's immediate infatuation. In some crooked fashion it fueled his attraction to her as well. What better way to retaliate for the slights of Dr. and Dr. Zambruski than to break their daughter's heart?

In time Jo and Ernie confessed the idiocy of basing their relationship on how they felt about her parents. Love grew long distance. He was intelligent, tall, dark, handsome, and fluent in his parents' native tongue. She graduated from Illinois and then followed him and his compassionate heart to Los Angeles. While he practiced medicine in a barrio, she attended UCLA, paying her own way.

She fell in love, too, with his work among the poor. Yet after becoming a doctor herself and joining a high-profile OB/GYN group in Beverly Hills, she got cold feet. His was not the life for her. The old battle with parental approval gained the upper hand. Eventually she left him and Los Angeles and replaced binge drinking with making and spending money. Her stockbroker and a real estate agent became her closest friends. When office space and malpractice costs skyrocketed, she didn't bat an eye.

Volunteering at the Hector Navarro Clinic began as a way to assuage guilt. Andie's question raised it onto a different level altogether.

Jo twisted around in her seat and looked at Andie. "Yes, this is exactly what I want. Shall we go inside?"

Twenty-Three

As they crossed the street to the clinic, Andie looped her arm into the crook of Jo's elbow. The sight of those hoodlums down at the corner nibbled at her newfound sense of adventure. Boogie boarding was one thing. Boys up to no good were quite another.

With a conscious effort to ignore them, she turned to her friend. "Saint Josephine."

"Andie, don't."

"It's true. I mean, I always thought you were a saint anyway because you're a doctor, but volunteering in a place like this cinches it."

"Actually my wildest dream is to use that vacant space there to the left of the clinic and work mainly with women. Speaking of saints." She leaned around Andie. "Char, hold on to Saint Molly before she heads down there to rescue those guys. I don't think they're in the mood."

Molly grinned. "Just let me go love on them. Love always disarms people."

Jo shook her head. "Disarms? Think guns, dear. Knives."

"Surely you exaggerate."

Andie gaped. "Molly!" she hissed. "Please!"

Char clasped Molly's shoulder. "Now, don't you two worry. I've got her."

Andie moved nearer to Jo. "Did you work with Ernie in a clinic like this?" Previously she had avoided mentioning Jo's old boyfriend, but the uneasy environment dispelled all propriety.

"Yes, this is very similar."

"Why did you ever stop?"

They stepped up the curb and crossed the sidewalk in a couple strides.

"You mean why did I decide to be a snob instead?" Jo grinned as she pulled open the glass door.

"Jo, I didn't mean—"

"I know. But it's the truth. You saw where I live, my office. Look at me." She gestured toward herself.

Andie admired Jo's chic appearance yet again. Even in blue jeans and plain white blouse she exuded wealth, but then she always had. Her initial reaction to the beach house as well as to Julian, along with snide comments about various things, indicated she was overly concerned with the material side of life. That she volunteered at the clinic was a delightful surprise. Although she would not have referred to Jo as a snob, Andie never would have guessed at such an altruistic side.

Following Molly and Char through the door, Andie paused in front of Jo. "How did you get here?"

"That sixteen-year-old girl who died on my watch."

Andie waited for more.

Jo shrugged. "I told you I nearly lost a birthing mother soon after that?"

She nodded.

"I called an AA counselor that night. Four hours later we touched on that one brief period in my life when I felt truly useful, truly happy." The corners of her mouth turned down in a self-deprecating smile. "It was working with Ernie. But it wasn't him. It was the people."

Inside the clinic's lackluster waiting area, Andie sat in a corner. Her chair resembled ones found in old-fashioned beauty salons. They had curved metal arms and legs, gray vinyl seats and backs. Padding showed through cracks in the vinyl. A slit under her own leg snagged at her slacks when she moved.

Half the seats were occupied with wheezing, hacking, and moaning people, a conglomerate of every age and ethnicity, complete with foreign speech and body odor. They were the ones who had awakened Jo's altruism.

Beside her, Char said in a low voice, "Our Jo is certainly full of surprises, isn't she? Who would have imagined!"

Andie smiled. That was Char's genteel way of expressing her chagrin. Living for a week in a replica of Grandmère Babette's humble home was acceptable. However, sharing space with the down-and-out offended her sensibilities.

On her other side Molly sat hunched, elbows propped on her knees, face buried in her hands. Andie knew she was not blotting out the scene. In their short time together, she had learned that when Molly went nonverbal on them, she most likely was praying. Either that or her hormones were doing their crazy dance routine.

Maybe Andie should knead Molly's hands, the next best thing to working on her feet.

Char murmured, "I wonder how long she'll be?" She leaned forward, eyeing a tattered *People* magazine on a low table before them. "I think I read that last December." She made no move to pick it up.

Jo had disappeared some time ago behind the reception counter after asking if they minded waiting for her. She wanted to see how things were going.

Molly straightened. "Should we offer to come back and pick her up later?"

"You mean *leave?*" Andie heard her voice go up a notch.

"Yeah. It seems obvious they could use her help right now. We can entertain ourselves for a while."

Char said, "Andie, do you have the map? I can find our way to that mall we've passed a couple of times, where those freeways come together. We can schlep around a bit, find a coffee shop, and then head back here late this afternoon."

"But you saw the traffic. It's probably impossible at rush hour!"

"Sugar, I drive on Chicago expressways all times of the day and night. You know what that's like."

"Well, I have the map, but we don't even know where we are."

"Of course we do. We're where tourists don't go."

Molly chuckled. "Come on, Andie. We're into adventure here. By definition that's an unknown outcome."

She felt a familiar tightness cut into her chest.

Molly went on. "Boogie boarding was an incredible first step for you. Let's take a second teensy-weensy one together. I know you're ready."

Char touched her arm. "As I live and breathe, you are most certainly ready. You don't see Molly or me out there in the ocean with you, do you? No way. Exploring in the car with us will be a cinch."

Molly patted her other arm. "You read maps better than I do. We need you, Andie."

If she mentioned her missing spunk again, Andie would dissolve into tears.

Jo interrupted. "Hey." She slid onto the low coffee table before them and crossed her legs. "I'm sorry for taking so long."

Molly said, "No, don't be. This is your day, and I think this is your place. You must want to spend more time here." She waved an arm. "My guess is they can use you right now."

"That's true. There's only a physician's assistant and one nurse on duty. Obviously their hands are full, but I don't want to sacrifice time with you guys. It always looks like this in here. I'll be back next week."

Molly and Char disagreed.

Andie tuned out their quiet debate and realized Molly was gently squeezing her arm. The light pressure conveyed her friend's concern. She knew that hormonal or not, Molly covered them all in prayer. To see just a short while ago Jo's first genuine smile since they'd reunited was evidence of God at work. And what else could explain her own courage to dive into the ocean?

How she longed for Molly's faith! For Jo's clear focus on what exactly she wanted to do with her time and energy. For Char's zest concerning every detail of everyday life.

"Hold on." Jo was turned, looking over her shoulder.

Andie followed her line of sight and saw a pregnant woman sitting off to the side. No, not woman. More girl than woman. A teen. A teen large with child. Tears streamed down her face.

In the blink of an eye Jo was at her side. Andie exchanged glances with Char and Molly. They waited.

Jo touched the girl's swollen abdomen. Their hushed conversation had a Spanish cadence to it.

As Jo helped her stand, she turned an apologetic expression toward them. "Five minutes."

Molly gave her a thumbs-up. Char swung her crossed leg faster than ever, mumbling something about car keys.

And Andie began to pray. Not for her own courage, but for the girl's.

⌒

"You! Over there."

Andie looked along with everyone else in the room at the receptionist. She had poked her head through the open half of the sliding window and was pointing a pen in Andie's direction.

"The redhead. Doctor wants you back here."

"Huh?"

"Now!" She slid the window and it shut with a decided click.

Andie stared at Molly. "Huh?"

"Jo wants your magic fingers and calm spirit." She grinned. "With every pregnancy I so wished for your grandmother's neck and back massages and mesmerizing voice. Go!"

When she was halfway across the room, Molly called out, "Tell Jo I'm praying."

Char slid further down into her seat.

With trepidation Andie went through the door leading to the examining rooms. Though she considered herself in the healing business, hers was not mainstream. Most people she met didn't have a clue what reflexology was all about. She didn't even have formal training, which really confused some. Grandmère Babette had taught her the subtle blend of science, art, and sheer hard work.

What in the world did Jo need from her?

No nurse, smiling or otherwise, directed her, but the cries of a woman settled the question of which room to enter. Andie opened its door.

Jo stood beside the pregnant teen, who was lying on the examining table. With one hand she held the girl's wrist and with the other buttoned up a white lab coat. Another woman stood at the far end of the table, slipping a mask up over her mouth and nose.

"Maria, this is my good friend Andie." Jo's voice was calm and authoritative as she addressed the young patient. "She's been through this twice."

Sixteen years ago! A twinge of panic squeezed her chest.

"She will help you." Jo looked at Andie. "No one is here with her. Just hold her hand. Knead her shoulders. Speak peace." She tilted her head one way, then the other, indicating directions. "Sink. Mask beside it. Gertie, physician's assistant, who prefers not to do this by herself."

The silver-haired woman gave a preoccupied half nod.

Andie said, "Not do what…?"

"Baby's a-comin'!" Jo slipped on a pair of latex gloves as she stepped around the table to take Gertie's place. "So is the ambulance, but my bet's on baby arriving first. Maria, how are you doing, sweetheart? Breathe like this." She demonstrated before setting her mask in place.

Andie heard Jo's words as if from a great distance. Baby? Ambulance? They did not immediately compute. "But this isn't a hospital."

"Correct." Jo glanced at her. Her eyes above the mask reflected Andie's own fear.

Like a robot, Andie dropped her purse on a chair, stepped to the sink, pushed her sleeves above her elbows, and methodically began to wash.

Jo was afraid. Jo shouldn't be afraid. She did this for a living! She had been at it for years and years. There were all those photographs on her wall, all those sweet-faced babies.

But they weren't in a hospital now! There was no *equipment!* What was Andie supposed to do? Molly was the strong, brave one. Molly had been through this four times. Why wasn't she in here? Molly could—

She turned to Jo and waited for Maria's cry of pain to lessen again.

"Jo."

"Hmm?"

"Molly's praying."

The mask moved and her eyes squinted. She was grinning. Her entire demeanor changed. "The Molly Effect. What else do we need? We're home free. Push, Maria! Push!"

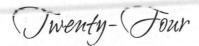

Twenty-Four

Char walked out of the clinic and pressed the speed dial key on her cell phone for Todd's number. As it rang, she shoved aside cans and paper litter with her sandaled foot, clearing a sunny spot in which to stand without paper whipping about her ankles. The afternoon breeze seemed to be a daily thing, as was her friends' needs to emote like adolescents.

Oh well. They were a hoot when not in the throes of angst. Char hadn't laughed so much in ages. And now the sun was shining—albeit rather low in the sky for them having done nothing in the past six hours but visit medical facilities—and she had a perfect excuse to call Todd before midnight, central daylight time.

He answered. "To what do I owe this unexpected pleasure?" Obviously he'd checked the caller ID.

"There was nothing else to do."

"Charlaine." He tsked. "Need I remind you that you are in San Diego? Of course there's something else to do."

"I beg to disagree. At the moment I'm stuck at this beastly urgent care clinic for low-income people who do not speak coherent English. The nearest tourist attraction is a group of gangbangers half a block away." A fancy silver BMW pulled alongside the curb. "A car just stopped in front of them. Oh my goodness. Look at that! Wow!"

"What?"

"I don't believe it. One guy pulled a bag out of his pocket and stuck it through the window. Now he's stuffing his fist into his pocket. I bet he's got a wad of hundred dollar bills in it."

"Char!" Alarm erased his Andy Williams croon.

"Do you think that was a drug deal?"

"Char!"

She turned toward the building as the car slithered past her. "Sugar, don't you worry. I'll tell them I didn't see a thing."

"Char!" He nearly shouted her name.

"If they get nasty, I'll execute my Tae-Bo kick on them. You know how well I can do that." She had demonstrated her exercise routine for him once.

The loud release of suppressed breath filled the line. "You're putting me on."

"Yes, Todd." She smiled. "Well, partially. The drug thing really happened."

"Don't do this to me."

"But your concern is so cute. I thought I'd prolong it."

"You're not playing fair."

She chuckled. They were even now. He hadn't played fair last night, talking in that sensual tone of his about how she was the glitter of the neighborhood and how he missed her.

"Charlaine, honest truth now. Are you safe?"

"Yes. They are paying no heed to me." She circled back round and surveyed the scenery. "There's a dollar-type store across the street. A taco stand next to that. Traffic is steady, and not all that many cars stop to purchase drugs from my friends." She grinned at his second loud expulsion of breath. "People are coming and going out of the clinic. I'm less than three feet from its door."

"What *are* you doing there? I thought this was supposed to be a birthday celebration. The doctor's."

"Right." She scanned the stucco wall behind her and decided against leaning. Her coral knit top was not getting anywhere near that filth. "And that's what I'm doing here. We promised each other to go along with whatever the birthday girl wants to do. No complaints allowed. And I'm not really complaining. I'm just a tiny bit bored. Jo was going to show us some boutiques and art galleries. Dinner was to be at a clubby, beachy sort of place. Though how clubby and beachy can be used to describe the same place, I have no clue. I think it's safe to assume I am not going to find out tonight."

"What happened?"

"We started out at her house and office. Both of them are absolutely gorgeous. Then Andie got all ooey-gooey over a display of baby photographs on Jo's wall. It was precious, truly. Somehow Jo got to talking about how that girl's death I told you about really shook her up. She can hardly work. Now she's on sabbatical. I don't know. She must have money from somewhere. Her parents were loaded, but I think they nearly wrote her out of the will when she took up with that Mexican."

"So how did you get to this clinic?"

"Well, Andie asked Jo what she really wanted to do and she said she would show us. We grabbed deli sandwiches and here we are, in the armpit of San Diego. Now she's in there taking care of a pregnant teenager. Andie's with her. Molly's working the waiting room like a salesman, moving from one sick person to the next, holding little kids on her lap. Who knows what germs they'll all carry back to the beach house!"

"Why is Jo taking care of someone?"

"Because she has a heart of gold. She likes to pretend she doesn't, but she does. I mean we simply *stopped by*, but she could not leave well enough alone and let the people who run things take care of this child, who should not be pregnant in the first place. Oh my word."

"Now what? Is that a siren?"

The wails grew deafening. Char covered her ear with a hand and shouted into the phone. "Hold on."

An ambulance screeched to a halt in the street, and the shrill noise wound down.

"Todd, you won't believe it. There's an ambulance right next to me. Medics are getting out." She watched a uniformed man and woman scurry to the rear of the boxy vehicle. "Now they're climbing into the back of it."

"You're not safe there. Why don't you go back inside?"

"Now, now. I am fine. It's just another big city. Chicago's not exactly the safest place on earth." Char watched the medics gather equipment. Out came a stretcher.

"But you *know* Chicago," Todd protested.

"They're coming— You're going in here?" She spoke to the emergency workers approaching the clinic. "Let me get the door." Char stepped to one of the double doors and pulled it open.

The young woman smiled as she passed. "Thanks."

"What's going on?" she asked them.

"A woman's in labor," the guy said. "Guess somebody missed the turn to the hospital."

Char let the door fall shut behind them. "Todd, they said someone's in labor. It must be Jo's teenager. Imagine that!"

"Your vacation is growing stranger by the minute."

"This is just life with the girls. I've told you some of the crazy stuff we used to do."

"But you're not kids anymore. This is supposed to be your fortieth birthday celebration too."

She was touched by his tender tone. "I'll have my turn."

"September twenty-seventh." He knew her birthday. Since he'd moved next door four years ago, he and his then wife had joined her, Cam, and other friends for dinner to mark the occasion. "Tomorrow. What did you decide to do?"

"We're going to Los Angeles. I promised myself I would buy one genuine designer outfit on Rodeo Drive. And we'll see Grauman's Chinese Theatre with all the movie stars' hand impressions on the sidewalk. We will make up for today's lack of glamour, I guarantee it."

"I'm sure you will, Miss Glitter. Why don't you give me the beach house address? Just in case someone wants to know where to send flowers."

The tickling sensation struck again. It was becoming downright habit forming.

Twenty-Five

Molly wondered if hearts could burst from an overload of empathy. Hers pounded with it as she sat in the clinic, a toddler on her lap, the woes of being poor and ill in America reverberating off the walls.

Char had stepped outside for some fresh air. Molly would have joined her, but she could not pry herself from the toddler she held. Jo and Andie remained behind closed doors. The cheaply made walls did little to muffle occasional gut-wrenching cries that Molly assumed came from the pregnant teen. She also assumed the cause of her distress was labor. The first indication had been when Jo touched the girl's abdomen, coached her in a breathing technique, and checked her watch. The second hint came when the girl stood. Molly knew a baby that low would soon greet the world.

Thirdly, all the waiting room occupants visibly relaxed. Though many were friendly before, most now became animated. What was happening? Everyone offered an opinion, most of them expressed in a combination of Spanish and English. They agreed that whatever was going on involved the pregnant girl. They did not mind waiting longer for their turn now. A birthing mother took precedence over coughs, flu, chronic aches and pains, and inexplicable rashes.

Birthing mother? Molly prayed. Jo seemed shaky and unsure of herself. The place was not a hospital. How could anyone give birth in it? Surely an ambulance was on its way.

The little girl on her lap took hold of Molly's hand and raised questioning brown eyes to her. She was a beautiful child with long black curls and dimples now deepening as the corners of her tiny mouth curled upward. Her mother sat nearby, clutching a feverish infant to her breast.

Molly nodded to the girl. "It's okay. Yes."

With a giggle she dug further into Molly's backpack, which she often carried instead of a purse. Fortunately she hadn't completely cleaned it out before the trip, so it still contained an array of small toys, books, and packaged crackers, buried treasures for little ones.

Molly felt a stab of remorse as she cuddled the child. She and Scott were content with four. Little Hannah came along a year after a miscarriage, and they did not want more. Still, when her body began to dance its hormone haywire number and she suspected ovulation had ended, she ached at the finality of it all.

She groaned inwardly. First she felt pity for every stranger in that waiting room. Then apprehension over Jo. Now inconsolable sorrow about a perfectly natural change of life. Oh! How she longed for those days when she simply told herself and others to "get out from under the pile!" Life was life. Deal with it. Sentimentality was hooey, a waste of energy better used elsewhere. Even her encouragement to the down-and-out had always emphasized the pulling up of bootstraps.

Yes indeed. The fortieth had been synonymous with entering a hazard zone.

The sound of a siren drew her attention from the toddler. Moments later two emergency workers wheeled a stretcher from the door across a corner of the room. The receptionist held open the door leading to the exam rooms, a distinct frown on her face, a reprimand imminent on the pursed lips beginning to part. One of the medics said something about a delivery truck blocking the back entrance. The door shut behind them.

A collective, puzzled smile went round the room along with more speculation. Molly caught some of it, the words spoken in English. Help had arrived. Was the girl all right? Of course. Probably false labor. They would check her out. They had special equipment. They could get her to the hospital.

Molly kissed the little girl's head, relieved that Jo had help, that all the sick people would now get their turn, and that she could pass the child back to her mother. She could get on with her loopy, menopausal life.

A tear trickled from the corner of her eye.

Good grief. She really needed to find a full-time teaching job.

Twenty-Six

"One more push, sweetheart." Jo encouraged calmly but loud enough to make herself heard over Maria's groans. "You can do it."

Andie ignored the death grip Maria had on one of her hands and smoothed hair back from the girl's damp forehead with the other. "You're doing a wonderful job, hon."

Maria gazed at Andie. Their eyes had been locked since the pushing began. In those few timeless minutes Andie had watched fear give way to the pain. Now sheer hard work showed in Maria's grimace and resounded in her cry. She was a runner crossing the finish line.

"Yay!" Jo's tone remained constant even in exclamation. "Here we go! It's a girl, Maria. It's a precious girl. Ten toes. Ten fingers. Beautiful color."

Gertie said, "Way to go, Maria!"

Andie whooped and not all that quietly. She could not contain the joy.

The baby whimpered and Maria did likewise.

Andie spoke soothing words and wiped her face with a damp cloth.

Jo laid the newborn on Maria's chest. "Baby needs her mama. It's bonding time."

Without hesitation Maria wrapped her arms around the child as Gertie wrapped a blanket around her. Andie noticed the attached umbilical cord and realized things were not yet over. Though she had worked with a few clients during their labor, she had not experienced an actual birth since Zach's sixteen and a half years ago. That took place in a hospital with all the accoutrements and all the nurses and Paul holding her hand. The memory had blurred somewhat, but she distinctly remembered that neither of her sons had been placed in her arms until after a nurse had completed some routine procedures.

It's bonding time. Jo's words echoed in her mind and tears pooled in her eyes. She missed her boys. She missed her husband. She missed what had been.

Maria smiled timidly.

Andie touched her cheek. "Congratulations, Mommy. May the Lord bless you and keep you from this day forth and forevermore." Silently she added, *You are a child yourself, but you can take care of this child. You will fight tooth and nail for her well-being.*

There was a short rap on the door and then it was opened. A young man and woman entered. Their clothing suggested they were emergency medical workers.

Jo chuckled. "Sorry, guys. You missed the fun part."

The woman grinned. "Aww nuts. I wanted to deliver the baby."

"Nothing like it, is there?" Then to Maria, "It's okay, sweetheart. This isn't as hard as the first part."

The medic asked, "Are you the doctor?"

"Yeah." Jo was intent on her work. "We're fine."

"Okay. We'll just wait until you're ready to transport." They left the room.

Andie went back to smiling at Maria. "Can I see her?"

She nodded.

Andie lifted a corner of the blanket. The baby mewed, her eyes shut, nose and forehead wrinkled as if she frowned. One hand was clutched in a tiny fist. She had a head full of dark hair.

"Maria, she is beautiful."

"What is your name?" the teenager whispered.

"Andie."

"Andie?"

From her puzzled expression, Andie assumed she had not heard of it. Perhaps the masculine *Andy* was familiar to her. "It's short for Andrea."

"Andrea." The girl's Hispanic accent rolled the *r*, put more emphasis on the second syllable, and added an *h* sound before the *a*. She looked down at her newborn. "Andrea. Andrea. Maria's baby."

"What?"

"I name the baby Andrea."

"What?" Andie heard perfectly well what Maria said, but it made no sense.

Jo said, "She named the baby after you."

"Nah."

"Mrs. Sinclair, it's a tribute. Just accept it and say thank you."

Andie recalled Molly giving Jo similar advice about receiving a compliment.

Maria smiled at her.

"But," Andie protested, "Jo did all the work, hon. The doctor. Jo. Josephine. Maybe Josephina? Isn't that pretty?"

The teen gave a slight shake of her head. "Andrea."

Andie heard a determined, womanly nuance to the child's voice. Evidently a baby had just been named after Andrea Sinclair.

And she thought riding ocean waves was a blast.

⁓

As she left the clinic with her friends, Andie was surprised that twilight had already fallen. They crossed the dusky street to Jo's car.

Jo said, "Char, I'm way too jazzed to drive. Do you mind?"

"Not at all."

"Thanks. The restaurant's not far." Jo gently tossed her keys to her and grabbed Andie's arm. "And thank you again. You made all the difference in there. I never could have gotten Maria to work with me like that."

Andie smiled. She had heard the praise countless times already. "It was so awesome." Nearly as high as Jo, she had reiterated her own phrase over and over. No other words sufficed.

Jo strode in a figure eight around and between them. "And thank you, Molly and Char, for being so patient."

Char laughed. "How do you know we were patient?"

"You didn't leave."

"Like we had a choice?"

Molly said, "The truth is, Char went outside and documented three drug deals. I myself was a basket case."

"A basket case?" Jo asked. "I thought you were praying. I was counting on the Molly Effect!"

"I prayed and then something snapped. I don't know."

Jo scooted to her side and pressed a hand to her forehead. "We've got to get you some hormones, dear."

They reached the car and climbed into it, laughing. Char and Molly complained good-naturedly about the long wait. Andie had paid no attention to time, only to the fact that she and Jo lingered with Maria and the baby. The baby. Baby Andrea. Her cheeks ached from grinning.

Jo refused to interrupt the bonding hour between mother and daughter or to let Maria out of her sight until she was convinced of her stability. Besides that, they took time for a photo shoot. Andie's digital camera, now tucked safely back into her handbag, held almost a dozen pictures. Baby and mommy. Baby and Jo. Baby and Gertie. Baby and EMTs. Baby and Andie. And, of course, baby by herself for Jo's wall.

From the backseat, Andie reached over and squeezed Jo's shoulder. "Josephine, you literally stopped a corner of the world to welcome that baby into it, didn't you? I mean, you kept Char and Molly, medics, and a roomful of sick people waiting."

Jo raised a fist in the air. "Woo! I did!" She twisted around in her seat to face the back. "And it felt so incredibly tremendous. Not that part, but the part where I didn't panic. And the part where I just sat down with Maria and asked how she was doing. Thank you for praying, Moll. And you for being patient, Char. And Andie—"

"You're welcome already!" Andie laughed.

"And you, Andrea," Jo rolled the *r* and poised her hand for a high five, "you had a baby named after you."

Andie slapped Jo's hand. "Woo! Yes, I did!"

Char started the car. "Where to, Jo?"

"The Chicken Pie Shop." She laughed again. "You are going to absolutely hate it."

~

Jo's prediction more or less came to pass. There was not much to like about the Chicken Pie Shop except the prices, a waitress who called them "honey," and—in Andie's opinion—the yummy mashed potatoes and gravy.

"But," Andie said, "it's the kind of place you love to hate."

The table nearly jiggled with the ensuing laughter. Jo's excitement was contagious. Their guffaws grew more raucous at every discovery in the large, noisy, 1960s-era diner.

Jo said, "Exactly. It's just so *campy.* I mean, the chicken decor is hysterical. Char, you are a good egg." She clapped her hands. "Egg! Get it?"

The others booed.

"Anyway," Jo continued, "I know this is driving you nuts."

Ever gracious, Char smiled sweetly. "Sugar, I'm just trying to catch up with you all."

Jo scrunched her nose in reply.

Char didn't miss a beat. "I think my mama knew someone who once ate in a place like this."

Andie's mouthful of soda nearly sprayed up and out through her nose.

Molly dropped her fork and doubled over.

Jo groaned. "You are going to make me pay tomorrow, aren't you?"

"Big time. But just think of all the money you saved tonight by coming here. Who could have imagined buying an entire meal for under five dollars? Color me flabbergasted."

With a straight face, Jo said, "Yes, it is amazing, isn't it? Potpie, potatoes and gravy, coleslaw, veggies, rolls, *and* a slice of pie, your choice. All for one low, low price."

"Well, hon, I'm not sure it's worth any more than that one low, low price." Char fluffed her short blond hair. "I swear, if I can't fit into my regular size tomorrow while trying on an outfit in some exclusive Rodeo Drive boutique, heads will roll." She paused. "Tell me again, what kinds of pie do they offer here?"

Jo grinned. "Like I said, you are a good egg. And you too, Miss Vegetarian. Are you all right?"

Molly's smile seemed forced. "Sure. No." She continued sliding poultry chunks from the potpie and piling them to one side of her plate.

"You're green."

"I'm fine. Just a little queasy. It might be the smell."

Grease dominated the restaurant's odors, a homey combination of fried chicken, roasting beef, and simmering soups.

Andie said, "I know the three of you have more discriminating tastes than I do, but I think the food is rather good. Well, the boiled veggies are a bit overdone. But the rolls and potatoes are great, and this pastry crust around the potpie is yummy. Oh, dear." She laid down her fork. "It's comfort food, isn't it?"

Jo laid a hand on hers. "Are you eating because you need to be comforted?"

"Hardly. Being in on that birth was the most exciting thing I've ever done. Not counting having my own kids, that is. No, I think I'm eating because I'm hungry and there was nothing else to order."

Jo squeezed her hand now. "Then just enjoy it, hon."

She picked her fork up again. "Okay. Besides, I can surf it off tomorrow."

Jo raised her coffee cup. "Here's to adventure." The others clinked a glass or cup to hers as she said, "To good friends. To celebrating this birthday twice." Tears seeped from her eyes and onto her cheeks. "I don't know what I'm going to do without you three."

And right there, in the middle of the Chicken Pie Shop while ordering cherry pie a la mode, Jo made up for the dozen years she had not wept.

Twenty-Seven

Molly sat with Jo at their usual breakfast table on Kono's patio overlooking the ocean. The early morning mist hung, thicker than she had seen it. Like actors on a stage, surfers, seagulls, and newspaper-reading patrons occupied their customary places.

Molly savored a black-bean-and-egg burrito, a welcome relief to her stomach still unsure about the previous night's potpie with chicken-based sauce and the unfiltered tap water. Fresh salty air erased traces of grease odors that had lingered in her nose through the night.

"It's what I want." Jo smiled.

The scene might not have changed, but Jo had. She did not wear sunglasses. Her eyes were puffy—and sparkling. A new, distinct glow emanated from her. She was steadily working her way through an entire order of pancakes, sausage, and eggs instead of half a plain bagel.

Molly said, "You're talking about the clinic."

"Yes. I want to spend the rest of my life in that place, caring for those people."

"That was my guess yesterday. You seemed so totally at home there."

"I was at home, even before I talked with Maria. Maybe that's why I cried. *Finally*, after twelve years." She shook her head. "I don't know.

134

I felt this rush of relief, like after a long, long absence I'd found my way home." She grinned. "But maybe that was just the overload of carbs pouring comfort into my bloodstream."

"Now don't talk yourself out of it, Doctor. You turned a major corner last night. You know as well as I do the cleansing effect of tears."

Jo chewed thoughtfully for a moment. "Yeah. I suppose your God had something to do with that too."

Molly winked at her. Yes, of course God had something to do with healing Jo's bottled up pain. Her friend never had taken her word for it, though. The seed was planted long ago. She let the matter rest, confident Jo's softening heart was fertile ground.

Molly said, "So now what?"

"I want to shop in baby stores today and buy everything Maria could possibly need or want for her little one. I wonder if they have baby stores on Rodeo Drive?"

"Char probably knows. But Jo, I'm talking about your work. What do you want to do after this sabbatical?"

"I just said it. I want to work in the clinic full-time." She took her last bite of pancake. "Open another space adjacent to it for women."

Molly heard hesitation in her tone. "But?"

Jo chewed, swallowed, and sipped coffee before answering. "You saw my house. My office. You just heard me say I want to spend a fortune on designer baby clothes and accesories for an underprivileged teenage mother."

Molly waited.

Jo drained her coffee cup and, after a moment, sighed. "Don't you see, Moll? I like money too much. I always have. The clinic would pay a pittance, not enough to invest, not enough for a Del Mar house mortgage, not enough for a gas-guzzling SUV, not enough for boutiques and specialty shops. I can count on one hand the number of times I've set foot inside a chain discount store."

"You don't like money too much."

"I do."

Molly shook her head emphatically. "It was always a substitute for your parents, hon."

"Alcohol was."

"So was money. So *is* money."

Jo wagged a finger. "I subscribe to Babette's list: 'A real woman knows her childhood may not have been perfect, but it's *over.*'"

Molly thought of another, one she'd been pondering. "'A real woman knows how to confront a friend without ruining the friendship.' Give me a chance?"

Jo set her jaw, its muscles visibly taut.

"What if you stopped leasing a plush office? What if you moved to an average-type neighborhood? What if you traded in your fancy car for something basic?" The answer seemed obvious to Molly, but it was for Jo to find and to name in her own way.

Through long moments Molly watched a myriad of expressions cross her friend's face. Maybe she wasn't ready to unearth it yet.

Jo flicked her eyes in Molly's direction. "Is this your new version of 'get out from under the pile'?"

"I'm only suggesting you ask yourself those questions. They seem to be the roadblocks to you doing what you really want."

Tightening her hand into a fist, Jo squished her paper coffee cup.

Molly raised her brows. "I hope you're not thinking about my neck?"

"Mary Catherine, yours has always been the voice I'd rather ignore."

"That's okay."

"I don't want to go there."

"That's okay," Molly repeated. "Don't."

"I mean, it's over. My childhood is over. Why isn't it over?"

Inwardly Molly breathed a sigh of relief. "It can be, more or less, right here and now."

"Last night I didn't want a drink before I went to sleep. I can't remember the last time…I was probably ten." Jo stood abruptly, scraping her chair across the uneven wooden floorboards, and gathered empty breakfast plates. Three quick strides carried her to the trash bin, where she deposited them. She loped back and sat again. "If

I downsize—give up my lucrative practice, my office, house, and car—
I will be a failure in my parents' eyes."

"And in your eyes?"

She took a long deep breath and exhaled it. "I'll be a free woman."
The corners of her mouth lifted slowly even as tears pooled in her
eyes.

"Now it's over, hon. Your childhood is over."

⌒

Molly did not lollygag with an unresponsive Jimmy Mack. With a
brief greeting she set his breakfast on the bench beside him and
excused herself. She and Jo hurried back to the beach house. The day's
schedule was tight.

They found Andie in the kitchen, still in her swimsuit, a large
beach towel draped over her shoulders, and her hair damp. "One sec."
She removed the carafe from the hissing coffeemaker and filled a large
colorful mug.

Giggling, the three made their way down the hall. Outside Char's
bedroom, Andie brushed her knuckles over the closed door. When no
reply came, they nodded to each other.

Jo mouthed, "One, two, three."

Andie pushed open the door and set the mug atop a dresser. They
tiptoed across the shadowy room, and, as one, pounced on a sleeping
Char and shouted, "Happy birthday!"

Char shrieked and sprang to a sitting position, yanking off an eye
mask.

"Surprise!" they yelled.

"In the name of all that is sane and holy, what are you doing?" She
patted her chest. "Besides giving me a heart attack?"

Molly went to the window and twisted open the venetian blinds.
"Rise and shine, birthday girl!"

Andie handed her the mug. "Fresh. In your favorite cup."

"Thank you. I think." Her tone whined. "Jo, you said we didn't have
to leave early!"

"Early for one is not necessarily the same as early for another. I think I mentioned nine o'clock?"

She glanced at the bedside clock radio. "It's seven-thirty!"

"But we want you to shower first. Birthday treat! Full pressure, no running out of hot water."

"You ladies are too good to me."

Molly picked up the discarded eye mask, fingering the silky black fabric. "I didn't think anyone really wore these things."

Char snatched it out of her hand. "It's my birthday. You cannot make fun of me. Jo, we did not do this to you yesterday!"

"That's because I was the first one up. Enjoy your coffee. I have to make some phone calls." She left the room.

Andie sat on the edge of the bed. "You don't really mind we woke you up early, do you?"

Char plumped pillows and leaned back against them with a moan. "Ask me later."

"We wanted to give you a special start. None of us had a special start on our real birthdays. Well, I guess Molly did, but it turned out not to be so special since she had to clean up the kitchen."

Char leaned forward and grasped Andie's forearm. "Andrea Sinclair, we've known each other since we were thirteen. You were my room-mate for two years. What do you remember about our mornings?"

Her eyes grew large. "But you have kids now."

"They've been making their own breakfast since they were *five*."

Andie blinked. "You want a bagel?"

She glared in silence.

"I'll go wash off my boogie board and call my mom."

Molly followed her to the door. "I'll call Scott."

"Molly."

She looked back and saw Char pointing to her cell phone on the nightstand.

"I'll just wait until Andie or Jo are done with theirs. You'll be getting birthday calls."

"Take it," she grumbled. "No one would believe I'm awake and civil at this hour."

Civil? Molly grinned as she unplugged the phone.

Molly busied herself in her back corner bedroom. It was a cozy size with braided rug, one window, and two single beds covered with patchwork quilts the color of desert pastels. Like the living room, Faith Fontaine's personality was revealed in knickknacks on the dresser and Georgia O'Keefe prints on the wall. Molly enjoyed Faith's expression of nature's subtle beauties.

"Moll." Jo spoke from the doorway. "Mind if I come in?"

"Nope." She shut the closet door. "I was just organizing things, waiting for Scott to land before I call him. He should be dropping Eli off at school about now. It's band day. He plays a trombone about the same height as he is."

"Hmm." She sat on a wooden chair that matched those at the dining table. "Have a seat."

"You sound so formal. Oh!" Molly slid onto a bed. "Test results already? In less than twenty-four hours? You must know people in high places."

Jo smiled. "Well, yeah, I do."

"So where am I in this crazy cycle? Please, please tell me it won't last much longer!"

"Well," she said again and stopped, her mouth partially open. She leaned forward, resting her arms on her legs.

"Come on. When do we start the hormones? Just give a wild guess how long it will last. I won't hold you to it."

"Molly. Hon."

She puzzled over Jo's hesitancy. "You can't possibly be like this with your patients, Doctor. Pretend that we haven't been friends forever. Give it to me straight. I'm looking at ten years, right? I'm only in— what do you call it? The premenopausal stage."

Jo straightened and pressed her hands against her knees. "I know how long it will last."

Molly tilted her head forward, eager to hear.

"Nine months."

"Not bad. From when?"

"From whenever the egg was fertilized."

In spite of teasing about out-of-body experiences, up until that precise moment Molly would have denied such a thing could truly happen when one was healthy and in her right mind. Jo's words, however, lifted a part of herself up and out. As if in a dream, she felt that other self walk smack-dab into the wall and have the wind knocked from her. While that one couldn't breathe, the one sitting on the bed had blurred vision and a rushing noise in her ears.

"Molly?"

The two selves collided back into one and the room spun. "What does an egg have to do with menopause?"

"Nothing." Jo was beside the bed, kneeling on the floor and grasping Molly's hands. "I know this is a shock, hon. You're pregnant."

"It's menopause! You said so yourself. I don't feel pregnant! How do you know— Oh my gosh. Menstruation stopped being regular ages ago. I figured— Oh my gosh!"

"I ran the test. It's routine. These things happen. You think you don't need birth control because your body fools you. I know this is a shock. Breathe, Molly."

"I can't!" she gasped.

"You have to. Come on. Let it out." She squeezed her hands. "Hey! You're the best mommy on earth! God knows what He's doing."

"Uh-uh. He doesn't."

"He does. That's what you'll say as soon as you start breathing. There's a brand-new life growing inside of you. It's His miracle."

Again her breath felt slammed back into her body and she wailed. "Jo! Hannah is six years old! I'm forty years old! Forty and a half! It's too late to start over!"

Jo sat beside her and wrapped her arms around her. "It just takes a little time to get used to the idea."

There wouldn't be enough time in eternity to get used to the idea. Molly burst into tears.

Twenty-Eight

Char turned off the hair dryer and studied her reflection in the bathroom mirror.

"Happy birthday." She cocked her head and grasped the collar of her hot pink terrycloth robe. "Well, so far forty looks the same as thirty-nine. Maybe even thirty-four. Not bad."

There were three factors to thank for that. One: her mama's genes for a Georgia peach complexion and a size two figure. Two: regular workouts at the gym. And three: the perfect hairdresser with a knack for keeping her blond hair very near its original shade without too many chemicals. He knew how to style it as well. The wind-tousled look had been his idea and suited her to a tee.

She opened a jar of moisturizer, SPF 25, and applied it, trying not to think of Cam's nonreaction to her haircut, her toned body, her success as chair of the Women's Club annual fund-raising gala last July, her—

She secured the jar lid with a quick twisting motion and surveyed her array of cosmetics. A hint of eye shadow would be appropriate for Rodeo Drive. The taupe color to enhance her almond brown eyes. Her outfit, too, should be understated. Probably the taupe slacks with a white silk blouse. She'd take along the new embroidered jacket in case they were gone late. Jo said Friday traffic might be extra heavy. Perhaps they would stay put in L.A. and have dinner before driving back.

Friday.

Todd was probably at the gym now. They sometimes rode together on Friday mornings, parting ways at the door as he went to the weight room, she to an exercise class made up of women who kicked and punched the air while savage music pulsated loudly.

Eye shadow brush poised midair, Char paused, her face close enough to the mirror to see the beige flecks in her irises. "Mama would never approve."

But then, Mama was dead and gone, long gone. Twenty-seven years long gone. Char had known her for only thirteen years.

Still, Ellen Cummins Stowe née Wentworth's impact permeated. Char knew she would not approve of the flirting with Todd Brooks. There was Southern belle charm that encouraged a general sense of well-being in a man, and then there was something else. Truth be told, they'd been into the something else for quite some time. As a matter of fact, she could identify the precise night it happened.

It happened on her birthday, one year ago. Cam treated friends to dinner at her favorite restaurant. The evening ended in their home. They'd scarcely begun a game of charades when Cam excused himself and went to bed. It was not unusual behavior, but for some reason it particularly stung that night.

Todd noticed. Not that he said anything. On the surface things remained even-keeled between them. He must have known, though, as she did, that their banter had taken on an edge. His recent phone conversations proved it.

A realization dawned within her. Todd Brooks wanted more than a flirting relationship.

She blinked.

What did she want? At forty, with two teenagers well on their way and a couch potato for a husband, who did not notice or seem to care whether or not she even breathed? *What did she want?*

She pursed her lips and shook her head. No, her mama would not approve at all.

Char heard a wail and opened the bathroom door just as Molly hurried past it, Jo on her heels. She followed them into the living room.

Molly strode toward the front door, her arms upraised. "This cannot be happening!"

Jo said, "I'll come with you."

"No!" Without a backward glance Molly pushed open the screen door and stepped outside. She was halfway to the boardwalk before it slammed shut.

Char asked, "What's going on?"

Jo turned to face her. "The test results came back."

Char caught her breath. Obviously Molly was upset. Would tests for menopause show something like cancer? "What is it?"

"Molly's pregnant."

"Oh." Stunned, Char went to the couch and sat down. "Oh, my. She's forty years old! With four kids already!" She herself would absolutely die. But then Molly was different. "Were they planning it?"

"From her reaction, I'd say no way." Jo sat in an armchair. "She figured she was in menopause."

"Where did she go?"

"A walk down the beach."

"What should we do?"

"I don't know. She said she needed time alone. I imagine she'll call Scott when she calms down."

Char recalled seeing a cell phone in Molly's raised hand. Char's cell phone, the one with the number that friends would soon begin calling to wish her a happy birthday.

With a sigh, Jo stood. "She'll get used to the idea and postpone full-time teaching a little longer. I'd better get back to my calls."

"Where's Andie?"

"Walking to the pier. See you in a bit." She headed down the hall.

Char glanced about the empty room. Cool, calm Molly was borderline berserk—with Char's phone—somewhere down the beach for however long it was going to take her to get used to the idea that she was pregnant. Plump Andie—who'd been content to sit for the past fifteen years massaging feet—was off *walking* all the way to the pier after already *swimming*. Jo—who had adamantly unplugged from work—was suddenly plugged back in. Two of the three still wore their early morning attire—dreadful sweat suits not fit for public viewing. More than likely Andie still wore hers as well; Char hadn't heard the other shower running.

And in less than an hour they were to leave for Hollywood!

Char crossed her arms. "Happy birthday to me."

Twenty-Nine

Back in April when she turned forty and realized life needed a major adjustment, Molly hit bottom. Learning she was pregnant redefined the word "bottom."

She strode from the beach house to the seawall, quickly scaled it, and sank her feet into the sand. Like mud, it pulled at her feet, cutting her stride to an amble. Annoyed, she tucked the cell phone into a pocket, rolled up her pant legs, and yanked off her loafers. Stubbing her bare toes the entire way, she reached the packed sand at the water's edge and turned south. Her long quick steps soon propelled her into a jog.

She knew the exact date it happened. In July. Up the Elk River. A picnic. Beneath seven-hundred-year-old trees. The nearest living mammals bear and elk. *Outdoors*, for heaven's sake. Like two kids caught up in the passion of the moment.

They should have known better.

In their quest for recovering an old love lost somewhere between child number two and planting a church, she and Scotty worked hard at entering each other's worlds. Never the traditional pastor's wife, Molly did not play the piano or sing or do office work. She didn't even visit sick people with all that much grace. He never insisted she take on tasks for which she was not especially gifted. God always brought someone forward to fill those slots. While she focused on the Sunday school and homemaking, he focused on being the pastor and bread-winner. Their paths diverged.

That day in July they hatched a plan to converge those paths in a new way. She arranged play dates for all four children and joined Scott on a forest job counting trees or some such thing. They were going to *work* and *talk*. She packed tofu sandwiches and potato chips and did not imagine it necessary to bring along anything related to birth control.

Evidently more than their paths converged.

Out of breath now, Molly slowed. Her cuffs had unrolled and were damp from dragging in the wet sand. She pushed strands of hair fallen from her ponytail back behind her ears.

In truth, she hadn't paid much attention to birth control over the past year. Everything pointed to her body shutting down. What with that and four busy children and divergent directions, there hadn't seemed to be a need.

Was it the stress? The stress of turning forty and feeling unfulfilled and trying to fix that? She applied for nonexistent teaching positions in the children's district. She considered applying at another school located an hour's drive away. An hour's drive when there was no fog, hurricane-force winds, or road work. Then Eli's soccer career took off, Betsy broke an arm in gymnastics, and Abigail and Hannah got strep. Molly knew she did not have an extra two to three hours in a day to spend on the road. She settled for substitute teaching.

Meanwhile, convincing Scott how desperate she was for his atten-tion occupied the rest of her energies. It should have been a no-brainer. As a pastor who counseled married couples, he should have been a little more in tune.

He came around, of course. He loved her, and he was a godly man. In time they reconnected.

Oh, yes. Indeed they reconnected!

"Lord!" She bent forward, hands on hips, and tried to catch her breath before a sob broke loose. *Why?*

I will be fifty-eight before this one graduates from high school. Fifty-eight!

She straightened and blew out a frustrated breath. She had to talk to Scott right now.

Maybe the test was wrong?

She pulled the cell phone from her pocket. Hands shaking, she flipped it open, and tried to remember her home number.

No, the church was more likely—

No, he was at his other job. Surveying up the Elk River. He was provided a cell phone for work, but it wouldn't function from there.

"Curses on the Elk River! I wish it would dry up!"

She swallowed back another sob.

Maybe he hadn't traveled too far yet. What time was it? What was his work number?

She heard a small voice coming from the cell and put it to her ear. "Scotty?"

"Scotty?" a male voice said. "Come on, sugar. I know I'm on your caller ID."

"What? Who is this?"

"Char?"

"What?"

"Sorry. I must have the wrong number."

As if emerging from a mental fog, she realized with sudden clarity that someone was calling Char. "No, you don't have the wrong number. This is Char's phone. But I'm Molly."

"Molly! Hi!"

"Cam?"

"Nope. Todd."

"Todd?" Char's son wasn't named Todd, was he?

"Friend. Char has spoken of you. Is she around?"

"Um." She glanced at the ocean, as if it would produce the owner of the phone. A turn toward the boardwalk revealed that Molly was nowhere near the beach house and Char certainly was not in sight. "No."

"Do you know when she'll be back?"

Back from where? The mental fog settled in again. "Nooo."

"Well, don't tell her I called, all right?" He chuckled. "I want to surprise her. I'll just catch her later. Bye."

"Bye." Molly pushed the "End" button.

Who was Todd? Why was another man calling Char on her birthday?

Char's birthday. They had plans. She should go back.

The sob finally erupted. Molly sank onto the sand, sitting at the water's edge, facing the horizon, her back to the people jogging by. She propped her elbows on her bent knees and covered her face with her hands.

She was pregnant. Pregnant!

The tears were not going to stop any time soon.

Thirty

The roommates had not surfaced by the time Char finished dressing. Frustrated with the situation, she decided to take a walk herself and buy a newspaper. She slid some change into a pocket, sunglasses onto her nose, and thought about the boardwalk route to a vending machine. It would take her past numerous sardine-packed houses, a youth hostel, a motel, and countless interesting-looking people. If the previous two days were any indication, she would more than likely run into either Julian, the boor of a neighbor, or Zeke, an audacious, Bible-toting black man who probably struck up conversations with fence posts.

Char headed out the side door and down the street, a narrow one-way affair lined with garages, carports, and the backs of other small cottages. Half a block from theirs, she turned off it and onto one of the sidewalks that served as passageways from the beach to the business district. On either side of it sat tightly packed houses of all shapes and sizes, their front doors facing the center. The quiet area, profuse with plants, resembled a courtyard.

The walk took only a matter of moments. She reached the main street district, a traffic-filled boulevard and home to all kinds of trendy restaurants, beachy shops, and sports equipment rental places. She paused and scanned the area until she spotted a newspaper vending machine about three blocks away.

She strolled, not wanting to perspire, a given in the bright sunshine. A warm breeze blew against her face. A helicopter flew over, adding racket to the traffic noise.

Well, Molly had said turning forty could be hazardous to one's health. Evidently her friends had reneged on their pledge to make hers different. As far as she could tell, hers equaled theirs in the disappointment category. What was she doing walking in a strange hot city all alone in search of a newspaper without her cell phone or car keys? With fun plans indefinitely delayed? At least at home she would have reminded the kids to tell Cam. Even without enthusiasm or an especially thoughtful gift, his response amounted to something. He never remembered the exact date itself without prompting; she hadn't bothered to prompt anyone before she left. The kids would never think of it on their own. Would Kendra clue them in? Surely her friend had called by now and left a voice mail message.

She sighed. The only bright spot at the moment lay in Todd's hint that he would send flowers. They could be there by the time she returned.

But then she would have to explain Todd to Molly, Andie, and Jo. Oh, hang it all.

She comforted herself with thoughts of his attention. Even inappropriate, at least it was attention.

Twenty minutes later, newspaper in hand and still thinking of little else but Todd, Char approached her turn. Three uniformed policemen stood at the sidewalk's corner. They were rather cute in their shorts and sunglasses, without hats. But she was in no mood to chitchat. She smiled tightly at the one who looked at her and attempted to sidestep him.

He blocked her path, his eyes hidden behind dark lenses. "Excuse me, ma'am. This way is closed."

"But I'm staying in a house down there."

"Sorry. You'll have to find another route."

"It's not far." She peered around him. "Just the other side— oh my word." She spotted a fourth officer crouching beside a gate. "He has a gun."

She didn't know guns but it was obvious this particular one was not just any old pistol sort. It was long and huge with all kinds of attachments. A rifle?

"Ma'am, we're in the middle of a situation here. For your own safety, please move on."

"As I live and breathe, I am going to get shot on my birthday. What is going on?"

A voice came from behind her. "Nothing out of the ordinary for this neighborhood."

She turned and saw Julian.

He grinned and looked over her head. "Right, Justin?"

The officer laughed. "Squatters, vagrants, druggies, thieves. We got 'em all. And that's just for starters this morning."

"Shh. You're going to frighten our guest." He nodded toward Char.

"Sorry, ma'am. Nothing to worry about. Have a good day, Julian."

"Thanks. Stay safe. Shall we, Char?"

"Shall we what?"

"Move."

"Oh." Did she have a choice? "I suppose. But I'm sure I can find my own way."

"Unfortunately, the police have the whole area surrounded. We can't get to our houses from either the back way or the boardwalk."

"You're joking." She walked beside him along the busy street, noticing his billowy white linen shirt, baggy brown slacks, and sandaled feet.

"Afraid not. This happens now and then. Did you notice the helicopter?" He pointed skyward.

"I guess I did hear one." She peered up and saw it now. It banked, low enough for her to decipher "Police" printed in large bold letters on its underside.

"Always a clue. It's been circling for a while. That cottage directly behind your carport seems to be precisely in the center."

"Which means?"

"The thieving, vagrant squatter high on drugs was or is currently inside Sapphire's home."

"Who's Sapphire?"

"A free spirit you wouldn't have met. She's down in Mexico this month."

"And a vagrant is using her house?"

"That's my guess. I'll let you know when I get the full story." He stopped. "How about breakfast?"

They had reached a corner restaurant with patio seating along the sidewalk.

"I never eat breakfast." How to get rid of the annoying man? She glanced across the street. A shop displaying sandals in its windows was a possibility— No, it was obviously closed.

"Something to drink then."

She looked further down the street. Hadn't she seen a bathing suit store nearby?

"I won't bite," he added.

"I know." The reply flowed automatically, though in all honesty, he gave her the heebie-jeebies. She hadn't forgotten his insinuations that night on the beach when he talked to her after she'd been on the phone with Todd, making her feel she owed him an explanation of the private conversation.

"But," she went on, "I'm sure you have better things to do than entertain me. I'll be just fine. I can go, um…" She had turned nearly a full circle, studying the shops. The bike rental place was open. Not exactly her cup of tea…

"But it's your birthday."

She swung back to face him.

"I overheard you." He smiled and pulled open the patio gate. "They have these great iced caramel chocolate whipped cream coffee drinks for birthday girls."

He really did have a nice smile and gentle eyes. She really was too hot to continue hiking up and down the blasted street waiting for the cops and robbers to finish their silliness.

And it really was her birthday.

She flashed a smile. "Well, all right, sugar. Lead the way."

Char removed her sunglasses and fanned herself with the menu. "Why is it so unbearably hot today?"

Across the table, Julian smiled. "Santa Ana. Feel the wind?"

"Yes."

"Straight from the desert. Dry heat blows in, pushing the temperature above normal." He looked back down at the menu.

They sat on the busy restaurant's sidewalk patio. Located near an intersection and practically within reach of a traffic light pole, it was a noisy place.

He said, "They serve nice bagels here. Oh, but you said you don't eat breakfast."

"Well, if I'm going to have that luscious iced coffee you described— What was it? Caramel, chocolate, *and* whipped cream? I'd better have a bagel to take the edge off all that sugar and caffeine." She replaced her sunglasses. "How long do you think we will have to wait before the perpetrator is apprehended?"

"It could take all day." His face was deadpan. "Four o'clock, maybe."

"Four o'clock! Why, they can't possibly keep people out of their houses until four o'clock! Or in them, for that matter! We're not prisoners! For goodness' sake! It didn't sound like they were after some armed guy with hostages! What kind of a crazy place is this?"

Julian's eyes crinkled behind his glasses. "Santa Ana is hard on tempers."

She sputtered. No words made it off her tongue.

"I am joking this time, Char. Thirty, forty minutes tops."

A young waitress stepped to their table and greeted Julian by name. He also knew her name and chatted with her about her dog.

After ordering, Char said, "My word, do you know everyone?"

"It's an outdoor community, paths always crossing."

"How did you ever get from Scotland to here?"

"Jesus."

"Hmm." A Molly clone for sure.

His crows feet crinkled as his mouth curved lazily into an enigmatic nonsmile. "That's the short version."

Okay, she thought, *I'll bite.* "We're not going anywhere." She tilted her head and smiled sweetly. "What's the long version?"

"I grew up in Scotland. Work brought me to the States. I was in software. I designed what some considered to be a spectacular creation." He shrugged. "By forty-five I'd had two heart attacks and lost my family. I sold out and moved here."

"Oh my goodness. What happened to your family?"

"I was not a fun person or even all that nice. Business consumed me. I never blamed my wife for leaving. We've made our peace. She remarried; someone else raised my son and daughter. They're grown now and visit occasionally."

"How sad to miss out on their lives."

"I was devastated, ready to check out. Permanently. I went so far as to purchase a gun. Then my neighbor Faith Fontaine and Zeke got hold of me, which is synonymous with Jesus getting hold of me. He let me crash and burn, the only way I'd turn to Him for help. And the rest, as they say…" He spread his hands. "Is history. Have you met Zeke yet?"

"Oh, yes." Yes, indeed. And she wasn't about to pursue any subject related to him! "What do you do now?"

"I keep on eye on Faith's house and the guests. I work with Zeke." Zeke again. "But what do you do?"

"I live."

Obviously the man was wealthy. He lived on the beach in Southern California in what she assumed had to be a multimillion-dollar home. She mustered up manners that had been scattered by the day's events and decided not to pry further. "I see."

He gave his little smile again. "You're wondering how a beach bum can afford this. As I said, the software creation was considered spectacular."

"Hmm. Well, good for you." Definitely time to change the subject. "Speaking of spectacular, we had quite a day yesterday. For starters I watched three drug deals go down."

"Here?"

"No. It was in some neighborhood Jo took us to. Jo's the doctor, the *single* doctor." She lifted her sunglasses just long enough to give him an exaggerated wink. "Remember? Anyway, we were at this clinic." She went on to describe the events of the day, from her friend's beautiful office to the gang members on the street to the baby's birth to chicken potpie. "Let me tell you, that is not going to fit onto one postcard."

"How is your family?"

"Just fine last I heard, which was yesterday when Savannah called to whine about her volleyball practice."

"No birthday calls yet?"

How ironic that of all people on the face of the earth he would know the day simply because he overheard her mention it! "Molly has inadvertently taken off with my cell phone. I feel downright lost without it. I am far too attached to that thing."

"Your husband must be frustrated, not being able to get a hold of you."

She gave him her pert smile. Why pretend? "Honey, without me at home reminding Savannah so she can remind him, Cam has been glued to his patients since sunup with nary a single thought as to the date."

"You didn't remind her on the phone to tell him?"

"No. I'm on vacation."

"When was the last time he remembered on his own?"

"Cole was two. He is now thirteen." She shrugged. "Not that I've been counting."

"I'm sorry."

Sudden tears stung her eyes, and she turned toward the street, grateful for dark glasses hiding the inexplicable from this stranger.

"I think," Julian spoke in a careful tone, "old Cam just needs some encouragement."

"And what would you suggest?" Too late she heard a bitter note.

"Straight talk often works. Tell him how things like this hurt you."

"It's not that big of a deal."

"Your marriage isn't that big of a deal?"

"No, I meant forgetting my birthday. I always organize a dinner out with friends. We'll do that when I get back. After all, I am the one who chose not to be home on this date."

"You are worth it, Char. Worth the attention."

Wanting to flee the conversation that seemed to be doing a number on her equilibrium, she pushed her chair from the table, a half-formed excuse on the tip of her tongue.

The waitress arrived just then, delivering bagels and iced coffees, one of which had a small pink birthday candle stuck into the thick whipped topping. "Happy birthday, ma'am. The candle *was* lit, but I think it's hopeless in this wind."

Char couldn't help an inward sigh. Then, calling on a lifetime of ingrained propriety, she found her voice. "Oh my goodness. How did you—" She glanced at Julian and back at the girl. "I guess I don't have to look too far. Thank you, sugar."

"You're welcome. Enjoy." She left.

Julian's eyes crinkled again in his nonsmile, the corners of his mouth hardly lifting. "Happy birthday, Char."

Not knowing how to civilly excuse herself, Char sipped the special coffee through a straw and tried not to think who had ordered it for her: a Jesus freak with penetrating eyes that were beginning to make her squirm.

The coffee was quite tasty, a pleasant surprise for such a dive of a restaurant. "Thank you. This was hardly necessary."

"It's always necessary to extend kindness." He was smooth. Too smooth in her opinion. "So how did you and Cam meet?"

"In college." She spread cream cheese on the grainy bagel that appeared to have more seeds than wheat. However in the world did it stick together? Molly would love it.

"I bet he swept you off your feet."

"Of course. If he hadn't, no way would I have quit college and worked—even before we got married—to help put him through dental school. Not that I was ever all that interested in classes. Nine to five in the university admin office suited me to a tee."

"How did he sweep you off your feet?"

"How?"

He nodded. "How."

"It just happened."

"In the usual way? I mean like...let me take a wild guess. He was the best-looking frat brother, you the sorority darling. Perfect match. Everyone thought so. He wooed you with surprise gifts and romantic walks in the rain and made a great tennis partner."

She stared at him. "You're a psychic."

He chuckled. "No. Just a lifelong observer of people. What was the clincher? Why him instead of one of your many other admirers?"

Her memory bank presented an old scene: Cam lifting her over a mud puddle, promising to always carry her over life's mud puddles.

Char blinked and saw Julian across the table, quietly spreading cream cheese on his bagel. "Security. That was the clincher. He was going to be a dentist. People will always need dentists. He was taking over his father's practice in a Chicago suburb. His parents were much older; his dad was retiring within five years. Everything was in place."

"Have you felt secure?"

Seventeen years of routine and enough money to prevent concern over making ends meet? "Yes."

"But you didn't only love him for security."

Imagining Cam in tennis shorts made her smile. "No. He was a hunk. And he made me feel special. No one else had ever made me feel that way." She shrugged. She did not want to remember Cam in tennis shorts and she certainly did not want to imagine him in them now! "Well, not counting these crazy girlfriends of mine, anyway. They made me feel special by promising a trip to Hollywood. Then they all disappear. Tell me there is still time to get there."

"I'm sure there is."

"Hey!" The voice came from somewhere behind Julian's shoulder. "Charlaine Wilcox!"

A figure came into view on the sidewalk.

A dark-haired man in need of a shave, waving a bouquet of flowers, wearing wrinkled khakis and a lime green polo shirt stretched over well-toned pecs and biceps. Dark sunglasses hid his eyes, but she knew they were chocolate brown.

"Hey," he said again, this time gently, in an Andy Williams croon. *As I live and breathe...*

"Todd?"

Thirty-One

"Yow!" Jo flinched and yanked her left foot clean out of Andie's grasp.

"Sorry. It's your adrenal gland." Andie repositioned Jo's foot on her lap and massaged with less pressure. "Experiencing a little stress, are we?"

Jo considered the question rhetorical. "Your grandma never made it hurt like this."

"Molly remembers excruciating pain." Andie smiled. "You never were one to admit pain."

Jo thought of her previous night's sobs at the chicken pie restaurant. That was pain exploding like fireworks. "Last night was progress then."

"Yes."

She studied her friend's face. A dramatic change had taken place in the three short days since Andie's own collapse into tears. The pale freckles were not covered with makeup. Her hair, twisted back and held in place with a banana clip, had not felt the heat of hair dryer or curling iron since her arrival. Her spunk was back, apparent even in the way she carried herself. Without a doubt the real Andrea Sinclair was emerging.

"Andie, I'd say we're both making progress."

She tilted her head in question, still methodically kneading Jo's feet.

"You're boogie boarding, dear. Assisting at baby deliveries. Cruising the boardwalk all by yourself. Having lengthy conversations with that strange man Zeke. Maneuvering your way through a police cordon to get back home."

Andie grinned. "And then there's the major first step. I came here."

"Yes. You came, you saw, you conquered. Bravo. How do you feel?"

"Exhilarated. Scared." Her bright blue eyes shone. "Like how Balboa or those other explorers must have felt sailing from Europe to America and discovering whole new worlds. I ask myself, now what? What do I do with this new world? How do I take it home with me?"

Her questions startled Jo. "I think…that's how I'm feeling too, though I hadn't put it into words yet. I mean, I know I can't take 'this' home. 'This' is the realization that I don't want my old life. I don't want to go home, so to speak."

"But a new life is staring you in the face."

"But not without tremendous upheaval and changing my entire lifestyle. I have doubts I can do that."

"That's the scary part."

"How is it scary for you, Andie? You just go home, take the new spunk with you, and your family benefits like crazy."

Her hands stilled, and she looked down at Jo's foot. "The new spunk doesn't quite know what to do with Paul and his girlfriend."

"Oh, hon."

"But I am narrowing down the choices." She flashed a smile. "Anyway, Molly has been gone a long time. Should we try to find her?"

They had discussed the situation earlier. Andie had missed the departure scene when Molly declared she needed time alone to think. Trusting in past experience, they knew that was how she operated. Since childhood she had truly meant it whenever she said she wanted to be alone. Still, she had never encountered a surprise pregnancy at the age of forty.

Jo said, "Yeah, let's go find her. If the cops are still out there, you'll have to lead the charge. I've never faced a gun before."

Andie giggled and set Jo's foot gently onto the rug. "I simply asked the police officer to escort me to the door, which was only a short distance and within sight from where he stood." She straightened and glanced sideways toward the open door. "Molly!"

Their friend pulled aside the screen door and entered the room. Her eyes were puffy.

Andie went to her, arms ready to embrace her.

Molly fell into the hug. "Ladies." She inhaled shakily. "I can't do this one alone."

Thirty-Two

"Todd!" Standing beside the table, Char laughed into his shoulder and returned his hug. "What on earth are you doing here?"

"Delivering flowers to the birthday girl." With a flourish he handed the tissue-wrapped bouquet to her.

"My word!" She giggled, fully aware of how the sound revealed her totally discombobulated emotional state. What was he doing there?

Todd reached across the table and stretched his hand toward Julian. "Hi. Todd Brooks. Chicago neighbor."

"Julian. Beach house neighbor. Have a seat."

"Thanks." He pulled out a chair and sat.

"Would you like something?"

"Iced tea would be great." He picked up a napkin and wiped his forehead. "I feel like I've been driving round and round in the desert. Of course, a convertible with the top down in this sun didn't help matters."

Char bumped her knee against the table as she slid back into her chair. Buying time to gather any semblance of aplomb, she burrowed her nose into the fresh flowers, unaware of any particular scent or species. "Mmm."

"Afraid they didn't have your favorite—gardenias, right?—at the airport," Todd said. "What a nutso place! I think I almost found your house, but cops have all the alleys cordoned off. I couldn't get near it. Then I hit this red light here and noticed a familiar blonde sitting in the corner restaurant."

She smiled.

Julian signaled the waitress and called to her, "Iced tea, please."

"So. Sugar." A half moment passed before Char managed to come up with another word. "What are you…" Her mind quit again, offering no help to complete the sentence.

"I'm on my way to Phoenix. Remember?"

They had discussed the subject the other night. "Business. *Tomorrow.*"

He shrugged. "I thought, why not go early and swing by San Diego to surprise you? I got you, didn't I?"

"You sure did. I owe you one. I still can hardly believe I'm looking at you. Didn't we just talk?"

"Last night. I was on my way to O'Hare to catch the red-eye." He grinned. "I called you first chance I had this morning to wish you a happy birthday, but Molly answered."

"Oh, yes. Long story."

Julian stood. "If you'll excuse me, I think I'll move along. Nice meeting you, Todd."

He shook his extended hand. "Please, don't go on my account."

"I have work to do."

"What line are you in?"

"I rescue stranded women." Again that little nonsmile. "By the way, if you need a place to stay, I have a spare apartment. You're welcome to it. Happy birthday again, Char. See you." With a wave, he meandered off toward the restaurant's door.

Char guessed he was going inside to pay. And she hadn't even thanked him!

Todd made a tsking sound. "Turn my back on you for three days and another Prince Charming steps to the plate."

"Prince Charming? Julian? Hardly. He was just keeping me company. The police should finish up their business anytime now." She leaned back in her chair, still unnerved by Julian's digging into the past and unearthing fond memories of Cam. Not to mention Todd's sudden appearance. "What *are* you doing here?"

A smile spread across his narrow face. His intense gaze heightened her discomfort. "Charlaine, you really have no idea? You really didn't pick up any of my hints?"

Hints? What hints? Harmless long-distance teasing about missing her? Wishing somehow things were different? She shook her head.

He placed his hand atop hers, the one that still clutched the bouquet lying on the table. "I'm here to steal my neighbor's wife."

Thirty-Three

With a feeling that a vise gripped her heart, Jo watched Molly as she blew her nose and added the tissue to a growing pile beside her on the couch.

What was it about the beach house? Jo finally admitted to herself that there was a *presence*. Some undefined influence emanated from the walls—sunflower yellow walls at that—and made them feel safe. How else to explain the softness creeping into her heart? How else to explain strong Molly's display of total uncertainty?

A stray tear slipped onto Molly's damp cheek, and Jo handed her another tissue. "Thanks."

Jo said, "You're welcome. What are vacations for, if not to come unglued? At least we're taking turns at it."

Andie smiled. "We'd better add Kleenex to the grocery list."

Molly said, "Maybe they sell them on Rodeo Drive."

They shared a laugh, a welcome relief, Jo thought, after the litany of woes Molly had recited concerning the pregnancy.

I'm so old! There is a greater chance of birth defects. The career is on hold. Interminably! Eli could have a kid of his own in eight years. I would have a grandchild and this one in the same school system at the same time!

165

Molly had wailed at that point. She sat, shoulders hunched and legs crossed, not buying into any positive comment Jo and Andie suggested. Now her face puckered anew, a hint of a forthcoming sob.

Jo said, "What is it?"

"I just had a horrid thought." She clamped her mouth shut and covered her face with her hands.

Andie said, "Oh, hon, no matter what, we won't love you any less."

"Moll." Jo scooted across the couch and placed an arm around her shoulders. "Come on. You've seen me at my absolute ugliest. It never stopped you from loving me, did it?"

She shook her head and wiped fresh tears from her cheeks. "After Abigail, before Hannah...I had a miscarriage. Part of me hopes—" A sob cut off the sentence she didn't have to complete.

Jo hugged her tightly. "Moll. You know you don't mean it, not truly, not deep down inside. If nothing else, you are all about life. You feel guilty eating seafood because some fish has to die."

Andie sat on the arm of the couch and embraced Jo and Molly. "Honey, it's understandable, just now when you're upset."

Molly only cried harder.

Jo heard the door open and looked up to see Char walk in, followed by a man.

Char hurried across the room, a bouquet of flowers in her hand. "Another cry fest!" She knelt on the floor, placing her hands on Molly's knees. "And I almost missed it! You all should have called me."

The tone underlying the Southern drawl puzzled Jo. Char sounded almost glib.

Molly raised her head. "Oh, Char. We couldn't call you. I have your phone!"

"Now, now, sugar. I know that." She cupped Molly's face in her hands. "Shh, it's going to be all right. A baby is wonderful news. He or she will be such a bundle of joy in your old age. Although I admit I am glad it's you and not me. You're a natural with kids. You always were. Come on now. Time to get out from under the pile."

Char was trying, but Jo didn't think she was quite getting there. What was going on with her? She seldom faked ooey-gooey; her compassion was always sincere even when she disagreed with them. And who was that stranger leaning against the doorjamb, a cockeyed grin on his face? He looked like an aging version of a has-been yuppie.

The man shook his head now as if in disbelief and cleared his throat. "Excuse me."

Jo felt Andie raise her head. Char turned. Molly leaned to peer around Char.

He went on. "Did we forget this is the twenty-first century? Women have rights over their own bodies."

As one, the four of them glared daggers. Jo knew she wasn't alone, sure as she knew anything. Though only two of them were still practicing Roman Catholics, there were certain beliefs they held in common, as much a part of their makeup as a beating heart. Abortion would not be an option for any of them.

He held up his hands as if being arrested. "Whoa. Sorry. Don't mind me. I just stopped by to wish Char happy birthday."

Char chuckled nervously. "Where are my manners? This is my neighbor Todd Brooks. This is Jo, Molly, and Andie." She pointed to each and then turned back to the group hug. "He was on his way to Phoenix and came here first to say hey."

Jo wasn't sure when San Diego had been moved to a new location between Chicago and Phoenix, but she was sure a major wrench had been thrown into the schedule.

So what else was new?

Thirty-Four

To Char's relief, the group hug dissipated. Molly seemed recovered enough, though she still wiped at her eyes. Jo faced forward on the couch, and Andie stood by the fireplace.

Char rose from the floor and sat in one of the overstuffed chairs, still holding the bouquet, and smiled. "Y'all don't mind if Todd tags along with us, do you?"

Of course they would mind. She knew that even before his thoughtless comment about pregnancy in the twenty-first century. He was an anomaly to them. A male friend who not only remembered her birthday but flew halfway across the country to surprise her? How heroic was that? But it would make no sense to the unromantic, the unadventurous. There was no place for it within the stuffy sense of propriety she'd felt the others bundled themselves in like mink coats on a warm summer's day.

Todd, naturally affable, stepped further into the room and sat in the nearest chair with a gracious smile. "I said I would take her to Beverly Hills myself, but she has her heart set on spending the day with you three. My rental is a four-seater convertible, otherwise I'd drive the five of us."

Molly blew her nose.

Jo coughed.

Andie said, "It's your day, Char. Of course we don't mind if you bring along another friend. The more the merrier. Though I can't imagine a man all that interested in a women's gabfest and shopping on Rodeo Drive."

It was as near a lecture as Andie would deliver. Char suspected the others would hold their tongues for a while. Still, the palpable tension wasn't exactly what she'd planned on for her birthday. With friends like them, who needed enemies? Todd Brooks included.

While the others changed clothes, Char waited with Todd outside on the patio. As usual the whole area was bathed in sunshine. They sat at the round table under its umbrella. The chairs were plain white inexpensive resin—not an Adirondack in sight!—but she had improved their looks and comfort with floral cushions from a closet.

"Char, I am sorry for intruding. I thought my visit would be a lark for you."

"It is! Don't you worry none. They'll be fine." She paused. "I do have one favor to ask you though."

"What's that?"

She smiled. "Please don't repeat that line you used on me about stealing your neighbor's wife."

His wide grin lifted his cheeks and dark sunglasses. "Sounds like an invitation to blackmail. You have to give me something if I promise not to tell."

"Todd Brooks! You are audacious!"

"I hope so." He stretched out his legs and leaned back in the chair, a little smile on his lips, the same kind worn by a cat assured that the mouse had to come out sooner or later.

Char shivered in delight. He had sworn at the restaurant that his comment was a joke. But...the way he looked at her—eyes at half-mast, head tilted—she knew he left the next move up to her. Whether or not it remained a joke was her choice.

Well, she was choosing to treat it as a joke.

Which only made the flirting all that more luscious.

~

They zipped along the freeway in Jo's SUV. Char sat between Andie and Todd in the back seat. The two of them chatted on and on about their sons while she mentally scolded herself. Surely the tension she felt was simply her imagination run rampant.

Except when Jo and Molly entered the picture. Jo drove in total silence, Molly a mannequin beside her in the front passenger seat. They brooded, no doubt about it. No imagination involved whatsoever.

Honestly! Those two still act like they own all the rights to a blue funk. At least Andie knows how to behave in a civilized manner.

Todd leaned around her now, making some conversational point with Andie. His shoulder rested against Char's. The physical contact was unnecessary, given the fact that the backseat was spacious and he wasn't that big of a guy. As a matter of fact, he was nowhere near as tall as Cam.

But that wasn't the point.

The point was his touch increased the tension. She wrestled with emotions. On the one hand she tingled. On the other, she squirmed.

Then Molly's words of three days ago resonated in her mind: *Friday is your day, Char. All I can say is beware. Turning forty can be hazardous to your health.*

She remembered conveying the conversation to Todd during one of their late-night phone chats.

"Pff!" She had fluttered her lips. "Stuff and nonsense."

Todd laughed. "I don't know, Charlaine. When what's-her-face hit her fortieth, she yawled like a banshee for days, inconsolable. She was convinced her life was over."

Of course Char knew he referred to his now ex-wife.

She puffed again. "Pff to that too. We know her cheese had slid right off her cracker, which she proved by leaving you two years later. I believe I am still in full possession of my mental faculties. And I really don't give a hoot about finding a few gray hairs, unlike what's-her-face."

"You'll make quite an attractive mature woman. I see your hair as pure snow white, though, not gray. And not for years to come."

"You sweet talker, you." She had smiled, filing his words into her heart like a piece of chocolate hidden in the cupboard to be savored later. "Anyway, my day won't be like theirs. In the first place, I'm not an alcoholic. I don't have Jo's struggle. Secondly, I am not discontent over the fact I don't have a career. All Molly can talk about is how much she wants to teach full-time. Thirdly, I would not be devastated if my husband forgot to tell me happy birthday like Paul did Andie. How could I be? Cam forgets every year."

"You are one confident thirty-nine-year-old." He chuckled.

"Do I sound horribly boastful? I don't mean to. It's just that Mama— Well, you've heard this before. She taught me a thing or two about self-control." She clung to Ellen Stowe's promise that a genteel disposition and self-discipline would carry Char through any upheaval life could throw at her.

But her mama had never reached the age of forty. Apparently the guarantee expired because this birthday had turned into one foul kettle of squid.

From the moment she awoke—too, too early for her sensitive nature—the day had indeed been a nightmare. Control had been swept right out of her hands. She had no control over Molly's baby news or Andie's need to take a hike or Jo's sudden interest in work calls, all at the precise time her friends should have been getting ready to leave for Beverly Hills. She had no control over an army of police blocking her path or Julian coercing her into breakfast. She certainly had no control over Todd Brooks showing up to confuse the situation and—of all things—attack their beliefs right off the bat.

Despite the blast of cold air aimed directly at her in the backseat, Char broke into a sweat.

Charlaine, sugar, horses sweat, men perspire, ladies only glow.

Right, Mama. But I can't even breathe at the moment. I am sweating.

Her chest felt tight as a drum.

Suddenly Jo broke her silence with a loud groan.

Char focused through the windshield and deciphered the reason. Just over the crest of a hill was a string of red brake lights. They stretched across all five lanes of bumper-to-bumper traffic and headed north as far as the eye could see, which must have been for miles. The car slowed to a stop.

Jo flipped on the radio.

Todd stretched his arm across the back of the seat and lightly touched her neck. "Welcome to Southern California."

She moved her head in a circular motion, releasing a knot from her neck as well as his hand.

Yes, indeed. The day had become a hazard zone. And there was no relief in sight.

~

Sixty minutes later Char practically fell out of the car. Desperate for air and space, she tangled her own two feet together.

Todd grasped her elbow and guided her descent. "You okay, birthday girl?"

She grunted in reply.

Jo shut her door. "Char, I am so sorry."

"It's not your fault."

They had exchanged the ridiculous phrases ad nauseam during the past hour.

They were in Del Mar, the city they had seen the previous day when visiting Jo's house and office. With a serious accident somewhere up the freeway and predictions of three-hour delays, Beverly Hills flumped into a pipe dream. Jo had maneuvered her car onto the shoulder and down an exit ramp, promising the entire slow way superb boutiques and an excellent lunch.

Andie shut her door and grinned. "I have an idea! Let's all get new outfits, not just Char. I need something spunky. Jo, you need something with color. That beige is getting tiresome. And Molly, you need maternity! Todd, you can carry packages or go find a men's store."

Char stared at her along with the others.

Andie wrinkled her brow. "What?"

Jo burst into laughter. "Who is this cheerleader inside Andie Sinclair's body?"

Molly added, "Make that bossy cheerleader."

Andie shrugged. "Turning forty is hazardous to one's well-being. Let's go ease the pain."

~

Molly's expected lecture came as Char inadvertently paired herself alongside her on the narrow sidewalk. The others walked ahead of them.

"Char, I am sorry I've had your phone all this time." She removed it from a pants pocket and handed it to her. "It hasn't rung."

"It's set to vibrate."

"Oh. I might not have noticed that."

Char quickly scanned for messages. There were none. The tightness in her chest increased a notch. Not even Kendra had called. Of all her friends she thought at least Kendra would have phoned by now.

"Has Cam called?"

"No."

"It would tell you if you missed a call?"

"Yes." Char snapped shut her jaw as well as the phone. The woman did not live in the same century! She had probably missed the last century as well! She got herself pregnant at forty years of age and didn't know the first thing about cell phones.

Molly said, "Todd called, though. It was at the same time I tried to call Scott. I started to punch in his number. Does it answer an incoming when you hit the number one?"

"Mm-hmm." She stifled a frustrated sigh. "Have you talked to him yet? Do you want to keep the phone?"

"No. He's unavailable until late this afternoon." They walked in silence for a moment, a few steps behind the others. "Char, it's none of my business, but are you and Todd…"

"Are we what?"

"Involved?"

"We're good friends. Cam and I are good friends with him, and were with his ex-wife until she dumped him."

"I just can't imagine having a male friend who would fly all this way to see me. Not to mention Scott would go berserk…" Again her voice trailed off.

"But then you live in the backwoods of Oregon."

"Yes, I do." Her tone hardened subtly.

By that point Char didn't care. She had enough problems interpreting her own feelings, let alone Molly's. She was nuts about Todd, totally flattered by the fact he had flown all that way.

But things niggled, things that interfered with the romantic image.

There was her mama's voice. When Ellen Stowe died, Char lost the only person who loved her fully and unconditionally. Left with no siblings, no grandmother, and an emotionless father, she clung to the memory of her mother's sweet voice. She filled a notebook with Ellen's words. She memorized her expressions of undisguised love for her child as well as ironclad principles by which Southern gentlewomen abided. One swirled now in Char's mind: *A lady shares physical intimacy only with her husband.*

Another vexation was the disapproval of her friends. They might as well go ahead and shake their fingers at her. She might as well see their wagging digits in broad daylight as to just imagine them.

And there was the Julian conversation, talking about those early courtship days with Cam. She didn't want to think about them! They were long gone.

"Besides," she said now to Molly in a huffy tone, "Cam is not Scott. Cam would not go berserk. It's simply not in his makeup."

"Does he know Todd is here?"

"Molly, *I* didn't know he was here. I had no idea he was coming until he showed up at the restaurant a while ago."

"Will you tell him?"

Char didn't reply. She had no reply. Was there a point in telling Cam?

Molly said, "What would Cam do?"

"Change the channel."

With that she hastened her steps and put distance between herself and Molly the prude.

Thirty-Five

Andie worked her way through a rack of clothes. Very spunky, attention-grabbing clothes. Wild colors, wild styles, wild price tags. She couldn't help but add up how many clients' visits for reflexology treatments it would take in order to pay for one T-shirt alone.

She hadn't yet gathered the courage to remove an outfit from the rack. Jo had held up a poppy red silk blouse and asked her if it was bright enough. Before the words were out of her mouth, a salesclerk swooped upon them, snatched the blouse right from Jo's hand, and whisked it off to a dressing room.

Were they even called salesclerks in boutiques?

Behind her Jo and Molly carried on a quiet conversation. Across the small shop Todd and Char laughed as they studied the shoe selection.

Andie had no idea what could be so funny about shoes.

She felt a light tap on her shoulder and turned.

Jo said, "I'm trying to figure this out." Her tone was hushed. "I mean, are you comfortable with the situation?"

Andie needed no further explanation. "He's...nice enough."

Jo clenched her teeth and widened her eyes. "Andie! Are you comfortable?"

She shrugged.

"Well, I'm not! Call me a retroactive Catholic, but *I* feel guilty for her. Isn't this adultery?"

Molly neared the clothes rack. "From a strictly physical aspect, I don't think they've reached that point. In Jesus' eyes though..."

176

"Close enough, cousin," Jo murmured. "I don't want to judge, but it just doesn't seem like we should stand by and do nothing. You two are the married ones. Is she throwing her life down the tubes or what?"

Andie went back to swishing hangers along the bar and gazing at clothes that would never show up on the streets of Madison, Wisconsin. "I don't think you're judging. I think you're aching because yes, she is throwing her life down the tubes."

"Then what should we do? I know you guys. You're hurting as much as I am. Friends don't let friends drive drunk. They surely don't let them commit adultery, do they?"

Molly said, "She must be in a bad way, though how could we tell? She never opened up with us when we were young. Naturally she does so even less now."

"Moll," Jo said, "what would you want us to do if you were in this situation?"

"I can't imagine. Sit on me? Haul me off to the airport? Talk to me? Yeah, talk to me. Find out why I hurt so much."

Andie looked at them. "And then we'd know you had your reasons. Just like Char does."

Jo and Molly stared at her, busy jaws suddenly slack.

She continued. "She doesn't feel loved by Cam. She feels rejected by him. I know this because it's me. The reasons are probably different. Paul's having an affair. She describes Cam as a couch potato, not a Lothario. But—" She bit her lip, her nerves wavering.

Molly said, "But what, hon?"

Andie turned sideways again and touched a spunky outfit. "But, wrong as it is, I've wished some man would give me a *fraction* of the attention Todd's giving her." She lifted a pair of capris and matching top from the rack. She held them to her cheek. "What do you think? Apricot work?"

They nodded as one.

The salesclerk descended like a vulture from the sky. "I'll start you a room!" She flew off. Andie whispered, "There's really only one thing we can do. Pray."

Jo and Molly followed Andie down a hallway. She spotted the orangey outfit hanging outside one of the dressing rooms and went to it. They entered a carpeted area, brightly lit and spacious enough to accommodate all three of them. It consisted of padded stools and floor-to-ceiling walls covered with mirrors.

Andie hung the clothing on a brass hook and noticed Molly in one of the mirrors. "You look green."

"I feel green." She grimaced. "Is it the power of suggestion? I've been feeling nauseous now and then, but it has intensified since this morning. It's like with knowing the cause, I've given my body permission to release the full-on effect."

Jo said, "You're hungry. We should have eaten lunch first. Breakfast was hours ago."

"I gave my last snack to a little girl in the clinic yesterday."

Andie opened her purse and dug around in it. "I think I have…yes. Here you go. Crackers."

Molly smiled weakly and tore the cellophane. "You guys want to kneel?"

In reply Andie sank to the floor. The others joined her. She and Jo held hands while Molly ate.

Andie said, "I haven't done much of this extemporaneous prayer stuff. Will you, Molly?"

Molly smiled and brushed crumbs from her chin. "Just talk to Him. You can do it."

"Okay." Andie closed her eyes. She felt Molly slip a hand around hers and squeeze gently. "Lord, we need Your help. No, Char needs Your help more right now. We don't know what to do, but we trust You. Keep her from making a huge mistake. Keep her from throwing her life down the tubes. Tell her You love her. Thank You, Jesus."

Molly said, "Amen."

Andie looked at her. "Amen."

Jo let out a noisy sigh. "Amen."

Thirty-Six

Jo promised Char an excellent lunch. They would go to Jake's and sit by a window with an ocean view, indoors out of the heat and incessant wind. They would eat salads with scrumptious things like warmed Camembert cheese and cranberries and toasted pecans.

But when they passed the deli where they'd grabbed sandwiches the day before, Molly the vegetarian mumbled something about going inside to buy salami, pastrami, and provolone. Char must have heard the desperate tone and declared it was lunchtime. Jo heartily agreed and opened the door. She didn't want to linger over a meal in a nice restaurant trying to make conversation with that snake Todd Brooks.

"It's my treat," the snake said now in an oily tone, a sly smile on his too-thin lips.

Standing beside him at the counter, Jo straightened to her full height. It put her eye-to-eye with the serpent. "We find it easier to just pay for our own." *Unless I'm the one paying.*

He flipped a credit card to the cashier. "Don't let her pay." Then to Jo, "Let me at least try to make up for disrupting your day."

She didn't protest that comment. Beyond a shadow of a doubt he had disrupted their day. "Thank you."

She left him to finish the transaction and headed to the washroom. What she wanted to do was put on running shoes and take off down the beach for however many miles it took to fill up the entire afternoon and evening. Maybe cold water would do the trick instead.

She spent a long time splashing it on her face. The problem was she didn't know what to do with emotions that had been dumped on her like trash from a garbage truck. She had filed away feelings for so many years her body had become unaccustomed to dealing with the abstract.

She suspected her blood pressure was up. What exactly was she supposed to do with feelings? With compassion for Molly's predicament? With perplexity over Andie's about-face? With rage at a stranger tempting a friend she hadn't seen in twelve years? With discomfort over Char's choices? Discomfort! She wanted to shake some common sense into the woman.

Her feelings weren't all negative. What was she to do with the sweet ache of praying with Molly and Andie right there in a dressing room? She hadn't felt such love since she was a child in church. And what of the explosion of hope that burst upon her after delivering that teenager's baby?

Well, fear was taking care of that last one. Fear and extreme doubt she could ever make such a lifestyle move. Work in a low-income section of humanity?

She studied her eyes in the mirror, searching for the cool, calm, collected doctor. All she saw was a woman on the verge of tears.

She bent over the sink again and splashed more water on her face.

Jo eventually joined the others. They had pushed two dollhouse-size tables together. Char and Todd sat at one, Molly at the other with a vacant chair. Andie straddled both, her iced tea on one, her salad on the other.

Obviously Andie was still in bridge mode, trying to close the gap between uncomfortable friends. Wounded in her own marriage, she seemed able to empathize with Char in ways Molly and Jo couldn't.

Jo sat. "Moll, you look better. Nutrition hit the bloodstream?"

She nodded, her mouth full.

Andie said brightly, "We were just telling Todd about Grandmère Babette."

Char nudged him. "If it weren't for Babette, these three never would have allowed me into their circle."

Andie's blush was instantaneous. "Char, I'm sorry."

"Oh, sugar. You all have apologized on more than one occasion over the years. And you are forgiven." She tilted her head toward Todd. "You know how thirteen-year-old girls can behave."

He laughed.

Char said, "His daughter is thirteen."

Molly perked up. "We were insufferable. Why would we be nice to this cute little thing who moved up from Georgia? Her accent drove me nuts."

Jo said, "And she was so *not* gangly. Petite was a dirty word in my vocabulary."

Char laughed. "The thing was, nobody befriended me. That all-girls parochial school was full of snobs and everyone already had their own clique."

The other three nodded in agreement.

Todd asked, "What happened?"

"Well." Char took a breath. "Mama died. Andie felt bad for me. Her grandmother suggested they could be nice to me."

Andie smiled. "She read us the riot act."

Jo said, "In French, so it shouldn't have mattered, but her gestures and frown and raised voice convinced us otherwise."

Andie added, "She lost her own mother when she was twelve. I think she would have forbidden us to visit her—which was our most favorite thing to do—if we didn't attend the funeral and bring Char along the next time we went to Grandmère's."

Char said, "They were so kind to come to the funeral. And after that they asked me to eat lunch with them in the school cafeteria. I think it was only a couple weeks later that I first went to Babette's apartment. She lived downtown."

Todd said, "What was so special about going to see her? Why was it your favorite thing to do?"

Char smiled. "The adventure of riding the train and acting like a grown-up. And being treated like one by her."

Molly said, "She fed us pastries and chocolates."

Andie said, "I felt at home there, unlike the house I lived in with my parents."

Jo held up her hands. "What can I say? It was the occasional sips of sherry."

Molly pointed a finger at her. "And you ruined that little treat by absconding with a bottle, didn't you?"

As they shared more memories, Todd faded from view. Eventually they talked about the List for Real Women, attempting to recite all its points.

"A real woman has one friend who always makes her laugh."

"A good piece of furniture not previously owned by anyone else in her family."

"A youth she's content to leave behind."

"Amen."

"A real woman knows how to have a good time at a party she'd never choose to attend."

"She has something perfect to wear if her employer or date of her dreams wants to see her in an hour."

Char said, "Which reminds me, we have shopping to do! The date of my dreams may want to see me in an hour."

Char's silly remark reminded Jo of Todd's presence and the situation. It also reminded her of another list item: A real woman knew how to confront a friend without ruining the friendship.

It was time to act like a real woman.

~

Jo lingered with Char in the shade outside a maternity apparel shop. Andie and Molly had gone inside; Todd was down the block talking on his cell phone.

"Char?"

"Hmm?" She studied the display in the window as if fascinated by maternity fashions.

"Can we talk?"

"Sure." She turned to face Jo and pushed her sunglasses atop her head. "This is really very nice here. Thank you. Warm though, huh?"

"Yeah. Sorry about Beverly Hills and the Santa Ana. But I guess I can't quite control those things."

"No, you can't, Miss Hostess with the Mostess."

Jo smiled briefly. "Char, I know we've grown apart through the years. All four of us have."

She nodded. "It's life, I guess. We followed different paths. Moved away. Etcetera, etcetera."

"Mm-hmm. But even after all this time without regularly communicating, I still care about you. We shared something unique that doesn't go away."

"I agree. I feel the same way."

"Okay. So I love you and I'm going to say something out of that love."

"Here it comes. Lecture number three." She dropped the sunglasses onto her nose again so they covered her eyes. She pressed her lips together in a straight line.

Jo felt her own hackles rise but kept her voice even. "Look, your relationship with Todd is your business. I'm just asking you to take care of yourself. If you were drunk, I'd take the car keys from you. If you want to sleep with Todd, I can't stop you. All I can do is point out that in both cases you're playing with dynamite. Except for the possibility of AIDS—"

"Jo! Honestly! You think he sleeps around?"

"Do you know for a fact he doesn't?"

"He's my best friend. I would know."

Jo forged ahead to complete her thought. "Except for the possibilities of AIDS or getting pregnant—"

Char blew out a loud breath of disgust.

"Except for those, the damage won't be physical. But you will forever change the lives of your kids and not for the better."

"You're an expert? The *unmarried* daughter of parents who are actually still married and working together?"

Jo felt an urge to throw her arms around Char. She resisted.

"Jo, I'm forty years old today. I'm running out of time to be happy."

She heard Char's bravado but felt her pain. She stopped resisting and enveloped her in a hug. "Hey, I'm just being your friend, asking the hard stuff. It doesn't mean I don't still love you."

Char remained stiff as a board.

Jo held on anyway. "Babette's list. A real woman knows how to confront a friend without ruining the friendship. I won't let go until you hug me back and tell me it's not ruined."

Char gave her a quick hug. "It's not ruined."

Jo stepped back. "Thanks."

"I guess you're entitled to your opinion."

"And you yours. It's good to explore other people's points of view. Okay?"

"Sure."

"Promise you'll take care of yourself?"

"I'll take care of myself." She brushed bangs off her forehead. "Julian says the Santa Ana is hard on tempers."

Jo didn't argue. The wind and heat and changes in air pressure had nothing to do with emotions running amuck. She suspected the Molly Effect had joined forces with something new: the Andie Effect. With two of them praying, it was hard to say what else the spiritual forces were capable of prompting.

Telling a friend she was crazy and then hugging the anger right out of her was enough to turn Jo into a believer.

Thirty-Seven

Molly clutched Jo's cell phone in her lap and bit her lip.

Lord, I can't do this alone.

You're not alone.

I understand, but—

Shh. No buts. I'm here.

Lord, have mercy.

She sighed. Of course the Lord was with her. Of course He would not leave her. Of course He was intimately acquainted with the baby, already saw every future day of his or her life. But still...

She felt as though she were walking a tightrope across a black yawning chasm of despair, an entity eager to swallow her up. When her steps faltered, she turned back to prayer, imagining the Lord's responses.

Andie interrupted her thoughts. "Line still busy?"

"Yes." She hadn't yet talked with Scott and was exhausted from carrying their news all by herself for nearly nine hours now.

Lord, I can't do this alone.

Molly, Andie, and Jo sat on the patio outside the beach house, frazzled from a day of shopping, hot wind, and Char's horrendously awkward situation. The birthday girl and Todd had just left. They had spoken of vague plans to sightsee and eat dinner and welcomed the other three to tag along. *Tag along.* Molly doubted she, Jo, and Andie would have accepted even a heartfelt invitation.

Jo broke the silence with a loud sigh. "Do you think he's gay?"

An out of the blue remark, but Molly understood she referred to Todd. In unison she and Andie replied, "No."

Andie added, "He watches Char the way Paul watches certain women. Women he finds attractive."

Molly stared at her.

Her eyebrows went up and down, like a facial shrug. "Char probably has more male friends than women friends. She probably still scares most females just by being herself. Cute and petite and charming."

Molly said, "Yeah, who wants to compete with that? Not to mention 'sugah this and sugah that.'" She dropped the Southern accent. "We should have locked her up in her room."

Andie shifted in her seat. "Maybe that's not the point." She glanced at both of them and then turned to face the house. "This place keeps Grandmère at the forefront of my mind. She would say, 'Char ees hurting.'" The guttural *r*'s were reminiscent of Babette's voice. "'She makes zee wrong choice. She pays zee piper; we don't. We just love on her. *N'est pas?*'"

"Ah *oui*, it is so." Molly smiled.

Jo crossed one leg over the other and swung it. "What is it about this beach house? You feel Babette, and I get this weird sense of— I don't know what. Of safety. No, more than that. Of intense security."

Molly blinked. "You feel secure here?"

She held up a hand. "I admit it. Atrocious as far as beach houses go, this place affects me positively. Probably the same way Babette's apartment did."

"Wow."

"Yeah. Wow."

Molly twisted around in the chaise lounge and studied the reddish-orange cottage. Its two picture windows either side of the front door reflected people strolling along the boardwalk. The last rays of sunlight shone. There was a timeless solidity about it that comforted her. The tightrope walker felt muscles relax.

She said, "I wonder if something lingers after a faithful person departs. You just know Faith Fontaine filled this place with prayer. Maybe angels still guard it."

Jo blew out a breath, a sound of astonishment. "Okay, make that *angels*, Babette, and a sense of security. This place offers it all. Now I ask, what else could we possibly want?"

Andie said, "Maybe Chinese for dinner?"

Molly laughed with her friends. Indeed, she was not alone—even if her husband did not yet know their world had been turned upside down.

⌒

"Good evening, ladies." Julian's voice turned their attention from the house. He stood on the other side of the white picket fence.

As usual, Molly felt drawn to him and smiled. Like Jo's question regarding the beach house, she asked herself, *What is it about the neighbor?* He didn't say much, but when he did talk his soft voice was like a soothing whisper. His dark eyes always twinkled behind his glasses and conveyed a distinct warmth.

"Hi," she said.

Jo's stiff response indicated that, unlike the house, he hadn't yet grown on her.

Andie, on the other hand, greeted him with a smile. "Julian, is there a Chinese restaurant nearby where we can get carryout?"

"Chang's, two blocks north on the main drag. No MSG."

She laughed. "You're better than the yellow pages. Come on in and have a seat."

At Andie's invitation, Jo straightened in her chair and crossed her arms as well as her legs. Molly wondered at her defensiveness.

Julian stepped onto the patio and joined Andie at the table. "You missed the sunset."

Molly glanced at the ocean. The sun had disappeared already behind a bank of clouds on the horizon. "Aww, we did. There goes that tradition."

Andie giggled. "After three times straight. Oh, well. I guess there was just way too much on our minds. I'm glad I got in my boogie boarding before the day went bananas on us."

Jo rolled her eyes as if to say *Don't go there.*

Julian said, "The waves were great, weren't they?"

Molly thought he must have caught Jo's expression and politely didn't ask about the "bananas" comment. She tuned out their ensuing discussion of the morning's wave situation and picked up the cell phone. She hadn't figured out the redial shortcut, and so she punched in the string of numbers yet again. A moment later the busy signal buzzed in her ear. Her stomach tightened.

Lord, I can't do this alone.

You're not alone.

"Still nothing?" Jo said.

"No. I can't understand it. A busy signal for hours? Scotty and the kids would not be on the phone or Internet this long."

Julian said, "Excuse me. Molly, you're from Oregon, right? The southern coast?" The guy had quite a memory.

"Yes."

"I just heard they're getting pounded with storms and high winds. Phone lines are down, power is off."

"Really?" A sense of relief flooded her. "That's great."

Three puzzled expressions faced her.

She shrugged. "Hurricane-force winds are no big deal. I used to panic when we first moved there, but I'm used to it now. I'm sure my family is fine. I'm just glad to know why I can't get through. Thanks, Julian."

"Sure. Always glad to be the bearer of bad news." His smile barely curved the corners of his mouth.

Jo said, "You watch the Weather Channel?" Sarcasm dripped from her innocent question.

"It's a favorite."

Andie stood. "I'm hungry. Julian, would you like to eat Chinese with us?"

"Thank you, but I have plans. I'd be glad to show you the way to Chang's."

"Great." She turned to Molly and Jo, pointing at each in turn. "Anything with seafood. Lots of veggies and extra for whomever should wander by in need of a meal. Anything else?"

They shook their heads.

"Okay. Back soon. I have money." She followed Julian around the corner of the house.

As the sound of their footsteps and voices faded, Jo uncrossed her legs. "Remember what she said about Char and Todd?" she murmured.

"Which part?"

"The part about how she wished some guy would give her a *fraction* of the attention Todd's giving Char."

The insinuation felt like a Ping-Pong ball ricocheting in Molly's head. It wouldn't settle in. "Andie and Julian?"

"He convinced her to swim in the ocean. She sat here with a loony grin on her face like a moonstruck teenager while he talked about weather. Now they're off to buy dinner together. He probably declined her invitation because we're here."

"No, Jo."

"Maybe, Molly."

"No, not Andie."

"If you were married to Paul…?" She let the thought float where it would.

Molly grimaced. She never had cared much for Paul Sinclair. An overly aggressive sales type, he'd latched onto the spunky redhead because—Molly had always assumed—she brought to the table every grace he lacked. Which was every grace under the sun. Andie made Paul more presentable and the guy was smart enough to figure that out.

"Molly, you and I both know he never was trustworthy. For goodness' sake, he made a pass at me the night of their rehearsal dinner."

"He did? You never told me that."

Jo closed her eyes. "We both had too much to drink."

She waited a full minute, debating with herself whether or not she wanted to hear any more. At last she said, "Jo?"

"We didn't. Ernie was picking me up." She opened her eyes and looked at Molly. "Otherwise a few stolen kisses would not have been the end of the story. He's a donkey's behind and so am I."

All for one and one for all? Molly saw the pain on Jo's face and bit back the smart remark. It wasn't necessary. "She'll forgive you."

"She shouldn't."

"God shouldn't forgive any of us. But Jesus came and He does."

"Should we pray?"

Molly's throat tightened. Now Jo wanted to pray? Char was out on a date with Todd. Andie was on a semi-date with Julian. Jo was confessing to Molly as though she were a priest who wanted to hear such things. Molly herself was pregnant—the last thing on earth she wanted or expected or needed—and she couldn't even tell Scott about it. Where had prayer gotten them so far? Seemed like into a heap of trouble. What was that verse about seeing the back of God? As if He were walking away. In disinterest? Or was it anger?

Suddenly chilled despite the lingering heat, she stood. "I need a sweatshirt." And then she went inside the beach house.

~~~

Molly sat with Andie and Jo at the kitchen table. The house remained warm after the hot day, and so they did not build a fire in the fireplace. Molly missed the cheery snap and pop, the warm glow of flickering flames.

They ate steamed rice and kung pao shrimp and moo goo gai pan with chopsticks straight from cartons. The meal was the quietest they had shared in four days. Maybe in their entire lives, not counting the times one or the other of their parents deigned to include the girls in a family gathering.

Molly said, "I hope I don't stifle my kids' freedom of expression. Never, ever."

Jo and Andie turned puzzled faces toward her. Jo said, "How did you get to that?"

"I was just thinking how quiet we are tonight. It reminded me of how we'd all go silent when we were at each other's homes eating dinner with family. Except for your dad, Andie. He never stifled us. We let loose with him, didn't we?"

Her smile was wistful. "We did—if my mom wasn't nearby. She stifled him as well as anyone within shouting distance."

"How is your mom?" Jo asked.

"Unavailable."

The adjective fit all three of their mothers. Of course, it fit Char's too, but they never used it in front of her.

Andie went on. "She adores Florida and her fourth husband. How are your mothers?"

Together Molly and Jo replied, "Unavailable."

Andie nodded. "Why is it they were unavailable and yet had the power to stifle us so?"

Jo raised a shoulder. "Because we could never live up to their expectations. We grasped that fact by the time we were nine, and it choked us. Why bother revealing our loathsome little selves to their scrutiny? We were in survival mode."

Andie said, "Molly, I'm sure you make your kids feel safe."

"I try. I've had the best example from my mom of what *not* to do. My goal has been to create an environment the exact opposite of what I grew up in. Now I wonder if I've been dismantling all the hard work, creeping out my kids with this wacky post-forty routine."

Jo speared a wonton. "You're just showing them a bit of real life. Mom is human; she has feelings too. I seriously doubt they are harmed by a few months of not having their itch scratched before they even notice a prickling sensation."

Molly felt suddenly weary of Jo's superior attitude. It had always been there, of course, and Molly had always accepted it. At the moment, though, she couldn't muster a whit of sympathy. Yes, given her home environment, Jo had scant chance of *not* adopting a superior attitude. But so what? They all had their cross to bear.

Jo bit into the wonton and chewed as she spoke. "You're like Andie's dad when it comes to unconditional acceptance. You're nothing like our mothers."

"You still talk with your mouth full." Molly was startled to hear her voice utter the thought.

Jo swallowed. "Comes from eating alone while watching the news and telling the talking head exactly what I think."

"I'm not going to feel sorry for you, Jo. We all make our own beds."

"And I'm not going to feel sorry for you just because you're going to have a fifth child to perfectly mother."

Andie's chopsticks clattered into an empty carton. "Well." She sat up straighter, her face aglow. "Speaking of my dad, guess who reminds me of him?"

Molly stared blankly at her.

Andie smiled. "Right here in San Diego."

Molly shook her head.

"Right next door."

"Julian?"

"Yes. I mean the accent is different, but he has a funny little one just like my dad had a funny little one. And the pitch of his voice is the same. Or maybe it's the cadence. Soft and gentle. I'm surprised I can hear him when a wave crashes over us. My dad was bald, whereas Julian has a head full of thick hair. But still I keep thinking of— oh, this is so silly."

Molly said, "It can't be as silly as me mentioning Jo's lifelong chewing habit."

"Or as silly as…" Jo scooped a crab rangoon from a box, popped the entire thing into her mouth, and chewed. "As silly as me telling Molly she's a perfect mother when I know darn well she isn't because no one is. So what do you keep thinking of, Andie?"

She sighed. "My dad and me swimming in Lake Michigan."

"I'd forgotten he liked to do that," Molly said. "He took the three of us a few times. What were we, about ten?"

"Mm-hmm. He and I went all the time as far back as I can remember, until he started traveling more. Anyway, the point is, Julian makes me feel safe like my dad did."

"That's not silly," Molly said. "We all long to feel safe, at any age. Even forty."

"Hmm," was Jo's noncommittal response.

Andie said, "Remember our first night here? I was so afraid of every single thing from the freeway to going outside in the dark. I only felt safe in my cozy room. And then you prayed, Molly, and took me outside to see the midnight ocean."

"Spunky Andie woke up."

"She did. And she's making spunky plans for her day tomorrow."

Molly exchanged a horrified glance with Jo. "Oh, Andie! We totally forgot!"

"That's okay."

Jo set down her chopsticks at last. "No, it's not okay. Saturday is your day, birthday take number two. Thank goodness that snake won't be around to disrupt our time together. He did say he was leaving for Phoenix tonight, right?"

"Yes, but the thing is, about my day   "

Molly held her breath. But the thing about her day, what?

Oh, Lord, please don't let her say she's spending it with Julian!

"Well, I've been thinking long and hard about what I need most. I know that's not the point of our second birthday celebrations. Then again, maybe they are the same thing. What I need most is also what I want most. That would make it a celebration, wouldn't it? Then again, it's such a selfish thing." She bit her lip and lowered her eyes. "I mean, we're all here together and should—"

"Andie." At Jo's harsh voice, Molly jumped. "It's your day. Just spit it out. There is no right or wrong answer here. What do you want to do? Or need to do? There is no difference!"

Andie blinked at her. "I want to spend the entire day and night without any of you." Her shoulders sagged. "Oh, that sounds too selfish. I'll think of something else. There are the museums."

Jo flashed Molly a "I was right" glance.

Molly said, "Andie, it's okay if you want to spend the day without us."

"It's not that I don't *want* to be with you. It's what I *need*. I've been facing fears since I decided to make this trip. Now I want to face the granddaddy of them all: spend a day by myself, eat in a restaurant by myself, spend a night in a motel by myself. No friend, no Grandmère Babette reminders in a cozy beach house, no kids." She hesitated ever so slightly. "No Paul."

"By yourself," Molly repeated and looked sideways at Jo. *Maybe you weren't right.*

"Yes. It probably sounds silly to you two—"

"Andie!" They reprimanded in unison.

"All right, it's not silly. But that kind of stuff terrifies me. Now I know what I need to do. Be alone with God in the midst of my fears and let Him create a safe place inside of me."

Molly nodded in understanding, a slow smile spreading across her face. "Okay. Go for it, girl."

Jo said, "Yes, by all means. What exactly will you do? You can use my house, if you'd like."

"Well, I reserved one of those little motel cottages just down a ways, the ones on the pier." She grinned and made her eyes wide. "Right *on* the pier. Do you believe it? The ocean whooshing twenty-five feet below a few planks supported by a few stilts. In earthquake country!"

"Wow," Molly said.

"Great idea, huh? I can move in at ten tomorrow morning. Then I'll just do whatever." She giggled. "Julian said he's very proud of me."

She told the neighbor? Molly didn't dare look at Jo.

Tears pooled in Andie's eyes. She reached between the little cartons that covered the tabletop and extended a hand out to each of them. They placed hands in hers and she squeezed tightly.

"Jo, I never could have imagined doing this if you hadn't gotten me here in the first place. And, Molly, never without your prayers. Thank you two. Thank you so much."

Molly smiled. "You're so welcome, hon."

Jo thrust her arm in the air, hand fisted. "Yes! Spunky Andie rules!"

Glad for her friend's courageous plans, Molly thought how the conversation had diverted her attention from other matters. Perhaps she could cope with life after all.

The peace was fleeting. At that moment her stomach rumbled and she knew the kung pao shrimp declared it would not be following the usual route through her system.

She ran to the bathroom.

Thirty-Eight

Char warmed her hands on her coffee cup as she gazed through the wall of windows at the ocean. Exterior spotlights captured the white-caps. There was no beach, giving the effect that the restaurant floated right atop the water.

With a smile she turned to Todd across the small table for two. He was attractive in a white open-collared shirt and tweed sport coat. The look did not disguise his athletic physique. Or was that simply her visual of him in workout attire?

She blinked away the image and focused on the elegant surround-ings complete with candles, soft jazz, and white linen tablecloths.

"Todd, what a perfect setting! That dinner was magnificent!"

"Just like you." His eyes reflected the candlelight.

"Oh, sugar." She resorted again to prattle and defused the unset-tling effect of his penetrating stare. The trick had worked all day and gave her some semblance of control. "You are too sweet to me. I can still hardly believe you are actually here. And that you found this restaurant. It's exactly what I had in mind for an extra special cele-bration. I don't know if Jo would have come through or not. I told you about the chicken pie place!"

"Well, I do have some idea of your tastes. Not to mention I know how to find an endless supply of restaurant possibilities on the Internet." He smiled. "You look chilled."

"I'm fine," she fibbed and sipped warm coffee. The little sleeveless, backless black number had been the best buy of the afternoon but a poor choice for the evening. If they'd had time to continue shopping, she would have found a wrap to go with it.

"Here." He removed his sport jacket, carried it around the table, and draped it over her shoulders. "Now, how about dessert?"

"Of course. But please, not one of—"

"Not one of those complimentary tokens with a birthday candle and waitstaff singing."

She laughed. "You've been paying attention, my dear."

"Yes, I have." He grew somber and leaned forward. "Charlaine, you mean the world to me." He reiterated words he had spoken on the phone earlier that week. "I'm not talking only about how you got me through the divorce. I'd like to be totally candid. All right?"

The prattle died in her throat. Perhaps it was his coat around her, the faint scent of his cologne, the feeling of being cared for. Whatever it was, she felt beat down. She was so tired of keeping up the pretense that she was not attracted to him, tired of feeling guilty for an emotion.

She said, "We haven't been totally candid?"

He tilted his head, brows raised.

Of course they hadn't been. Totally candid would mean no teasing, no nuances. She swallowed. "All right."

"I don't have to go to Phoenix tonight."

Movement behind his shoulder diverted her attention, which in all total candidness probably wanted to be diverted. She shifted her eyes again to a table she had been watching through most of dinner. A man sat there with two teenagers, a boy and a girl. They hadn't exchanged but three words. All of them appeared incredibly sad.

"Char, I—"

A server materialized with a carafe. He refilled their cups and left.

Todd cleared his throat. "As I was saying— Well, hold that thought. Here comes the waiter now."

The friendly young man recited his inventory of dessert choices complete with descriptions and his own opinions.

He reminded her of Cole, an older version. Her outgoing son would make an excellent waiter and, in the right setting, earn great tips. Not that he would need to help pay for college, but the experience could be an education in itself. She would mention it to him.

The waiter left with their order.

"Char, you're zoning out on me. Are you disturbed by what I said?"

"He reminds me of Cole. I was thinking…" She saw his stare and knew he wasn't buying it. She repositioned herself in the seat. "You only said you don't have to go to Phoenix tonight."

"Yes. But I think you're zoning out on me because you heard what I didn't say." He paused. "And you're not quite sure about that."

Goose bumps sprouted, but she didn't reply.

"You and I connected the very first time we met four years and three months ago. Remember? Instant kismet. We get along like we've been lifelong friends. You are adorable. If you weren't married, I would ask you to marry me. What I am proposing is… Well." He reached across the table and caressed her hand. "I want to express this feeling we have between us in a fuller way. Will you spend the night with me?"

She blinked. There. He had said it. Out loud. Voiced her own desire.

He went on. "I promise to have you back to the beach house before your friends wake up. I understand if that's bothering you. Their level of sophistication isn't quite where yours is, but their feelings matter."

"I'm married." It was the objection that would not go away, an echo of her mama's advice.

"Our becoming lovers won't change that. Char, I want you so much."

She glanced off to the side. The sad family she had observed walked past them now. There was a hole in their unit. They were incomplete without a wife and mother. Where was she? *You'll forever change the lives of your kids and not for the better.* Jo's voice joined her mother's.

"Char, I am discreet. You know that. I would never jeopardize your family. I like your family. No one need ever know. I just don't know how long I can go on without holding you. Without kissing you."

His words went straight to an arid part of her, a place dried up through lack of such sentiment.

I'm married, she argued with herself.

But Cam never says things like—

Not since—

Not since whenever.

Still.

Still, he was her husband. She owed him—if only technically—one last chance.

Char slid her hand from under his and pushed back her chair. "Todd, excuse me. I need a few minutes."

He smiled. "I'm not going anywhere."

She shrugged off his jacket, grabbed her little bead-covered black bag, and hastened toward a hallway she hoped led to the ladies' lounge.

~

"Savannah!" Char hissed her daughter's name into the cell phone.

"Hi, Mom. I'm on the other line. Emmy's on hold—"

"Get your father on the phone this instant!" She paced the nicely appointed sitting area that was part of the ladies' washroom.

"Huh?"

"This instant!"

"Are you okay?"

"No! Just get him!"

"Mom!" Borderline panic laced her tone. "What's wrong?"

"Sugar." Char took a quick breath. "I'm all right. I'm just upset and I need to talk to him."

"He's asleep."

"I know that! Wake him up! Now! Please!"

"Okay, okay."

Char flopped onto an overstuffed floral chintz chair and closed her eyes, ignoring the sporadic parade of women in and out of the powder room. The line went silent. She assumed Savannah put her on hold to tell her friend on the other line goodbye.

She had called the home phone, to no avail. Cole was gone on an overnight with his Scout troop. Cam would be asleep since it was after eleven in the Midwest. She wondered why she hadn't dialed Savannah's cell first.

The breeding of a gentlewoman unraveled right then and there on her fortieth birthday. No amount of tongue gliding along her teeth was going to disperse her anger. It had been accumulating far too long.

Her daughter's voice was audible again. She was talking with Cam. There were muffled sounds.

"Char?" He came on now, his voice full of sleep.

Hot with near rage, she hadn't prepared two coherent words. She let the emotion have its way. "It's my birthday, Cam! You forgot my birthday!"

"I did?"

"Again! Like always!"

"I don't always—"

"Yes, you do always! Unless I mention it to the kids and they tell you, you have no clue."

"I know it's at the end of September. I knew you wouldn't be here this week for it, but we planned to celebrate when you come home— Savannah, hon." His voice faded as he must have turned to their daughter. "It's all right. It's your mama's birthday today…yeah. Today. And we forgot…Mm-hmm, that's why she's upset. You go on. I'll bring your phone to you when we're done."

It's your mama's birthday.

Cam was a northerner, but he had fallen in love with a Southern belle and her speech. Sometimes he unconsciously mimicked her accent. Often he used her phrases. And, like she with her mother, he had always referred to Char as "mama" to their children, even now, years after they had graduated to "mom" and "flaming fossil."

He cleared his throat. "Savannah says happy birthday. I say happy birthday. I'm sorry. I am very sorry."

"That's not the point!"

A woman walked by as the words exploded from her. At her surprised expression, Char slipped off her heels and curled her legs beneath herself, turning a shoulder toward the door.

"Char, what is the point then?"

"The point is—" Hopelessness choked off the words. Where to begin? The point was seventeen years worth of dwindling affection. It wasn't explainable via the telephone.

Her only choice was to cut to the chase. "I called because Todd is here."

"Todd?" Complete bafflement filled his tone.

"Todd Brooks."

"Todd Brooks." He repeated the name, his voice confused.

"Our neighbor Todd Brooks."

"Really?" Pleasantly surprised now. He liked Todd. He didn't even mind that she and Todd went to the gym together. It saved on gas. "He's out there? You ran into each other?"

"Cam! Put two and two together!"

"Huh?"

"It is not a coincidence! He's here because I'm here! He's here because you're not and it's my birthday and we've been flirting for four years and now he wants to do something besides just flirt!"

Silence.

Char felt like a word-gushing fire hydrant. "If you cared at all, maybe you would have noticed. Maybe you wouldn't just sit and watch television. Maybe you'd remember September twenty-seventh and at least have called. Maybe I wouldn't be sitting here in this fancy restaurant seriously considering my alternatives with the neighbor guy!"

More silence.

Tears streamed down her face, but the fire hydrant's nozzle twisted shut and the flow of words stopped. The anger was gone as well. She wondered dazedly what percentage of wives called their husbands to discuss plans to commit adultery.

A heavy sigh blew in the line. "What are you going to do?"

"I don't know. What are you going to do?"

"What can I do?"

"I don't know that, either."

"I care, Char."

"You could have fooled me, C.P. Goodbye."

She disconnected before he could reply. At that point, there was absolutely nothing he could say that would make any difference whatsoever.

Thirty-Nine

Jo sat on the edge of the bed and pressed a damp cloth to Molly's forehead. Even in the low lamplight her face appeared drained of all color.

"Moll, I can get something for you. I've got my prescription pad with me. A pharmacy is down the street."

She grimaced. "Throwing up comes with the territory, especially when I'm stupid enough to eat the spiciest kung pao I've ever tasted in my life. Promise me you won't say 'Chinese' in front of me for a long, long time?"

"Sure."

"Hey. Don't look so worried. I'm fine. I will be fine."

"Can we get you anything else?" Jo glanced at the nightstand, where she'd placed water bottles, saltines, and her cell phone for Molly to use.

"What else is there?" Her mouth twisted, a brave attempt at a smile. "I can't believe Andie walked three blocks in the dark to buy those crackers. Make that Spunky Andie. Let's keep calling her that so she doesn't lose sight of it. Okay?"

"It's a deal. Think you can sleep now?"

"Mm-hmm." She closed her eyes. "You'll leave the door unlocked for Char?"

"Yes, Mother."

"You'll wake me if she doesn't come home soon?"

"No. Why would I do that?"

"So we can go find her."

"Yeah, right. Go to sleep."

Molly smiled through a groan. "One for all and all for one."

Jo stood. "Do you want this light on?"

"Yeah." Her eyes remained shut. "Maybe I'll read."

"Okay. Yell if we can do anything."

"Mmm."

"Moll?"

"Hmm?"

"I'm sorry for being such a smart mouth about the way you mother your kids."

"No worries. I'm sorry for attacking your chewing habits."

"That hardly mattered. I attacked you personally."

Molly looked at her now through dark lashes that obscured the gray-green eyes. "And I'm sorry for thinking you're a snob who will never get it."

"I am a snob." She waited, unsure if she wanted to hear more. "I'm still envious of your thick eyelashes."

"Chicken. You're changing the subject."

Jo thought of Andie fighting her fears with every ounce of courage she could rally. And of Molly, so intensely searching for herself during a few short days away from everyday distractions that surely could not leave her time to think.

Wasn't all of that the point? The reason Jo had wanted to be with her friends? To feel their collective strength and battle her own fears and find that piece of herself she had lost?

"Okay," Jo said. "I am a snob who will never get what?"

"That God loves you unconditionally."

She sank onto the bed again, pushed there by two giant hands, one emitting God's radiant love, the other His blazing fire. It was the Molly Effect, full-on assault.

"Moll," she whispered. "I can't reconcile the fire and the love. I'm the poster child for filth. If I get close, He'll burn me up."

"I keep telling you, that's why Jesus came. He forgives the junk. All you have to do is ask. Andie will forgive you too. All you have to do…sorry, I…" A soft snore rattled in her throat.

Molly was fast asleep! God oozing from her every pore and she was fast asleep!

Of all the nerve.

⌒

Jo walked out into the living room. Andie was nowhere to be seen. Except in Jo's imagination.

She'll forgive you too. Molly's words referred to Andie, to Jo's confession of making out with Paul after the rehearsal dinner.

Maybe she would just go to bed. Sleep in the beach house had been deeper than she'd experienced in a long time without the aid of a pill. Whether it was angels, leftover Faith Fontaine vibes, recalled Babette memories, or a combination of all three, that beach house *presence* induced rest. Soul-soothing, dead-to-the-world slumber.

Now, though, thoughts of her friends intruded, zapping the need to escape. If a friend would not let a friend drive drunk, neither would she ignore needs she might be able to meet. Molly was ill, Char was confused about where she stood with them, and Andie…

Andie needed to hear how she had been wronged by Jo. The air between them needed to be cleared. Perhaps that sort of thing gave more space to angels, Faith vibes, and Babette memories.

Perhaps it gave space to the radiant love that wasn't so ethereal anymore.

⌒

Jo found Andie outdoors standing in the dark at the seawall, gazing toward the ocean.

"Hey." Jo stepped beside her.

"Hey. How's Molly?"

"She's asleep. She should have dinner out of her system, anyway."

"Poor thing."

"But it's so worth it, right? At least that's what I hear, especially from mommies when they first hold their brand-new baby. By comparison, what's a few months of barfing, a few hours of working a howling ball from the womb?"

Andie chuckled. "That's true. It is so worth it."

Jo faced the ocean but didn't see it. She saw only her old friends giving birth. Eight children between them. Why hadn't Jo been a part of even one's entrance into the world? *Distance and marital status.* Those seemed silly excuses.

"Jo, it must be unbearably hard. Delivering all those babies and not having your own."

She leaned heavily against the wall, pushed again by those giant hands. No, only by one this time. The one emitting blazing fire. She deserved His wrath.

Andie said, "It's none of my business—"

"Of course it is, Andie. We reunited because we had a great friendship and wanted to experience that closeness again. That closeness of sharing all our business." She turned and slid sideways up onto the wall. "I'm not sure how I ended up an obstetrician. I never really planned on having children. My parents cured me of any innate tendency in that area. But when I was going to school and helping Ernie at the clinic, I most loved working with the pregnant women. And so it seemed an obvious choice to go that direction. I think it had something to do with observing the miracle of life over and over. I couldn't get enough of that. Still can't."

Jo stopped short of addressing Andie's comment about the profession being difficult for her. Did she really have to go there? Must she describe how some days it was indeed unbearably difficult because a hysterectomy at age thirty-six made it so?

All Jo's determination to reconnect with her friends fizzled. Maybe their deeply personal journeys were no one else's business. She swung her legs over the top of the seawall and twisted around to face the ocean.

Andie sat beside her. "Oomph," she grunted as she pulled her legs up one at a time. "In the water I feel so light and athletic! This wall is a little reality check. I should have skipped the fourth egg roll." She sighed loudly. "It just went down so easily. There was Paul in my mind, talking me out of tomorrow's flight of fancy. 'Andrea.'" She lowered her voice. "'Do you truly believe that going to a motel is really the best use of your time and money?'"

Jo patted her shoulder. "Of course it's the best use of them. It'll be like one of those camps where they challenge people to move way beyond their comfort zone by staying out in the woods all night alone or rock climbing."

"That's what I think. I also think while I'm out there, maybe I'll find some new tapes to play in my head. Twenty years is quite long enough to filter every thought through 'But Andrea, if you do it my way, won't that be better?'"

Jo shivered. The night air remained balmy, but the thought of Paul, year after year, crushing the spunk right out of Andie chilled her to the bone.

Was it really her place to add even more weight to the power he held over her friend?

But which was the worst offense? To add weight or to withhold the truth?

The truth would free Jo of some guilt. It would clear the air between them.

But it would hurt her…

And yet, maybe telling the truth was like Andie's work, like kneading toxins loose in order to open the way for healing energy to flow.

Andie said, "You must think I'm such a ninny. You're so strong and independent."

"Hon, I spent years drinking myself into oblivion on a regular basis. That makes me the ninny. You've just been doing the best you could, taking care of your children and home while living under a smothering personality. And from the descriptions of your sons and your work, I think you've done a superior job."

"I'm not too sure about that."

"Well, you should be. You know what I've noticed since we arrived?"

"What?"

"Our first two days together, you said 'Paul' in every other sentence. He thought this, he thought that, he would say this or that. You're bringing him up less and less."

"Really?"

"Mm-hmm." She paused and looked at Andie. "But I have to bring him up. There was…uh…something happened. A long time ago."

She turned toward Andie.

"I want to ask your forgiveness. I did a stupid, stupid thing." Jo felt her throat close up. Her pulse raced. Her head pounded. "I'm so sorry."

"For what?"

"I drank too much at your wedding rehearsal dinner."

"Jo, I forgave you for that—"

"I know. You always did. Every time I messed things up you did. But that's not what I'm talking about. Paul drank too much as well. And after he took you home, we met at a bar. He made a pass. I let him make another one. We sat in a booth and…made out. Then I remembered Ernie was on his way to pick me up after his shift. End of story."

Andie's face was hidden by shadows, unreadable.

"It was a drunken flirtation that meant nothing to either one of us. I only saw him twice after that, at Char's and Molly's weddings. We never spoke of it or even hinted at that night. There were lots of other people around. A big party." She caught herself before saying "other women." Hard telling what the guy had gone on to do that night. "He probably doesn't even remember anything. I'm sorry."

"Well." Andie's breathing sounded uneven. "Why are you telling me now?"

"I need your forgiveness."

"You didn't cover this the last time you went through the Steps."

Jo shook her head. "No, I didn't. And I'm not going through the Steps now. I just...want to get right with you. And God."

"He'll forgive you."

Jo waited.

"I..." She slid off the seawall. "I... it shouldn't matter now. So long ago. And kissing you in a bar one time was a mere drop in the bucket. He, um, he hasn't been faithful since...maybe never. I-I don't want to talk right now." She hurried across the boardwalk toward the house.

Jo's heart pounded and she whispered to herself, "Hang in there, Spunky Andie. Hang in there."

Forty

The refrigerator in the beach house kitchen was a nice one. It even had a light bulb in the freezer section. Like the noonday sun, that light illumined the compartment and the one item—besides ice cubes—stored in it, namely a carton of ice cream. Black raspberry chocolate ice cream. A half gallon. Unopened.

The container was turned sideways, allowing the label's list of ingredients to catch the full impact of the light, making the fine print easily readable.

Fat grams. Saturated.

Carbohydrate grams. Not the complex kind.

Sugar.

Corn syrup.

Mono- and diglycerides.

Sodium phosphates.

Artificial flavoring.

Artificial coloring.

The fan kicked on. Frosty air blew on Andie's face.

She closed her eyes and let the blast cool the hot anger that burned. Her cheeks must have been as red as her hair.

She had always imagined it had been Char. Char, the out-and-out flirt, turner of men's heads, not yet engaged to Cam at the time of

Andie's wedding. Not cynical Jo, always disdainful toward Paul, so enamored with Ernesto Delgado she almost didn't make it to the church in time for the rehearsal.

Well, in reality Paul smooching with Jo in a bar was not what happened the night before her wedding. True, that knowledge cut her to the core and she would have to deal with it, but it was not the main source of her pain.

No, he had been with someone else, maybe even Char. Not that he confessed such a thing. She just knew…The dark circles under his eyes…The exchanged snickers with the groomsmen… His uncharacteristically felicitous attention toward her, overmuch even for a wedding day…She had asked, "Okay, what'd you do?"

Joking.

"Andrea, I married you." The wink. The grin that freed a mass of butterflies in her stomach. "That's what I did."

And she let it go.

Was that the first swing of the ax? The first leg to be knocked out from under her spunk?

Andie stared again at the carton, at the enlarged depiction of luscious fruit and chocolate chunks surrounded by thick textured raspberry-colored sweetness.

How could Jo…? Countless other times, her behavior had been easily forgivable. Who could blame her? She truly had never felt loved by her parents or siblings. She drowned her pain with alcohol. She had only her three best friends and Grandmère Babette.

But now, Andie wasn't all that eager to forgive.

Jo and Paul could rot in Hades.

She slammed shut the freezer door.

⌒

Andie knocked on Julian's patio door, the one facing the beach. Slivers of light shone around closed vertical blinds.

The blinds moved. Julian pushed them aside and slid open the door, concern immediately creasing his face. Music poured out. Majestic classical music enveloped her.

"Andie." He spoke loudly. "Come in. Let me take that."

She shrugged the large overnight bag from her shoulder into his hand and stepped inside. "Thanks."

He shut the door behind her. "Have a seat."

She gave the room a cursory glance. It was large and comfortable, lit by two floor lamps. Though sparse by Faith's standards, it was nicely furnished. Blue tones dominated. Overstuffed couches and chairs and a sound system filled the front end. Behind a dividing counter, she spotted the kitchen area.

He picked up a remote from the coffee table and pointed it at the receiver. The volume lessened.

"Have a seat," he said again.

She remained standing, feeling dazed. A short while ago she had looked at her overnight bag, already packed for tomorrow's adventure, and was struck with the sensation of freefall, like how a baby robin pushed from its nest must feel. Instinct kicked in, activating limp wings of dormant faith. She flew to the nearest tree branch, trusting in the shelter available there.

"Julian, I need a place to sleep."

"The apartment upstairs is ready and waiting." His rental space.

"The couch—"

"Wouldn't think of it."

"I'll pay—"

"I don't charge friends."

Look at the birds in the sky. They do not sow or reap or gather into barns; yet your heavenly Father feeds them. Are you not worth much more than they are?

He tilted his head to the side and studied her for a moment. "Do you want to talk?"

She shook her head.

"Cry?"

She hesitated. Well, yes, she wanted to cry. Above all she wanted to cry. And a shoulder reminiscent of her dad's would be the perfect place to let her tears fall.

But Julian was not her dad.

Once more she shook her head.

"I'll get the key." He went into the kitchen.

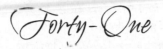

Forty-One

Jo watched from the beach.

Earlier, after confessing to Andie, she had walked a long time, barefoot, at the water's edge, soaking in the deep quiet, giving Andie space in the house.

Now she stood, rooted in the sand as her friend walked to the neighbor's, a large bag hanging from her shoulder.

Julian opened his door. Andie went inside. He shut the door and the blinds.

Jo could hardly blame her. Why would Andie want to hang around her any longer? Why would she bother to pretend she didn't want another man? Any other woman would have left that scoundrel Paul ages ago.

But she wasn't any other woman. She was Andie. Jo had never known anyone else like her. Molly was good, solid, but earthy too. *Get out from under the pile.* Andie was good, not solid so much as shot clear through with purity.

Lord.

Jo sank onto the sand where she stood. She dug her feet through the cool top layer, damp from the night ocean air. Beneath it her toes touched pockets of warmth where the sun's heat lingered.

Why did it hurt so to do the right thing? It had been right to reveal her true self to Andie. It had been right to not give that abortion pill to the sixteen-year-old girl. It had been right to gather her old friends together.

Images flashed through her mind.

The liquor store three blocks away.

Her wallet on the dresser in her bedroom.

The tall plastic cups in the cupboard.

She would use plastic. Glass was prohibited on the beach. Of course, so was alcohol, but she wasn't about to get sloshed inside Faith Fontaine's house. Come to think of it, she doubted she could even walk through it in order to get money for the sole purpose of buying booze. That *presence* she felt in the house—whatever it was—kept chipping away at her desire to escape real life.

Maybe the salesclerk would extend her credit until tomorrow.

"God!"

Other images chased off pictures of herself sitting in the sand with a bottle and a plastic cup.

Molly needing something more substantial than saltines. Soup. Toast.

Char coming home. Alone. Scared.

Andie extending forgiveness. Molly said she would. Molly's word was synonymous with promise.

I will stay sober for them.

Oh, God. Only by Your help.

She blew out a breath. "I guess that was a prayer. I wonder if He heard?"

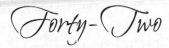

Forty-Two

Char sat on the seawall at least a dozen doors south of the beach house, in a spot between the circles of light where the shadows were darkest. She clutched the little black beaded purse in her lap. Thanks to her mama's admonition, she had stocked it as usual with the woman's survival kit, an updated version of what a woman needed when faced with the unforeseen: lipstick, a fifty-dollar bill, her American Express card, and cell phone.

"Oh, bother." She reached up the sleeve of the itchy sweatshirt and scratched her forearm. Cheap fabric. No surprise there, considering she'd purchased it and the too-large matching black pants at a discount department store. Though the place offered convenient hours—good grief, it was open twenty-four/seven—it fell short in its selection of petite sizes.

But the uncomfortable clothing kept her warm enough in the post-midnight air. She only hoped the pretty black dress wouldn't snag on the concrete wall where it draped down behind her. How odd she must look. She wore the sweat pants under the dress, the sweatshirt over it, and floppy canvas deck shoes. Her heels lay next to her.

Never, in her wildest dreams—or wildest nightmares—could she have imagined a worse fortieth birthday. Or any birthday, for that matter. And the ending was far too putrid to ponder. It qualified for a level infinitely beyond hazardous.

"Char?"

She jumped almost completely off the wall and spun around. "Oh! In the name of all that is sane and holy! Julian! Don't do that!"

"Sorry."

She placed a hand on her chest and tried not to gasp again. She thought she'd been paying close attention to the vacant boardwalk, but she hadn't seen or heard him approach.

He sat beside her, one leg bent so he faced her. "Are you all right?"

"I have no idea." She yanked the sweatshirt hood onto her head. Evidently Julian had recognized her by her hair or profile. Surely nothing else resembled her.

"Incognito?"

"It's none of your business." She looked at the ocean.

"Just being neighborly. Can I help with something?"

"No." She gave a sharp laugh. "I think I've had quite enough help from men for one lifetime."

"Now, now. Don't throw us all out the window."

"I will if I want to."

"Very well."

The quiet swish of waves filled the air. She watched skinny legged birds race about at the water's edge. They'd stop momentarily and poke long pointy beaks into the packed sand.

She could easily lose her mind if she sat there much longer.

"So," she said, "can I rent your apartment for tonight?"

"I'm sorry, but someone is staying in it."

"Oh."

"Shall I walk you to your house?"

"No. Thanks."

He didn't move or say anything else.

"Julian, you can go home. I'm fine."

"I'd rather not leave you out here alone. It's two AM."

"They hate me."

"Who?"

"Molly, Jo, and Andie."

"Why would you think that?"

"I don't measure up to their prudish expectations. I went out with Todd tonight. They're all in a snit over it. He was just being neighborly." She glanced at him and quickly turned back toward the ocean. "Kind of like you and my birthday breakfast."

"Perhaps then it's your imagination that they're disturbed."

"I lied. He wasn't just being neighborly. But I'm guilty as well. I encouraged him. Every day on the phone since I got here. In every conversation of the previous four years. I did everything short of hang a sign on my neck with 'Available' written on it. Why wouldn't he put the moves on me?"

"The only wonder is it took him four years."

She had questioned that too. She didn't think it was because he was married most of those years. She suspected more went on during his business trips than he discussed. Or after PTA meetings, when that Penelope what's-her-name was president, before she moved away.

Which happened about the time Todd suggested he and Char go to the gym together.

"Char, they'll be worried."

"More likely they're thinking good riddance."

"Has no one ever worried about you? Been concerned over your whereabouts?"

If a semi had roared up from the ocean floor and charged across the beach toward her, Char could not have been more jolted into action. She spun around, away from him, sweeping her legs up and over the wall. She hopped down and planted her canvas deck-shoed feet onto the sidewalk. *Hang the worry of snagging the dress.*

He caught up with her lickety-split. "You forgot your shoes."

"Thanks." She accepted the heels from him without slowing her pace.

He stayed beside her.

"I don't need an escort."

He silently strode along.

She heard his questions in the dull thud of their hurried steps. *Has no one ever worried about you? Been concerned over your whereabouts?*

"My mother was concerned. But a drunk driver took care of that." Her voice rose to nearly a shout. "Broadsided her in the middle of the day. I was thirteen!"

"I'm sorry. What happened after that?"

She halted. "What happened after that?" She yelled now. "What a ridiculous question! My mother was gone! What do you think happened?"

A lamp shone on his face. Even in her rage Char saw compassion in the line of his jaw, the set of his full lips, the eyes staring back at her.

He said, "I think your world was shattered."

Her throat felt held in a stranglehold.

"Char, did it ever get fixed?"

She took off again and broke into a jog. Without a backward glance she hastened to the beach house and went through the gate and across the patio. An outdoor light was on; a lamp glowed behind the window curtains. A welcome sign?

The doorknob turned in her hand. At least they hadn't locked her out. She went inside and swiftly locked the door behind her.

As if whatever pursued her could be kept at bay.

Forty-Three

Molly pulled the phone away from her ear. The distance failed to diminish the effect of Scott's whooping and hollering. He was going to wake the kids. Then he'd have to explain to them that they were going to have a sister or brother, blah, blah, blah.

His earsplitting response to her pregnancy news was not what she expected.

Not yet out of bed, she slid back under the covers and waited for him to stop shouting praises to God.

Praises. And thanks. For ruining her life?

"Scotty."

"Oh, Molly! You are so precious! I love you! Hallelujah! Thank You, Jesus!"

"Scotty!"

"What?"

"I don't want to be pregnant!"

That silenced him for a long moment. "But you are," he whispered. "It's a baby, Moll."

She cried then. It was unbelievable how many tears the body could produce within a twenty-four period.

"Sweetheart, it's okay."

"But don't you understand? I'm forty! Eli is eleven! I'm going to teach! Full-time!"

"Yeah?" His singsong tone said *so what?*

"I am not Superwoman!" She wailed into the pillow, drowning his response.

Long moments passed before she could speak again through her tight throat. "This changes everything." She reached for a tissue on the nightstand and blew her nose. "I mean, we were starting a new season."

He didn't respond.

"I suppose I should just merrily say, 'It's okay, God. I don't mind if You slam all those doors You just opened up!' Oh, Scotty, I'll never find myself again."

Still no response.

"Scott? Are you there?"

No reply.

She looked at the phone. Its tiny colorful screen had gone black. She pushed the power button, but nothing happened.

The battery was dead.

She bounded from the bed and searched the nightstand and floor. No power cord! Why wouldn't Jo leave that too?

She opened her door and trudged down the hall, past Char and Jo's closed doors. Should she wake one of them? Maybe Scott would call Char's number. Knowing her, though, she'd sleep through the ringer's rendition of a brass band playing "When the Saints Go Marching In."

Early morning gray afforded enough light to see that there was no cord or cell phone lying about the living room or kitchen. She went to the area off the kitchen where she could see Andie's door. It was open.

"Andie?"

Molly noticed that the bathroom door was also open. She stepped into Andie's bedroom. Could she be out in the ocean boogie boarding already? At six-thirty in the morning?

She found a note on Andie's bed and picked it up.

"Started my birthday early. See you Sunday morning—your day, Molly. Start planning! Love, Andie."

Start planning. Sure. Like planning mattered.

She didn't even want a second birthday. "No thanks, Lord. One fortieth was quite enough."

Her stomach somersaulted. She sat on Andie's bed and waited for it to right itself. It didn't. Betsy's gymnastics routine came to mind, the one where she did one forward roll after another, all the way down the mat, from one side of the gym to the other.

Molly groaned.

The crackers seemed to help. At least they had stayed down.

She stumbled into the kitchen and found the box on the counter. She tore open the waxy paper around a stack of crackers, pulled out the top one, and took a bite. She hated saltines, but the instant salt and white flour turned mealy on her tongue, the forward rolls slowed.

Fresh air would help. She found her sweatshirt left at the kitchen table the previous night and slipped it over her flannel pajamas. Barefoot, bag of crackers in hand, she went outside. The patio chairs were covered with condensation from the nighttime mist. Munching on her third cracker, she walked between a pair of joggers and a bicyclist to the wall and sat.

While her stomach settled, Molly breathed in and she breathed out. There really was nothing else she could do.

~

"Morning."

Molly turned around the seawall and saw Jo nearing. "Morning."

"How are you?" Jo plopped beside her.

"Better, thanks." She noticed Jo's haggard appearance. "Are you okay?"

"Mmm. Yeah." Settling her bare feet atop the wall, she hugged her knees to herself and rested her chin on them. "No. Andie left last night. I waited up for Char. Two o'clock."

"What? Andie left? Char came in at two o'clock?"

Jo closed her eyes and sighed.

"Jo."

"I told Andie about...about making out with Paul. When is it she'll forgive me?" She looked at Molly, her expression that of a lost little girl.

"Aww. What did she say?"

"More importantly, what didn't she say? She didn't say all was or ever would be well between us."

"She will come round. She sounded fine in her note."

"Note?"

"In her room. She started her birthday early and would see us tomorrow morning."

"Okay." The word was more a release of breath.

"But she left last night? Where did she go?"

"Julian's."

"No." Molly stared at the large white neighboring house. Glass nearly covered the entire three stories that faced the ocean. It was sleek and grand, probably beautiful to those who cared for contemporary styles.

"I watched her from the beach. I saw him let her inside."

"It's a huge place. Lots of rooms. Didn't he mention something about renting out the upstairs?"

"But they *connected*, Moll."

"Enough to sleep together?"

"All I know is she desperately needed someone to connect with her. I guess we didn't fit the bill."

"Sort of like you and that street pastor, Zeke."

Jo straightened, surprise on her face.

"You connected, right? Before you really opened up to us."

"Yeah."

"If it's that sort of connection, a spiritual one, then they're not getting physically involved. He seems such a straight-arrow kind of guy, not into one-night stands. The voice is Sean Connery's, but he's no James Bond."

"Exactly. He's just what she needs because Paul is such a jerk." Jo lowered her chin again to bent knees. "Because I am such a jerk."

Molly touched her foot. "You're not responsible. Neither are we responsible for Char. Two o'clock, huh?"

"Two-eighteen. I heard her come in but didn't talk to her."

"Did you hear Todd?"

"No."

"I can't remember the last time I stayed up until two — Yes, I can. It was three years ago. Abigail had the flu. She got sick right after dinner and kept on going straight through the night." She remembered how then the other kids came down with it, one by one. It dragged on for a month. An eternal month. Add another child to the picture, and she could easily be looking at a lost six weeks every time a germ went round. Her heart sank.

Jo stood. "I can't face this without coffee. Are you up for our walk to Kono's?"

"I don't think so."

"I'm not, either. I'll go make coffee. Want some tea?"

Molly nodded her head and said, "Herbal tea sounds great."

"Okay, I'll make that too. Did you talk to Scott yet?"

She told her what had happened.

Jo tugged on her arm. "Come on. Let's go plug in the phone. You can talk while I fuel my caffeine habit."

They walked toward the house. The morning gray and mist lingered, but a hint of desert warmth scented the air. Would that hot wind blow again? Molly hoped not. She wasn't up for that, either.

As a matter of fact, she wasn't up for much of anything. Especially not for Scott's inability to empathize. He related right and left to a congregation. He understood what *trees* needed. Turn her life inside out and he was once again—or still?—clueless.

That shot any so-called new understanding between them right out of the water.

Inside the house, Jo headed for the coffeemaker. Molly ignored her directions concerning the cell phone's power cord and instead found a bath towel. She would dry off the patio chairs. They could sit in the fresh air and drink their tea and coffee.

And then Molly would breathe in and she would breathe out.

Forty-Four

Char's eyelids flew open. Startled, she sat up in the bed. Seven o'clock? *Seven?* Why was she awake?

She touched her face. She'd forgotten to wear her eye mask, and now dawn intruded.

Or was it a bad dream? Something hung in the foggy edges of her mind. What was it?

Todd.

Cam.

Julian.

Molly. Jo. Andie.

Discount store sweats.

She looked down, and a sweatshirt hood moved with her head. She brushed it off and glanced under the covers. Rough black fabric covered her from head to ankles.

"Oh my word!"

Where was the dress?

She spotted it on a chair at the foot of the bed and remembered. In last night's craziness she had removed it and put on the first thing within reach—the sweatshirt—in order to crawl into bed as quickly as possible.

Away from that unseen hounding *whatever*.

Char sprang from the bed and whipped off the offensive clothes. Within moments she stood under the shower's spray, vigorously scrubbing a loofah over her skin. She shampooed her hair and dug her acrylic nails into her scalp. Eventually the hot water cooled, and with reluctance she turned it off.

She wasn't ready to get out. She felt coated in…gunk, black as night.

⁓

Char helped herself to coffee from the carafe in the kitchen. She spotted Jo and Molly through the window, sitting on the patio with mugs in hand.

Her throat and chest throbbed. Her heart felt like a ricocheting pinball.

Like that time in high school.

They were sixteen years old. Or rather the others were sixteen and had their driver's licenses months ahead of her. Jo's parents bought her a fancy car for her birthday. Like always, they provided her with the trendiest, most expensive new thing on the market. She called them guilt gifts, purchased in lieu of the time they didn't spend with her. She should have pranced about like a spoiled princess, but she never did. Though she had the superior attitude of most brainy rich people, it wasn't the type that caused her nose to bruise from frequent contact with the ceiling.

That September day Jo arrived at Char's house. Molly and Andie already sat in the backseat of her sporty convertible. Char remembered seeing them as they drove up the driveway. It was a hot Saturday, ten days before Char's birthday, and they wore shorts. They were going to the mall.

Her heart pounded. Her throat ached from wild activity in her chest.

She didn't want to go. They didn't really like her. They put up with her because Babette convinced them to do so and because, to put it bluntly, the cutest boys were attracted to Char. Given that their all-girls parochial school limited male attention, going to the mall was a significant event. Char's attendance was a necessity.

But she didn't want to stay home either. Home...such as it was.

Just a few minutes before the girls' arrival, Char's father had informed her he'd asked what's-her-name to marry him. That woman in the kitchen. Her mother's kitchen. The woman who cooked breakfast that day. The one who giggled when her father said the sunrise brought her.

Sunrise. *Pff.* Like Char didn't have ears. The woman had spent the night.

In her mother's room.

It hadn't been the first time, and now she was going to *live* in it.

Heart pounding, Char stood rooted to the floor. Jo honked. Andie waved. Molly made a goofy face. Char didn't budge.

Until she heard the woman's laugh from somewhere in the house.

Char joined her friends. Jo backed out of the driveway. Molly asked what was wrong. Andie squeezed her shoulder.

She didn't tell them what was wrong until they all sat in a booth at her favorite restaurant, the table piled high with gaily wrapped birthday gifts. They had planned the surprise for her. That was when she knew they weren't just putting up with her.

The story of her dad's betrayal spilled out. They listened. They loved her through it.

But that was twenty-four years ago and she hadn't been the one hurting others.

Char carried her mug and went out the back door.

~

Behind the house, Char sipped her coffee and scanned the narrow one-way thoroughfare. No one walked along it. She stood in what should have been the backyard area but was in reality a dry patch of dirt not much bigger than her walk-in closet back home.

The area did not afford much privacy. Low fences and concrete walls divided tiny yards. Without turning she could see windows from a dozen homes, most of them tall like Julian's. Directly across was a small one-story cottage where that vagrant had been hiding out.

Char shivered.

What an odd place. Brilliant sunshine and heat yesterday, eerily misty this morning.

She heard a noise coming from Julian's and stepped nearer Jo's SUV in the carport. The last person she wanted to see was the neighbor! If she slipped along the far side of the vehicle, perhaps he wouldn't notice her.

She stole a glance toward his yard and froze.

Andie?

Touching Julian's arm?

In a gesture of familiarity, Andie rose as if on tiptoes and leaned into him.

He leaned down toward her, his hand on her shoulder.

She kissed his cheek.

She kissed his cheek?

And he smiled.

Oh my word.

They parted, calling out goodbyes.

Andie turned left onto the alley and spotted Char. Her smile faded as she walked toward her. A large canvas bag hung from her shoulder. She wore what she called the "spunky outfit" she'd bought yesterday, a flowing top, floral print, apricot-colored linen, and matching cropped pants. It was a perfect look for her.

"Hi," Andie said.

"Hi."

Andie stopped before her. "You're up early."

"I...am." Char was speechless, totally unable to segue from her jumbled thoughts to greeting her dyed-in-the-wool, Miss Goody Two-shoes friend at seven in the morning as she left the neighbor's house. The neighbor's arms.

They stared at one other for a moment.

Finally Andie said, "It's not what it looks like." She finger-combed her red hair. It was damp like Char's, as if she'd just showered. "Oh, fiddlesticks. I can't help what it looks like. How are you today?"

"Um." Words still failed her.

"You look like you've got a hangover, but I know you don't drink." She shook her head.

"Fortieth birthday?"

She nodded.

"Told you so."

Char stared in disbelief.

Andie shifted the bag from one shoulder to the other. "Well, I'm off to re-celebrate my fortieth. You'll have to schedule a do-over for yourself in the near future. See you tomorrow." She turned.

"Where are you going?"

Andie faced her again. "You didn't talk to the others? I'm spending the day by myself. I guess to face my fears. Bye." She walked away.

What in the world was going on? Andie at her spunkiest had never been abrupt, never borderline rude.

Andie twirled around and called out, "Char?"

"Yeah?"

"Did you sleep with Paul?"

Char's eyes felt as if they might bug right out of her head. "Of course not! You're my friend. He was always yours."

Andie nodded once and then turned again to continue on her way.

Char watched until the mist enshrouded her friend and wondered again what in the world was going on.

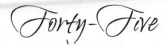

Forty-Five

Jo left Molly on the patio and went inside the house to refill her mug. Char stood at the sink filling the carafe.

"Char! It's not even seven-thirty!" She stopped short of reminding her that she'd just gotten home a few short hours ago.

"Hmm. Morning. I'm making more coffee. I drank all yours."

"No problem. Molly's into tea today. I had most of the first pot to myself."

"Hmm."

Jo sensed something off-kilter. Char appeared dressed for the day in pale pink slacks and a white knit top. Her hair was damp. She showered already? And not dried her hair? And she didn't say much. Even tired and grouchy, Char always bubbled over with words.

Jo said, "Are you hungry? I'm going to make toast."

"No. Thanks."

Jo busied herself with bread and the toaster. "I'll bring coffee out if you want to go sit down."

"I'll wait."

"Molly's feeling like a semi ran over her."

Char flinched.

"She ate spicy Chinese."

"Hmm."

"Did you have a good dinner?"

"Yes."

Jo gathered peanut butter and jam, knives and plates, and waited for Char to expand. She didn't.

"So," Jo said. "Where did you eat?"

"The, um, Marine Room."

"Ah. Nice."

She nodded.

"Char, are you okay?"

"Mm-hmm."

"I was just wondering because five minutes have passed and you haven't called me 'sugah' yet."

One corner of her mouth slid inward enough for a dimple to appear. "Yesterday was…"

The toast popped up, but Jo continued gazing at Char. Something akin to panic gleamed in her friend's eyes.

Jo said, "Let me fill in the blank. Yesterday was hazardous to your well-being."

"You could say that."

"Welcome to the club."

"I had no plans of joining."

Jo gave her a sympathetic smile.

~

They sat round the patio table, nibbled on toast, and engaged in stilted conversation about the weather. When Char wasn't watching, Molly threw Jo a befuddled look. She shrugged in return. They had agreed earlier that they would not interrogate Char about her evening. Jo's question about which restaurant she and Todd ate in was their self-imposed limit.

Char picked up her coffee cup. "Andie told me she's spending the day alone."

They exchanged a glance. Andie had just told them last night. When would Char have learned—

"I saw her this morning."

"You saw her?" Jo asked.

"Leaving Julian's. In the back. You didn't know…?"

Jo pulled at the neck of her sweatshirt. Now she would have to tell Char as well. Suddenly she thought of yesterday and how she had lectured Char on her plans with Todd. Her face felt hot.

Jo said, "I knew. She left last night because I-I hurt her. She got angry."

Char simply blinked.

"The thing is, after Andie's rehearsal dinner twenty years ago, I made out with Paul in a bar." She abridged the story. Being drunk was disqualified as an excuse. "I told her that last night."

"Oh, my."

"I imagine she didn't want to spend the night in the same house with me."

"Well, I don't think she spent it with Julian either."

"I saw her go into his house."

"Appearances can be deceiving." Char's face, so soft and Southern, hardened.

"I know. Char, I am sorry for chewing you out yesterday. I know I come across like a know-it-all, like—"

"Sugar, stop right there and think about this. If Molly or I had cornered you at that bar, literally sat between you and Paul and told you what an idiotic thing it was you were considering doing and what a louse he was anyway and hardly worth it and how sad you would make Andie, would that have changed the outcome?"

"I was drunk." There went that resolution.

"A part of you wasn't. That part deep inside of you that always listened to us no matter how plastered you were."

Jo stared, now the one at a loss for words.

"I didn't sleep with Todd."

Gratitude flooded Jo. Molly smiled.

"And Andie didn't sleep with Julian. He and I talked at two o'clock this morning on the boardwalk, down a ways. I didn't want to sleep here, either. Guilt and shame." She shook her head. "I asked him if I could use his upstairs apartment and he said someone was in it. If that someone wasn't Andie, I'll snip every single one of my credit cards in half."

Jo said, "Appearances."

Char went on. "Yes, but you were on the mark with my appearances. With Todd, I— Well, you can imagine. I should thank you both for the lectures. No." She paused, batting eyelashes damp with tears. "What I want to thank you for is showing me how much you care. Even after all this time."

Molly reached over and clasped Char's hand on the table. "And even if something had happened last night, we would still love you."

"Something did happen! I went out with him, with motives nowhere near resembling innocent. I have flirted shamelessly with him for years. I feel so guilty." She cackled in an unladylike way. "Probably because I am."

Molly said, "It doesn't change our love for you or God's."

"Oh, Molly. He can't want me!"

"Yes, He can."

"But I drained the hot water heater this morning trying to scrub all this gunk off of me."

"What gunk, hon?"

"This *whatever*. It feels like *tar!*" She pulled at her sweater sleeve. "And I keep looking over my shoulder. Something is *there*. I know it! I can feel it!"

"Char, we need to pray. Right now."

Char's face crumpled. "Okay."

Molly held her other hand out to Jo. She placed hers in Molly's, took Char's free one, and tried not to think about pedestrians not a dozen feet behind her gawking at them.

Molly closed her eyes. "Lord, I praise Your holy name. Come be with us right now and touch Char in a special way. She feels the weight of her sin. It feels like guilt and shame. Like tar. I know You're listening to her now." She paused. "Char, you can pray out loud if you want or not. You know all about confessing to a priest. Well, your Holy Priest is here right now, waiting to hear from you. Ask Him to forgive you."

Even if Char had wanted to pray aloud, Jo didn't think she could. Her sobs were too great.

After a time, Molly said, "Lord, help Char to receive Your forgiveness, to accept Your death as the payment she owes. Thank You. Amen."

Molly let go of their hands and scooted her chair closer to Char's. She put her arms around her, and for a long time Char cried softly against her shoulder.

"Oh, Molly." She sat up and whispered as if in awe. "When I told Him all about how I wanted to commit adultery, how I already had in my heart, it was like I could see Him on the cross and all that tar was covering *Him!* Then all at once I felt sparkling clean, inside and out. Everything seemed bright and I thought 'It's over, it's over,' only it wasn't exactly me thinking that. It was more like a knowledge put deep in my heart. He really forgives me, doesn't He?"

Molly smiled. "Yes, He really does."

Jo felt as dazed as the other two looked. Evidently the Molly Effect had struck again.

Forty-Six

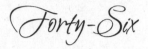

Char shook toast crumbs from a paper napkin and blew her nose into it. The first rays of sun broke over a roofline, bursting through the morning's cloud cover and casting glorious brilliance everywhere.

It was exactly how she felt on the inside and the outside, covered in brand-new, scrubbed-clean baby skin.

The tar was gone.

A sense of being followed was gone.

Sunshine filled her being. There was no other word for it.

"Oh, my. Oh, my." She couldn't stop repeating the phrase. She couldn't think of anything else to say. And she couldn't stop smiling.

Molly laughed.

"Molly! Whatever did you do?"

"Nothing. Well, I talked to God, who is right here with us. His Spirit did the rest."

Jo said, "I call it the Molly Effect."

"Jo, it's not my power."

"I know. But you tap into it."

"Whatever." Char laughed, for no good reason she could think of except it bubbled out. "Wait until I tell the kids— Oh!" She clapped a hand to her mouth. Cam! She had told him she was about to commit adultery and then hung up on him!

"Char, what is it?"

She shoved back her chair and stood. "It's Cam. I have to talk to him. Right this very instant!"

The screen door fell shut with a thud behind her.

⁓

No one in Char's family answered the house phone or their individual cell phones.

She sat in her bedroom on a small, old-fashioned, straight-back padded chair and stared at her phone as if it could explain.

Savannah *always* answered hers unless she was in a class. It was the weekend; she wasn't in school. She was at a friend's or the mall. Cole would be at football practice. Cam might still be with patients; he kept Saturday morning hours. Not that he ever answered his phone, but he had one and, given last night's information, one would *think* he'd carry the thing in his pocket, the power switched on, and that he'd answer even while in the middle of drilling someone's tooth!

Hang it all. She wasn't about to call the office and leave a message with his staff.

Obviously last night's information had not made an impact. By morning he could have thought he dreamt the whole thing.

Even couch potatoes breathe. It was Julian's voice, referring to C.P. He had said it that night he saw her talking on the phone with Todd. He thought she was having a tête-à-tête with her husband until she set him straight about that relationship.

What else had Julian said? Something about her. She wasn't sure whether it was a compliment or not.

Do you know what I see when I look at you? An attractive, delightful blonde with an irresistible zest for life. Somewhere in old Cam's heart lingers a yearning to have a tête-à-tête with you. And yesterday morning as they drank special coffee at the restaurant. *Old Cam just needs some encouragement.*

That was it. Both times she had figured Julian meant it was all her fault romance had died with Cam.

It takes two, sugar. Her mama's voice now. *Two to tango, two to fall in love, two to disagree.*

No, it wasn't all her fault. Perhaps Julian simply meant what he said. Cam yearned.

"Color me flabbergasted."

She pondered the new thought for a moment. If it was true...then she should tell him he had a funny way of showing he cared.

Or maybe she should just shut up for a change.

Well, for now her choice was clear. He couldn't exactly listen to her if he didn't answer her calls. She would have to keep her mouth shut as far as he was concerned.

She closed up her phone and headed back out to the patio.

"Last night I told Cam about Todd." Char lifted her coffee mug and met her friends' stares of disbelief over its rim.

Molly said, "You what? You told him about Todd?"

"I did. I called him from the ladies' lounge."

Jo said, "The ladies' lounge! What? In between courses?"

"Before dessert." If only she had left things alone. Just listened to her conscience and told Todd to take a hike and not bothered phoning Cam.

"What did he say?" Molly asked.

"He was stunned. I reamed him. Told him he should have noticed. He should have been aware."

Jo said, "That's probably true enough."

"But I left him hanging. He said what am I going to do, and I said I don't know. And then I hung up."

"Yikes," Molly said. "And now he's not answering?"

"No."

"He's hurting."

Jo said, "And madder than a hornet."

Char set down her cup. "I honestly can't say which or if either."

"You don't think he cares?" Molly asked.

"Well, he pays the bills. That says something."

They exchanged uncertain glances.

Molly said, "It does say something."

"He didn't call me yesterday. That more or less sums up how things are between us, even if he does pay the bills. As far as I know, he loves the television remote more than he does me."

Jo said, "But he's not like Paul, is he?"

"No, he's not in the least like Paul. He respects me, I have to say that for him. He did respect me, anyway...before last night..."

Molly patted her arm. "Last night is where love kicks in. I'm sure he loves you, hon."

Jo said, "Of course he does. What's not to love about our charming Georgia peach?"

She smiled at their encouragement. "Any number of things, I'm sure."

"As Andie would say, fiddlesticks!" Jo shrugged. "So do you want to tell us about the rest of last night? What happened over dessert?"

"Pff." Her lips vibrated with an expulsion of breath. "Dessert! I skedaddled right out of the place. I didn't even go back to the table. I just made a beeline for the front door. I told the valet I had a most distressing phone conversation and would he please tell the guy who would come out to pick up the red convertible that his date had to leave. It was a dire emergency. I should have tipped him, but I only had a fifty and there was a taxi at the curb."

Jo laughed. Molly clapped her hands and whistled.

Char's suspicions were true. They really, truly did not like Todd in the least.

"The valet said no problem and opened the taxi door for me. I hopped in and said to the driver please just go. He wasn't too swift. He'd never make it in Chicago. I think that was when I yelled."

They both hooted now.

"Something like 'Get out of this parking lot!' I didn't know where to go. I didn't want to come to the house for fear Todd would show up and I'd have to talk to him. Did he come?"

They shook their heads. Molly asked, "Has he called?"

"I turned off my phone after I talked to Cam last night. Just now I skimmed through the missed calls looking for Cam's number—he did not call, by the way—and noticed Todd's number. I didn't check voice mail. I'm sure he got the hint." She paused. "Also I didn't want to come here because I simply could not face you three."

Now they nodded.

That memory jumped at her again, the one from her sixteenth birthday, more vivid than earlier. She saw Molly, Jo, and Andie in the restaurant booth, nodding vigorously, compassion and understanding clearly written on their youthful faces. She heard Andie's invitation as loud and clear as she had that day: *You can live at my house.*

They were right there with her, all those years ago and now today. They knew shame kept her away last night until the wee hours of the morning. They understood she would have blamed them for her feeling that way.

Oh, God! How could I have been so blind?

After a deep breath, she went on. "Anyway, back to the taxi. I was absolutely freezing, so I told the driver to take me to any store that stayed open past ten PM. He found one of those discount superstores miles from here and waited while I bought sweats and shoes. Then he dropped me off a few blocks from here." Last night's loneliness struck her anew and tears stung. "I figured I'd wait until the coast was clear."

"Oh, hon," Molly said. "What did you do?"

"Sat on the seawall and nearly lost my mind trying to make sense of my life. Then out of the blue up walks Julian. I jumped about a foot." She felt them tense. "I swear, the entire boardwalk was empty as far as I could see in both directions. Nobody came by that whole time."

Molly looked relieved. "Promise you will not do that again?"

"Okay, promise." She had no desire to do that again. "Like always, Julian just barged right in on my space, asking questions. The more he talked, the thicker that tar felt. He said you all would be worried. Somehow my *mother* came up in the conversation! What is it about that guy? He really gets under my skin, but you know what? He entertained me on my birthday morning when no one else was around, and he got me home last night before I totally flipped out."

"He doesn't add up," Jo said. "I mean, a beach bum from Scotland who lives in Southern California in that multimillion-dollar house?"

Molly said, "He seems genuinely interested in our well-being. Like he's responsible for making sure we enjoy the beach house. He helped Andie get over her fear of the ocean. Evidently he gave her a place to sleep as well."

Char said, "That's what he does. Seriously. He told me at breakfast yesterday. He watches over Faith's house and guests. But I don't think he's a bum. He has money." She filled them in on Julian's story. "And he works with that lunatic, Zeke. Oh, maybe he's not a lunatic, either." She laughed.

Molly said, "Maybe Julian is one of Faith's leftover guardian angels."

Jo groaned.

"You never know." Molly turned to Char. "Whoever he is, I am glad he brought you home."

She basked in the concern that showed on their faces as blatantly as their noses. Why hadn't she always seen it there?

"Me too," she said. "Me too."

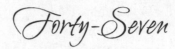

Forty-Seven

They raised the patio table's red umbrella to block the sun. Molly sat in its shade beside Char and read with growing consternation a long list of phone numbers on the tiny cell phone screen. Char scrolled through the "missed calls" record. There were thirteen.

Eleven from Molly's home number.

She felt flushed. Three possible explanations told her it wasn't a hot flash. First, the desert wind blew again; its heat crept onto the patio. Second, she was pregnant, not exactly on the doorstep of menopause. And third, she had hurt Scotty, an action guaranteed to produce discomfort.

She said, "Talk about guilt and shame."

Char pressed the keypad of her phone. "Molly, dear, whatever you said to your husband can't hold a candle to what I said to mine."

"I unloaded all my anxiety on him and got upset when he more or less told me I was looking at it all wrong. The battery went dead about then. I didn't call him back to finish the conversation. I didn't want to hear any more of his nonempathy. Which I'm sure he knew because that's what I told him on my birthday."

Jo stood. "He probably called on my phone too. I'll go get it." She went inside the house.

Char said, "I'll get his voice mail for you."

"No. I feel bad enough. I'll call him with Jo's phone. Let's keep yours open for Cam."

"Okay. First I guess I should see if Todd left a message. I'll have to put closure to this mess one way or another." She held the phone to her ear and listened for a few moments.

Molly heard a male voice and watched Char's face redden.

She hurriedly moved the phone and pressed a key. "Well. Enough of that."

"What did he say?"

"A lady would never repeat such things." She lifted her shoulders and let them fall. "Hmm. Okay. That's that then. I'd say he got the hint loud and clear."

"Char, what will happen when you go home? With him living next door?"

"I haven't really considered that yet." She sat silent for a moment. "Our houses are large enough and far enough apart; a fence and hedge separate our backyards. None of us have to see each other unless we make a point of it. And...there's a woman over one block. Younger. Single." She gave a self-deprecating smile. "He has noticed her. Of course, she's not nearly the catch I am, but he will not lack female companionship."

Jo returned to the patio with her phone. "Looks like you've got one or two messages from him." She sat at the table. "Moll, is there anything we can do?"

She shook her head.

"I think..." Jo began, a sheepish expression spreading over her face. "I think if we were in your shoes, you would have been praying for us by now."

"Of course. You're my good friends."

"Does it work on yourself?"

"What do you mean?"

"You're in need, Moll. I don't have the connection you have with God. I can't do it for you. Can't you do it for yourself?"

"Sure." When she felt like it. She didn't feel like it. She was too ticked at what had happened. At what God had allowed— Or was it simply the consequences of their stupid actions? But God knew—

"So." Jo glanced at Char and then looked back at Molly. "Do you want us in on it?"

Char nodded in agreement.

"On what?" Molly asked.

"On prayer. For you. We could sit with you while you pray."

"For what?"

"Molly!" Frustration spiked Jo's tone. "I don't know for what. You're upset about being pregnant. You're mad at Scott. You made this trip to find your identity in God, but for all I know you're mad at Him too."

Molly winced involuntarily.

"Now I may be all wrong here, but it seems like He would give you some relief. You've almost convinced even me that He loves all of us unconditionally. Wouldn't He answer your prayers for the ability to accept the situation?"

Char leaned toward her and said gently, "Sugar, you know it's not like you have a choice. The situation is what it is."

"But," Molly heard the ugly whine in her voice and swallowed. "Yes, Jo, He would answer that prayer. But…I don't want to ask it."

There was a glint in Jo's narrowed eyes. "You're saying you don't want to get out from under the pile?"

Molly's jaw dropped. "You snot!"

Jo looked at Char. "Hormones."

"Not the menopausal kind though!"

"Nope!"

Molly said, "Ha-ha. You two are hilarious."

Jo's smile lessened. "Seriously now, why don't you want to ask it?"

Her head felt like it could pop. "Because then I have to accept that I am after all only Pastor Scott's wife, mother of Eli, Betsy, Abigail, Hannah, and Number Five. I have no identity, no permanent role outside my home, and I never will have. Hold it! On second thought, maybe I can—when I'm sixty years old."

"And," Jo said, leaning in now, her voice soft, her eyes tender. "What is so wrong with that?"

"Easy for you to say. You've got your role, this…this major identity that affects hundreds of lives. You can't imagine what it's like not to have that. We are smart women with college degrees. I should be doing more with my life!"

"My so-called 'major identity' means that if all my patients' names were listed, my obituary would be long. Whoop-de-do. There will be no 'survived by' names of people who called me wife and mom. People who knew the real me."

Char reached across the table and touched Jo's hand. "You'll have us."

Jo smiled a thank-you. "Molly, maybe we can't have it all in this life."

But didn't God promise it all? Didn't He give her the desire to take on full-time teaching? Couldn't she do more for Him in that capacity? Instead He placed her in a tiny town with no job opening less than an hour and fifteen minutes away? Instead He gave her a pewful of children?

Oh, Lord. I am not walking my talk right now.

That was a pitiful prayer. Sort of.

At least it was a prayer.

Jo said, "I almost had it all. Moll, I've been where you are, from the other side."

Molly started and Char straightened. There was something different in Jo's tone. A pain.

"Four years ago I was pregnant. Unplanned. Some birth control expert, huh? I can't even blame it on being drunk. It…the baby was a girl. I miscarried at five months. There were complications. I had a hysterectomy. The father…transferred to Seattle. True love it wasn't."

"Oh, Jo." They both offered condolences.

Molly said, "You didn't tell us."

She shrugged. "You've all mourned enough for me through the years."

Molly's head hurt. "I can't imagine what awful pain you endured. To lose the baby and the ability to ever have any? Oh, Jo. I am so sorry. Have you mourned? Have you cried?"

"You didn't ask if I drank." She winked. "Amazingly, I did not. Seattle Man was good that way for me. But, yes, I did mourn and cry. You know I did because you were there, the other night in the restaurant."

"Jo!" they cried again in a mutual tone of combined disbelief and sympathy. "The other night?"

"It's okay. I'm learning. I've cried every day since, but less and less. It helps." She paused. "The father and I mourned when it happened." Her brows went up in a mocking gesture. "We did care for each other and were thrilled about the pregnancy. We planned to marry. Anyway, we had a little ceremony on a beach, just the two of us, and told her goodbye. Want to know what I named her?"

They nodded.

"Catherine Michelle Wentworth Zambruski."

"Oh, Jo!" they said once more. The name incorporated the middle names of Molly, Andie, and Char.

"A mouthful." Jo cocked her head. "Which reminds me, Char, I have a bone to pick with you. I mean, honestly, Wentworth for a middle name?"

"Oh, right. Like Zambruski is any prize for a last name. It sounds like a beer."

It was an old joke between them. While they bantered, Molly massaged her temples. Exhaustion was closing in, but she grasped Jo's point. She interrupted their chuckles. "What you're saying is that you accepted not having it all."

Jo's broad smile shrank until only the corners of her mouth remained upturned. "No, not totally. I've just been waiting for you to show me how."

Overwhelmed with trying to process Jo's news and the way she challenged her about prayer, Molly stood abruptly. "This is too much. I need a nap, and I am taking your phone, Josephine."

She handed it to her. "Chicken."

"Whatever. Excuse me."

Jo's chuckle followed her to the door. "God will find you!"

She looked over her shoulder. "Well, He'll find you too."

"I hope so!"

Molly changed into shorts and a T-shirt, made the bed, and laid down on top of it.

She should have rejoiced over Jo's pressing her about prayer and the comment about hoping God would find her. She should have had an answer to Jo's reminder that she made the trip to find her identity in God alone—not the kids, Scott, or teaching, full-time or otherwise.

But Molly's head pounded and her stomach was doing a gymnastics warm-up, an indication of a full-fledged routine to follow. She grabbed a cracker from the nightstand. It tasted stale.

Scott answered on the first ring. "Molly?"

"Scott!" She felt relieved. He should have been gone by now, to work up the Elk River. "You're still at home?"

"The trees can wait. You're more important."

"Mmm. Will you say that again?"

He said it again. And again. Until the cracker was eaten and her eyes were closed.

Forty-Eight

Andie leaned on the railing and gazed out over the broad expanse of ocean. She stood on the pier in a small area located behind her motel room. The room was actually a cottage, one of several lining both sides of the pier. They were angled in such a way as to create private decks in back and parking spaces in front. She thought the white cottages cute and inviting with their Delft blue trim and window boxes, from which colorful flowers spilled. Jo would think them decidedly not Southern California.

As the morning's gray cloud cover receded, so did Andie's anxieties. She breathed in the moist salty air and watched a surfer catch a wave.

"So far so good. I have made it to the motel."

Molly's words came to mind. *You know He's closer to us than the air we breathe.*

She smiled. "Thank You, Lord. Thank You that I am not alone."

A short while ago she had awakened in Julian's upstairs apartment, surprisingly refreshed for falling asleep in a strange place with images of her husband and good friend kissing in a drunken embrace.

Refreshed but shaky, she gathered every bit of faith and courage she could muster and dressed for the day in her new spunky apricot outfit. She packed the pretty sandals in the large overnight bag and laced up her sensible tan oxfords. Char would never approve of the fashion statement, but the motel was a good hike from Julian's.

With trepidation she went down the outdoor staircase to Julian's door. He refused again to accept money for the overnight use of his place. For a few moments she basked in his fatherly attention. He wished her a good second, independent fortieth celebration. Standing beside him she felt an inpouring of hope that she would not spend the next twenty-four hours curled in a fetal position.

Not ready to speak to her friends, she had taken the back route and ran into Char behind the beach house. In spite of her crisp just-so clothing and stylish hairdo that was attractive even wet, Char looked a mess.

Andie remembered her the previous night, gaily going off with Todd, and something zapped her heart. In the blink of an eye her emotions solidified into an ugly chunk of grim satisfaction. So. Little Miss Georgia Peach suffered right along with the rest of them. Aw. Poor thing.

Andie spoke like a smart aleck to one of her oldest friends. Walking away she was struck with a new thought. Her remarks were a smoke screen. They hid a pain she wanted to avoid. That pain was rooted in Paul, of course. In his infidelity. But it was also rooted in a dark suspicion about Char, something Andie let remain unacknowledged for twenty years.

Suddenly she understood the entire week was about her confronting something much more important than her daily fears. It was about addressing the pain. Time was running out.

And so she had spun around and asked Char point blank if she'd slept with Paul. Char's horrified reaction melted Andie's distrust of her old friend on the spot.

The exchange doused her with courage. Overwhelmed, she had no words to explain things to herself, let alone to Char. She turned away again. The new courage spurred her on down the alley and on to the motel office two hours early to ask if her room was available.

She smiled again at the ocean.

Point-blank. That was how her day had begun. That was how she wanted to finish it. That was how she wanted to fill every moment in between.

Point-blank. Maybe it could become a habit.

Andie stood at a busy intersection, long purse strap crisscrossed over her shoulders, sunglasses and visor in place. She studied a pamphlet, trying to decipher bus routes.

San Diego was a huge place.

Andrea. It was Paul's belittling voice. *That outfit doesn't exactly flatter you. Maybe it's the color. Or the style. And what are you doing standing on the street corner waiting for a bus? Go rent a car, for crying out loud. People will think one of Madison's top real estate agents is a cheapskate if they see his wife on a bus. You're not really going to attempt to go through that silly list—*

"Hey, sister!"

She looked up to see Zeke, the wiry Rastafarian-looking street pastor. He approached the bus stop. She smiled. How could she not? His grin split his face in two. Dreadlocks sprouted every direction in such a carefree way. She wished her boys could meet him.

Julian had introduced Andie to him on their way to boogie board. She saw him again another morning on the boardwalk, and they'd chatted a while. He absolutely glowed with joy, the type, she figured, not of this world.

"Hi, Zeke." she said.

He stopped and shook her hand. "How's it going?"

"Fine. Except I can't figure out which bus to take."

"Where you headed?" He took the pamphlet from her.

Paul's voice murmured in her mind, casting doubt on her plans. She thought of the paper in her pocket. Earlier, while sitting in a café eating an omelet she wrote a list of things that scared her. Instead of seeing it as a list of fears, though, she titled it "Andie's Adventure List."

The first item was to eat breakfast alone in a restaurant. That one was checked off. Number two read *Explore an area of San Diego I can't walk to; take a bus to get there.* The "there" was what she had planned to do with her friends on her special day.

On second thought, she could change her plans. Do something easier. Jo wouldn't mind driving her and the others there sometime during the next two days.

See, Andrea? You're being sensible. You don't have to go chasing off— Take a hike, Paul. I boogie board in the ocean.

She smiled at that thought and said out loud in a determined voice, "I want to go to the Museum of Art in Balboa Park."

Zeke didn't laugh or look at her as though she were nuts. He simply studied the schedule. "Well, sister, I do believe we are taking the same bus. You'll have to transfer before I do, but I'd be glad to show you."

"You would?" Relief flooded her. "Thanks. Where are you going?"

"Home." He gave the pamphlet back to her. "Time for a little sleep. Been up all night. Let me tell you, it was some dark night here at the beach. I'm talking spiritual realm. The evil one was busy. Here's our ride now, sister."

The bus ground to a halt near them, and they boarded it.

Andie wondered at Zeke's words. He was in tune with more than she wanted to know, but she sensed a connection with what he said. Evil touched good things. Things like her marriage. Like her friendship with Jo, Char, and Molly.

They sat down together and she asked, "You don't live around here?"

He chuckled. "My Father owns the cattle on a thousand hills, but ain't no way I can pay rent in this neighborhood. He provides plenty for me, don't get me wrong. He got me a nice little apartment and a solid job. I work at a convenience store, mostly third shift. Last night I was off, so I spent it down here where the real work is done."

"Do you live near family?"

"Yes, I do. Mama, two brothers, two sisters, their spouses, bunch of nieces and nephews."

Andie guessed from his unlined face that he was younger than her, but not by much. There was a depth to him that added years. "You're not married?"

He shook his head and smiled. "Got me a girlfriend, though. Maybe even fiancée. We shall see. Most women don't want nothing to do with the way I live. First 'cuz I was so messed up, now 'cuz I'm always off doing Bible studies and some such. But, Lilly, now she's different. You haven't met her yet?"

"No."

"Oh, she's pretty. She comes with me sometimes to the beach."

"Why do you come here if it's not close to home?"

He grinned. "That's what my mama always asks. She says I ought to preach on my own street. But the Lord brings me here. Back before He got hold of me, I sort of lived in this neighborhood at one time. You seen all the homeless folk?"

She nodded.

"That was me, sister. Down-and-out without a hope in the world. Then my friend met Jesus and he told me, and then I met Jesus. Amen. The fellowship grows and grows, but not everyone knows Him yet. And there's a heap of sorrow here. Lot of ways I can help since I know from my own experience what it's like for these lost sheep."

"That makes—" She shook her head. She almost said it made sense that he traveled to preach on a beach, but in all honesty it did not make sense. "Zeke, I can't relate to your lifestyle."

"'Course not. You're called to something else. What do you do?"

"I'm a wife, a mom with two teenage sons, and a reflexologist."

"Say what? Reflex-what? I never heard of that."

She explained her work to him.

He nodded. "See, that's where you're called. You heal people right there in your own neighborhood."

"But my husband doesn't want me to." She unintentionally blurted the words. Thinking of how she loved her work reminded her of Paul's incessant complaints about her job. She might as well admit that there was no way he would ever permit her to open an office in their house. What a pipe dream she'd been engaged in!

Zeke said, "You mean he doesn't want you to heal others?"

"He doesn't really consider it healing or even helping people all that much."

"How come? Don't you do that stuff to his feet?"

"No. He has sensitive feet. He says it hurts too much."

"Mm-mm. I am sorry to hear he doesn't support what you do."

Me too.

"A husband and wife need to support one another." He shook his head. "Could be the Lord has some other kind of ministry planned for you. Just keep looking up, sister. Just keep looking up. You mind if I pray?"

Andie smiled. One thing she was sure of that day was that she could use all the prayer she could get.

⌣

Ancient religious paintings of every shape and size filled the walls in a large, high-ceilinged room of the San Diego Museum of Art. The only sound came from the echoed footfalls and hushed voices of the handful of other visitors.

Andie sat alone on a marble bench and studied a spotlighted canvas before her. It was good-sized, probably six by eight feet, but not the largest in the room. It was not exotic the way some of them were. There was no gruesome depiction of Jesus bleeding on the cross or of saints battling with grotesque demons. What had captured her attention the moment she entered the room was its gentle portrait of human nature. The note read *Virgin and Child with Saint John, Attributed to the Italian school, Fifteenth Century.*

Baby Jesus, perhaps five months old, sat on His mother's lap. John, a toddler, leaned against her, holding his hand out to Jesus, showing Him a small bluebird he held. The children were chubby and rosy-cheeked, real in appearance without the usual halos. She wondered at the family relationship. Presumably Mary and John's mother, Elizabeth, were kinfolk. Cousins perhaps? How heartwarming the thought that perhaps the boys had played together as children!

Andie longed to hold her own sons again at those ages. Overcome with a sense of missing them, she had sat down on the bench. She remained glued to the seat because an intense feeling of connectedness with Mary had taken hold of her imagination. Mother to mother, woman to woman.

"It is quite emotional, isn't it?"

Andie jumped at the sound of the voice and turned to see a woman sitting beside her.

"Oh, I am sorry," the elderly woman said. "I startled you. And probably ruined your concentration as well." Her hair was white and wispy, her face as downy soft in appearance as the ones in the painting.

"No, you didn't—" Andie caught the woman's knowing smile and returned it. "Well, yes, you did ruin it, but that's all right."

"It was just that your rapturous expression spoke so clearly, I thought we were already having a conversation!"

Andie laughed with her.

The woman had a delightful laugh, like high-pitched wind chimes tinkling in the distance. She was short; her feet didn't touch the floor. She wore tea rose pink—cardigan, blouse, and skirt. Pink lipstick. Pink rouge. Pink purse on her lap. No doubt she would call it a pocket-book.

Andie said, "My grandmother and I would go to the Art Institute in Chicago. We'd sit and look at paintings we liked and talk and talk."

"My husband and I used to do that right here." She turned from the picture to glance at Andie. Her eyes were large and watery powder blue behind square, silver-rimmed glasses. "He's been gone ten years now."

"I'm sorry. My grandmother has been gone fifteen."

The woman bowed her head slightly.

Swell. Now Andie missed her babies *and* Babette. And, truth be told, she probably missed a husband who sat with her in wonder at works of art. But...was it even possible to miss something she'd never had?

She said, "How fortunate your husband shared in your enjoyment of art."

"Well, actually, I shared in his. He was a painter, as a hobbyist. I didn't know the first thing about art until he taught me." She smiled. "I was not always the best student. Later in life we spent weekends at art festivals up and down the coast, selling his work."

"That sounds lovely."

"It was. If I may ask, did your grandmother introduce you to art?"

"Yes. She was French and grew up in Paris. According to her, there was only one true art museum in the world."

Like a little girl, the woman swung her legs back and forth. "The Louvre."

"Naturally. I was at least thirteen before I knew not all painters came from France."

Her laugh tinkled softly. "Oh, what a treasure of a grandmother!"

Andie smiled. "Yes, she was. I fell in love with art because of her."

"Did you pursue it in a formal way?"

"I studied art history in college for a couple years before I married."

"Falling in love with a man does tend to change things."

"Mmm." Not wanting to think about Paul, Andie gazed at the painting again. It washed over her and seeped into her heart. After several moments, she could no longer contain herself. Words spilled out impulsively. "Why is it so emotional?"

"Tell me what you see."

"I see a young mother loving her children. Of course, from the title I know they're her son and a relative. I see a moment of pure joy, of purest truest love, of the power of nurturing that only happens between mother and baby." Her breath caught. "I think that moment is a two-way street. A mother not only gives, she *receives*. All that joy and love and nurturing even as she's giving them away."

"Ah. You see yourself then."

Andie turned to her in surprise.

The woman smiled. "You're a mother."

"It shows?"

"Naturally."

"I miss those days."

"As do I."

They both turned back to the painting.

After a time, the woman said, "Mary must have carried quite a burden of responsibility. I don't suppose she knew at the age she is depicted here what her Son would do when He grew older, but surely His miraculous conception concerned her."

"Mm-hmm. To say the least. She must have known His would be no ordinary life. I wonder if she was anxious over the unknown future? It seems since she was visited by an angel that she wouldn't have a tendency to worry."

"I'm not too sure. We all have our angel moments, when our deep hearts recognize His presence and care. Nothing quite as radical as what happened to Mary, of course. Do you know what I mean?"

Andie thought of the time not too long ago when she sat in church and heard the clear message that she was to fear not. Somewhere between her eardrum and her heart the priest's voice had changed to a whisper from God. Beyond a shadow of a doubt, He was taking care of her.

She said, "Yes, I know what you mean."

The white head bobbed. "Yes. Still I can fret and stew and be afraid of the unknown. Even about my children who are grown up and doing just fine. I think Mary had her bouts with worry. And then she would pray and remember Gabriel's visit." With something of a hop, the woman sprang to her feet. "Well, it's time for tea. So nice chatting with you…?"

"Andie." She shook the woman's hand.

"I'm Jelly."

"Jelly?" Andie couldn't help but smile.

"Yes. It's short for Anjelica. With a *j*. My grandchildren call me 'Grammy Jam.'" She laughed, her face lit up with sheer joy. "Now, dear, I've taken up enough of your time, but you're quite welcome to join me for tea if you like."

Andie didn't need to think about it. "Why, thank you. I'd like that very much."

"There's a lovely spot right next to the museum. Do you have photos of your children?"

As they walked toward the doorway, Andie gave the painting one last look. If Jesus had a mother who worried over Him, then surely He could sympathize with a fearful woman like Andrea Sinclair.

And love her.

Forty-Nine

Standing at the kitchen counter, Char hummed to herself and sliced cucumbers and peppers for a salad. Too wound up to sit still, she had volunteered to prepare a late lunch since none of them felt like going out.

From the sound of running water, Molly was still in the shower. Jo helped in the kitchen. Her long braid made a damp circle on the back of her T-shirt.

Char said over her shoulder, "Shall we eat inside? It's cooler in here, don't you think?"

"Yes." Jo removed plates from a cupboard and elbowed her arm. "Hey, you sound way too perky for being up half the night and not indulging in a nap like your two sensible friends did."

"No. I sound way too perky for behaving like a complete idiot and for not fixing things with Cam yet. I do so worry for him. What must he be going through? But at the same time I feel this bubbly sensation, like I'm drinking fuzzy champagne nonstop."

"Oops. Don't compare the Molly Effect to champagne. She'd have a conniption."

Char laughed loudly. "She's not like that anymore. I mean, she hasn't told us to get out from under the pile."

"Not yet, anyway. I might have goaded her into considering it since I told her to do the very same." Jo opened the refrigerator, leaned inside of it, and called out, "What do you think Cam will say?"

Char refocused on the vegetables and cutting board. "Well, I don't think he'll mumble to himself 'Where's the remote?' The thing is, I truly do not know if he gives a hoot about our marriage or not. He may very well welcome a way out."

"The question is…" A deep male voice resonated from the screen door.

Char whirled around, quite sure she was hearing things. Even when her eyes landed on the shadowy figure of her husband of seventeen years standing on the other side of the beach house front door, she wondered if he were a figment of her imagination.

"Cam?"

For Char the world shifted into slow motion. The knife fell from her hand and landed with a thump on the rug, its cool blade coming to rest against her bare foot. The effervescing bubbles popped one by one, and a sensation of her entire body deflating from within spread from her head to her fingertips, down through her legs to her toes. She felt her face freeze into creases of incomprehension.

"The question is," he repeated, making no motion to enter, "do you give a hoot?"

She lifted a foot, moved it forward, and set it down. Then she did so with the other.

Walking across the room was like swimming in tar.

Eons later, she reached the door and stared at Cam.

He was still very tall, still very blond, still broad of shoulder. Still the friendly family dentist. Still her husband.

Did she give a hoot?

She was tired of duck soup, of him being uncommunicative, of him forgetting her birthday, of him being a couch potato, of him gaining jowls, of his belt buckle hiding under his belly. She wanted chateaubriand.

But there he stood. The fact that he'd made a spur-of-the-moment flight halfway across the country—after what she'd told him!—certainly approached chateaubriand.

"Oh, sugar! I do give a hoot."

"So do I." His lips formed a straight line. His arms resembled two boards at his sides.

"Will you please come inside?"

He opened the door, stepped through it, and guided the door to a soft close behind him. He halted and set a gym bag on the floor. Then his arms stiffened again.

Char burst into tears.

Fifty

Above the noise of Char's sobbing, Jo heard the refrigerator kick on and realized she still stood partially bent over in front of its open door, a bottle of salad dressing in hand. She straightened and shut the door.

Like witnessing the aftermath of a car accident, she watched, glued in horror. Her heart ached at the scene of Char's collapse before a robotlike Cam. The physician side of her twitched to go help.

But this wasn't a collision on the freeway.

Jo slipped quietly to the back of the kitchen-living room area and down the hallway to Molly's room. She tapped on the closed door and then let herself in, whispering, "Sorry."

Molly stopped toweling her hair and looked up. "What?"

Jo eased the door shut behind her and whispered, "Cam's here."

"What?" She lowered the towel to her shoulders. "Cam?"

"Yeah. He just showed up!"

"No kidding?" She sat on the bed and smiled. "Wow. Good for him. Good for them."

"Except she's falling apart."

"I imagine so. She really did a number on him with that Todd business. What's Cam's demeanor like?"

"Like a rotund Santa-type who may never find jolly again."

"This has got to be a glimpse into hell for him. Imagine being wakened in the night with such awful news and then traveling all this way. That says something for him. Even if she didn't think he cared, he must."

Jo nodded. "Before we saw him standing at the door, we were talking, probably loud enough for him to hear because my head was inside the fridge. She was saying she didn't know if he gave a hoot, and then we heard him ask if she gave a hoot. She said yes, and he said he does too."

Molly closed her eyes. "Thank You, Lord."

"Amen, but Moll! They look so hopeless out there."

"Then let's pray." She held out a hand.

Jo glimpsed that love again, God's love streaming forth from her friend. No longer a trickle, it expanded into great waves that doused His fire. Like a little girl, she longed to splash in those waves and feel clean and giggle with joy. Molly knew the way.

Jo sat beside her, put out her hand, and saw Molly grab the bottle of salad dressing she still held.

They broke into simultaneous giggles.

And Jo knew nothing was hopeless.

Fifty-One

Char held a wad of paper towels to her face. One sheet by itself was not going to absorb the unladylike stuff produced by her sobs. There wasn't even a ladylike term for the sobs themselves. No two ways about it, they were gut-wrenching.

She still stood facing the front door Cam had walked through a few minutes before. Evidently he had come in far enough to retrieve the towels from the kitchen counter, but he now stood again between her and the door, the thick roll in his hand, not near enough for them to touch. He hadn't said a word since entering. She couldn't read his bland expression.

Confession and apology stumbled over each other, at times incoherently. "I'm sorry. I'm sorry. Nothing happened. I'm sorry. I left the restaurant right after I talked to you. Nothing happened!"

At last the crying slowed and she stopped talking. Cam hadn't said a word since he'd stepped inside.

He cleared his throat. "But something did happen."

Like a physical blow, his words nearly knocked her over. She went to the nearest armchair and sank onto it. Hugging herself, she rocked back and forth. She felt icy cold.

"Y-yes." Her teeth chattered. "I flirted. I egged him on."

Cam pulled the ottoman to the chair and sat on it. "I don't understand." His deep voice fell to new depths of bass and was toneless, as if he were tired beyond measure. "You talk to everyone. You flirt, you tease. That's just you. You make people feel good. You're the most outgoing person on the face of the earth. Why is this different? When did it become…egging him on?"

"Last year." She knew exactly when. "After my birthday dinner. We were all playing charades and you went to bed."

"That…wasn't so out of the ordinary." His hushed voice cracked.

Through blurred vision she watched pain etch itself onto his face. Everything sort of crumpled, his high forehead, puppy brown eyes, regal nose, and wide mouth. She was responsible for it.

But still… "I was tired of not feeling loved, of not being noticed. By you, Cam. By *you*."

"Do you love him?" He skirted the underlying issue, but she followed his lead.

"No. He simply gave me the attention I craved. It was never physical, though. I had no idea he would follow me out here with such intentions."

"But last night you made me believe you wanted to follow those intentions."

Still shivering, she felt an onslaught of heat. "I'm sorry. I thought I did. But when I came face-to-face with the real possibility, I knew I couldn't. It was wrong. I'm married to you."

"How could you even think it?"

"Because I was so very desperate for your attention."

"My attention?" His voice rose, making him sound surprised.

"Yours, Cam. I'm not totally blaming you for this, but— Oh, hang it all. You're responsible too. I mean, you *never* comment on how I look, *never* notice a new outfit or hairstyle. You *never* make eye contact. Not even when you're checking my teeth! You *never* say you love me. And physical intimacy! Well! Don't get me started!" Did she really have to explain his obvious lack of interest? If one were interested, wouldn't one act like it?

"I *never*?"

"Oh, once in a blue moon. Not enough!"

"You should have said something."

"I shouldn't have to!"

"Then how am I supposed to know?"

"Because a husband should just know these things!"

"Well, you should just know I love you!"

"How should I know that?"

He sighed heavily. "Because I go to work every day."

"That makes a lot of sense!"

He stood up abruptly. "I'm tired. I'm going to find a motel. The cab passed a Best Western a few blocks—"

"Camden Wilcox!" She leapt to her feet. "That is exactly what this is all about. Don't you dare quit on me! Don't you dare go take a nap and ignore me!"

"Char, I was up all night making arrangements and packing and then I flew here as soon as I could. What more do you want from me?"

"I want you to fight for me!"

"Well, if Todd Brooks were here, I'd punch him in the nose."

"Really?"

He shook his head. "Probably not. I am not a knight in shining armor. I'm just your everyday overweight family dentist who needs a shower and a bed and time to think."

"There's plenty of room here—"

"I have to be alone." He walked to the door and picked up his bag. "I'll call you later."

Engulfed with another weeping fit, she sank back onto the chair and picked up the roll of paper towels. The door fell shut behind him.

He needed this. He needed that. What about what *she* needed? Like a hug? Like his presence? Like a flaming knight in shining armor!

She ripped off a paper towel and pressed it to her face.

"He came, Char. All this way." Molly sat on the ottoman and yanked tissues from a box. "Here."

Char dropped her wadded paper towel onto the floor and accepted the softer tissues. "Thanks." She had just relayed her and Cam's conversation to Molly and Jo, most of which they'd probably been able to hear from the back of the house.

Standing behind Molly, Jo said, "Sounds pretty close to knight in shining armor to me. He had to move at steed pace and pay a king's ransom to make such an impromptu trip."

"But he didn't even hug me. Not that he ever does unless I initiate it, but how could I this time? He stood there like a stiff-armed robot! I've never seen him so upset."

"He has a right to be upset."

"I know that, but it's not exactly the sort of attention I need from him."

"At least he didn't say 'Where's the remote?'"

Char shrugged.

Jo said, "He obviously gives a hoot. Besides getting here, he must have canceled patients. Didn't you say he keeps Saturday hours?"

Char nodded. "Mornings."

Molly said, "And he must have made arrangements for the kids as well, right?"

"I suppose. His parents still enjoy Cole and Savannah, and the kids, surprisingly, are okay with them. They would come and stay. He must have asked them."

"All right! Three pluses for the guy," Jo said. "And his remark about going to work every day? That's just his way of saying he loves you. It seems to be how men are wired. I think it's a caveman sort of thing." She growled for emphasis.

Molly squinted her eyes and glanced over her shoulder at Jo, who shrugged.

Char said, "But I want words. I need words."

Molly said, "So tell him that. Again. Very specifically which ones and how often."

"Pff," she fluttered her lips. "If he bothers to listen."

Molly hugged her. "He bothered to come. He knows you betrayed him, and that cuts him deeply. It will take him time, but the fact you did not go beyond flirting has to mean something. Last night was a wake-up call for him in more ways than one. He will bother to listen."

"And just think," Jo added. "You can go off somewhere and talk and even spend the night away—and your roomies won't be upset in the least!"

Char smiled halfheartedly. "Well, I don't have a knight, but I am grateful for my ladies-in-waiting."

Fifty-Two

Andie thought that by now the Adventure List would have become easier to follow. But her heart hammered in her throat, and she gripped the round metal railing with clammy hands and hunched inward like a turtle when the roller coaster roared past.

She stood in line, ticket crunched in her hand, waiting for her turn to climb aboard. No one in front of or behind her appeared close to forty years of age. It was a young person's adventure. Why in the world…? She could simply scribble this event off the list. Not check if off, but pretend that she'd never written it down.

After all, seven of the twelve things were already checked off: Wear the spunky outfit. Eat breakfast alone in a restaurant. Explore an area of San Diego; take a bus to get there. Eat lunch alone in a restaurant. Look at a huge ugly snake up close. Pet a goat. Talk to a homeless person.

She'd added that last one after the conversation with Zeke. The event had been accomplished in Balboa Park where she saw a woman wearing one too many coats for a sunny day and hauling a stuffed trash bag. The talk did not go well. Evidently the woman wanted to be left alone; she refused even to take the ten-dollar bill Andie held out to her. Still, that counted and she had checked it off, knowing that later on the boardwalk she could make eye contact with the homeless, perhaps even talk with them. If they wanted to.

A short zoo visit had taken care of the snake and the goat. By the time she boarded the bus for the return trip to the beach, she was flying high. She had faced fears, prayed for courage, and forged ahead like that elephant rushing across his playground. Ba boom. Andie felt invincible.

Only five items remained: Talk to a pierced and tattooed teenager. Eat sashimi in a Japanese restaurant where strangers were seated together. Spend the night alone in a motel. Spend twenty-four hours without friends or family. And…ride the roller coaster.

Her legs wobbled like jelly.

Jelly. Anjelica. What a delightful time they'd shared over tea. Andie had even shared her Adventure List with the woman and won her hearty approval.

Now that could be an item: Show the silly list to a stranger. She could cross off roller coaster and still have an even dozen adventures.

Silly.

The word stopped her short. That would be Paul's voice. Her recognition time of his pernicious influence had shrunk considerably.

"It is not a silly list." She had even begun to speak out loud to him. Out loud and point-blank. "And, by golly, just for even thinking this is silly, I will ride this thing!"

"Lady, you okay?"

Andie blinked and saw that the roller coaster attendant was speaking to her.

"What?" She had to nearly shout over the noise of the rattling contraption.

"I said, are you okay?" He was young, his hair no more than an eighth of an inch long, his shirt a sleeveless tee. A silver ring hugged one nostril. A reddish-orange flame outlined in black rode up his bicep.

She smiled. "I'm scared to death. I have never, ever in my life ridden one of these things."

"You're kidding!" He smiled back at her. "Nothing to worry about."
He went on to explain the safety features.

A few moments later he pushed the seat's bar into place snug
against her and promised her she would be fine. "All you have to do,
ma'am, is let go."

Andie grinn ?d as she followed the cute little Asian hostess through
the crowded dining room.

All you have to do is let go.

Yes! What better way to describe soaring on a roller coast? Or, for
that matter, her entire day? She had been letting go point-blank for
nearly twenty-four hours.

She felt the spunk in her step. The grin stretched. Was she strutting
like a peacock on her way to join seven strangers for dinner? Probably. But what else could one do?

Nine out of twelve adventure items checked off the list! Make that
nine and a half. She was already in the Japanese restaurant. She was
even looking forward to her first bit of raw seafood.

It's full of bacteria and God knows what else. You'll get—

Stuff it, Paul.

She joined the seven strangers already seated at a table shaped like
a half-moon. Spanning the space between its tips was a gray slab
where, she assumed, a chef would cook the food. Or slap seaweed
around a piece of uncooked fish…

The others welcomed her as she sat at one end beside a smiling
redheaded woman about her age who said, "Great color on you! I'll
have to try it."

They were a friendly bunch, a group of siblings and spouses and
their widowed father, celebrating one of the guys birthday; he was
forty. With gusto they included her in their conversation and talked
her through menu choices. By the end of the meal she wanted sushi
recipes to add to her collection.

Laughing, she bid them goodnight and headed to the exit, mentally checking off item number ten. Now, if she didn't succumb to the desire to call her boys and if she didn't bolt from her little motel cottage before dawn, she could check off number—

"Andie!" Char emerged from the crush of people meandering in the foyer.

She smiled. "Char! Hi!"

They hugged as if they hadn't seen each other for ages. It felt good.

Andie grasped her friend's shoulders and looked into her eyes. Their unusual camel color had always intrigued her. No. Point-blank reality? They had always made her envious. *Now* they intrigued her. Now she admired them.

She lowered her head in order to be heard above the din. "Char, I am so sorry for snapping at you earlier."

"Oh, sugar! Don't you worry your pretty little redhead about it. We've all been on edge what with—" She laughed and waved her hand in dismissal. "I don't need to get into that. Look who's here."

Andie followed her line of sight and saw a tall man next to them. Blond hair, distinctly square jaw beneath the smile. "Cam?"

"Hi, Andie. It's been a long time." He thrust out his hand.

She shook it, recalling how they used to tease him about avoiding hugs. She thought his height interfered. Well over six feet, he was easily the tallest man in the restaurant. Still good-looking, though he had put on quite a bit of weight.

"What a surprise!" she said.

"Good to see you. Excuse me. I need to put our name in for a table."

Andie let her mouth drop open as she turned to Char.

"I know!" Char said. "Halfway across the country."

"What's going on?"

"I called Cam from the restaurant last night and told him about Todd, and then I left Todd there and this morning Molly prayed with me and— Oh! There is so much to tell you! I'll fill you in later. How was your day?"

"Great."

"You ate here? All by yourself?"

Andie smiled. Char knew her phobia of eating alone. It dated back to school cafeteria days. "I ate with a group of strangers!"

Char laughed. "That's even better than by yourself!"

"Now I'm off to my motel room."

"Okay. Go for it, Miss Spunk. See you tomorrow."

They hugged goodbye and Andie made her way through the crowd to the door, smiling to herself. Molly prayed *with* Char? Cam showed up? Wow.

Night had fallen, but the streets were brightly lit and the sidewalks lined with restaurants and people. Taxis weren't plentiful in the beach community, but the motel was within walking distance. Andie headed for it.

Check off number ten. She had eaten sashimi with strangers.

Her heels felt wound up with springs. They bounced her along the sidewalk.

She had just talked with Char. Uh-oh.

She halted.

Did that cancel *spend twenty-four hours without friends or family?*

Well...she hadn't really *spent time* with her. And their meeting was by accident. It wasn't as if she'd sought her company. It wasn't the same as, say, calling the boys—which she still longed to do simply to hear them laugh at what their uptight mother had done.

But she didn't really need to hear their laughter before tomorrow. After all, she was feeling God's pleasure at her *fearing not.* Somehow that more than made up for any momentary loneliness.

She resumed her spunky strut.

Check off number eleven!

Fifty-Three

Char sat across from Cam in a booth at the Japanese restaurant. Unlike Andie's experience, they chose to dine in a quieter room and let the chef cook their meals out of sight.

The thought struck her that they hadn't eaten dinner alone without friends or family at the table in—well, who knew how many years?

She choked on a sip of water.

"You okay?" he asked.

She nodded and coughed into a napkin. Did he have any idea? Instead of blurting out the question, she held back. She was measuring her words tonight, trying to stay on track.

Like an angst-ridden teen, she had sat in the beach house all afternoon, phone in her pocket, mind racing, stomach churning. Regret over her actions and anger over his inaction duked it out, neither one winning the struggle. She was wrong. He was wrong.

But he had come. He *had* come. Like Jo said, three pluses for the guy.

At last he had called at six forty, suggesting dinner. He was hungry. She wasn't, but obviously that didn't matter. They needed to talk.

Understatement of the year.

271

Jo and Molly had helped her prepare by asking what his favorite food was and locating an appropriate place not too far away. On her third change of clothes, they convinced her she looked presentable. She wondered why she was concerned. It wasn't as though he would notice.

Jo gave her the keys to her car with an exaggerated wink. "Don't hurry back. If I should need the car in the morning, I know which motel you're at."

She had picked up Cam at the motel located a few blocks from the beach house and driven to the restaurant. They hadn't exchanged any words of significance. He appeared rested but was still standoffish. It was as if after his leap into the action which got him to San Diego, he forgot the point of his heroic efforts.

Which was just fine with her. If he didn't get the point—to fix things between them—she wasn't going to explain it. She wasn't even sure she wanted a hug. She knew for certain she wasn't going to give one first.

After they ordered, he said, "You're so quiet tonight."

"Maybe I've prattled on too much through the years."

"I like listening to your prattle."

Huh? She felt her head bob. He listened to her prattle? And liked it?

"I like your teasing and flirting and making people feel good. I guess…" He shrugged. "Well, I've thought about what you said earlier, how I don't tell you things. You know, I talk all day at the office. I guess I get talked out."

So his patients and staff were more important to him than she was? She squeezed her hands together on her lap, determined to let him talk.

"And at home or when we're out, you always speak for both of us, and that's okay by me. You're much better at it. I've told you that."

The compliment sounded vaguely familiar. He had told her…

"Twenty years ago," she quipped and bit her tongue so hard an "Ow!" slipped out before she could stop it.

"What?"

"I bit my tongue. I didn't mean to sound sarcastic."

"Well, twenty years *is* a long time. I'll give you that." His puppy brown eyes shimmered as if full of tears.

And she wilted.

He said, "It's mostly you I talk about all day long. You and the kids. Patients always ask. I tell them all about your volunteer work, how you run the school and the women's clubs. I tell them about what you cook. About your trip here with old friends. About your latest—what is it? Kickboxing?"

Close enough. She nodded. "I had no idea."

"I assumed you would know." He paused. "You don't love him?"

"Todd?" A flirtation, a crush, a coping mechanism. But love? "No. I love you."

"Yet he can give you what I don't?"

"To a certain extent. He gave me attention, Cam, the kind women want."

"But I take care of you. I work and pay the bills. Isn't that more important? Isn't that attention enough?"

"You just described what my father did for me. I don't need another father. So, no, it's not enough." She thought of chateaubriand and knights in shining armor. How could she make him understand?

"It's not enough," he repeated her words, his forehead creased. "Okay. Where do I start? I can't undo the past. I can't conceive the future. What do you want from me right now this very moment?"

That was an easy one. When she whispered to God in her heart that morning, walls of pride crumbled and His forgiveness poured in. A few bricks remained, though. She saw that clearly now because she hesitated to reply. But honestly! In the deluge of her "I'm sorrys," he hadn't once extended forgiveness. Why should she be the first one to ask for it? After all, if he'd been a better husband, they wouldn't be in this mess.

And then she saw the tenderness in his raised brows, in the downturned set of his mouth. He longed to understand.

Well, somebody had to go first. "What I want, what I *need*, is your forgiveness."

"You have that." Not even a heartbeat separated his words from hers. "That goes without saying."

Relief flowed through her. Quick on its heels, though, came frustration. Nothing could go without saying! That was the problem! Why couldn't he— She gulped in a lungful of air and held it. Her husband had forgiven her.

She released the breath. "Oh, Cam. Thank you. I don't deserve it, but I don't know how I would go on if you didn't forgive me."

"I hear the dumbest stories from patients. Either about themselves or others, about how they'd rather be bitter and self-righteous than to forgive a spouse." He shook his head. "Divorces right and left."

She simply stared at him. All right, she did believe aliens could inhabit humans.

"Char, you don't want a divorce, do you?"

"Oh my word!" Her voice rose several octaves. "No! Do you?"

"Of course not. What would I do without you? You keep me going."

"I do?"

He gazed at her, and she suddenly realized he had maintained eye contact since closing the menu. "You didn't know that?"

"Not a clue, sugar."

"I should have said something?"

She nodded.

"Will you forgive me? For not saying things I should have? For not noticing you?"

There was only one answer to that question.

"Yes, of course I forgive you."

For the first time in ever so long, he smiled directly at her, his entire face engaged.

Like a thirsty desert nomad coming at last upon an oasis, she tasted the water cautiously, taking tiny sips, giving the dry pockets of herself time to absorb it.

And hoping with all her might that it flowed from a perpetual source.

An unobtrusive waiter served the many dishes Cam had chosen. As usual he inhaled his miso soup, sushi, and an entire platter of tempura. But he also managed to talk nonstop.

Char, dumbstruck at moments, nibbled and wondered what had uncorked him. First his ears—so obvious in the way he heard her—and now it seemed his vocal cords were set free as well. At times she couldn't get a word in edgewise.

Halfway through his yakisoba, he said, "Char, he's our neighbor. I can't pretend that nothing happened."

"I don't expect you to."

"He should apologize."

"Yes, but I doubt that'll happen. He left a voice mail, cursing me up one side and down the other. I think he will avoid us at all costs."

"He swore at you?"

"Yes."

"He's always seemed like a nice, regular sort of guy. Friendly. Returns my tools in good shape."

"Cam, he's a womanizer. And I fell for it."

Chopsticks in midair, he gazed at her. "You were that desperate for attention?"

"Yes."

He set down the sticks, the bite uneaten. "Char, I am sorry. I just didn't know."

She shrugged.

"Thank you for calling last night. I know you're giving me another chance. I don't want to blow it this time. Tell me what I should do. Tell me how to be. I want to guarantee that you won't need a Todd anymore."

Whew! He got it! Molly must have been praying up a storm. Cam actually got it! And he was giving her carte blanche!

She blinked back tears of gratitude. "Cam, that's like handing me a blank check."

"Well, fill in the blanks and I'll see what I can do."

Batting her eyelashes like crazy did not help.

Fill in the blanks?

Punch Todd Brooks in the nose for real.

At the least, call him a few dirty names to his face.

Turn off the television.

Lose fifty pounds.

Give me surprise gifts. Flowers will do.

Just pay attention.

Tell me what you're thinking. Communicate.

Remember my birthday.

No. None of those were it, not exactly.

"There's really only one thing." Her voice was unsteady.

"Okay."

The floodgates threatened to split open again. She locked her jaw into place.

He leaned forward. "And that is…what?"

Fighting for control, she whispered quickly, "Call me honey-buns."

"Call you—huh? I do call you that. I've always—"

She raised her brows.

"I do! I distinctly see myself coming home after work and saying—"

She cut him off with a tilt of her head. "When was that?"

"When?" A sheepish expression spread over his face. "When we lived in the apartment."

She nodded.

"Maybe our first house too."

"Fifteen years ago."

"I'm sorry."

Thank You, God.

Looking lost in thought, he picked up his chopsticks, set them back down, and then leaned toward her again. "Why is this little thing such a big deal to you?"

She sighed inwardly. They weren't at square one. They were in a subterranean basement with no exit posted. Evidently the closure of one battle only cleared the way for another. She was not going to give up now, though. If she had to explain until she was blue in the face, she would do so. She swallowed the weepy feeling.

"Cam, sugar, 'honey-buns' is a big deal because it speaks volumes to me. It says you give a hoot. It says you notice me. It says you won't leave me."

"Leave? You thought I would leave you?"

"I didn't consciously think it." Her heart felt squeezed as if in a vice.

And then, right there, with a plate piled high with sukiyaki in front of her and Asian music twanging from a speaker overhead, she put two and two together. The feeling was old, familiar. It was one of great loss.

She looked at him. "Mama left. Daddy left, in a sense. He was so incapable of expressing emotion, and then he married what's-her-face. One by one Jo, Molly, and Andie left."

"And I left. Physically with long hours at the office. Emotionally." She whispered, "Yes."

"I'm sorry." He held his hand out to her.

She untwisted the napkin from her fingers and laid a hand in his, unable to speak.

"I think I have the funds to cover that check." He smiled. "Honey-buns."

They went to the beach and sat side by side on the seawall, facing the dark ocean.

Char slipped her hand into Cam's. "Sugar, I am so glad you came."

"So am I." He squeezed her fingers. "Honey-buns."

She smiled. He had called her that at least a dozen times in the past half hour.

He said, "I didn't know what I was going to do once I got here. I didn't know what you would do. I only knew I had to get here."

"Why?"

"I didn't want to lose you."

"Why?"

He didn't reply immediately. "That's obvious, isn't it?"

"Pretend like it's not."

"Well, because I love you!"

"Thank you. I like hearing that. And I love you."

He touched her face. "I'm sorry for being so slow."

"But you came after me, halfway across the country."

"You shook me up, honey-buns." He lowered his hand and gazed toward the water. "You made me feel anger and fear."

"I'm sorry."

"No, don't be. I haven't felt anything good or bad for a long time."

"What?"

"The truth is, Char, I'm bored silly with life."

"Huh?"

"I hate dentistry."

"Cam! You've always enjoyed it."

He shook his head. "Nope. Never have. It was the thing to do, what with Dad retiring and the business all in place. I'd grown up under his tutelage. It was the easiest thing to step into. And it took care of the money issue. I wouldn't have to think about that." He held out his hands, inspecting them. "Look at these. They should be doing something else, like playing football."

"Football?" Char couldn't think straight. He'd played in high school. "You want to play football?"

"No. It's just that these are not dentist hands. My mind is not a dentist's. There's got to be something more to life!"

Chateaubriand. He had an inkling that matched hers! He too was tired of duck soup! He wanted complexity!

"Honey-buns, you woke me up. I can say it out loud now. I don't want to be a dentist. Whew! That felt so good I'll say it again. I don't want to be a dentist! Think about it. We live in Chicago, one of the most exciting cities in the world, but day in and day out, five and a half days a week, year in and year out, I'm staring into people's mouths. I might as well be in the middle of Nebraska! Do you know what I want to do?"

"What?"

He grinned. "Own a restaurant."

"A restaurant?" Someone could have knocked her over with a feather. "A restaurant?"

"Yes. I have always wanted to do that."

"You have?" News to her.

"Yes. I never told you that?"

From somewhere deep in her throat a laugh started. "Camden Wilcox! You never tell me a darn thing!"

He laughed with her. "That makes us even."

"Okay. Even steven. Now you know what I want, and I know what you want."

"So what do you think?"

"You're serious? A restaurant? Well, uh, color me flabbergasted." She scrambled to find encouraging words for the most bizarre thing he had ever uttered. "It, uh, sounds…interesting. You…you like food. You know food. Are you thinking maybe you could buy a place already going? Sort of have it on the side, like a hobby?"

"No, Char." His smile stretched. "I want to open my very own. I want to run it myself. Day-to-day operations."

She felt her eyes bulge.

"Not the cooking part, of course. I'd have to find a really good chef. That's the secret. And location. Like in that strip mall they're renovating on Fifth. Imagine starting from scratch. Creating menus. Hiring staff. Advertising. Outfitting the place. Maybe make it a California theme. This beach environment here is stimulating, isn't it? Imagine replicating it in the Midwest." He stopped, and his smile faded. "We'd lose money. Prestige. We'd all have to pitch in. The kids too." He heaved a sigh. "That's why I never pursued it. Shoot, I never even thought much about it, let alone pursued it. Ah, forget I said anything."

She blinked, still digesting his wild ideas. He actually had a dream! He was talking! And now he was giving up?

"No, Cam, I don't think I will forget you said anything. As I live and breathe, this is the first heartfelt thing you've communicated to me in eons. I will not ignore such an event." She paused for effect. "I do, however, have one question."

Shadows hid his eyes, but he faced her. The streetlamp cast light on his mouth, now settled back into its habitual straight line. Oh! How she had already—in a short couple of hours—grown accustomed to its upturn! To its free movement releasing words upon words!

Come on, Cam. Don't leave me now.

Molly would pray. Well, she could too.

Dear God, help. Please?

She said, "Do you want to hear the question?"

He shrugged.

She elbowed him. "You can do better than that."

He cleared his throat. "Okay. Ask it."

"Can we serve chateaubriand?"

"Chateaubriand?"

"You know. Double-thick beef tenderloin."

"Center cut. With sauce?"

"And fixings. Potatoes, other vegetables. As complex as we can make it."

A slow grin made its way across his broad face. "Sure. Whatever you want, honey-buns."

"Okay, Cam. Then you should think about it. Dream big."

"You mean it?"

"I mean it."

They smiled at each other.

And then he kissed her. And she kissed him back. And she knew she wouldn't be returning Jo's car to the beach house until sometime tomorrow.

Fifty-Four

Andie awoke with a start in the middle of the night. Where was she? Where was the clock? Odd shadows filled the room. The steady whoosh of the ocean was loud, very near.

And then she remembered. *Spend the night alone in a motel.* She had added a postscript to the final test: *with the window open.*

When she had gone to bed, she imagined Molly's baby in a similar environment, one of uttermost safety. The rhythmic sounds and the sensation of floating had lulled her to sleep.

Snuggling deeper under the covers, she smiled. She felt no fear. Then why was she awake? So wide awake?

She moved around until she saw the digital clock. It read two forty-seven. Not exactly time to get up.

But that was what she wanted to do. She felt a sudden urgent desire to not sleep through her all-night adventure. Something might be missed!

She rolled from the bed and wrapped herself in a blanket. Although she hadn't packed a robe, she had brought along herbal tea bags and now brewed a cup. Like that first night after Molly had dragged her outside to the seawall, she felt drawn to the mystery of ocean and stars. She carried her mug out onto the tiny deck area and leaned against the railing.

The evening's cloud cover had dissipated and the stars shone.

"Lord, You are awesome! To think You made all this and bother to notice me. We made it through that list of fears with flying colors, didn't we?"

What a day it had been! She thought of Julian, Zeke, Jelly, the roller coaster attendant, the woman beside her in the Japanese restaurant. "You surrounded me with angels, didn't You?"

She had never felt so contented, so at peace, so loved, so spilling over with love, love to give away. Did all this have to end? Three days remained to spend with her friends, and then it would be time to go back home and pick up life where it had left off what felt like an eternity ago. Then what? Would it all end?

Spunky Andie was not going to fit into that mold.

"Point-blank, Lord. I am tired of kowtowing to a man who tells me with every glance I am worthless and who has a girlfriend and probably has had others in the past. I know You died for him, Jesus. You took these sins against me into Yourself. So with Your help, I can forgive him." Her shoulders dropped, as if the struggle left her. "Yes, I do forgive him. But I refuse to accept the status quo."

She winced slightly and waited.

No fire rained from the heavens. No voice boomed condemnation. No fear rattled in her chest or choked her throat.

"Okay." She calmly sipped her tea. "Now what do we do?"

At four AM Andie curled up with her cell on the chair next to the cottage window and listened to another phone ringing. Not wanting to disturb the boys by calling the house, she had dialed Paul's cell number. The thing was like another appendage for him.

Her heart pounded away, doing its thunder rendition, resonating in her chest, throat, and ears.

Lord.

The ringing stopped. "Hi there!" Paul's exuberant voice came through above another one that sounded like a newscaster's. "Hold on. Let me turn this down." The noise dimmed. "Miss me already, darlin'?"

Andie's heart went into double-time and felt as if it would bound from her chest. He hadn't checked the caller ID. He was driving.

He said, "I miss you too."

Her booming heart muffled his voice,

But his words were like lightning flashes that preceded thunderous booms. They seared themselves into her mind.

God! Please!

"Hello-oh. Are you there?" His singsong tone teased.

Andie wanted to crawl back around the corner and into the mouse hole, back into her warm cozy nest where ignorance was bliss.

No! She did not want to do that. She wanted a point-blank life. Candid. Forthright. Free-spoken.

She swallowed and reminded herself that her husband's words now proved what she had already suspected. She wasn't the guilty one who should crawl away.

"Paul, it's me." Surprisingly, her voice did not quiver. Her heart decelerated a notch.

Silence.

Instead of clueing him in, she waited and twisted around in the chair, the better to catch the sea breeze coming through the window.

"Andrea!" Disbelief was in his tone.

She cringed. No one called her Andrea. They never had. Twenty years ago she thought it romantic that he did. When had it begun to sound condescending? Controlling?

"Yes. So you must not be with her?"

"What?"

"You answered 'Miss me already?' I figured that meant you *were* with her, but you aren't now."

"Her? Andrea, what are you up to? It's the middle of the night there! Is everything all right? You haven't called all week."

Well, of course she had called and left several voice mails. He hadn't been available. She didn't want to talk about that.

"Paul, let's not pretend anymore. You're not at home."

"Ho, ho." The fake laugh. "Okay, you caught me. I didn't want to concern you. There was that bash at Valentino's for Dick Green's retirement last night. Some of us stayed on. You know, celebrated a little too much. Good old ever-sober Marty hauled me to his house. I slept there. I thought it was him calling to make sure I made it home."

"You called Marty 'darling.'"

"You know how I rag him."

"Mm-hmm. And I was born on Mars." Her voice gained strength as she spoke. "I need to say a few things. One, I know you're seeing someone. I doubt she's the first. Two, you have a week to end it and make an appointment with a marriage counselor. Three, I'm spending another six days out here."

"You're doing what? Andrea, what has gotten into you? What's going on?"

"The truth is going on. I've decided that your infidelity is not my fault. I forgive you and am willing to work through things, but your fooling around will not continue if you want to live under the same roof with me."

"Have you been drinking?"

"Grow up, Paul. I'll be home a week from Tuesday."

"A *week* from Tuesday? Hey, listen. I don't know what those friends of yours have been saying, but you and I make a good team."

Translation: I cook your meals, keep your house, entertain your clients and coworkers, do your laundry, and look the other way when "urgent meetings" happen all times of the day and night.

He continued. "Whatever is bothering you, we will talk it over when you get home *the day after tomorrow*."

"Will you admit you have a girlfriend? Or was tonight just a one-night stand?"

"Andrea! Where did you get such a crazy idea?"

"Goodbye, Paul." She closed up her phone.

And then she broke down. Even as she sobbed, though, she thought about how she could check off number twelve. She had made it through the night alone in a motel with the window open.

Come to think of it, she had added one more fearsome thing to the adventure list: Confront Paul.

And she had completed that as well.

Make that thirteen adventures. A baker's dozen. All checked off. *Finis.*

Fifty-Five

Jo propped her elbows on the table and closed her eyes to shut out the gray morning as well as other diners on Kono's deck. She rubbed her temples.

Hangovers had never felt this bad, had they? Before spending five days in a beach house with her old friends, she hadn't cried. Nor had she addressed issues that made her feel slit open by a scalpel without benefit of anesthesia. Neither had she felt the desire to attack her life with a battering ram, smash it to pieces, and start over with nothing but her physician's credentials—a sure formula for disaster. Drinking sounded a lot less painful.

Jo continued massaging her temples, eyes shut. At least the weather forecast promised a more typical day: blue skies, seventy-two degrees, no Santa Ana winds. Maybe that would help matters.

She had placed breakfast orders and found a table. Molly was around the corner at the coffee kiosk line, extra long because it was Sunday morning. They hadn't seen Char yet. That meant either things went well or Cam had morphed into an ogre and done away with her. Andie had not been heard from—except for her note—since she'd left to spend the night before last with—make that *at* Julian's.

"Hey. Thought I'd find you here."

Jo opened her eyes and saw Andie now standing at a neighboring table, asking a man if she could take a chair from it. He nodded, and she dragged it across the wood decking. Then she sat down, across from Jo, a huge grin on her face.

Jo smiled tentatively. "It's our morning spot."

"It's great. Ocean view, out of sight of the madding crowd." Her blue eyes were puffy but bright as if the sun itself shone through them. "I saw Molly in line. She's almost to the counter, so cheer up. Coffee is on its way."

Jo nodded. "Do you want breakfast?"

"No, thanks. I ate a while ago. This place wasn't open yet, but I walked down that main street a ways." She fluttered her hand indicating the direction. "And found a restaurant."

"So how was your day? And night?"

"I'll tell you all about it when Molly comes, okay?" She paused. "Jo, let's clear the air. I forgive you."

The tight band behind Jo's eyes felt suddenly released. "Andie, I am so sorry I hurt you."

"I know. But you admitted it and I accept your apology. Will you accept my forgiveness?"

"I don't deserve—"

"You don't, but then none of us deserve God's."

The Andie Effect was in full swing. Between that and the Molly Effect, Jo figured she might see Jesus Himself any minute now, probably out on a surfboard catching a wave.

Andie said, "I needed to hear the truth about Paul. That's what finally came through loud and clear."

"I didn't mean to make him out to be the bad guy."

"But he was. He is. I've just been ignoring it. You helped me deal with reality." Her shoulders rose and fell as she made a show of taking one deep breath and letting it go. "I called him this morning. From the way he answered his cell phone, it was obvious he thought I was his girlfriend. He refused to admit it, though. I told him I knew, that I forgave him, and that I want him to break it off. And I told him we have to see a marriage counselor."

Jo could only stare at her.

"He denied and evaded. We'll see what he does about it. If nothing, well, then I guess that's that. Spunky Andie is not going back to being Mousey Andie." Her face puckered up.

"Oh, hon. Are you okay?"

"Yes. I cried for a while." She lifted her chin and the creases smoothed from her forehead. "I'm sure I'll cry again. But now I know I'm not alone. My perception of God is that He is very close to me. And even though I don't live near you three, I feel you're all available to me again, like in the old days."

Jo nodded.

"I asked myself why I married him in the first place."

"I remember when you wanted to be a nun."

"Yeah." Her smile was wistful. "Then my dad died. My mom was a major loose cannon. Grandmère was in the nursing home, totally in some other world. I didn't see myself finishing college under that scenario. Paul was older, graduating, a gung-ho business major with definite plans. He offered security. I don't know what he saw in me, except that I was pliable and naive. The perfect wife."

"Andie."

"It's true. Anyway, I love you, dear friend, and I forgive you."

Jo hadn't even felt the sutures being stitched into place, but they were there. She knew because the pain, no longer exposed to the elements, was alleviated.

"Thank you, Andie."

⌣⌒

While Jo and Molly ate their breakfasts, they listened in amazement at Andie's tale of how she spent the previous day by herself surrounded, it seemed, by angels posing as humans. Jo thought Molly's expression probably mirrored her own: wide-eyed and grinning. They laughed from Zeke to Jelly to the tattooed kid, but soon sobered as she told about gazing at the middle-of-the-night stars and planning a conversation with Paul that would alter her life from that moment on.

"Andie." Molly set down her fork. "God can change anyone."

"Spots to stripes?" She smiled. "I don't know that Paul would want Him to. We'll see. In the meantime, Paul has a week to take the first step. I told him I'm staying here until a week from Tuesday. I already switched my plane ticket."

Jo laughed. "Spunky Andie just keeps on percolating."

She shrugged. "The motel has a room available so—"

"No!" Jo cried. "Stay with me. Stay at my house."

"I couldn't—"

"Of course you could. If you want."

"Well, of course I would want."

That was when Jo knew beyond a shadow of a doubt Andie had forgiven her. They exchanged a smile.

Andie said, "Thanks. And that's my story. What did you two do yesterday?"

Jo blurted, "Worried about you."

Molly patted her shoulder. "I did lots more. I stopped throwing up spicy Chinese. I napped. Twice. I helped Char choose an outfit for her dinner with Cam. I let the good doctor here start me on progesterone."

"Is that because of your miscarriage?"

"Yes. I used it when I was pregnant with Hannah."

Jo looked at her two friends. She saw compassion on Andie's face. She never could hide that. Color had returned to Molly's cheeks, and she didn't seem to be in sewer depths of despair anymore about the pregnancy. She had even asked Jo to figure out the due date. Though she was trying hard to rally her enthusiasm, she hadn't quite returned to normal. Jo wondered how long it would take.

"That's it?" Andie asked. "No sightseeing?"

Jo glanced at Molly. That wasn't quite it. She said, "And…I put my house up for sale."

Andie's breath caught. "You're going to do it! Move to a hovel and minister to those poor people at the clinic. Expand the OB/GYN care."

"I wouldn't go so far as to say I've made up my mind to do all that. I simply met with a Realtor friend at my house and…" It wasn't easy to say it aloud. "Uh, signed the papers."

Andie smiled.

"Stop grinning like that."

"I'm so proud of you."

"Don't be, Andie. I don't deserve that, either."

"Yes, you do. This one you do."

Jo shook her head, but couldn't stop a smile from forming. Maybe Andie would like to spend an entire month with her.

Sunshine slowly regained control of the skies. While the cloud cover dissipated, they lingered at Kono's. Molly and Andie drank herbal tea. Jo, caffeine addict and health expert, savored her third cup of coffee.

Andie said, "Molly, today's your turn! What are the plans for your do-over celebration?"

"Mmm. I'd like to do over a day up the Elk River with Scott."

Jo and Andie smiled at each other. They'd heard the picnic story.

Jo snickered and then laughed out loud. "Oh, Moll! I can't help it. I have to say it again. Get out from under the pile!"

"Ha-ha. Andie, why don't you say it too? Then you can both feel better for finally getting back at me."

Andie chuckled. "Okay, here goes. Get out from under the pile, Mary Catherine."

"Ooh, good one. Extra points for the name." She glanced over Jo's head and waved. "Here comes Char. We'll give her a turn too."

"Hi, y'all." Char joined them at the table, a tall paper cup in hand. "I was hoping you'd be here."

While Molly clued Char in on the topic at hand and Char added her own "get out from under the pile," Jo tried not to stare. The change in Char, however, was too obvious to ignore. It took her a few moments to identify the difference in her.

Jo never would have described the petite blonde's demeanor or physical attributes in the least bit harsh—until now, when an absence of harshness glared. A new softness about Char suggested she might just float away. She smiled, but it was different somehow, not that annoying, pert variation she often pasted on her face.

"Jo, sugar, do I have spinach between my teeth?"

She shook her head. "No. It's just...just...you look so different!"

"Oh, my. Does it really show?"

They nodded as one.

Char beamed. "All I can say is that I feel different. Cam and I have been *communicating*. We talked and talked for hours and hours and then—well, obviously I didn't come back to the beach house! But you don't need to hear all *those* details. Anyway, we talked like we haven't since we were first married."

Andie smiled. "That's wonderful."

Jo said, "Bravo!"

"Super!" Molly added. "Do you feel reconnected?"

"Most definitely. And you'll never guess. He said he hates being a dentist. He wants to run a restaurant!"

"No way!"

"You're kidding!"

"Wow! Where did that come from?"

Char laughed. "I am in shock, absolute shock. He left just now for the airport because he still has to be a dentist tomorrow and the day after that, but..." She held up her palms. "He wants to investigate turning his business over to some other dentist he knows." Her smile shrank into the pert one, her eyes glowed too brightly. "Is there an epidemic in the medical profession I haven't heard about? I mean, does he sound like you, Jo, or what?"

She nodded in surprise.

"But you don't support a spouse and two children!" The tiny smile kept slipping, and her voice rose from its usual purr. "I adore him for making such an effort to get here and for how he listened so sweetly and forgave the Todd thing and understood how I need *daily* assurance that he loves me, but my word! What will I ever do if he quits his job?"

No one had an answer.

Jo thought of her own fears of total upheaval, of downsizing, of financial unknowns. Char's fears would be multiplied along those lines. Then there was Andie's confrontation with Paul, which placed a huge question mark on her future. Good old solid Molly was a mess over the glitch in her future plans. Now this healing of Char's marriage stirred up a host of things for the Wilcoxes.

But... "Ladies," Jo said, "we are moving forward, right? Not one of us is staying stuck in a corner."

They looked at her with puzzled expressions.

"We're forty years old. We've been pulled from the status quo. We've turned corners and have glimpsed the unknown. That's scary, yes. But I don't think any of us would choose to go backward. No, it's onward and upward. The only choice is whether or not we..." She looked pointedly at Molly. "Get out from under the pile."

"Mm-hmm," she muttered. "Thanks for the pep talk, coach."

Jo smiled sweetly. "Care to show us how it's done? After all, this is your day, and for the moment, none of us can change a thing about our iffy tomorrows."

"You're paying me back for making you celebrate your second fortieth."

"*Au contraire.* I'm repaying the favor because I will be forever grateful that you yanked me out of my corner. So, birthday girl, what would you like to do?"

Molly's smile was not sweet. "Go to church."

Church. Jo felt her own grin disintegrate.

Not funny. I don't care if your name is Saint Molly.

Since her second year in college, the mere mention of attending a Sunday church service filled Jo with loathing. Weddings and funerals held in churches did not count. She had no problem with mere social events nor the buildings themselves.

No. It was the clear memory of finger-pointing that still unraveled her.

As a child she participated in traditional church practices, from Sunday mornings to confirmation to thirteen years of parochial school with required daily chapel. She complained and rebelled to a certain extent, but she went along with it. After all, it was just what the Zambruskis did. It was on the same level as dinners in the formal dining room in appropriate dress, as ski trips to Switzerland between Christmas and New Year's, and as August cottage stays in Michigan.

Until her second year in college.

Molly's fault, of course.

One Sunday morning, with nothing better to do than nurse a hangover, Jo tagged along with Molly to a church service. By that winter the Molly Effect had gained momentum. Jo's saintly roommate could not get enough of church. She visited a myriad of denominations and seemed to enjoy every single one. For her, Jesus had become a real entity. She got excited learning different expressions of worship.

Jo didn't understand it.

That particular day they went to what Jo called a hopping place. No one could say three words without exclaiming *Praise the Lord!* Praise the Lord this, Praise the Lord that. And the hand clapping and foot stomping! Somebody should have called the cops. The peace was definitely being disturbed.

Jo's headache did not go away.

But she endured the hullabaloo.

Then the preacher took the stand. Or rather pulpit.

And then came God's fire. It rained in that place.

Jo had been around church enough to catch on that God had His fiery side. On occasion she recognized it in Molly, a ramrod demeanor at times overshadowing her compassion.

The preacher that day was a large man, height as well as widthwise, with a booming voice to match. His eyes were pinpricks in a florid face. His smile was that odd inverse kind in which the corners of his mouth dipped downward instead of up.

But it was his forefinger she remembered most clearly.

He pointed it at her. Directly at her.

She and Molly sat off to one side, in the back row. She did not imagine his aim.

He pointed it at her as he shouted his most explicit words of condemnation: *You are going to hell!*

Twenty-one years of sins, venial and mortal, confessed and unconfessed, raced through her aching head. And those were just the ones she knew about. Her heart pounded. Bile rose in her throat.

Of course she was going to hell.

But she didn't have to sit there and listen to a raging bull tell her so.

His voice followed her out the door, something along the lines that if she left that place, she would never get saved.

She had avoided Molly for days after that. The first thing she said to her was, "I will never, ever go to church again." Except for funerals and weddings, she had kept her word.

And now, on her friend's second fortieth birthday celebration, she was committed to doing whatever Molly wanted.

Saint Molly, of course, wanted to go to a Sunday morning church service.

Fifty-Six

Molly led the way from the dining patio, Andie and Char close behind; Jo brought up the distant rear.

Molly felt Jo watching her like a hawk. Perhaps they had pushed each other too far this time. Her friend's silent wariness was eerie.

Their pertinacity to challenge each other had gotten out of hand. Jo wouldn't let go of the old phrase, "Get out from under the pile." Molly felt guilty for not being able to do so, for not even wanting to do so, for not walking her talk. She felt guilty for Jo not accepting all Jesus had to give.

That was why she went for the jugular, "I want to go to church," knowing full well Jo's promise to avoid it at all costs after that disastrous service they attended during college.

The meeting had been so thick with God's condemnation it suffocated His love. Years later Molly could see that, but not before a judgmental Miss Goody Two-shoes had thoroughly engrained herself and taken a good hold of Molly's persona.

Molly reached the busy boardwalk now. Char and Andie veered toward the pier to pick up Andie's overnight bag at the motel. They were deep into a conversation about husbands. Molly waited for Jo to catch up and then fell into step beside her.

"Jo, the service is on the beach." She nudged her with her elbow. "No shoes required. Probably no shirts, either, for that matter. You could wear your swimsuit."

"Mm-hmm."

"If things get weird, you can leave."

"Nope. We're committed to sticking things out with the birthday girl. No complaints allowed."

"I got carried away. I know how you feel—"

"That was a long time ago. Don't worry about it."

Molly glanced off to the side. Jimmy Mack wasn't on his usual bench. She looked around but didn't spot him. At least she hadn't disappointed him by walking by without a gift of food or money.

Good grief! Did she really think she could rescue everyone? Not even Jo was within her alleged power.

"Jo, I'm sorry."

"For what?"

"For everything. For being Miss Goody Two-shoes all those years. For causing you to think I really am Saint Molly."

"But you are. A saint and very, very good. You always were. You are the most together woman I've ever met."

"I am none of those things. On my birthday I saw myself for what I am: a one-woman razzmatazz overly concerned with being right and priding myself on carrying the whole load while Scotty did his thing."

"Superwoman."

"Yep. And I don't like being that, but now I'm thinking again that I can do it all. I can have a fifth child and teach full-time. That's crazy, even with Scotty's help and understanding. Then I get upset with God for dumping this load on me. Not very saintly or good."

"You said you came here to find Molly and to depend more on God because your real identity lies in Him. Right?"

Jo's memory could be most annoying. "Yes."

"How are things going?"

"Not well."

"What would 'well' look like?"

She gave her a sidelong glance. "I wouldn't be such a mess over being pregnant. I would function just fine without talking to Scott and the kids all the time to make sure someone hasn't forgotten to wipe their nose."

"In other words, you wouldn't be real?"

Molly stopped and stared at her.

"You would look like Superwoman, the perfect saint, and Miss Goody Two-shoes all wrapped into one human being with a perfect family to boot?"

"That's not it. It's about me not walking my talk."

Jo smiled and took hold of her elbow, steering her back into the pedestrian flow. "Only I would notice, dear. And that's only because I'm searching for shades of gray. If you don't have any, walking your talk doesn't mean a thing to me. Let's get to church."

Molly wanted to join in the singing, but she was way too busy with other things.

Like digging her bare toes into sand and listening to guitars and drums and seeing new acquaintances in the congregation. Jimmy Mack swayed to the music. Zeke clapped his hands. Julian closed his eyes and sang.

Like basking in the nearness of her three old friends who gallantly tried to sing unfamiliar words and tunes.

Like wondering, *Lord, why is it that while I'm letting You down Jo is paying more attention than ever? This does not make sense.*

After a time, they all sat down on blankets shaded by a large canopy. A sweet-faced young man stepped to the microphone and introduced himself as Pastor Jamie.

Molly nearly groaned. She knew what Jo would be thinking, that the kid never drank a beer or said a cuss word in his life. He got saved as a three-year-old, married his darling next-door-neighbor childhood sweetheart, and they had two point five rosy-cheeked, well-behaved kids. She knew Jo was thinking all that because, details aside, it was the gist of how she once described Scott and his Bible college friends who were groomsmen in their wedding.

Lord, You know Jo needs someone who—

"Let be then: learn that I am God…"

Suddenly Molly stopped being busy with other things. She tuned in to the sermon.

Jamie was their age and had a history to turn one's stomach.

Molly stopped the internal rescue dialogue. Jo and Andie and Char and Jimmy Mack and her children and Scott and every Oregon school kid slipped from her thoughts. She stopped telling God how to fix them all, how to save them. She stopped thinking she let God down— as if He couldn't do things without her being Superwoman, Miss Goody Two-shoes, and a perfect saint all wrapped into one human being.

Instead she heard what was intended for her alone.

"Let be then: learn that I am God…"

Let be. Let go. Cease striving. Pause a while. Stand silent. Be still. Let be and be still. I am God. Lord, You alone are Yahweh.

"Yes, Lord, You are. You alone."

Molly murmured praise softly. She sat cross-legged on a thin rough carpet in a corner of a musty old bookstore, surrounded by floor-to-ceiling bookcases. Bibles lay about the floor, a myriad of translations and paraphrases, all open to Psalm 46. How many ways could "shhh, it's okay, I'm here" be expressed? Would she ever comprehend what it meant to take her hands off? Could her soul ever absorb the enormity of His mighty power and audacious love?

In the beach house over lunch, the four women had discussed the church service. As one they agreed that their futures—what Jo had referred to as their "iffy tomorrows"—were in God's hands. No amount of anxiety would change a thing. Easier said than done, Jo unnecessarily pointed out, but she had smiled and even thanked Molly for making her go to a service again. That Jamie guy was "all right, lots of grays in him."

Molly felt a new peace settle about them all. They decided to spend the day in quiet activities, things like browsing in secondhand bookstores and strolling through a desert garden at Balboa Park

"Molly," Char said now. She shared the small "Religion Section" corner with her and sat on a child-size wooden chair. "May I interrupt?"

"Sure."

"I was skimming through this and found a verse someone highlighted in yellow." Char looked down at the Bible in her lap. The book was small with a pretty blue cover and gilded page edges. "It says 'I know the plans I have in mind for you—it is Yahweh who speaks—plans for peace, not disaster, reserving a future full of hope for you.'" Her eyelashes flittered quick as wings on a moth approaching a porch light.

Molly waited. She was into being still.

Char looked up. "So. Is that for me?"

Molly smiled and whispered, "The Holy Spirit is speaking to your spirit."

Char's eyebrows disappeared under her shaggy bangs. "He won't let Cam buy a restaurant! I felt it!" She sprang to her feet. "I'm going to buy this Bible."

Molly resisted the desire to catch her by the arm as she scurried from the corner. It was that business about being still. It slowed all her reflexes.

But shouldn't she explain how sometimes God's plans could easily look like disaster to a person? That He used difficulty to mold and shape and pour out His love?

Take, for example, an unplanned, undesired pregnancy at the age of forty.

Molly sighed loudly. Char was God's responsibility, not hers.

She picked up the nearest Bible and began flipping pages in search of Char's verse. Somewhere in the twenty-ninth chapter of Jeremiah was reassurance of a future full of hope.

Molly emerged from the store. The business district was borderline shabby, made up mainly of shops carrying used items such as books, clothing, and furniture. But little trees lined the sidewalk, and her friends waited in the shade of one. Like herself, they held plastic bags full of treasures unearthed on the bookshelves.

"Okay, Jo, where to— What's wrong?"

Andie was grinning, but Jo and Char wore expressions that reminded her of Hannah's when she stuck a bobby pin into an electrical outlet.

Andie said, "Jo got a phone call."

"A phone call? Aw, come on, you guys. You agreed to turn those things off for the afternoon. We're having a 'be still, let go' day."

Andie said, "Well, we discussed it and decided we wanted Scott to be able to get through."

Molly tried not to roll her eyes. She had already talked to him and all four kids separately.

"And there's Cam, who we think will definitely call Char as soon as possible. And I want to be available to my boys in case Paul goes off the deep end. Who knows what he's going to do? Anyway, then there was the real estate agent." Andie paused for effect, her eyes wide, laughter imminent in her wide grin.

"Real estate agent?"

"He sold Jo's house!"

"No way! In one day?"

They all nodded.

"Whoa!"

"Exactly!" Jo said. "As in whoa, Nellie. This is happening too fast for comfort. I don't even have a hold of the reins yet!"

Molly laughed with Andie.

Char said, "What are you going to do?"

"I don't know!"

"Oh my word. What will I ever do when Cam says he's selling *our* house?"

Jo's glance would have withered a lesser woman.

Char reached into her bag of books, whispering to herself. "Jeremiah. Plans for peace, not disaster."

Molly turned to Jo. "Can you take some time to think about it?"

She shrugged. "What's to think about? Two offers came in. It turned into a bidding war. The final one is more than I was asking. Lots more. It's an outrageous amount the house would never appraise out at. A bank wouldn't give such a loan, but the agent told me this guy doesn't need a loan! He's paying cash!"

Andie threw an arm across Jo's shoulders. "Will you make enough money to lease that space next to the clinic?"

Jo tilted her head onto Andie's shoulder and sighed. "And remodel. Equip. Hire staff. The whole shebang."

Char looked up from the Bible in her hand. "But where will you live?"

"Um, well, one idea has crossed my mind. I own this apartment building…"

Molly pointed a finger. "Josephine Zambruski, admit it. You've been thinking about this. You have a place to move to. You want to do this!"

"But a week ago I never could have imagined such a crazy thing. Which makes it sound truly demented."

Molly cocked her head. "And your point is what, dear?"

She moaned. "It's your fault, the three of yours. Why don't you all just go home?"

Molly giggled with Andie. Eventually Jo and Char smiled and snickered. Before long the four of them had to sit down on a bench, doubled over in hysterical laughter, tears streaming down their faces.

~

Not far from the shopping district, they all sat in Jo's car across the street from her apartment building. As one they exclaimed over the flourishing palm trees and bougainvillea. The building itself was three stories of pale pink stucco with no distinguishing features. Small bungalows sat on either side of it, an elementary school down the block, a church across the street. Parked cars lined the curbs, older models, nothing fancy. Nothing particularly extra nice or attractive.

Jo did a lot of shrugging. "It's investment property. A management company runs it. Gardeners care for the yard. I don't do a thing except take full advantage of its write-off benefits. It's rather ugly."

Molly playfully punched her arm. "Jo, it's great. Just think. It could be your future home."

She shrugged.

Char said, "Sugar, I am glad to see you are not a slumlord. I must admit I was concerned a few blocks over. Are we near that clinic?"

"Yes. The neighborhoods run together. This area is nicer, but obviously it's not high-end rent. If I..." She swallowed as if the words were difficult to say. "If I lived here I'd be ten minutes from work. Housing would cost less. I'd spend a pittance on gas."

"What are the units like?"

"Last I saw when I bought it seven years ago, they were all right, clean enough. Updated electricity and plumbing. All are one bedroom. Old-fashioned with a lot of wood. Nothing fancy. It was built in the twenties."

Andie said, "It reminds me of the beach house."

Jo twisted around in the seat and gawked at her.

Now Andie shrugged. Her smile wrinkled her nose. "Same era. Is there an empty apartment?"

"No, so this talk is a waste of time. Year leases are in effect, with the first one up in February. I wouldn't kick someone out. They're all the same people who lived here when I bought it. Everyone pays on time. No one complains."

Molly said, "Anyone have moving plans?"

"No!"

Molly added her own shrug. "Let go and know that God is God."

"He'll kick someone out?"

"If He needs to."

Char reached over the back of the seat and squeezed Jo's shoulder. "He got Cam off the couch and out to San Diego."

"You're all nuts." Jo started the car and pulled away from the curb. "This discussion is over."

After a bit, their chuckles slowed. Char and Andie engaged in conversation in the backseat.

Jo glanced at Molly. "I'd say you're walking your talk again."

"Really?"

"Yes, and all that glowing peace is so obnoxious." She winked. "Does this mean you've come to terms with things?"

"I-I don't know."

Let be then: learn that I am God.

I'm forty, I'm pregnant. And I'm not drowning in anger, not struck useless with dread.

She placed a hand on her tummy, which hadn't gone back to anywhere near flat since Abigail's birth. Plenty of space for a little one to take up residence and keep it a secret for a while.

A little one. Technically, counting the miscarriage, this was the sixth to move in.

Thou didst weave me in my mother's womb.

"Oh, Lord," she whispered, "there really is a person in here."

"What?" Jo asked.

She cleared her throat. "I didn't want to come to terms with things, but I guess maybe I am closer than I was."

"What do you mean you didn't want to? Isn't acceptance of the situation simply an act of your will?"

Your will, not mine. Yours, Lord, Yours.

She said, "I could fight tooth and nail against filling a pew with my own kids. I could deny and complain and blame others. Those are powerful tools. I'm sure I'll use them yet because they give me a sense of control." She shook her head. "No, my only act of the will was to consciously, all day long, let go of what seems like control."

Jo drove in silence, her mouth a straight line.

A few blocks down the road, though, she flicked a finger at the corner of her eye.

Molly found that gesture more hopeful than anything.

Fifty-Seven

Andie relished in the peaceful Sunday with her friends. Occasionally a wave of panic would wash through her, engulfing her heart with fear. To think that twelve hours ago she had said what she said to Paul! Was it horribly unfair to him? Was it horribly ugly?

Then Molly, Char, or Jo would say "Let it go," referring to whatever subject they happened to be discussing at the time. It fit everything they talked about. Since the church service on the beach that morning, the phrase had become the byword of the day. It kept making her smile, and the panic frittered away like waves on the shoreline.

They strolled through an enormous desert garden. She had no idea such numerous succulents existed—and in all shapes and sizes. Their scents were subtle, a sweet dryness.

"Incredible!" Molly said, not for the first time. "Look at this cactus. It's got to be twelve feet tall!"

"Oh, look at this one!" Char exclaimed from another path. "Then I'll come see yours."

A synthesizer version of a Bach minuet sang out energetically from Andie's purse. She jumped.

Char, Jo, and Molly swung to face her, their expressions not as calm as a moment before.

"Sorry!" she called out and unzipped her bag.

304

They should have listened to Molly and never turned on their cell phones. But then Jo would not have heard her news, and that had been such a wonderful thing to share as it happened. The timing too meant they were able to see her building, her potential new home.

She read the ID screen and shook her head at Molly. It wasn't Scott. It wasn't Paul's cell either. "My house."

As the others went back to roaming through the cacti, she answered. "Hello."

"Hey, Mom." It was Zach.

"Mom?" And Jadon on an extension. "How's it going?"

Zach said, "Catch any waves today?" They both laughed. They were still incredulous over her atypical behavior.

"No, not today. I skipped the boogie boarding and went out for breakfast instead. How are you guys?"

They chitchatted for a time. Andie discerned they had no idea about the morning's conversation with their dad, and she was grateful he had not confided in them.

"So, Mom," Zach said. "We have something of an emergency here."

"Emergency?" Quick as a heartbeat, panic swelled in her chest.

"Don't worry," he said. "We just need a permission thingamajig signed and Dad's not around. But Coach said if you call him, he'll accept Aunt Jen's signature. She said she'll sign. It needs to be turned in tomorrow."

Jen was Paul's sister, their nearest relative.

"Okay." Andie swallowed, trying to steady her voice and to not yell *Where is your father?*

"Give me the coach's number. Wait." She rummaged in her purse for the nifty notepad and pen that should have been in their own special compartment. She couldn't locate the compartment, but her blurry eyesight and shaking fingers finally found a scrap of paper and another pen. "All right."

Zach provided the number. "Thanks, Mom."

"Mm-hmm. So where is your dad?"

"I think he said Milwaukee. Some meeting early tomorrow. He left this morning."

Milwaukee was not a whole day's drive from Madison. "Why did he leave already?"

She could almost hear Zach's shrug. Neither of her sons was interested in the real estate business. Zach wanted to coach; Jadon wanted to be a forest ranger.

"He said something about setting things up. For a seminar maybe? I don't know."

"Are you going to spend the night at Aunt Jen's?" They hadn't done that for ages, not since declaring the little cousins were monsters to be avoided at all costs.

They groaned in unison.

"Mom, I'm sixteen. Jadon is almost eighteen," Zach complained. "We have a car, we have food, we have money. We can get ourselves to school on time. We're not afraid to spend the night alone. Heck, we did last night. I don't know what time Dad came in."

After six AM.

"He had a party to go to. By the way, Zach and I were in by eleven."

"That's great, but…but…." She bit her lip.

Zach said, "But what? We're fine. You don't have to worry."

"But you're not grown-up. You're still only teenagers!"

"It's football season. No girls, no booze, no partying if either of them are involved. No skipping class. Okay? We promise."

Sports meant everything to them. They wouldn't jeopardize their eligibility. They were disciplined beyond what she could have hoped for. They were good boys. At times she had even been embarrassed when other moms complained about their teens and she had nothing to add to the woeful conversation.

"But—"

"Mom," Zach said. "Will it help if we tell the Smiths and the Hadaceks we're here alone?" He mentioned neighbors who would pay attention if informed.

"I suppose." She wanted to tell them of her plans to stay longer in San Diego. How could she do that now? "I feel like your parents have abandoned you."

They hooted. "Mom!" Jadon said. "Let it go!"

Let it go. Let be.
All right, Lord.
Her sons were fine.

~

The desert landscape provided no benches, no grass, only narrow blacktop paths and dirt. Lots of dry dusty earth.

And a few big rocks.

Andie lunged toward one and plopped onto it before her legs gave out. Like a downed soldier, she waited. Within moments Jo, Molly, and Char surrounded her.

"What happened?"

She told them about the conversation with Zach and Jadon.

Char laid a hand on her shoulder. "They sound so grown-up, sugar. They'll be just fine. You've done a great job with them, Mom."

Molly said, "Milwaukee is not that far away. And surely he'll call them."

"I don't know. A week ago he didn't have any business scheduled in Milwaukee. Maybe he's not even that far away. Maybe he's just at *her* place. Maybe he'll check in with them. Oh! How can I ever tell them I'm leaving their dad? I couldn't even tell them I'm not coming home until next week!"

Jo scrunched down on her haunches. "I know I'm the inexperienced one in the group as far as husbands and kids go. But it seems to me you have just described a highly undisciplined, sneaky, self-centered man. You think they don't know this about him?"

She stared at Jo.

"They're obviously smart kids. My bet is they've deduced a whole lot more about him than you might realize."

Molly said, "It would explain why neither one are the least bit interested in his work. From what you told me before, the only thing they all have in common is him watching them play sports."

Char leaned over and hugged her tightly. "Let it go, sugar. Let it go."

⤳

They ate dinner in a starkly decorated restaurant. Footsteps and voices echoed in a low drone off the wooden floor and high ceilings. Framed prints for sale hung about the large open room. They were of a postmodern style Molly would have to study for an incredibly long time to comprehend the astronomical price tags. Rich coffee aromas mixed with those of exotic spices. Only organic fruits and vegetables and whole grains and hormone-free meats were served, not counting the dessert menu they'd already perused. Plenty of regular old fat and sugar available there. It was definitely a Molly place, perfect for her do-over celebration.

"Hey!" Char exclaimed. "I just thought of something! Maybe Paul is on his way here! Like Cam!"

Andie couldn't help but smile at Char across the table. Her expression was that of a little girl who'd just opened a gift and found exactly what she wanted.

"I bet he is coming."

"Paul wouldn't—"

Three frowns cut off her statement of disbelief.

Char said, "Who would have ever imagined Cam waking up like he did?"

"He didn't have a girlfriend."

"Well, no. Still, he just needed to hear what was on my mind. You told Paul what was on your mind. Trust me, it has thrown him for a loop. He'll see what he's about to lose and then he'll hightail it out here. Flights from Madison simply take longer than Chicago's."

Molly said, "What would you do, Andie? If he came?"

She turned to her. "I don't know what I'd do if he showed up. It's almost impossible to imagine it happening."

"Try?"

"Hmm." She thought for a long moment, picturing Paul on the front doorstep of the beach house. He wasn't smiling nor wearing a look of contrition or even concern. He should be doing at least one, but try as she might she couldn't paint his face with any of those things. Judgment and condemnation had been there far too many years. Funny. She hadn't realized that until now. He was always…polite about it.

Molly touched her forearm. "Imagine him doing everything you told him to do."

Admit his transgression? Break off the relationship? Call a marriage counselor?

She shook her head. "He can't do it because he doesn't love the spunky me. I'm changing. I'm no longer naive and pliable. No longer the kind of wife he needs. He hasn't done a thing I've asked him to do in— Oh, he probably never has, not really. Not unless it was in his best interests."

Char said, "God might whack him over the head."

"He might." She smiled and changed the subject. "I'm ordering the triple chocolate cake. This letting go exercise needs a little coping support at the moment."

"I hear you." Char nodded. "I'm having apple pie à la mode. Organic sugar has less calories, right?"

"Right."

Jo laughed. "Okay, you talked me into it. I'll keep you company with the raspberry cheesecake."

"White chocolate mousse for me." Molly raised her water glass. "One for all, and all for one!"

"Hear, hear."

"Hear, hear."

They clanked their glasses together and, as one, signaled the waitress.

Fifty-Eight

Char's phone rang as she rode in the backseat of Jo's SUV on their way to the beach house after dinner.

As when Andie's had rung earlier in the desert garden, everyone stopped talking and waited with breaths held. They probably also did what she did: wonder why they hadn't stuck to their agreement to leave the flaming things turned off. The bothersome fake musical notes tended to shatter peaceful environments.

She dug it from her bag and flipped it open. The ID screen lit up in the dark car. It was her husband's cell phone number. He was using his own phone! "It's Cam!"

A delicious tickle went through her. Thank goodness she hadn't turned hers off. Imagine! C.P. calling her!

"Hi, sugar!"

"Hi, honey-buns!"

She giggled. "You're using your phone."

"Of course. I wanted to tell you that I love you."

"Oh, Cam!"

"I even remembered you programmed your number into my cell. You're number one. In all ways."

She laughed. "You are such a fast learner."

"Third in my class at dental school. Think how great I'll be once I get going on something I like to do."

"Mm-hmm," she hummed an enthusiasm she didn't feel. "How was your flight?"

"Just fine. The kids are just fine. My folks enjoyed their short stay. Guess what else is fine? Besides you, that is."

"I have no idea!"

"That retail space on Fifth is available."

"Oh."

"The Realtor took me through. It's perfect. Guess what."

"I-I don't know."

He chuckled. "We're meeting tomorrow to sign the lease!"

"Oh." Char pressed the automatic window button and lowered it. "Well." She stuck her face through it. The air whipped her hair at eighty miles an hour. "Oh, my. Uh, color me flabbergasted, sugar."

"What'd you say?"

The wind must have muffled her voice. She pulled her head back inside. "I said color me flabbergasted."

"That's what I thought." A grin was evident in his tone. "Listen. It is such a great deal, I couldn't pass it up. I'll tell you all about it when you get home. I'll go to the bank tomorrow and apply for a business loan. There will be remodeling costs right off the bat. We can probably sign those papers on Friday. What did you do for Molly's birthday?"

"Uh, how about I call you back in a bit? We're in the car and I'm sure the girls don't want to listen to me jabber away."

In unison they whispered loudly, "Jabber away."

She waved a hand at them. "I'll call you, Cam."

"Okay, honey-buns. Love you."

"Love you too! Toodle-oo!"

Char closed up the phone and gazed through the open window. Numb.

Andie patted her arm. "Hon, do you mind if we shut the window? It's a little cool."

She shook her head but didn't budge. He signed a lease? He was getting a loan?

The window went up by itself. The movement caught her attention. Jo must have used the driver's control button.

"Oh. Sorry, ladies."

"That's okay," Andie said. "Anything you want to talk about?"

"Oh, my. Oh my word." The first syllable was a sigh. The following ones disintegrated into one long drone.

"What is it?"

Where to begin? "Dear Cam. He called me honey-buns and he asked what we did and he told me he loved me. Twice. Can you imagine? All in one little old phone conversation."

"That's wonderful!"

"Oh." It was the drone again. "There must be some weird real estate phenomenon in play. He's signing a lease on a retail space tomorrow and borrowing money to open a restaurant in it!"

Her friends remained silent, obviously at a loss for words.

"Exactly." She crossed her arms and stared out the window. "There is nothing to say."

Fifty-Nine

Last to troop through the front door, Molly waved at Julian as he walked past the beach house. Lamplight reflected off his glasses and revealed his enigmatic smile.

"Goodnight, ladies!"

"'Night!" Molly called out, chuckling over what he must think of them, together one night and not the next. He probably chalked it up to women being women. Maybe that was why he wasn't married.

At her elbow, Char whispered, "Our guardian angel, out on his nightly crusade to help the helpless."

Andie smiled. "And offer hope to the hopeless."

"Uplift the downtrodden," Molly added as she shut the door.

"Encourage the despondent," Andie chortled.

Char said, "Rescue damsels in distress."

Giggles overtook the three of them.

Jo rolled her eyes. "You three probably want to invite him inside to play Trivial Pursuit."

"Nope," Char said. "I have to make a phone call."

Andie walked across the room. "And I want to put on my jammies. Then I'll find the game. I know I saw it in one of these closets."

"Good." Jo sprawled facedown onto the couch and moaned. "I'm not up for company. I don't want to see another piece of cheesecake for a long time!"

Molly followed Char into the hallway, unbuttoning the waistband on her slacks. "Jammies sound good to me. Gotta make room for the popcorn."

Char laughed. "Popcorn! We just ate. You are pregnant, girl." She walked into her room and Molly went to hers.

She shut the door and sat on the edge of her bed. Something besides her waistband felt binding. It was probably in her spirit.

"Okay, Lord, what is it? I'm listening now. I'm done whining. For the moment, anyway. You understand that, right? I'm only human."

Fussing had consumed a lot of energy, energy put to better use when she took her mind off herself. She slid to the floor and knelt beside the bed.

"Lord, I praise You. You alone are God and worthy of praise." She touched her abdomen. "I don't like this situation. It's not what I wanted for my future. But You're in charge. I'll try to let You be in charge. I guess…"

She hesitated, knowing full well she still held back, her fist squeezed around a puny sense of control.

"I guess— Oh! Like You don't know what I'm thinking. The thing is I do not want to pry my fingers apart and let go! But if I don't, I'll just be miserable. So I guess I'm asking You to…" She buried her face in her hands and whispered, "Change my heart. Please change my heart."

The prayer was a familiar one. *Change my heart. I don't want to leave Chicago. I don't want to marry a pastor. I don't want to quit teaching. I don't want more than two children. I don't want to live in the Northwest. I really don't want to live in a dinky one-horse town in the Northwest. I don't want to admit marriage and children have not fulfilled me.*

God always answered, and she always felt, in the end, that He enabled her to go with the flow, His holy flow.

But this one? This one was the hardest of all.

Sixty

Back at the beach house, Char went into her room and shut the door. What was she going to say to Cam? This was not what she had in mind! But how could she discourage him at this point? He was so open with her! So thoughtful of her!

Well, except for the part about blasting their financial security to bits.

She sat on the bed and stared at her cell phone. She thought of silly calls with Todd. She thought of that tar feeling. She thought of Jesus on the cross, covered with her gunk, and of that fresh wholesome feeling.

Maybe she should ask Molly to pray.

Molly said she could do it herself, though. Anytime, anywhere, with whatever words came to mind.

"Lord," she whispered and closed her eyes.

Something didn't feel quite right. She glanced about the room. What was it?

"I'm not in church. But Molly says anywhere works. I guess I could..."

Feeling rather silly, Char scooted off the bed and knelt beside it.

"Yes, that's better. Lord, I'm new at this. I guess You know that, though. Are You listening? Molly says You are. I don't know what to do.

Imagine that! I'm at a loss for ideas. Fresh out of words for Cam. So I'm asking for Your help. Amen. Oh, thank You for Cam. Thank You for how he has changed. As I live and breathe, I never would have imagined that, either! Amen. Oh, and will You help Andie too? Paul sounds like such a nincompoop. Can I say that? Okay. Amen."

She opened her eyes and stood. "Here goes nothing."

The phone rang on the bed. She picked it up, saw Savannah's cell number, and answered.

"Honey! Hi!"

"Mom!" Her daughter wailed so loudly Char moved the phone from her ear.

"Sugar, what is it?"

"It's Dad!"

"What's wrong?"

"He won't let me go to Evan's tonight!"

"Well, of course not, dear. It's a school night."

"But he never says no! What did you do to him?"

Char covered the mouthpiece and laughed.

Savannah's voice continued to ring out loud and clear. "He's a flaming fossil! Grandma and Grandpa were going to take me. Evan's mom said she'd bring me home. He invited me and Allie. Just us to study algebra, and she gets to go!"

"You know the rules. Boys and school nights—"

"Dad doesn't have to do a thing. Grandma even liked my outfit. Then Dad walks in, takes one look, and laughs. 'I don't think so,' he says. And then he says I'm not going anywhere anyway on a school night at seven o'clock. And then he smiles and says—get this—he says 'I love you.' What has gotten into him?"

"Oh, sugar." Char didn't hold back her laugh. "Your daddy had a lesson in verbal communication, that's all. And he loves you. Do you know how fortunate you are to hear him say that?"

"I want my couch potato dad back! This dad is ruining everything. Allie will get Evan now. Just wait and see. She'll move right on in. My best friend and the guy I love! My life is over!"

Char waited for her daughter's tears to slow. Evan had been her main crush since August. He hadn't given any indication the feeling was mutual. An invitation to his house must have excited her to no end.

"Savannah, sugar, it will work out. Now you just mind your daddy."

"Why should I? Grandma thinks he's being ridiculous. She'll still take me."

"No, Savannah. Your daddy knows what's best for you and all of us."

"You're no help!"

"Some day it will make sense. Bye, honey."

"Goodbye!" She disconnected.

Char replayed her advice. He knows what's best. For all of them. Did she really believe that?

It was so new, the concept of Cam participating in family life, of offering opinions, of setting boundaries for Savannah. What a change! What an incredibly good feeling it left inside of her!

Char thought she had known best. Where had that taken them? To the brink of disaster.

Cam knew about financial security, and now he knew about expressing his love, which he thought was synonymous with providing for them. No way was he going to hurt them.

Of course he knew what was best.

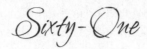

Sixty-One

Jo pulled shut the fireplace screen and admired her handiwork. The crackling fire chased away the cool, damp night air and did its magical thing on the environment, which was to make it perfectly cozy.

The game board was set up on the coffee table between the couch and love seat. Bone china teacups and saucers graced end tables.

Jo smiled. It was their second to last night together and already she was missing her friends. At least Andie would be staying another week.

"Hey, everyone." Jo retrieved a bag she'd placed on a chair and joined the others on the couches. "Before we start, I have gifts."

"Jo!" Andie said. "Gifts? After all you've done for us? Not the least of which was bringing us together. You shouldn't have!"

"They're just little mementoes to remember our time together."

Char clapped her hands like a delighted child. "Well, sugars, hang on. I've got to go get mine."

"Your what?"

She only giggled and raced off to her bedroom.

"Me too." Molly uncurled herself from the couch and moved in her languid way.

Andie stood and shrugged. "What's a birthday—even a make-believe one—without gifts?" She headed to her room.

Jo said to the empty room, "Guess I didn't exactly bowl them over with my thoughtfulness."

Within moments they were all passing around plain bags to each other, laughing at the impromptu gift exchange, oohing and aahing over each other's creative keepsakes.

Char described how she had found colorful scarves at a kiosk the first day she strolled down the boardwalk. Andie gave them boxed note cards from the art museum's shop, illustrated with French paintings. Molly surprised them with used books, easily purchased right under their noses as they'd browsed separately among the stacks of three shops.

"But you win, Jo," Molly said, "for being most surreptitious. How did you manage this? We were all together looking at these things. What was that artists' colony called?"

"The Spanish Village." Jo smiled, rather pleased with her findings. She had given Andie a glass-blown paperweight for her future office; Char, handmade earrings, the gaudiest she could find; and Molly, a beautiful set of pottery, a child-size cup and bowl for the new baby. She thought someday she'd send gifts to her other four children. As soon as she learned their names and ages.

Hugs and giggles went round the circle.

Jo said, "I just want to thank you three for…for everything. For putting up with me all those years and this past week. I have missed you so much. You've always been like moms to me. Not that I know from experience what a true mom is like, but I do know I have been mothered by you. Nurtured is the word." The speech could have gone on, but her vocal cords refused to cooperate.

Andie said, "We did mother each other, didn't we? We were 'Super-girls' from the very start."

Molly nodded. "Yes. We were mature little things. Aware of each other's needs when we should have been playing with dolls. I distinctly remember at nine years of age receiving laundry tips from you, Andie, and solace from you, Jo, when I failed a spelling test."

Char sighed. "I do believe your moms were as *unavailable* as mine." She tilted her head, as if waiting.

Jo perceived she wanted the adjective to sink in. *Unavailable.*

Molly responded for the three of them. "You knew we called our moms that?"

"I overheard Jo say it once."

Jo raised her hand. "The big mouth."

Char smiled. "We were about eighteen. I've appreciated that you never wanted to say it in front of me. The fact is, I think your moms were more unavailable than mine. Even after Mama died, I had those thirteen years to cherish in my heart, thirteen years of something none of you ever had. If she had lived, I don't think Mama would have lost herself in a career like yours did, Jo. Or been so enamored with society like yours, Molly, that she missed most of my accomplishments. Or been like yours, Andie, so childish and ill-equipped to face the real world. Mama was never self-absorbed."

Jo said, "Oh, Char. You are something."

She patted her hair and fluttered her eyelashes. "Why, I'm just your everyday Georgia peach."

When their chuckles faded, Andie said, "I wish we could have known your mama."

"I wish she could have known you all. The three nerds who took me, the blond ditz, under their wings."

Molly said, "We were such snots to you."

"And you weren't a ditz, Char," Jo said. "You were smart and funny and disgustingly charming. Still are, for that matter."

Molly and Andie nodded.

Jo said, "We were desperate for some class in our tight little nerdy threesome. Thank God for your glitter."

The others turned surprised expressions to her.

"What?"

"Thank God?" Molly smiled.

Jo shrugged. "I suppose we could thank Babette for every good thing in our life. Shall we play the game?"

"Sure."

As game pieces were distributed, Jo felt the outsider again. Not married, no kids, no church affiliation, no connection with God.

Good grief. Talk about a tight little threesome!

<hr/>

"Jo!" Molly's panicky cry came from the hallway.

In the living room, Jo dropped the game pieces she was boxing up and raced toward her, Andie and Char on her heels.

Molly met them outside the bathroom, her face scrunched into a question mark. "I'm spotting."

Jo grasped her hands. "How much?"

"A trace."

"Any cramping?"

"No."

Thank God. "Okay. This happens."

Molly nodded, returning Jo's squeeze. The adrenaline surged between them. They both knew it happened, and they both knew it could be a precursor to a miscarriage. Or not.

Jo clung to the *or not.* "Let's get you into bed."

Molly nodded again. There wasn't anything else to be done except stay off her feet for a while.

Like a swarm of bumblebees, the four moved down the hall and into Molly's room. They all tucked her in, Andie doing the covers, Char patting her feet, Jo brushing hair back from her forehead.

"Moll, it's all right. You know it doesn't necessarily mean anything is wrong."

Char said, "It happened with both my pregnancies."

"Let's pray," Andie said.

Jo and Char looked at her; she looked back at them. An unspoken "uh" hung in the air. Even with Andie's gallant efforts in the boutique dressing room, Molly was the prayer woman.

Jo tried not to think of Molly's half-formed thought the day she'd heard the news, that a part of her almost hoped for another miscarriage. She hadn't meant it. She really hadn't meant it. *She didn't, God.*

Andie turned to the patient. "How do we pray?"

Molly's facial features were still wrinkled together. "I want this baby." The furrows unknit themselves a centimeter at a time. "Three hours ago I could not have said that. In all honesty, I've been a totally unavailable mother. When I finally prayed, all I could ask God to do was change my heart." Her eyebrows rose, the only movement in her now smooth, peaceful face. "I guess He did."

Andie nodded and reached out to hold hands. The others did likewise until the circle was unbroken.

"We praise You, God, for changed hearts. Please keep Molly and her baby safe."

Jo tucked herself into the twin bed on the other side of the nightstand from Molly's.

"Jo, you don't have to sleep in here."

She smiled at her and turned off the lamp. "Who said anything about sleep?"

"Don't you dare stay awake!"

"Then I'd better stay put. There's a better chance of me sleeping in here than across the hall."

"Jo." Molly sighed. "You know there's nothing you can do for me. I promise not to get up and go jogging on the beach."

"Ha-ha. Go to sleep."

"You too." She yawned noisily. "My goodness, you are one hovering hen of a doctor. Scotty will have a fit over your bill."

"I'm sure we can work something out. Like you could name the baby Josephine."

"Or Joseph."

"That works too."

"Betsy's named after you, remember?"

"Mmm. *Betsy? Elizabeth?*"

"You don't remember." Molly had the grace to chuckle at Jo's memory lapse. "'Anne' is her middle name, you dork."

Anne. The same as Jo's. "Really? Wow. Thank you."

"You're welcome. I never could work in 'Wentworth' so I didn't even attempt 'Michelle.'"

She thought of how she herself had used the others' middle names for her miscarried baby. "That's okay. I took care of those."

"Yes, you did."

Silence hung between them, interrupted only by the surf's constant whishing sound through the open window. Jo recalled how Molly had always raised a window at night, even in the dead of a Midwest winter or in summer's ninety humid degrees. No matter blazing furnace or overworked air conditioner, she craved fresh air.

Jo loved that earthiness about Molly. It added to her aura of solidity.

"Hey, Jo."

"Hmm?"

"Jesus loved children. I think the unborn ones who don't make it here go to be with Him. If that's true, then I have one with Him and so do you."

Jo stared into the dark.

"Who knows?" Molly's tone carried a smile. "Maybe they're playmates. Maybe mine is a girl too."

"Hmm."

"Maybe. We can hardly begin to imagine what God has in store for any of us."

Jo continued staring into the dark. After a time, she heard Molly's breathing pattern deepen. The doctor could go to sleep as well.

But the almost-mother heart beating in her chest could not.

⌒

Jo's eyes remained wide open, yet images danced about in her imagination. Two chubby toddlers frolicked in a meadow. Both girls. One with black hair, one with light brown. Giggles echoed in her mind.

Ridiculous.

But it felt…nice. Good. Wholesome. Complete. Downright precious.

Childhood had been too painful of a passage for Jo. She vowed to never be a mother. Even as a little girl playing with dolls, she had cast herself as doctor, never as mommy. No one needed to point out the obvious. She simply imitated her own mother.

Whenever her best friend, Molly, envisioned the future, it always involved kids. Kids by the hundreds in the classroom and a couple of her own, one boy and one girl. The girl, of course, would be the best friend of Jo's daughter. Sometimes Jo played along just to humor Molly.

As a doctor she did all she could to ensure healthy beginnings for parent and child, but her participation ended there. She cared for women with biological clock issues, but she never heard the ticking of one until she became pregnant. When the heartbeat of her in utero baby chugged like a minuscule train in her ears, a primal wave of intuition flooded her.

She would have been an okay mommy.

Why did You take her away from me?

Jo bit her lip until the cry sank back down into her chest and dissolved there.

The two little girls jumped into her mind's eye again. They laughed and ran through wildflowers, hand in hand.

You are not fair!

Scarcely conscious of her movements, Jo got out of bed and slipped to her knees. As a child, that was how she addressed God. It was just the way things were done.

God, You are too full of fire. But I am tired of fighting and I want to see my daughter. I want to see Catherine Michelle Wentworth. Cathy. Jesus, if You are real and You love me like Molly says, give me the faith I need. I'm sorry for all the terrible things I've done. Please forgive me or just burn me up right now.

And please, oh please, don't abort Molly's new one. If You are the Great Physician, keep this baby safe. Please, God, please keep the baby safe.

Jo remained on her knees for a long time, wrestling and bargaining with God. She told Him everything, exhausting her supply of thoughts and emotions and promises to care for poor people if only He would keep Molly well. When there was nothing left to say, she stopped.

Amen.

The images of prancing toddlers were gone.

But that nice feeling lingered. It grew into a peace unlike anything Jo had ever experienced. She climbed into bed, almost asleep before she laid her head on the pillow.

I prayed. I really did.

What is it about this beach house?

Sixty-Two

Andie awoke with a start. The bedroom was middle-of-the-night dark. Except for the rhythmic swish of ocean, everything was quiet.

It must have been the chocolate. Until dessert that evening, she hadn't eaten sugar for some days. Her body was simply reacting—

Like a black fury out of nowhere, her conversation with Paul the previous morning rushed at her. It whirled, a funnel cloud inside of her, stirring up fear and anxiety. *You have a week to end it and make an appointment with a marriage counselor. I'm spending another six days out here.*

What had she done?

She had drawn a line in the sand and dared him to cross it.

The sinking sensation was not an unfamiliar one. If she'd been standing, she would have had to sit down as the loss of feeling crept through her limbs.

Paul would not cross that line. He was not on his way to California on a red-eye flight. He would remain on his own side and do as he pleased and drag her back across because that was where he needed her.

She would go because they shared two sons and a home and church and friends. How could she jeopardize all of that? If she didn't go back, what irreparable damage would she inflict upon Jadon and

326

Zach? What would people think? How would she pay bills? Keep up the house?

Marriage was for as long as they both should live. For better, for worse.

Panic bubbled in her chest and cut off air to her lungs. She gasped. Sheer terror roared, a dragon flinging itself about the small room. She couldn't breathe.

"Lord Jesus!" she cried aloud.

Instant calm enveloped her, as if a door had been shut against a raging thunderstorm. Peace filled the room. She struggled for a breath. And then all was quiet.

Was He that near? That real?

She climbed from the bed, went down on her knees, and bowed her head on the quilt.

"I am terrified by myself," she whispered. "Are You here? Will You take care of me?"

Her eyes were closed but a scene developed before her, not exactly within her imagination but somewhere beyond it, in some undefined territory between dream and reality.

She was on the beach, walking along the ocean's edge. Cool water tickled her feet and ankles. Salty humid air filled her nostrils. Someone moved along beside her, a taller, masculine presence. She could not see a face, but the arm brushing against her left one felt solid as a rock.

She could not hear a voice but, without aid of an eardrum, words imprinted themselves upon her mind. "Andie, I am so fond of you. There is nothing to fear. I will always take care of you."

As if a curtain dropped, the scene vanished. Her left arm tingled, nerve endings remembering a touch.

Joy engulfed her then. Unspeakable, uncontainable, incomparable. Laughter and grateful tears spilled from her.

Sixty-Three

Molly gave up trying to convince Jo she was going stir-crazy lying in bed. Instead she simply changed into a T-shirt and sweat pants and carried her pillow out to the front room couch.

"Jo, it's no worse than last night. I'm okay." She settled down on the cushions and tried to set her face into a compliant expression.

Jo loomed over her. "Don't you dare move until I get back."

Molly held up two fingers. "Scout's honor."

"Mm-hmm."

Andie nudged Jo aside with her elbow and handed Molly a cup of tea with a neat array of saltines on the saucer. "Go get her some real breakfast. The eggs are gone and we only have a few crackers left."

Molly smiled. "Thanks, Andie. How were the waves?"

"Super." She sat on the edge of the couch at Molly's feet. Her hair was still wet from her early morning swim. "How I wish there were an ocean in Wisconsin!"

Char entered from the hallway, her eyes at half-mast. "How I wish there were coffee in San Diego. Is there?"

Andie laughed. "I didn't expect you up already! But the pot is ready to go."

"I didn't want to miss any of our last full day together." She moved to the kitchen counter and flipped on the coffeemaker.

Molly exchanged a smile with Andie.

Jo said, "Char, do you want a breakfast burrito? I'm going to Kono's."

She wrinkled her nose and headed for the loveseat.

"Okay, nothing for you just yet."

Molly said, "You won't forget Jimmy Mack?"

"I will deliver breakfast to him only if you promise not to move off of that couch."

"I already promised."

"You said 'Scout's honor.' We were never Scouts."

"What a stickler! I think I'm glad you weren't around for my other pregnancies, Dr. Josephine." Molly caught sight of Jo's shoulders sagging and dropped her mocking tone. "I wasn't serious."

"I know."

"I promise not to move."

"Okay."

Andie cleared her throat. "I'd like to say something."

Molly laughed. "Andie, your face is lit up like a Christmas tree."

Her grin stretched even wider. "The most amazing thing happened last night. I got all fearful again, all anxious and mousey sometime in the middle of the night. Just woke up with it. But I prayed. And I sensed—you won't believe this! But it really happened. I sensed Jesus was with me, and I know beyond a shadow of a doubt I'm going to be all right whether Paul changes or not."

Molly thrust a hand in the air. "Amen!"

From the other couch Char warbled a subdued version of her rebel cry. "As I live and breathe! Me too!"

Molly laughed. "You too what?"

"I prayed last night, and then I talked to Savannah and then I figured out—no, I didn't figure anything out. I just knew Cam loves us and God will take care of us. No matter what."

"Amen again," Molly said, more quietly because a feeling of awe was filling her. Both Char and Andie had prayed! And they both felt a new peace.

Jo turned abruptly and walked to the door. Molly knew she was eager to go. She wore shorts and athletic shoes, planning to jog to Kono's. She had missed her routine exercise all week.

But Molly knew she also felt left out of the conversation. Her heart ached for Jo. What could she say?

Hand on the screen door latch, Jo turned. "Egg and black bean for you two?"

"Yes, please," Andie said.

She didn't wait for Molly's reply but walked out the door. It fell shut behind her.

Dear Lord—

The door reopened and Jo stepped back inside. "Well, okay. I guess I'm supposed to tell you. I had my own come-to-Jesus meeting." She raised a hand and closed her eyes. "I mean no disrespect, Lord."

Tears sprang to Molly's eyes.

Jo walked across the room. "I confessed everything. Old and new stuff. I told Him I really want to see my baby girl. I told Him if He keeps your baby safe, Moll, I'll work in that clinic." She sat on the edge of the coffee table. "I'll take care of every poor pregnant woman in San Diego County. Of course, that was an exaggeration, but I will try my hardest." She sounded breathless.

"And?" Molly prompted. There was more in Jo's eyes.

She gulped. "I didn't hear voices, but…I came up with an idea. The thing is, my life needs a major overhaul. The only place I can figure out where to begin is with you, Moll."

"With me?"

"I mean I want to just hang with you for a while. As in for months. As in I want to deliver this baby. As in I don't want you flying home tomorrow. I want you to come home with me." She glanced at Andie. "And Andie. Then, when you're ready—that is, when I'm ready to let you go—I'll pay the flight change fee. But I'd rather drive you home to Oregon."

Jo rushed her words together. "We could probably leave in a few days, be there by Friday. And then I want to stay and rent a place to live until Joseph-slash-Josephine arrives in April. I want to figure out what to do with my future—like I mean, honestly, can I live in an old one-bedroom apartment, work in a clinic, and not charge an arm and a leg above public aid payments? I just hope He doesn't send me to Africa!" She drew in a deep breath. "Moll, the bottom line is I need to watch how you live in the grays. Is that too much to ask?"

Molly wasn't precisely sure what Jo had asked, but she heard rumblings of a newborn faith and of a desire to see it change her life. She smiled. "No, it's not too much to ask."

Jo brushed impatiently at her eyes. "I think I even want to invite Julian and Zeke over for dinner." She shrugged.

Molly grinned with Char and Andie as they all nodded. "Sure. Why not?"

Andie said, "Oh, Jo! What an adventure for you! I want to come. Can I come? Just till next week? I could fly home from Oregon. I'd love to see where you live, Molly. What do you think? I can help you drive." She opened her mouth into an *O* and her brows rose up her forehead. "Me, driving in California! Yikes!"

Jo hiccupped a tearful laugh. "Yes! Spunky Andie lives! Of course you can come with us."

Andie turned to Char. "How about you?"

"Thank you, sugar. We haven't had a road trip in ever so long. It would be such fun, but…" She smiled. "The thing is, Cam called already today. Isn't that the sweetest thing you've ever heard? The man who hasn't called me in fifteen years wakes me up today because he can't wait to talk to me!" The smile went crooked. "And, well, he got the business loan approved—*this morning*. He was on his way to sign the lease for the restaurant space. If I don't get home tomorrow, he'll be choosing wallpaper without me. His decorating skills are not something you would envy."

Andie said, "Oh, dear. Talk about yikes. Are you okay?"

Char's smile disintegrated. "I will be. I think I need a group hug. Maybe even one more cry fest?"

Molly set her teacup on the end table and held out her arms. Andie scooted along the couch and grasped one of her hands. Char bustled over from the chair and sat next to Molly on the couch, taking her other hand.

Jo slid to the floor beside them and caught the two available hands, closing the circle. "What is it about this beach house, anyway?"

Epilogue

September 27, One Year Later
San Diego, California

Dr. Josephine Zambruski studied the five-by-seven framed photograph displayed on her desk and smiled. The picture always made her smile. How could she help but grin at that awful reddish-orange so-called Southern California beach house? In front of it, she, Molly, Char, and Andie stood, caught in the middle of a belly laugh. Her friends' faces were a sure guarantee of a smile. The memory of their week in the house a year ago would forever produce a rush of joy.

They had waited until the last morning, right before Char left for the airport, to pose for the "official" reunion snapshot. Char had snagged Julian, that odd duck who lived next door, as he walked by and shoved the camera into his hands. He said something about cheese in his Sean Connery accent, Andie mimicked him, and that was all it took. They clung to each other to keep from rolling on the patio's flagstones.

Andie was at her spunkiest, wearing a black wet suit, damp hair springing all directions. Char wore the huge earrings Jo had given her, a genuine smile—not the pert one—and a colorful hip outfit that only an attractive diminutive Georgia peach could get away with. Molly, dear Molly, always comfortable in her own skin, wore a T-shirt and shorts and an open-mouth grin that made her laugh nearly audible.

Peace reigned in her face even as her body threatened to reject the tiny new life which had barely begun to live.

Although Jo herself smiled in the photo, she appeared in shock with eyes too wide and bright. Of course she was in shock. By then she had more or less decided to sell out, move to a dinky apartment, work in an underprivileged, crime-infested neighborhood, right after spending six months of R & R in, of all places, rainy Oregon with a pastor's family.

Jo's office door opened and stopped just short of bumping one of the two chairs in front of her desk. Rearrangement wasn't possible in the cramped space. She had learned to make do.

The receptionist, a widow and gem of a grandmotherly type, poked her head inside. "Dr. Jo, there's a man on the phone who wants to make an appointment for his pregnant wife after eight o'clock some night next week. I said we don't do that, but he said, quote, 'You tell Sister Jo this is Brother Zeke.'"

Jo laughed. "They're pregnant?" She clapped her hands. "Yes, Ginny, by all means make the appointment for whenever they need it. I owe that man a lot."

"Okay. You're the boss."

"Thanks. Hey, isn't it after five? Please go home."

The woman smiled. "Like I have something better to do on a Saturday night? When are you going home?"

Jo glanced down at an open file on her desk and the stack of folders beside it. "Uh…soon."

"Mm-hmm. That's what I thought. How about fish tacos for dinner?"

She grinned. "Perfect. I have to make some calls."

"I'll lock up and be back in a flash. With extra guacamole." Ginny shut the door.

Jo stood and turned her straight-back chair around to face the window. There wasn't enough space in the office for her swivel recliner, but the chair she used was padded. And if she situated it just right, she could lean it back against the desk and prop her feet on the windowsill in between potted plants. Healthy potted plants, she added, marveling at the green thumb she never before knew she possessed.

She gazed through the prison-like metal bars that covered the window and saw a patch of autumn sky above a palm tree. The blue deepened. Somewhere quite a number of miles west of where she sat, nowhere near within her sight, the sun sank into the Pacific.

She reached for her telephone.

A Chicago suburb, Illinois

Char's cell phone lay on the white linen tablecloth. She had left it out with its ringer set to vibrate. The date was September twenty-seventh and she hadn't heard yet from Jo.

She sat alone in a booth at The Wilcox, listening to piped-in soft jazz, admiring the eclectic nouveau style of artwork and chinaware, smelling luscious garlicky pasta and roasted meat scents, and tried not to count customers. Cam admired her head for business, but she thought she sometimes got carried away. A night like this one with every table full, people waiting in the foyer, and waitstaff running expertly to and fro made her want to climb up on the seat and shout hallelujah!

She had done that one night after closing. The chef still teasingly referred to her as a closet Jesus freak. She wasn't sure. She only knew that God had caused the impossible to happen. Cam called her honey-buns every single day of the week and the restaurant paid the bills. Her husband was carrying her over life's mud puddles just as he'd promised all those years ago. Who wouldn't shout an amen or two?

The phone buzzed like a bee. Before answering it, she read Jo's name and number on the ID display. "Hi, sugar!"

"Hi, sugar, yourself! Happy birthday, Char!"

"Thanks."

"I'm sorry to call late. Are you in the middle of dinner?"

"No. I'm sitting in our favorite booth with coffee, debating what to have for dessert. Cam's over checking on Savannah. This is her first Saturday night on the job as hostess. Cole is so cute bussing tables and advising her on where to seat people."

"And how is she taking that from Little Brother?"

"She is learning the art of being gracious. I imagine Cole's willingness to share tips with her has something to do with it."

Jo laughed. "Is the place bursting at the seams?"

"Oh, yes."

"Isn't that great? So how was your special day? Hopefully turning forty-one was not hazardous to your health?"

"Not in the least. First off, Cam remembered! Roses and breakfast in bed."

"Aw."

"Then we ate lunch downtown and shopped. He picked out a gorgeous red dress at Saks, which I'm wearing now, of course. He never in his life has chosen a dress for me! And I quit shopping at Saks months ago, but he insisted. Jo, it was a wonderful day. Oh my word!" She watched as an enormous cake was rolled into the dining room on a cart.

"What is it?"

"Oh, my— It's a cake with *sparklers!* It looks like a wedding cake, it's so huge. It's even tiered. It's beautiful. But there's no reception— Oh!" She squealed. "Cam is pushing it this way!"

"It's for you! Okay, I'll let you go. Char, happy birthday!"

"Thank you so much for calling, Jo! Love you!"

"Love you too. Bye!"

The cake approached, sparklers sizzling, their light reflected in Cam's smiling eyes. Waiters and waitresses, Savannah, and Cole approached from every direction, and they all began singing "Happy Birthday" to her. Patrons around her added their voices. As the song drew to a close, applause and cheers resounded.

Talk about hazardous to her health! She could scarcely catch her breath. She just might hyperventilate!

Cam leaned over and kissed the tears streaming down both her cheeks. "Happy birthday, honey-buns. I love you."

Maybe health hazards could be good things.

❧

Madison, Wisconsin

Andie closed the front door behind a client whom she had convinced to come for a reflexology treatment on a Saturday evening. She watched the elderly woman and her husband make their slow way down the sidewalk to their car at the curb.

"Lord, please heal her sciatic pain."

The phone rang. She hesitated for a fraction of a second. Even quick prayers whisked her to another place. The fact that she had lived in the condominium less than six weeks added to her disorientation.

The phone rang again.

"Kitchen."

Andie walked through the living room, into the kitchen, and picked up the cordless from the table. "Hello?"

"This is your therapist calling."

She laughed. "Hi, Jo! Did you talk to Char?" Jo had asked for birthday reminders.

"Just now. Guess what's going on."

"I bet they were having dinner in their restaurant. Hmm. Let me think. I bet Cam did something special. What was it?"

"Well, as we said goodbye, he was pushing a cart across the dining room. There was a huge tiered cake on it."

"No!"

"Yes. With sparklers!"

"Oh, wow! He is the peach, isn't he?"

"Yeah. So…how are you?"

Andie did a quick self-assessment. Jo never asked the question frivolously. She understood that resuscitating Spunky Andie called for a major shot in the arm at times. And, bless her heart, Jo was there to give it.

The boys were fine. Surprisingly they lived most of the time with her in the small three-bedroom condo she leased rather than at the house with Paul. Jo thought it not all that surprising. And so the mothering part of Andie was fine.

Work was going exceedingly well. Old and new clients had found their way to her very own home office, aka the living room. The functional side of life was fine.

Bible studies, new friendships, and volunteering at a women's shelter occupied her off-hours. Spiritually and socially she was fine.

Then there was Paul. He had rejected her efforts at reconciliation, moved out, and filed for divorce. The dynamic duo of Andie and Jesus was not something he had bargained for. In the end, she didn't want the house. It was too big with too many reminders. It fed the mousey side of her. Using a different lawyer than his and a different real estate agency, she sold him her portion of it.

Last week, though, Paul's marriage to the "other woman" who hadn't even been the "other woman" in Andie's life was a major hurdle. The boys said she had worn a white wedding gown.

Heart-wise, she wasn't quite fine.

"I'm okay, Jo. Better than yesterday. Heaps better than last week."

"Day by day letting go?"

"Yes."

"Thatta girl. Hey, I have some good news. Well, not so good for Mildred."

Andie walked into the living room and sat on the couch. Jo had moved into her apartment building when a tenant unexpectedly became engaged and wanted to move out. Mildred was another tenant and ninety-six-years old. "What happened?"

"She had one too many conversations with her imaginary friends and phoned her son—again—at three AM to come join them for tea."

"Oh, dear."

"Yes. They're moving her into a home October first."

Andie heard the implication in Jo's silence, but played along, trying to ignore the delightful prickle of goosebumps. "Hmm. You'll need a renter then."

"Mm-hmm. I have someone interested in an eight-month lease. A Navy couple. When he ships out, she moves back to Kansas."

Andie smiled. "Really? Then you'll need another renter, say in early June?"

"Mm-hmm." She paused. "Oh, Andie. Do we thank Him for dementia?"

Andie thought about it. Jadon was working, saving money for college. Zach would graduate from high school in May. They both had fallen in love with San Diego when she took them to visit the previous Christmas. They planned to attend college together in California.

And she wanted to live there.

She said, "We thank Him for Mildred's good long life. We thank Him for the Navy couple. We thank Him for my friend who would welcome me as a neighbor and tenant."

Jo breathed a contented sigh. "Okay."

"Okay." She grinned. "And amen."

Southern Oregon Coast

"On your mark! Get set!" Little Hannah Preston popped up from her crouching position and shot down the hard-packed sand as fast as her six-year-old legs would carry her.

Eli sprang up, shouting "Go!" as he raced after his sister.

Betsy yelled, "Not fair, you two! Come back!"

Abigail stood up, spun around, and marched the opposite direction. "I quit," she announced huffily over her shoulder. "I'm walking with Dad."

Molly laughed so hard her bent legs gave way and she flopped backward onto the sand.

"Mom!" Betsy wailed, still crouching in start position. "It's not fair!"

Molly laughed harder. "No, it's not, hon." She wanted to add that *life isn't fair either, Betsy, you might as well get used to it.* But maybe that was too much information for her ten-year-old.

They were racing on the beach through twilight, one mad dash after another. Finish lines became starting blocks at rock piles, runoff streams that cut through the sand, and smooth, gray-white logs washed ashore.

"Hey!" Scott called out.

She turned to see him wave the cell phone.

Abigail and Betsy shouted together, "It's Aunt Jo!" Another race ensued.

Molly would have to wait in line for her turn to talk. Jo called so regularly on Saturday nights the kids expected her. Even Eli spoke to the woman they now called "Aunt." The honorary title evolved naturally during her Oregon stay. She spent five months in a small rental house down the street, spoiling them rotten like any respectable aunt should. They missed her.

Molly smiled at Scott as he approached. The two girls now brought up the rear, excitedly sharing the phone as they filled Jo in on their new school year.

Scotty reached for her hand, pulled her up off the sand, and kissed her cheek. They continued walking slowly, blatantly eavesdropping on their daughters' conversation, silently chuckling at stories of childhood woes and delights.

Molly thought of the new school year and how she wasn't even subbing. *No, Bets, life isn't fair.*

As if he sensed the path her mind wandered, Scotty squeezed her hand.

His simple act affected her like little else. Though life seemed wilder than ever for the Preston family, he was beside her in every which way, doing his best to prevent her from taking on the role of Superwoman. Some days she despaired over her lack of teaching career and devised elaborate plans to show how they all could successfully function if she were gone ten hours a day. Then Scotty would do something special for her. He would say, "Next year," and she would ask God to pry her fingers from the control stick once again. *Let be then.*

The family gathered at the foot of a steep winding path that led up the hillside to the parking lot. When the kids had finished their chats with Aunt Jo, Molly took the phone.

"Hey, Jo."

"Hi, Moll. How's my Joseph?"

Molly smiled. The question was always Jo's first to her. "He wants to talk." She caught hold of Scott's arm as they started the climb.

He stopped and grinned as she held the phone up to the five-month old baby boy in the carrier on his back. Joseph Michael Wentworth Preston squealed on cue.

He was awfully cute with chubby cheeks, black hair that stuck straight out every direction, Molly's wide mouth, and Scott's sleepy-slant eyes. With three names derived from his mother's girlfriends, he had to be awfully cute.

"Joseph, say hi to Aunt Jo."

Molly could hear Jo's giggles and silly talk punctuated with her own version of squeals. Hard as she tried, Jo could not hide her favoritism toward Joseph. That she had delivered him only partially explained his number one status with her. More important was her unshakeable belief that Joseph was God's direct answer to her prayers. Who could argue with that?

Molly put the phone back to her ear and resumed the uphill hike behind Scott. "How is life?"

"Oh." Her voice went unnaturally high. "Full of surprises."

Sensing disruptive news, Molly halted on the path and turned. Dusk nearly hid her view of the sentinels, those enormous boulders scattered just offshore. They always reminded her of God's faithfulness. Even in the dark they were there, keeping guard. The incoming tide crashed against them.

"Jo? What's up?"

"Well." She sighed. "You know how I say now and then, only a little bit jokingly, that I hope God doesn't send me to Africa?"

Molly stifled a laugh. "Yes."

"He answered that prayer. I don't feel convicted to go to Africa. Not the least bit." She paused again. "It's India."

"Hmm." She feigned nonchalance. "For how long?"

"Three weeks."

"Ah. Nice. A short introductory visit. Then, who knows? Once you've been and you learn about opportunities for missionary doctors—"

"Be quiet."

She could contain herself no longer. A belly laugh erupted and sang out above the rushing surf below. "Woo, Jo!" she shouted. "I am so proud of you!"

"Control yourself. All I did was agree to think about it."

"Yeah, right. When do you leave?"

"Uh…October twentieth."

Molly thrust an arm in the air and danced around in a little circle. "Yes! Yes! Amen!"

At last Jo joined in her laughter. "Oh, Moll. What an outrageous year this has been! I don't even want to think about turning fifty!"

Grandmère Babette's List

A Real Woman Has...
A nest egg for personal use
Something perfect to wear if the employer or date of her dreams wants
    to see her in an hour
A youth she's content to leave behind
A set of screwdrivers, a cordless drill, a hammer, and a black lace bra
A black dress and a white silk blouse
One friend who always makes her laugh
And one who lets her cry
A good piece of furniture not previously owned by anyone else in her
    family
Eight matching plates, goblets, and a recipe for a meal that will make
    her guests feel honored

A Real Woman Knows...
How to fall in love
How to quit a job
How to confront a friend without ruining the friendship
When to try harder...and when to walk away
How to have a good time at a party she'd never choose to attend

That she can't change the length of her calves, the width of her hips,
    or the nature of her parents
That her childhood may not have been perfect, but it's over
How to live alone...even if she doesn't like it
Whom she can trust, whom she can't, and why she shouldn't take it
    personally
Where to go...be it to her best friend's kitchen or a charming
    inn...when her soul needs soothing
What she can and can't accomplish in a day, a month, a year

Discussion Questions

1. Reaching age forty can be one of life's major turning points. Four old friends meet in San Diego to celebrate their fortieth year. Why does Jo initiate the reunion?

2. How does Andie approach the meeting? How does Molly? How does Char?

3. Why were Jo, Andie, and Molly disappointed in their birthdays?

4. What happens on Char's birthday? How is she affected by events?

5. What is a turning point you've faced in your life? How did it affect you? Were you changed by it? What did you learn from it?

6. In what ways is the beach house like a character?

7. Is there a place—manmade or natural—that significantly affects you? How?

8. Where was each woman in her faith walk at the beginning of the story? Where are they by the end?

9. Did you identify with one of the women? In what ways?

10. How do the friends influence each other?

11. Have you lost touch with a significant friend who was a good influence on you? Can you imagine reuniting? What roadblocks stand in the way?

12. How do Julian and Zeke offer insight to the women? Do strangers ever affect your point of view? How so?

13. What corners do the women push themselves out from? How have you faced a fear and pushed yourself from a corner?

14. The verse "Let be then: learn that I am God" particularly affects Molly. In what ways do they all "let go" of an area of life?

15. What areas of life have you or would you like to "let go and learn that God is God?" How does one let go?

Other Books by Sally John

THE OTHER WAY HOME SERIES
A Journey by Chance
After All These Years
Just to See You Smile
The Winding Road Home

IN A HEARTBEAT SERIES
In a Heartbeat
Flash Point
Moment of Truth

THE BEACH HOUSE SERIES
The Beach House

About the Author

Sally John is a former teacher and the author of more than ten books, including the popular Other Way Home series and In a Heartbeat series. Illinois natives, Sally and her husband, Tim, live in Southern California. The Johns have two grown children, a daughter–in–law, and two granddaughters.

Sally always appreciates hearing personally from you, her readers. Please feel free to contact her via mail at:

Sally John
c/o Harvest House Publishers
990 Owen Loop North
Eugene, OR 97402

or
via her website at:
www.sally-john.com

or
via e-mail at:
sallyjohnbook@aol.com